KAILANI

LILISA

ABY

ORABEL

THE BARREN SEA

N

W E

S

ELECTRICAL
DISTURBANCE

THE B

THE

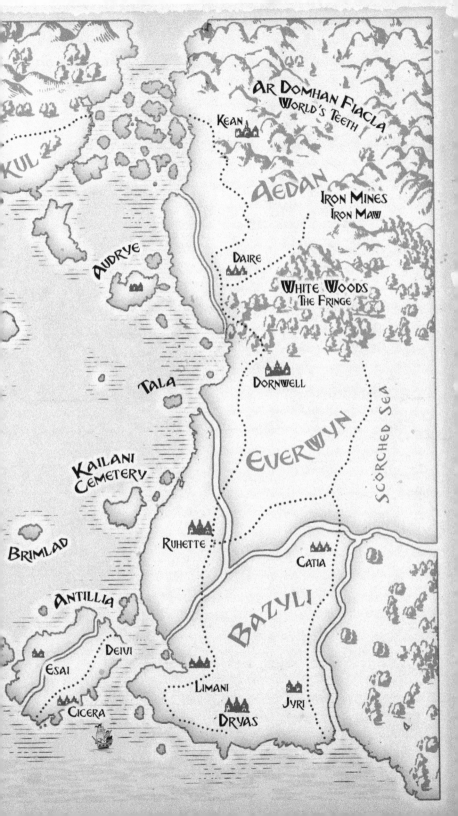

# Beyond The Horizon

*Book 1*

K. J. Cloutier

First edition February 2023

Front cover image/design by Natalia Junqueria
Map design by Natalia Junqueria
Character art by Alana Meyers-Echegaray

ISBN: 978-1-7778562-1-2 (paperback)
ISBN: 978-1-7778562-0-5 (hardcover)
ISBN: 978-1-7778562-2-9 (ebook)

Published by Meraki Books

www.kjcloutierauthor.com

*For my mom,*
*who's always been my biggest fan.*

# Part One

## *The Outsiders*

# Chapter One

"You're overreacting," Liam scoffed. "It's just a sea monster."

"No, Liam." Emery stared at the white pinprick on the horizon, barely breathing. "It's definitely a ship."

Her twin snorted. "That's ridiculous."

Emery leaned forward, squinting at the never-ending void of blue that was the sea and sky, ignoring the way the branch groaned under her bare feet and the rush of waves against the rocky cliff far below. An eternity of silence seemed to pass as the dawn sun crawled higher and the white pinprick grew. She squinted harder and details began to emerge. Three tall masts, half rolled-up sails, a giant wooden hull, multiple decks. She could even make out the wheel. Cold dread prickled along her skin.

Liam sucked in a breath. He could see it now, too.

"Who's ridiculous now?" Emery whispered. Her brother had no retort this time, and the frigid fear seeped into her chest. "We have to warn everyone."

"It'll turn around." Liam leaned casually against the redwood's trunk, but she saw the way his hands shook behind his crossed arms. "They always do."

This was true enough. In all of Emery's seventeen years, they'd spotted a total of three ships on the horizon. Each time, the ship turned around before ever coming close to their island.

"But what if it doesn't this time?" she asked.

"They haven't found us!" he snapped, betraying his anxiety. Liam never snapped. "This ship's just lost, they'll probably turn around any moment. And even if not, they'll never find the Break."

Emery pressed her palms against the rough bark of the tree, hoping the familiar texture would center her emotions. Inside her, the cold fear waged war with the warming ember of something else entirely.

*Exhilaration.*

Because there were only so many possibilities as to who could be aboard that ship. They could be the Ungifted humans who have hunted Emery's kind her entire life. But they could also be refugees, elemists like Emery and everyone else on the island, seeking asylum from the cruel outside world.

If it was the latter, it would finally mean new people to talk to. Maybe even her parents were on board, finally returning for them after so many years.

But if not, if it was the humans...then her home would be doomed.

Emery and Liam watched with thundering hearts, waiting for the ship to turn around like all the others. But the ship sailed closer and closer, heading for the northern edge of the island, straight for –

"They're heading for the Break!" Emery cried.

"But...that's impossible," Liam said, his arms slack at his sides.

The Break was the only gap in the island's perimeter of high rock, the only external access point to the island within, so narrow no one would even notice it from the sea unless they already knew it was there.

The ship glided on, still on course for the Break, and then vanished from view around the bend of the island. Whether they continued to sail passed the island, or turned for the Break, Emery couldn't tell.

Regardless, no ship had ever gotten this close.

Emery stared down at her brother.

He stared back, his face drained of color. "Sweet Eldoris," he whispered.

Emery scrambled down the tree, leaping the last few feet onto a bed of moss and pine needles, and together she and Liam sprinted through the woods, so quickly that branches snagged their hair and ripped their tunics.

They skidded to a halt when they hit the beach. The islanders there were all peacefully occupied; frolicking in the bay, sitting in the sand weaving mats, or practicing with their *lims*. At Emery and Liam's dramatic entrance, several stopped and stared.

And then the ship slipped through the Break, emerging inside the bay like a silent predator.

A stillness fell across the beach, like the trembling calm before an almighty storm. The islanders stopped whatever they were doing – frolicking in the bay, sitting in the sand weaving mats, practicing with their *lims* – and stared. Nobody moved. Nobody made a sound.

A shriek pierced the silence, then another. The islanders erupted into a flurry of movement. Parents grabbed their children as most people dashed for the trees and the chance of safety their homes beyond provided. Emery swallowed down the sour taste of her panic. She knew she should probably run too. A degree of protection lay behind the trees. If a fight ensued, this beach would see the first bloodshed. But she could not bring herself to flee. Whatever happened next, she refused to miss it. If she had to fight, then so be it.

The villagers remaining on the beach began huddling together, hastily beckoning Emery and Liam over and pulling them into their cluster.

Emery swallowed down the sour taste of panic. She understood. A chance of safety remained behind those trees. But on the beach, that's where the bloodshed would happen.

The ship still glided though the bay. Its sails were rolled, but paddles were poking out from both sides, guiding it through the water. The ship moved as if it belonged there, as if it knew exactly where it was going.

The wind shifted and Emery's long dark hair began to whip her face. The sand beneath her was vibrating, the water at the bay's edge frothing. Beside her, everyone stood rigid, hands raised and fingers curled. They were reaching out to the elements, manipulating them to their will, ready to strike. Emery had never wished more ardently that her own abilities would finally awaken properly.

Several young islanders beside her widened their stance and reached for the *lims* strapped to their backs. Emery reached for her own, holding the long, smooth piece of wood with a bulge at each side aloft as she'd always been taught. She held her breath, waiting for the battle to erupt. Her people weren't going to go down without a fight.

She held her breath, waiting for the battle to erupt. The ship glided to a stop, then floated silently on the turquoise water. The elements around Emery and her people roiled with energy now. But nobody moved.

Then, a smaller boat was lowered into the water at the ship's side and three outsiders clambered in. Emery squinted, desperate to glimpse any clue that could explain who they were, but they were too far away to make out any details. Her people gasped as the boat skimmed across the water towards the southern edge of the bay – the area closest to where the Arch-Elemists lived. The boat landed on a small patch of sand among the rocks, and the strangers disembarked, heading for the trees edging the beach, straight towards her leaders' home. Again, as if they knew exactly where to go.

Seeing the outsiders march towards their leaders seemed to finally spur the islanders into action.

The adults next to Emery stepped forward, raising their hands in unison, working together to lift up a monstrous wave from the bay. It took shape momentarily, like a giant watery serpent eyeing its prey, then shot straight at the outsiders.

It crashed into nothing. As if it had hit an invisible wall just before the shoreline. The sea simply fell back on itself, creating giant ripples in the usually calm bay.

The man next to Emery, Aryan, stumbled sideways, nearly colliding with her.

She grabbed his elbow to support him. "What just happened?"

Aryan's face was white as birch bark. "They...stopped it."

"The Arch-Elemists?" Liam asked.

"Or...the outsiders?" Emery added, limbs tingling with dread.

The Arch-Elemists were incredibly old, frail-looking beings, but they held immense power. They had raised the island itself from the depths of the seabed, one hundred and forty-nine years ago. All of Orabel stemmed from them, all bloodlines from the founding families they had brought with them, and so any important decisions concerning the island were left in their hands. It was they who consulted with the gods and elements, they to whom the gods would whisper the messages they shared with the islanders. Only four remained of the original fifteen. Emery had often wondered what would happen once they were gone. She hoped the answer was not unfolding in front of her right now.

Helplessly, Emery and her people watched as the outsiders slipped behind the trees bordering the beach. Through the foliage, the outsiders were barely visible as they approached the gigantic redwood tree that was the Arch-Elemists' home, undaunted and unscathed. Emery waited for them to be thrown backwards by the force of the Arch-Elemists' ancient, angry power, but again, nothing happened.

Instead, the outsiders marched right up to the tree, and disappeared inside.

# Chapter Two

E mery had spent most of her seventeen years listening to stories about people who lived beyond the island, but she'd never been particularly sure how much to believe the old tales.

"I've heard most of them have three heads," Liam chirped when they were back in the hollowed-out redwood her family called home, sitting at the table with their sister Ayana. "Those we saw earlier must have been the runts."

"Oh, shut it." Emery threw a pecan at his forehead.

He caught the nut as it bounced off and shoved it in his mouth, barring his teeth in a wicked smile. "Don't pretend you're not curious."

Their grandmother stood beside the table, thin lips pressed together and lines crisscrossing her face in places Emery was certain were smooth the day before. Their grandfather, similarly, was pacing round them, his steps soft on the packed-dirt floor. Despite Liam's bravado, fear had crept into the room like some sort of sickness, one that had spread and infected every single person since the outsiders appeared. Less than half a day had passed since their arrival, but it already felt like an age.

"Grace says some of them have wings," said Ayana with an attempt at cheerfulness, fluttering her frail fingers.

"That's ridiculous," Liam scoffed.

"And having three heads isn't?"

"That's enough!" their grandmother snapped. "Outsiders are just humans, like us. But most likely they'll be Ungifted." She straightened Emery's tunic and pulled a lose thread from the sleeve. "Do you have nothing without holes?"

Emery looked down at her attire. Her off-white cotton tunic and brown woolen trousers sported a fair share of grass stains, and the hole over her right knee was glaring, but they were the cleanest and most intact pieces of clothing she had.

Their grandmother turned to Liam. "Try to do something with your hair." She reached out to flatten it but he swatted her hand away.

"I'm not a child," he complained. "And why should we bother looking proper for the outsiders anyway?"

"Do as you're told," their grandfather ordered. "Or you'll be left behind."

Liam fell silent, his dark shaggy hair tumbling over his face. Emery pushed her own dark hair out of her eyes and watched as their grandfather peered through one of the tree's small round windows, as if expecting the outsiders suddenly to be standing outside, ready to kill them all. It was odd for either of her grandparents to snap, but clearly the anxiety was getting to them.

After the strangers had mysteriously entered the Arch-Elemists' home, a few brave islanders had rushed to their leaders' aid, ready to fight. But when they returned it was with unexpected instructions. The Arch-Elemists had sent them away, telling them not to be afraid, and instead to spread the word that there was going to be a gathering that night.

That was all they'd heard. Nothing was said about the outsiders, why they had come, how they'd found their way to the island, or if Emery's people were now in danger. All they had been expected to do was

wait. So, her grandfather continued to pace, her grandmother fuss, and her brother squirm in his seat, unable to sit still.

Ayana fiddled with the petals of a pink daisy growing in a pot on the table and whispered, just loud enough for her siblings to hear. "I heard the outsiders are only three feet tall and obsessed with daisies."

Emery and Liam snickered, ducking their heads when their grandmother shot them another glare.

Ayana's own laugh quickly twisted into a grating cough, rising from deep within her lungs like an awakening beast. Their grandmother's glare shifted into a worried frown and she took a step towards her, but Ayana waved her off as if it were nothing. As if her cough wasn't getting worse with every passing day.

The sound sent Emery's stomach into knots, and the thought that had been repeating itself since the moment the outsiders had landed on their shore returned once more. What if these strangers weren't there to destroy them? What if they could save her sister?

While her siblings sat picking through the bowl of nuts, she fiddled with the beads of bone and wood that were woven into her loose curls, then got up and began pacing around as well. She circled the table and chairs that had been carved directly into the base of the tree, making laps past the fireplace, a large cavity that had been gouged into the tree's red-brown inner wall with a generous hole leading outside to filter away smoke. Her grandmother was standing there, staring into the flickering flames. To distract her whirring mind, Emery began rearranging the wooden plates and cups that lived in the little hollow alcoves lining the side of the tree's trunk.

"Do you think it's...*them*?" Liam asked suddenly.

Emery almost dropped the cup she was holding as her brother voiced the other thought she'd been trying most to avoid.

*Them*, he had said. Not mother or father, but *them*. As if they were strangers.

But then, they had disappeared when she and Liam were only babies, Ayana barely two. If ever they did meet again, it would be as strangers.

Emery watched Liam as he spun a nut on the tabletop. His

face was impassive, as if his question hadn't been a kick in the stomach for all of them. Grandmother continued to stare at the fire, her own face bleached of color. Grandfather looked at Liam though, lips pulled into a frown and eyes pained. He opened his mouth, but he either changed his mind or decided there was nothing worth saying after all. The silence stretched, growing brittle.

And shattered when a knock sounded at the door, causing them all to jump.

"Time to go," her grandfather announced.

Emery smoothed down her tattered trousers and rubbed at a stain on her tunic, pulse suddenly racing. She took a deep breath, inhaling the homely aroma of damp earth, sap and sea salt before her grandfather pushed aside the layer of hanging vines and they stepped out of their home.

A crowd of islanders shuffled long the dirt path that wound its way amongst the giant redwoods, heading for the heart of Orabel. Emery noticed almost everyone was clad in tunics and trousers of cotton or wool, forgoing the often worn outfits woven from the island's foliage. Since the islanders made these outfits using their ability to manipulate the elements, the exact reason why outsiders hunted them, Emery wondered if choosing to not wear such outfits that night was a subconscious effort to remain hidden. Even if was clearly too late.

As Emery's family fell into step with the crowd, she could feel their anxious energy in the air, heavy and charged like a thunderstorm about to erupt. Everyone was eerily quiet, the only sounds their soft footsteps on the beaten dirt, the buzzing of bees in the flowers lining the path, and the annoyed clucks of a few chickens as they moved out of the way of the moving crowd.

Beside her, Ayana stumbled. Emery instinctively reached out to support her sister, but Ayana shook her off and hobbled along, leaning instead on her lim, her mass of black and silver curls spilling over her frail shoulders. Emery kept close behind, but glanced towards the beach. The island's circular bay peeked through the small gaps between the trees and somewhere beyond the Break, the sun hovered just over the horizon, turning the sky above and water below a furious blood red. The strange silhouette of the outsiders' ship, so out of place, bobbed in the water, as if taunting them.

Her spine tingled, but whether from anxiety or anticipation she couldn't tell.

Liam hissed, "I heard that, before the outsiders eat you, they fill their cups with your blood, then they drink it as they feast on your flesh."

"They also squeeze your eyes to make jelly for their bread," Ayana turned and added.

Emery cringed.

The crowd thinned as it spilled into the gathering space, a clearing at the edge of a perfectly circular lake. In the middle of the lake, marking the very center of the island, was the sacra, a giant boulder sitting on a raised portion of land. Ancient, curling symbols were carved into its sides, and upon it burned a fire that never went out, even in wind or rain. This was where the presence of the gods was strongest. Usually, the clearing was where the islanders prayed every morning while practicing statera. But sometimes, like tonight, celebrations or important meeting were held there as well.

All around them the land steadily inclined, giving the feeling of being at the bottom of a gigantic bowl. Rows of wooden benches had been grown directly from the ground here, on which the islanders now began to take their places, and in front of them stood a huge wooden dais. Its platform was solid and perfectly smooth, resting on four columns each formed by a dozen different types of wood twisting around each other in a sturdy rainbow of browns, greys, and reds. The columns also supported a thin roof made from interwoven branches and vines. Violet bellflowers sprouted perennially from the pillars, while white orchids sprinkled the roof like sea spray.

Emery's family fell forward to claim a spot, but she was too distracted by the unusual sight ahead to hurry after them. The four ancient Arch-Elemists sat in the chairs growing directly out of the dais. All four wore identical robes made from woven-palm leaves, and on each of their heads perched a small crown of twisted wood and vines. Their hands were clasped patiently, their sleeves rolled up to reveal the black tattoos of the elements etched upon their wrinkled skin, as they watched the islanders pile onto the benches. Emery eyed them with her usual mixture of curiosity and wariness. These beings were immensely important to Orabel, but they rarely left their tree, preferring to keep to themselves unless there was a dire need for them to do otherwise.

But this time it was not the Arch-Elemists causing Emery nearly to trip over herself for staring. Because there, sitting on a fifth chair next to them, was an outsider.

# Chapter Three

All the stories Emery had ever heard about the strangers who lived beyond the island ricocheted inside her head.

Outsiders had wings and three heads. Outsiders ate people, or enslaved them, or both. Some stories told they had blue skin, others red. Some described weapons that shone in the sun, so sharp they could slice through human flesh like soft mud. Outsiders were three feet tall. Or eleven. Outsiders were overly fond of daisies...

The possibilities described had been endless, and yet, as Emery stared at the outsider, she was almost disappointed.

This stranger had no wings, nor multiple heads. He wasn't blue, or red. In fact, he could have easily blended in with the islanders themselves. The only thing that really made him stand out was his clothing, trousers dyed a black deeper than she knew possible, polished black boots reaching up all the way to his knees, and a white tunic half hidden beneath a long and rather magnificent twilight-blue coat. Silver trimmings ran along it's cuffs and collar, and silver buttons shone like tiny moons along its parting. A walking stick of the same metal, upon which the man was drumming his fingers, leaned against his chair. His hair was cropped short, a sight uncommon on the island. He was sitting very upright, gazing around at the islanders with a mild, unreadable smile. Emery could just make out the color of his eyes, a deep green, like the needles of a redwood.

His traveling gaze met hers and locked on for a moment. A tremble ran the length of her backbone, and she quickly looked away and headed to where her family had taken their seats. Sitting down, she craned her neck to look for her friends Grace, Caelin and Fia, but her search broke off when the Arch-Elemists stood up. Custom dictated that islanders must never sit when they were on their feet, so the crowd quickly rose as well. A heavy silence settled over the gathering place, and Emery stood up on her tiptoes to get a proper view of the dais.

The outsider stood beside the Arch-Elemists, and now Emery could also make out a long blue cape attached to his shoulders, billowing behind him like ocean-formed smoke. Moreover, she realized with a jolt that four other outsiders were loitering just behind the dais, half hidden in the shadows cast by the maple and pine trees. Her heart hammered as she took in the details of their appearance: all men, all standing straight and attentive, all wearing similar clothing to the first outsider, but their jackets were shorter and less ornate. The sight of even more outsiders sent her pulse racing with unease, but the slight hope that had also swelled in her chest quickly shriveled. They weren't here parents. At least, none of them could be her mother since they were all men. But she supposed one could easily be her father and she'd have no idea. She didn't know what he looked like.

She shifted her attention to Arch-Elemist Dyzek, who stood in the middle of the group gazing at his people with watery eyes. Though he was thin, balding, and at least a hundred and seventy, his voice boomed with strength. "Sons and daughters, tonight is an important night for Orabel. We have made a vital friend, one who shall lead us to our salvation. We present to you Commissioner Tavor Thantos."

The crowd burst into a windy storm of whispers as the Arch-Elemists retook their seats. But while the islanders followed suit, the commissioner remained standing, leaning on his silver walking stick. The clearing grew quiet as he made his way to the center of the dais, so quiet Emery could hear the distant slapping of waves against the island's rocky cliffs. Only his footsteps sounded as they cracked against the smooth wood, punctuated by the soft thud of his stick as he moved with a slight limp.

Reaching his chosen spot, his steps cracked against the smooth wood, punctuated by a soft thud every time his stick connected with the dais. A long strip of cloth hung from his shoulders, billowing behind him like odd, blue smoke. e smiled a bright, warm smile, and finally spoke. The language he used was theirs, but his accent was strange, vowels at an angle and emphasis in all the wrong places.

"People of Orabel, it is an honor to finally meet you." His keen eyes swept across the faces staring up at him. Emery caught a few smiling back, several more frowning, but the majority's expressions were completely blank. "I've been looking for you a long time. But before I tell you more about myself and why I am here, I would first like to tell you what I know about Orabel."

Emery and Liam glanced at each other, brows raised. This Tavor shouldn't know *anything* about Orabel. The fact he even knew the island existed was unsettling.

"A hundred and fifty-five years ago, Orabel did not exist," the commissioner stated. "During that time, elemists such as yourselves lived peacefully with ordinary humans like me and my companions here." He indicated the outsiders standing behind the dais. "But then the Elemental War shattered our trust in each other. Even after the war had ceased, a way could not be found to repair that trust. Ungifted humans like us began to hunt the streets in bands called varens, who considered themselves responsible for tracking down and destroying every elemist they could find." He took a breath. "They still do."

Emery shuddered. Varens had haunted her nightmares her entire life.

"I acknowledge it has been a dangerous time for elemists," Tavor continued. "Understandably, after these attacks began a small group decided to create a safe place just for your kind. They set off for the edges of the known world, and, with their abilities combined, managed to raise rocks, coral and sand from the ocean bed, creating an island on which to hide. These elemists never left, choosing to remain forever instead of risking being killed by varens. That island, that haven they created, eventually came to be known as...Orabel."

He finished with another smile, and Emery couldn't help noticing how attractively it accentuated his features.

No one smiled back though.

Emery exchanged another look with her twin. The fear in his eyes mirrored her own. *How does he know?* she mouthed. *He's an outsider!*

Liam shrugged, equally baffled.

"Now it's my turn." Tavor's brilliant smile widened. "As you are all aware, I am not from here. I come from a city called Dornwell, on the coast of a land called Tala."

Emery shared another glance with her twin, this one full of intrigue. They knew very little about the lands outside of Orabel.

"I must confess," he continued, "Dornwell is nothing like your charming island. It is much larger for a start, and our homes are made of stone and brick, not trees."

"What's brick?" Emery asked her grandmother, receiving a shushing for an answer.

"And of course, the most notable difference is that, in my city, elemental manipulation is strictly forbidden." He paused for effect. "And punishable by death." Whispers of outrage and fear travelled across the crowd.

"And that's why I'm here. I want to change that. I want to restore the peace that once existed between our worlds, for them to be united again."

Silence fell again, but this time Tavor looked as if he had been expecting some sort of response. Instead, the islanders continued to stare at him, letting the silence stretch.

"He must be mad," Ayana whispered.

Emery nodded in agreement.

Finally, a middle-aged man near the front spoke up and when Emery craned her neck to see who, she realized it was Aryan, "How?"

The commissioner smiled. "I am very happy you asked, sir. I believe there are two aspects to this. The first iI'm a man of high importance in my village, and my opinion is highly valued amongst my people. s my hope that, over the next few months, I will have the great privilege of learning from you. The more I learn, the more I will understand you. The more I understand, the easier it will be to reintroduce you to the wider world, and it in turn to you. The second, and please forgive me if this sounds conceited, but I am a man of some...importance back home. I have the good fortune that my thoughts and opinions are, in general, highly valued. I intend to use this to *all* our advantage. I am convinced that, by combining my authority with the knowledge you are willing to impart to me over the next months, together we will be able to bring peace to our warring worlds."

The islanders began to murmur once again, this time less fearfully.

"He sure thinks highly of himself," Liam muttered.

Emery bit back a nervous laugh.

The villagers murmured amongst themselves again, the whispering less fearful, and more intrigued, maybe even eager.

Her own pulse was racing with indecision. Gods, how long had she yearned to see the outside world? And to do so without the fear of being executed...

But Aryan was not done with his questions. "What makes you so important?"

Tavor hesitated, glanced back at the Arch-Elemists. All four nodded once in unison. When Tavor looked back at the crowd, he appeared almost nervous for the first time. "I am the head of the varens. They are under my command."

Emery's stomach hollowed out with horror as a terrible silence settled upon the crowd. So the varens had found them after all.

And then people were standing and shouting. The wind began howling and the trees bordering the clearing began groaning as some of the islanders reached for the elements in panic.

One of the other Arch-Elemists stood up, woman named Nyneve. She was just as old as Dyzek, silver flowing her and dark, wrinkled skin, but also like Dyzek, her voice boomed as she shouted, "Be calm!"

Almost immediately, the shouting ceased, and the wind died down. Though some villagers remained standing, they gave Nyneve their attention.

Nyneve lowered her hands in a placating gesture. "We are safe. Tavor is here to help and nothing more. The gods have shown us our salvation, and it is him. Let him speak."

She sat back down. And slowly, the villagers who had been standing did the same, though many of them still appeared uneasy and unconvinced. But the Arch-Elemists had never been wrong in the century and a half they'd been the leaders of Orabel. They'd always kept their people safe. And Emery was certain it was this trust that kept the villagers in check for the time being.

"Yes." Tavor cleared his throat, his face a little pale, but when he spoke his voice was steady and confident. "I am here to help. Varens are not what we used to be. Our job is to simply keep everyone safe, ordinary humans and elemists alike. Though we are still tasked with hunting down elemists who use their gifts to harm and destroy, we leave peaceful elemists, like yourselves, alone. But with that being said, there are still some humans who dislike and distrust elemists, and so it's still dangerous for you out there. With your help, I want to change this. I want peace."

Emery's heart thrummed with Tavor's words, with the possible implications. And all around her, her people began whispering to each other again. This time they didn't sound as panicked. This time they sounded intrigued, maybe even eager.

"However," Tavor announced over the babble. "I have one slight problem."

The audience fell silent, their attention fixed and undivided on the outsider again.

"As I've just mentioned, I have an important role in my city. This means I cannot spend many days, let alone a few months, away from my duties, not even for something as important as this. However, your kind and honorable leaders" – he swept his arms wide, indicating the Arch-Elemists – "and I have devised a plan. One of you will be selected to come aboard my ship and travel with me to Tala. This way, I can learn all I can from you, without neglecting my domestic duties. That person will then become a peace ambassador, representing not only Orabel, but all elemists across the realm. If everything goes according to plan, we will soon have peace. All I ask for is one brave person to come forward. I will do the rest."

He finished with a dip of his head and limped back to his seat. He sat down as if relieved to be sitting again, but his eyes blazed with energy.

A slow, steady buzz began to sweep throughout the crowd, but

Emery could barely hear it over the sound of her own heart. She stared at the outsider, with his short hair and absurdly bright clothing, unable to process what she'd just heard. This strange plan, brought forth by an even stranger man, could very well change everything.

Peace meant freedom. Freedom meant leaving the island. Leaving the island meant possibly finding a cure for the Withering.

His plan might just save her sister's life.

# Chapter Four

After Commissioner Tavor Thantos had retaken his seat, the *Arch*-Elemists rose again. Emery and the other islanders followed suit and a heavy silence fell as Dyzek once more stepped forward to speak.

"We have consulted with the elements and our gods, the great Eldoris, Pyralis, Teralyn and Tadewin."

The islanders murmured quiet prayers at the sound of their deities' names.

"The gods have shown us the path they intend for us, and we must follow. With Commissioner Thantos's help, we can save our island from the Withering, and bring about the peace we so long for. Now is the time to act, we may never receive such a chance again. Furthermore, the sickness is no longer only striking the elderly, but the young as well."

A few people glanced at Ayana, who at nineteen was so far the youngest person on the island to become afflicted.

Dyzek's tone became even more somber. "It is also spreading at an increased rate, and striking the young. Just last night, Fynn Rothkin became the latest to come down with the illness."

Horrified murmurs rose from the crowd, and Emery whipped her head around to where Fynn was sitting with his mother. Sure enough, silver now streaked his dark hair, just liked Ayana's. The first sign of the Withering. Gods, he was only eight.

"If we do nothing, half of us are likely to die from the illness. The other half may survive, but will be left without their gifts."

With dread knotted in her stomach, Emery glanced at her sister. The death rate of the Withering did indeed seem to be fifty percent. But for some reason, survivors lost their abilities to manipulate the elements. Ayana's abilities had already vanished, and Emery could only pray to the gods that the Withering didn't take any more than that.

"Without our gifts," Dyzek continued. "This island will fall. But now there is hope! Which means we must be brave, and act. We will give you all a day to dwell on these matters, but by twilight tomorrow" – he surveyed the crowd before him – "we intend to have chosen our ambassador."

The Arch-Elemists and Tavor took their leave, stepping down from the dais in single file and disappearing, along with the other four outsiders, down the winding path that led back to the Arch-Elemists' tree.

Moments later, the remaining islanders swarmed together to discuss the inconceivable plan with which they'd just been presented. Emery's grandparents quickly vanished into their chosen huddle within the mass, and the siblings began fighting their own way through to their most trusted friends.

Soon the faces they were searching for emerged, and the six moved amongst the trees at the outskirts of the clearing where they could speak more freely.

"I don't like it," Caelin blurted imediately, just as Emery suspected he would.

The daylight had waned to almost nothing as Tavor and the Arch-Elemists spoke, and now the iridescent fungi that lined the clearing, and indeed all the paths in Orabel, were beginning to glow, casting a blueish glow across her friend's skeptical face. In this dim lighting, it was almost difficult to tell Liam and Caelin apart as they stood next to each other. Though Liam was slightly taller, Caelin had the same thin and gangly build. His hair was also equally shaggy, if a few shades lighter. It had become a running joke that Caelin was secretly their third twin.

"He's an outsider," Caelin continued. "Why should we trust him?"

"I don't like it even a little," Caelin continued. "He's an outsider. Why should we trust him?"

"The Arch-Elemists do," Fia answered, her red hair bobbing as she bounced on the balls of her feet. Seeming to glance sidelong at Liam, she added, "And he is incredibly good looking."

"Ew, don't," Caelin groaned.

Liam glowered.

"Definitely didn't have three heads," Emery said, bumping him with her hip.

"He only has the face of a god," said Grace, Caelin's older sister. She had one of her slender arms around Ayana's shoulders so Ayana could subtly take some of the weight off her weary bones. The fungi's glow dyed her golden curls almost silver, and the white flowers laced throughout her leaf gown glowed too, like little stars. She looked up to the heavens. The moonlight dyed her golden curls silver, and the white flowers laced throughout her woven leaf gown glowed like little stars. She had one slender arm draped across Ayana's shoulders so Ayana could subtly lean against her and take some weight off her own wary bones. "Or perhaps he is a god, in disguise, come to rescue us."

The girls giggled, but the boys didn't seem convinced.

"Definitely didn't have three heads," Emery said, bumping Liam with her hip.

"It doesn't even sound like a real plan," Caelin objected. "What does someone like him want to learn from us?"

"Oh, but Caelin" – Liam snapped a twig off a branch and began spinning it between his fingers – "don't you understand how *interesting* we are to such a...sophisticated gentleman?"

"Are you saying you trust him?"

"I don't know."

"So, you wouldn't go with him?" Fia asked, still bouncing.

Liam scoffed. "Of course, I would. How could you say no to something like that? To be the one to restore peace?"

Fia shrugged. "I don't know. Something seems...off. How did Tavor even find us? And how does he know so much of our history?"

"Perhaps the Arch-Elemists told him," Emery said. "They must have been in some form of contact before the outsiders got here. How else could they have made it through the Break?"

The Arch-Elemist's gifts were far reaching. They could read the wind, gleaning bits of information from the outside world, which is one way they'd been able to keep the island safe for so long. And they could also use the wind to send forth their voices, to communicate with whoever they wanted.

"Are you saying you'd say no if you were chosen, Fia?" Liam asked.

Fia bit her lip. "I don't know. I'd be happier about mingling with the Ungifted if most of them didn't want me dead but...I think I'd do it."

Caelin glared at the ground. "I don't trust any of it. Whoever they choose is being handed a death sentence. I would say no. Not that it really matters in my case."

An awkward pause followed, and Emery felt a twinge of pity for him. During infancy, babies often displayed small acts of elemental manipulation, usually when their little bodies couldn't contain a big emotion. Emery had frozen her bath water during a tantrum once, and Liam had sent a blast of air into a meal he hadn't wanted to eat, spraying their grandmother's face with food. Caelin had never displayed any small acts as a baby, and at one year of age, when the Arch-Elemists tested him as they did all babies born on the island, whether or not they'd shown signs of the gift, nothing happened.

Caelin, it seemed, wasn't born an elemist like everyone else on the island. He would never be able to bend the elements to his will. It was a rare occurrence, so rare it had only happened four times in Orabel's history. But though Caelin would never see it this way, she sometimes thought he was the luckiest of them all. He didn't have the gift, but he also didn't have the burden of power that would sentence him to death if he ever left the island.

"But Caelin, the plan has to work," Liam said, his voice dripping with sarcasm. "Didn't you hear how important the man was?"

The girls laughed again, while Caelin scowled.

"I'd go," Ayana said, suppressing a cough. She'd been quiet, and Emery suspected the day had worn her out. "They might have a cure out there."

A second awkward pause followed, after which Caelin's voice grew softer. "And what if they don't? Or what if you –" He caught himself, but Emery knew exactly what he was thinking.

*You might not live long enough to see it.*

"Don't care." Ayana pulled herself up as straight as she could, even though Emery knew it caused her pain. "I'd still try."

"I'd go with you." Grace kissed the top of her head. "And if there isn't a cure out there, I'd find all the stuff needed to make you one myself."

And Emery believed her. If anyone could do that, it was Grace.

The conversation continued but Emery stayed silent for the rest of it, fiddling with a couple of pine needles that had fallen into her pocket. She felt ensnared by her own thoughts. Perhaps Liam was right. Perhaps it would be worth all the risks. After all, it would be extraordinary to be the one who brought back the peace between the Ungifted humans and elemists.

And what if her parents were out there somewhere, waiting for her to take this opportunity finally to find them? And most importantly, there was Ayana. If there was a way to save her, to save everyone, from the Withering...

But Caelin was right too. It was dangerous for any elemist to venture away from Orabel. Death was everywhere in the form of storms, sea monsters, pirates, a whole society that wanted them dead. Was it even worth trying if she was killed the moment she stepped off the island?

When she crawled into bed that night, she lay awake for a long time thinking about it and in the end, she figured it didn't matter either way. Her abilities were still so weak, she would never be chosen to go. At least two thirds of Orabel were more qualified. What could the outsiders possibly learn from her?

EMERY WOKE with her heart thundering in her chest. Sitting up, she leaned against the curved wall the base of her bed grew up against and pressed her palms into her eyes until she saw nothing but darkness.

She breathed in and out, slow and steady. She'd been having a nightmare.

Though she was no stranger to nightmares, this one had torn her from sleep, causing her to wake in the full crush of panic and leaving her with an awful aching sensation that was taking a long time to subside.

She couldn't remember the last time she had suffered from one, but the outsider's speech had obviously left too many questions bouncing around her head.

Her bad dreams were always variations on the same theme. Sometimes her parents were suffering grotesque deaths, whether by the mouths of fierce monsters or at the hands of their own friends. Sometimes they were walking away from her, thrilled to be leaving her behind on the island because they'd never wanted her in the first place. It was always the same torture. Emery's parents always disappeared, and she was always powerless to stop it – as had been the case in real life.

As the nightmare gradually dissolved into flashes of colors and heartbreak, she gazed around her room.

Morning sunlight flowed through the round window, illuminating the dark wooden interior, the hollow alcoves in the wall containing her few belongings, and the curtain of vines gifting her with privacy from the rest of the home. As she blearily watched a few flecks of dust float along the sunbeam, she realized with a jolt that she slept in and must have missed that morning's statera. She couldn't remember the last time her grandparents had allowed her or her siblings to miss the gathering that happened at dawn every morning, where the villagers started their day by practicing statera and praying to their gods.

She crawled off her straw and goose feather stuffed mattress and pulled down a few clothing options. After choosing a pair of brown trousers and a white tunic, she thought back to the commissioner's bright attire yesterday evening. What she wouldn't give for something a little more colorful.

When she finished dressing, she grabbed her lim from where it leaned against the wall, slung its sheath over her shoulder and pushed past the curtain of vines to step onto the landing beyond. She glanced to her left, where thick, flat branches grew horizontally from the round wall. They snaked their way higher and higher until they ended beneath a second vine shielded room where her grandparents slept. All seemed silent up there, and Emery assumed they were already gone, or they slept in too.

On her right, two more vine curtains covered the entrances to a third and fourth room where her siblings slept. She parted Liam's curtain and peered inside, but the room was deserted. His woolen blanket lay in a heap on the floor, a few pieces of clothing littered beside it.

Inside Ayana's room, however, voices were murmuring.

"You'd have to go."

"Not without you I wouldn't."

Emery peered through the vines shielding Ayana's room from full view. Through the jungle of potted flowers filling the room, she could just see Ayana and Grace lying side by side on the bed, watching a blue-and-yellow butterfly fluttering above them. The butterfly danced briefly along the golden petals of a sun flower, circled a vase bursting with violet pansies, and then continued its journey in the direction of her window.

"I'd make you go," Ayana insisted. "I wouldn't let you say no."

Grace rolled so that her face was inches away from Ayana's. "What if we were soul bound? Would you let me stay then?"

Emery knew she should step away from the doorway. This wasn't a conversation for her to overhear, and she already knew how it would end.

"No, Grace." Ayana's frail voice turned stern. "I'm not going to bind with you."

"Aya, I don't care –"

"*I* care thou –" Ayana's voice rose momentarily before shattering into a rattling cough. She gasped, seemingly unable to catch her breath, and Emery fought the urge to barge into the room.

*Gods, what if this time she stopped breathing? What if –*

Mercifully, the coughing ended. Ayana was hunched over the end of the bed now, breathing in the aroma of a large, crimson flower Emery couldn't quite recognize. Grace was holding it for her and rubbing her back.

Ayana forced herself to sit upright and flicked her silver-black curls out of her eyes. "I'm dying, Grace. You don't really want to be bound to a dead –"

"You're not dead yet," Grace snapped, her voice beginning to warble with emotion. "And I love you."

"I know. I love you too." Her hand curled gently around Grace's arm. "Which is why I won't let you throw your life away when I might be...gone in a –" Ayana collapsed in another choking fit, and this time Emery backed away from the room, vowing only to stay until the coughing stopped again. Grace murmured something she couldn't make out. With her stomach in knots, Emery made her way down to the tree's lowest level.

In the kitchen, Liam was standing in front of the fireplace, a neat pile of kindling waiting in its belly. His own lim was sheathed and ready on his back. A small candle was burning in his hand and he stared at it with determination, assumedly attempting to compel the candle's flame to leap into the kindling.

Leaning against the table, Emery challenged her brother, "If you manage to get that fire started, I'll eat a pinecone."

Fire was notoriously difficult to control, and neither of them had managed to do it.

Liam's response was flat. "It warms my heart how much faith you have in me."

He continued to stare at the candle. For a moment the flame flickered towards the fireplace, and Emery's heart jolted with surprise, But then the flame danced straight back up again and she thought maybe it had just been a breeze.

Liam huffed, blew out the candle, and put it away. His scowl softened when he turned to look at his sister. "What's wrong?"

"I...overheard Grace asking Aya to bind with her again."

Liam smirked. "Accidentally, I suppose?"

"Does it matter? She keeps saying no."

Liam sighed. "She loves Grace, and she wants her to be happy, even if that means...being with someone else. I guess she's trying to be selfless."

Emery stared at her twin. "That may have been the most serious thing I've ever heard you say."

"Don't worry, won't happen again." He snatched two apples from the table and tossed one to her.

Emery caught it and took a bite. "I can't even imagine wanting to bind with someone. You know, loving someone that much."

Liam stared at his apple, his face falling. "I wonder if Mother and Father were soul bound."

Emery ran her thumb over a small bump in the surface of her apple, sighing, and admitted, Liam stared at his apple, his face falling. "

Part of me really hoped they'd be on that ship."

"I know," Liam said. "Me too."

They gave each other a sad smile, neither of them saying what Emery knew they were both thinking. Such hope was foolish. After sixteen years, why would they come back now?

"We're going to be late," Emert said instead.

Liam sighed, adjusting how the sheath sat against his shoulder. "I can't believe we even have lessons today."

"Did you go to *statera?*"

He grimaced. "No. You?"

She shook her head. "Grandmother must be really out of sorts not to come drag us out of bed."

The twins headed out into the bright sunlight. It was warm as usual, but a slight breeze caressed their cheeks, carrying with it the sharp scent of pine and the heady smell of blossom mixing with the salty aroma of the sea. Sunlight filtered through the branches above them, speckling the beaten paths with golden fragments as they headed for the shore.

Birds were chirping and singing, flitting from branch to branch, and all around them other islanders were wandering between homes, whispering and muttering about the plan the outsiders had brought with them and everything it could mean. Some were grinning eagerly, others wore stiff smiles, a few even glared whenever they looked out to the bay as if cursing the ship newly bobbing there. The day felt thick with suspense and possibility.

Old Hally stepped out to greet them as they passed her home, directing a gummy smile towards Liam in particular. "Word has it you've managed to create a small twister for the first time. Exciting tidings."

Liam grinned and stood a little taller, towering over Hally and her age-hunched back. Meanwhile, the familiar weight of embarrassment filled Emery's stomach like stones.

Hally must have sensed it, because her smile softened immediately. "Don't worry, my girl. Your time will come."

Heat rose in Emery's cheeks. She cast Hally a quick smile as to not be rude, and hurried on, leaving Liam to chat a little longer with Hally. She kicked a pinecone off the path in front of her, pouring her frustration into a good hard boot. Sometimes she hated living in a place where everybody knew everything about everyone, always. She knew very well her abilities were taking longer than usual to fully manifest, she didn't need to be reminded at every turn.

For their entire lives, Emery and Liam had been equal in their abilities to manipulate the elements in small ways. When they turned seventeen a few months back, their abilities should have surged, becoming more powerful. And Liam's had. But Emery's hadn't. Not yet. And she couldn't help but feel like Liam was leaving her behind while everyone watched.

Liam caught up with her, still grinning.

"Don't," she said.

"I didn't say −"

"You were going to."

"You don't know −"

"Yes, I do."

Liam sighed. "You're right."

"I know I'm right."

Remnants of morning fog still lingered along the bay's surface when the twins reached the shore. The outsiders' ship remained where it had been stationed yesterday, its ominous silhouette turning ghostly in the fog.

Behind it, just visible, loomed the Break. Turquoise water from the ocean beyond flowed through the Break and filled the circular bay, the water lapping gently at the white sand of the beach. the only hole in Orabel's perimeter of steep cliff face. The Break was so narrow one would never notice it from the sea, unless they already knew it was there. Through the Break the sea flowed, filling up their perfectly round bay with crystalline water, ringed by a continuous beach of white sand.

Emery always wondered why the Arch-Elemists bothered with the Break. If no one was supposed to come or go, what was the point of having an opening? Ayana said it was to give the illusion of freedom.

Emery always wondered why the Arch-Elemists bothered with the Break. If no one was supposed to come or go, what was the point of having an opening? Ayana said it was to give the illusion of freedom.

Emery and Liam's peers were standing in a circle further down the beach. The twins joined them, managing to melt into the group without their instructor Ezra noticing.

Most of the other students didn't either, in fact everyone looked unusually distracted. Arguably no surprise given the unnerving presence of the ship that felt like it was watching their every move.

Ezra, a lean, greying woman of around eighty, instructed everyone to run through the movements of *fleeting storm*, and the students slowly stirred, no one particularly motivated. Eventually though, everyone moved to stand in a line along the beach.

Emery reached up to pull her lim from its sheath, and thoughtlessly fell into the movements. Having done this nearly every day since she was twelve, it was all too easy for her mind to wander as she twirled the lim above her head in *gathering clouds*, quickly slashed down in a zigzag to perform *lightning strike*, before sweeping it low in *wild wind*.

Every day since she was twelve, she had practiced, moving carefully and deliberately in and out of these poses designed to keep her safe. Every day, just like every other child in Orabel, she had practiced the individual movements and combinations, and sparred with her classmates, all to help her fend off outsiders if any were ever to breach the island.

And yet here they were, outsiders on their very soil, with nothing even resembling a fight to be had. It made today's training seem more like a performance than practice, and she felt foolish just going through the motions.

"Partner up," Ezra instructed. "I want to see lots of *falling dusk* today. Rise to meet, sweep to deflect, and see if you can make your transitions quicker each time."

The students shuffled into pairs, Emery partnering with her classmate Dray. They bowed their heads towards each other, Dray's dark hair falling into his face, tapped the tips of their *lims* together and took a step back.

But before they launched into their movements, Emery said, "I'm sorry about your brother." Little Fynn Rothkin, the eight year old who'd recently fallen ill with the Withering, was Dray's younger brother, and she could only imagine the devastation his family must be feeling. When Dray didn't reply, she continued, "I'm here, if you ever need to talk about it."

When Dray finally looked up, pushing his hair back to reveal his face again, he looked impossibly tired. "Thanks," he muttered and launched into an attack.

Emery sighed inwardly. She and Dray had been more then friends once, but they didn't talk a lot anymore, and she supposed she couldn't blame him if he didn't want to talk now.

She hurried to catch up, matching Dray's footwork as they circled each other in *spattering of stars*. They both swung their lims in *arcing moon*, tapping each other's left shoulder lightly to ease into the sparring.

Emery's mind began to lose focus again. As she circled to face the bay, the ominous sight of the outsiders' ship came into view behind Dray. She could see movement on the ship, figures – outsiders – milling about on the decks. She wondered just how many outsiders there were on that ship. And she wondered what Tavor was doing right then, if he was one of those figures on the ship, or if he was still with the Arch-Elemists in their home, or maybe, if he was wandering their island right now. Distracted by the thought of an outsider casually strolling through her village, she accidentally caught Dray's ear with her lim.

But Dray hardly noticed. He too was now staring over his shoulder at the ship, his lim limp in his hand. When he turned to face Emery again, his tired eyes where hard. "What do you think they really want?"

Thrown by the question, Emery didn't respond right away. "I –"

But they both turned as, beside them, the slow and steady tapping of wood against wood switched to frenzied clacks.

Liam and Caelin were locked in battle, swinging their lims at each other in a furious blur, clearly done with taking it slow and steady. Liam laughed, putting in extra flourishes and dancing out of the way of Caelin's blows, all except one that caught him on the arm. Caelin, however, remained serious and precise, focused on speed and accuracy rather than spectacle.

The entire class stopped their own practicing to watch, spurring Ezra to sigh and step over to them. "Liam, one should always take these lessons seriously. You wouldn't be having them if they weren't important."

Liam stopped suddenly, leaving Caelin swinging his lim into the empty air and almost overbalancing, and

grinned provocatively. "And yet, there's a group of outsiders here, and none of them are attacking us. So, what's the point?"

To Emery's surprise, Ezra did not rebuke Liam. Instead, the older woman cleared her throat and shot a glance at the outsider's ship, as if hoping it had disappeared. The fog had lifted now, and bright sunlight was streaming down from the heavens. The water sparkled with radiance, but the ship itself remained a foreboding unknown.

"Nonetheless, statera-lim is important, Liam. We also don't know yet how this...situation will turn out."

"That's the problem," Dray spoke up, drawing the classes attention. "We *don't* know how this will turn out." Dray's voice was as hard as his eyes, and he turned to glare at the ship. "Father says they're not to be trusted, that they can still attack at any point. And we're just standing here swinging our silly sticks about, as if that could save us. Liam's right. What's the point? What's the point of anything?"

Dray tossed his lim into the sand so unceremoniously that most of the students gasped. Emery clutched hers closer to her chest. They had each been given one at age twelve before their first lesson, selected, straightened, and polished by one of their parents or guardians. It was theirs for the rest of their lives, to carry and care for, a symbol of their personal responsibility as they stepped towards adulthood and not a useless stick to be thrown on the ground. Even Liam, for all his bluster, looked shocked.

In the stunned silence that followed, Dray marched off into the trees, leaving his lim where it fell and a volatile feeling of dread in the air. Dray may have been the only one to say it, but Emery knew he was not the only one attempting to bottle up his fear. After all, every person on the island had been preparing for an outsider attack their entire lives, had lived in constant fear of it. But now outsiders were here, not attacking, and that fear didn't just go away overnight. It needed to go somewhere, to either be pushed down or channeled into something else.

As the day wore on, bringing them closer to that evening's meeting and the announcement of who was going to join Tavor on his quest, Emery could feel the atmosphere on the island turning more and more unstable, and she wondered when, and how, it would finally explode.

# Chapter Five

Emery peered into the bucket of water and examined her reflection. Her dark blue eyes were bright against her almond skin, more obviously now that her hair had been put into a single braid running down to the small of her back. The wood and bone beads adorning it caught the light nicely as she turned her head, the white feather braided tightly into her hair for the past seven years to honor the goose that had spent its life gifting her people with eggs swinging near her jaw. She pushed a loose lock behind her left ear, brushing the bone hoop that pierced the top of it.

She had often been told she looked like her mother, but had no evidence by which to judge this. Her heart ached at the thought of that woman, forever a mystery to her, but she shoved the feeling down into the shadows of herself, where it belonged.

There were more important things to think about that night.

On this special occasion she had put on a brand-new dress, one Ayana had finished only that afternoon. The bodice was comprised of palm fronds and grasses, woven together with a skill Emery could only admire. Her arms and shoulders were left bare, but layers and layers of ferns tumbled from her hips like a waterfall of foliage. Blue bellflowers dotted the dress here and there, and when she moved it sounded like wind brushing the forest canopy. She couldn't remember the last time she'd worn something so fancy.

"Teralyn's teeth, how did you make this?" she asked, fingering the soft leaves running along the top edge.

Ayana shrugged and continued placing layers of baby's breath in her own hair. "Grace taught me. It's not that hard."

"For you two, maybe."

Everyone in Orabel usually wove leaf garments by manipulating the required elements with their abilities, but Grace had always preferred to make things with her hands instead. When Ayana's elemental abilities had started to disappear due to her illness, Grace had kept her busy by teaching her to make all sorts of things without them. Clothing, trinkets, bowls, it didn't matter; Grace would find a way for Ayana to make them using only manual skill. And so Emery's sister could always feel she had something to contribute, even as she grew weaker.

Emery watched as Ayana put the finishing touches on her hair, hair that used to be glossy and black and so curly she couldn't get a comb through it without oiling it first. Now, premature silver streaks ran through it and the beautiful curls had wilted like the petals of a dying flower.

Her dress was much like Emery's, but her hair sported a blood-red carnation and a powder made from crushed rose petals sat in a thin layer on her cheeks in an attempt to mask the chalkiness of her skin. While Emery and Liam shared their mother's darker complexion, Ayana's skin was a few shades lighter, a trait she received from their father, or so they assumed.

Neither Emery nor Liam could remember him at all, and Ayana only had vague notions of memories, mostly a soft voice that contrasted with rough, callused hands. And unlike their mother, who had grown up on the island, the siblings couldn't simply ask anyone what their father looked like, for he'd been an outsider, a stranger their mother had met after she'd left Orabel. Emery's grandparents had only met him once, the night her parent's had abandoned her and her siblings, but it had been dark and he'd been hooded, so they'd hardly seen his face.

When Ayana stood, her back was so hunched now that she was shorter than Emery, who longed to see her standing taller than her again.

For three years she'd been watching her sister fade away, and soon, if a cure couldn't be found in time, there'd be nothing left of her.

"You're beautiful," Emery whispered past the lump in her throat. Because she was. She was still alive, still standing, even if she had to lean on her lim like a cane. Alive was the most beautiful thing one could be.

Ayana scoffed, and Emery didn't press the point.

Footsteps echoed along the tiny landing outside Ayana's room and Liam pushed his way inside. His hair was neatly combed, and he was wearing the cleanest, whitest tunic and crispest dark trousers she'd ever seen him in. "You two ready?"

Emery gaped at him in shock and amusement. "And who might you be?"

He grimaced and ran a hand through his hair. "Grandmother attacked me."

"I don't think I've ever seen you so...clean."

"Joke all you want," he said as he moved over to gaze into the bucket. "We all know I look unbelievably fetching."

Emery chuckled, then smoothed her dress and peered into the bucket herself one last time. Two nearly identical faces stared back at her.

"You both look so grown up," Ayana said. Emery looked up to see a sad smile on her face.

Their grandparents were waiting for them downstairs. As soon as Emery's feet were on ground level, her grandmother bustled over to straighten her dress. Her own woven-leaf gown rustled as she moved, and her silver hair was pulled back into a long braid too. She stepped back and admired the young trio. "You look wonderful, my dears."

Their grandfather stood by the door, dressed much like Liam

and with his grey-streaked hair lying similarly flat against his head. "Ready?"

Liam grinned. "Always."

Outside, other islanders were already strolling down the paths towards the center of the island, just as they had the night before. Unlike yesterday, the atmosphere no longer felt unsettled, if anything it was festive. Almost everyone had also pulled out or created more ornate clothes for the occasion. Most people were smiling and chatting away, strolling along as if this wasn't one of the most important meetings they would ever attend. Only most though. A few were still looking suspicious, whispering to each other in quick, tense undertones.

Though Emery's own stomach had wriggled with anticipation for most of the afternoon, she felt remarkably calm now. All day she'd fretted about what she'd do if she was chosen. Would she go, risking her life in the outside world and leaving everything she loved behind to bring peace and find a cure? Or would she say no, remaining behind like a coward in the relative safety of their home and leaving it to someone else? She'd wavered back and forth as the day wore on, but instead of deciding, she kept landing on the same thought: it didn't matter. She wouldn't be chosen as the ambassador. She wouldn't have to make the choice at all.

And so Emery's steps were light as she and her family joined the flow of islanders on the path.

When they reached the clearing by the lake, they found it had changed in the span of a day, as it was apt to. Instead of long benches, the clearing now sported dozens of large, round stumps with five or six smaller stumps sprouting up around them. The arrangement was clearly intended to serve as tables and chairs, and already more than half had been filled.

"Ayana!" Grace waved from where she was perched beside Caelin and Fia. Her hair had been elaborately bound with vines and she wore a spectacular dress made entirely of ropes of ivy. Emery wasn't entirely sure how she moved in the thing.

Emery's grandfather patted her head before following her

grandmother to a table already occupied by some of their own friends an Emery and her siblings wove their way through to Grace and the others.

Once they made it, Emery stood up on her tiptoes to see the dais over the heads of those still standing. The four outsiders who had stood behind the dais did so again. On the dais, the Arch-Elemists sat in their chairs, but this time a long, rectangular table had grown up from the platform in front of them. The ancient guardians watched with pensive expressions as their people gathered and settled.

Beside them sat the outsider, Commissioner Thantos, watching the swelling crowd with sharp eyes. He seemed to be examining every single person in turn, and Emery looked away as his gaze landed on her.

Her eyes found Dray, sitting at a table at the other end of the clearing with his family. She hadn't seen him since his outburst that morning, but it seemed like his anger had been spent. He sat blank faced now. His mother, Mel, sat beside him, and Little Fynn perched on his mother's knee, his head leaning on her shoulder and eyes closed, as if the short trek to the clearing had drained him. Dray's youngest brother, only two, sat in the grass next to the table playing with a wooden toy, full of the bouncing energy Fynn should have also had. On Dray's other side, his father, Aryan, glared at the outsider with thinly veiled mistrust.

A hush swept across the crowd as the Arch-Elemists rose to their feet, followed by the rustling of the other islanders doing the same.

Their leaders surveyed the crowd, then Nyneve raised her arms, her silver hair falling across her shoulders like water, and a small smile lifted the corners of her lips. "You may sit." The islanders took their seats. "My sons and daughters, prepare yourselves, for tonight is the beginning of our future. Tonight, the gods will speak, and one of you will be chosen to change the world."

The crowd murmured with anticipation.

"We must fight the illness that is spreading across this island.

We must help Commissioner Thantos bring peace between our worlds. The gods have already shown us who they chose, but now they will show you."

The Arch -Elemists moved in fluid unison, like a river down a mountainside, stepping off the dais and winding their way through the tables to the lake. The islanders spun in their seats to watch them, but Emery glanced back to where the commissioner still stood on the dais, the toes of his boots hanging over the edge as if uncertain whether to follow.

Dyzek looked back and beckoned him over, upon which he immediately stepped down. He swept past Emery's table, sparing a glance neither for her nor her friends. Instead, his eyes were fixed on the giant, round boulder – the sacra – etched with curling symbols sitting on a patch of land in the center of the lake, though Emery imagined it probably didn't look particularly impressive to him.

The four Arch-Elemists waded up to their knees into the lake, spreading out so they stood several feet away from each other. The islanders held their collective breath as their leaders closed their eyes and raised their arms skyward, the rustling of their robes the only perceptible sound.

The outsider remained on the shore, one hand behind his back and the other resting on his silver cane, still eyeing the sacra with curiosity.

Emery and the rest of the islanders held their collective breath as their leaders closed their eyes and raised their arms skyward, the only sound the rustling of their leaf-woven robes.

The Arch-Elemists began to chant an ancient language Emery didn't understand, a lilting, lyrical tongue that sent goosebumps racing along her skin. The words filled every space, every crack and orifice of the island, until nothing else existed. Something stirred in her chest, like a creature was beginning to rouse there. She couldn't resist the urge to place a hand on her breastbone just over the stirring, as did everyone else. The only two people she could see not doing it were the outsider and...Caelin.

Dyzek broke off his chanting while the other three continued. He gathered himself for a moment, then exclaimed, "We call upon Teralyn, mighty goddess of the earth, to keep us strong and steady through the turmoil ahead!"

A creaking, groaning sound announced itself above the chanting as, one by one, tiny flowers of every color and shape Emery had ever seen blossomed from the sacra's carvings, turning and opening to face the last rays of the sinking sun.

Dyzek slid smoothly back into the chanting and Nyneve broke off, exclaiming, "We call upon Eldoris, merciful god of water, to guide us!"

At first there was no obvious reaction. Then Tavor quickly stepped backwards as the lake began to churn. It was slow at first, but gradually built up speed until the entire lake seemed to be spinning, white-capped waves hurling themselves around the boulder.

Nyvene rejoined the chanting once more and the Arch-Elemist Aeolius paused to make his appeal. His white beard was so long it nearly touched the churning water at his knees. "We call upon Tadewin, fair goddess of the wind, to lift us up and give us courage when all seems lost."

A gust of air lifted Emery's braid from her back. Wind shrieked through the trees, along the lake, across the entire island, dancing across the earth and water, the skin of the islanders sitting at their tables. It joined the melody of rushing water, lyrical chanting and the heartbeats of the elemists watching eagerly.

The last of the Arch-Elemists, Celosia, ceased her chanting to announce, "We call upon Pyralis, fearless god of fire, to never let our hope burn out. Fearless god, show us the face of the one meant to save us."

The fire upon the boulder flared, brighter and higher, un-caring of the wind buffeting it from above or the water spraying it from below. The flames danced and twisted, reds, oranges and yellows smearing together so brightly Emery's eyes watered, but she didn't dare look away.

Shapes began to appear amongst the colors, obscure at first

but then sharpening into something recognizable. A pair of eyes, a nose. Brows, cheeks, a jawline and lips. The wind died down and the water began to slow, and Emery continued to stare as the face took shape.

Her lungs stopped working and the chanting began to echo in her skull, louder and louder until she thought it might burst.

That face...she'd recognize it anywhere, even in the depths of a flame.

Her lungs seized.

The Arch-Elemists, the other islanders, and even the outsider turned from the sacra to face the table at which she was sitting.

Emery slowly looked at her brother, his face pale and eyes wide.

"The gods have shown us the way," one of the Arch-Elemists announced. "They have chosen Liam Aalokin."

# Chapter Six

E mery's lungs refused to suck in air as her mind slowly processed the nightmare unfolding before her.

*No. Not Liam.*

Though the wind was no longer shrieking and the water no longer roaring, her pulse thundered so loudly she couldn't hear what the Arch-Elemists were saying as they beckoned her brother forward.

Her mouth opened in silent protest, her body too stunned to do anything else, as Liam rose from his stump and made his way through the tables full of people, head held high, shoulders thrown back.

She gripped the edge of the table so hard her fingers ached.

Emery had thought so hard about what she'd decide if she was chosen to be the peace ambassador, whether it would be worth all the risks, worth leaving everyone she loved behind. And yet, it somehow never occurred to her to worry about being the one left behind.

But surely Liam wouldn't go. He wouldn't leave her behind. Not after their parents...

Liam reached the Arch-Elemists, who now stood on the lake's shore. The commissioner stood beside them, sharp eyes sweeping over Liam while the rest of his expression remained unreadable.

Over her still pounding pulse, she could just hear Dyzek ask, "Do you, Liam Aalokin, accept this challenge, this great responsibility?"

No. He wouldn't. He wouldn't just leave.

Ayana grabbed Emery's hand and squeezed.

Liam didn't look back, at her or any of them. Ayana grabbed Emery's hand and squeezed.

"I accept."

The world seemed to tilt and go black. Blood thundered louder in her ears.

He would. He *was*. He was going to leave her, just like their parents. And he'd possibly die out there, too. Just like they might have.

All around her the islanders burst into applause, though a few still muttered to each other uncertainly. Emery tried to look proud and encouraging but couldn't. She couldn't be happy for him, no matter how noble the cause.

He was leaving, and he might not come back.

"On one condition," Liam added, raising his voice over the cheering. The clearing descended into silence, and Liam turned to look straight at Emery and Ayana. "I accept, but only if my sisters come with me."

Emery sucked in a sharp breath.

Murmurs began all around as heads swivelled between the siblings and the Arch-Elemists. The elderly leaders glanced at each other, then turned in unison to the outsider. For a brief moment, the commissioner's brows raised, then he quickly smoothed his features and looked over at Emery and Ayana, clearly studying them.

Emery didn't move, didn't breathe. She could feel Fia and Caelin staring at her and Grace practically vibrated next to Ayana, but she refused to look at any of them. She stared at her brother but he gazed right back, mouth set in determination.

Emery's emotions swirled inside her like a hurricane. Relief and dread and exhilaration and horror. She honestly didn't know whether she wanted Tavor to accept or deny her.

The outsider turned to the Arch-Elemists and nodded. "I accept the condition, in part. The healthy sister may come. The other..." Tavor hesitated, looking awkward and regretful. "I'd be afraid she wouldn't survive the journey."

Emery turned to Ayana, her heart splintering. "Don't worry. I won't –"

Ayana grabbed her hand, eyes brighter than they'd been in a long time. "No. You have to go. Both of you."

Emery shook her head. She couldn't abandon Ayana, couldn't leave her behind like their parents had. And her grandparents. They'd already been abandoned once too. "No. I'm not –"

Dyzek called her name. When she didn't move, Fia and Ayana shoved her from her seat. "*Go.*"

She felt sick. This was wrong. The gods had not chosen her. Her abilities weren't even fully awake yet. What help could she be?

She took a step forward. Then another.

She'd say no.

That would be the right thing to do. She'd stay with her family, and she wouldn't get in the way. And Liam...he'd head off into countless dangers, without her. He'd save their island, without her.

She wove through the tables full of people, her friends, her family, all watching. She looked at their faces as she passed, the faces of generations who had never left the island, who had lived in constant fear since birth, whose children would likely do the same if this mission failed.

There was Fynn, who without a cure might not live to see his tenth birthday.

There were her grandparents, eyes wide and faces pale. She would be leaving them, just as their daughter had before.

Didn't they deserve answers though? What if she could find them?

What if she died first?

She paused in front of her grandparents, opened her mouth to speak but she didn't know what to say. To her surprise, her grandmother smiled. She grabbed Emery's hand, gave it a squeeze, and lightly pushed her onwards. "Go child."

Breathless, Emery reached the edge of the lake, where her brother stood tall before their ancient leaders and the outsider, before the sacra and the gods. The outsider looked her up and down again, his expression betraying nothing. Was he already regretting this decision?

Emery's breath turned sharp and shallow. She couldn't do this.

But then Liam turned his deep blue eyes on her, full of promise and confidence.

*We can do this,* he silently said. *You and me, we can do this.*

He held out his hand. She took it, fingers trembling. And just like that, her fears quieted in her head. Together, they faced the Arch-Elemists and the outsider once more.

*Aeolius* looked at her. "Do you, Emery Aalokin, accept this journey? Will you bring peace to your people?"

Emery's fears reared again, stomach lurching. No. This was a horrible idea. They might die. They might –

Liam squeezed her hand, and the fears calmed once again.

They might die. But they might also succeed. They could be the liberators of their people. They could save Ayana. And they could do it together.

Glancing over her shoulder, she caught her sister's eye. Ayana nodded, and that was enough to seal her decision.

Emery swallowed, her throat as dry as bark. "I accept."

Cheers erupted, but Emery barely heard them. Her world narrowed to Liam's hand, grasping hers tightly.

She didn't hear what one of their leaders said that prompted a second wave of applause.

Beside her, Liam beamed, seeming not to notice the people who clapped more slowly or less enthusiastically. But Emery did. She noticed the way they glanced at each other, eyebrows raised, probably wondering why the gods had chosen two seventeen-year-olds to play such an enormous role. Frankly, she wondered the same thing.

She was half aware of being led to the dais and to the table upon it, where Dyzek coaxed up an extra stump next to the commissioner's so she could sit. Somewhere through the blur food began being served, and suddenly a bowl of sweet potato chowder was steaming on the table in front of her. Emery automatically picked up her wooden spoon but couldn't bring herself to take a bite. Her stomach still roiled with too many emotions, and she was very aware that the outsider sat right next to her, barely half and arm's length away.

When she glanced his way, he was already looking at her, smiling. Up close, that smile was even more dazzling. But she was saved from having to think of something to say when the Arch-Elemists began manipulating the fire on top of the sacra, twisting and morphing the flames into shapes to tell the story of their four gods and how they'd once roamed the lands, each of them able to summon and manipulate one element each, how they'd created the mountains and the trees and the rivers and the seas, how they'd borne children amongst themselves, and how, after generations those children were able to manipulate not one but all the elements.

As the fiery tale neared its conclusion, depicting how the gods eventually lost their corporal forms and instead lived on in the elements themselves, their souls mingling with that of fire, water, air ,and earth, Emery snuck another glance at Tavor. Emery knew the story, of course, and had hardly listened to it. But he watched enraptured, his own bowl of chowder forgotten and growing cool before him.

After the flames returned to normal and the formal dinner had ended, the tables and stumps retreated into the earth, leaving the clearing full of space once more. A bonfire blazed to life in its center, and people began playing on drums and flutes. Music and laughter swelled all around, and Emery felt once again like she couldn't breathe. She rose from her seat, intent on stepping off the dais to get some air, but a tap on her shoulder stopped her.

She turned to find the outsider standing too. He dipped his torso forward in what must be some kind of outsider greeting. "I think it's time we were properly introduced," he said, his accent strange and, this time, she thought, quite lovely really. Before she could respond, he took her hand and kissed her knuckles. "It's grand to meet one of the chosen ones," he said, his accent lovely and strange. "I'm certain we'll make history together, Miss Aalokin."

Her palms began to sweat, and she pulled her hand away, praying to the gods he hadn't noticed. "Thank you." She forced a smile. "I hope I can be useful, Commissioner Thantos." Her palms began to sweat, and she pulled her hand away, praying to the gods he hadn't noticed. "Thank you," she managed. "I hope I'll be of some use to you."

"Tavor, please." He smiled back, his eyes bright in the semi-darkness of the night. "And I'm sure you will be. I look forward to getting to know you better."

"When do we leave?" Liam asked, also standing from his seat, his eagerness clearly shoving any manners he possessed aside.

"I hope to leave in a week's time," Tavor said. "In that time, my men will finish readying our ship for the long journey and I hope to help you two prepare."

"One week?" Emery blurted. One week hardly felt like any time at all.

"Yes, I know it seems fast," Tavor relented. "But we need to leave before the wet season hits, or our journey will be even more dangerous."

"Wet season?" Liam asked.

Tavor rose an eyebrow at Liam curiously. "Do you not have seasons here? Fascinating. Well, out there we have a dry season and a wet season. During the wet season, hurricanes are a constant danger on the seas. It's best we reach the continent well before that season begins."

Emery mulled over Tavor's words, interest peaked. On

Orabel, the weather ranged from sunny to rainy and everything in between, but like everything about the island, elemental manipulation was used to control it, to keep the weather from getting too hot or too cold, too dry or too wet. But she'd been told stories about how in some places beyond the island, it got so cold ice fell from the sky, and so hot plants withered in the heat.

"How long will it take us to reach the continent?" Liam was asking Tavor.

"If the weather holds and no complications arise, about fifty days."

"Fifty *days*?" Liam's mouth fell open, and Emery exchanged a wide eyed look with her twin.

It only took an hour or two to walk from one side of Orabel to the other. Emery couldn't imagine how huge the world out there must be if it took fifty whole days of sailing to reach the continent. The thought of all the new things one could see in that time caused a peculiar mixture of unease and excitement to burn in her chest.

Tavor chuckled. "Yes. It's quite the journey. Your elders hid you well." Emery wanted to ask how, if that was true, Tavor had managed to find them, but before she could, Tavor clapped his hands together. "Now, enough formalities. We can prepare on the morrow. Tonight, shall we celebrate?"

Tavor led Emery and Liam off the dais but almost as soon as his boots hit the grassy meadow, a cluster of villagers descended upon Tavor full of questions about his world. Emery wanted to listen to Tavor's answers, but Liam was already pulling her away to the edge of the clearing, and she turned to see Caelin, Fia, Grace and Ayana breaking through the multitude towards them, their expressions encompassing the full range possible. As soon as they were within earshot they began talking over each other.

"I can't believe it!" Fia shouted, eyes bright as the stars above them.

"This is amazing!" Grace squeaked. "You'll get to see what's out there! Think of everything you'll learn. I've never been more jealous in my life!"

"This is bad," Caelin mumbled. "This is very, very bad. You should go back and say you can't do it."

Emery gazed at her friends as they babbled, soaked up their presence. How was she going to live without seeing them every day?

Ayana grabbed her elbow. "We'll discuss all this tomorrow. Tonight, we're going to be happy. Agreed?"

Without waiting for a response, Ayana grabbed Grace's arm as well and dragged them both towards the bonfire, where other islanders were whirling in time to the drumbeats.

Somehow, through the fog in her head, the numbness in her body, the music managed to reach Emery, and she began to dance, allowing herself to feel everything but to think about nothing. Even though Liam and Fia mostly danced with each other. Even though Grace spun Emery around and around so many times she thought she might puke. Even though Caelin mostly just stood there, staring into the distance.

Even though, in a few days, she'd be leaving them all behind.

# Chapter Seven

Emery's ears were still ringing with the boom of drums and the trill of flutes when she stumbled into her bedroom later that night. To her surprise, candlelight was dancing across the walls, and her breath caught when she realized someone was sitting on her bed. It was her grandfather. He lifted his head at the sound of her gasp, the candlelight starkly illuminating the lines on his face.

"You gave me a fright," she said.

"I'm sorry, my dear. I was just...reminiscing."

He was holding a small wooden figurine shaped like a goose, its feathers worn smooth from years of handling. He ran a finger up and down its long neck.

"Do you remember this?" Grandfather asked, running a finger down the goose's long neck.

Emery sat down beside him. "Of course. Liam and my ninth birthdays. You made him a goat."

Her grandfather chuckled, gazing down at the figurine again. "Yes."

Every year on their birthdays, he would manipulate a chunk of wood into a little gift for them. Emery had never tired of watching him. As he fiddled with the goose, Emery spotted the tattoo of an oak tree inked on his wrist, a tattoo he earned when he became masterful at manipulating wood with his abilities. In Orabel, every great achievement or big life moment was marked with a tattoo. When they mastered an element, went through the bonding ceremony with a partner, had a child. Liam was supposed to get his first tattoo shortly after they turned seventeen and his abilities had fully awoken. This would mark him as an official adult. But he never got his tattoo, because he wanted to wait for Emery so they could get them together. Only Emery's abilities still hadn't fully awakened and so it never happened.

A pit opened in Emery's stomach, wondering if they'd make it back here so he could finally get his tattoo, or if he'd squandered is only chance for her.

Shoving away that worry, Emery reached past her grandfather into a little nook in the wall where she kept the figurines he had made for her over the years, pulling out the newest one. She and Liam had their birthday a few months ago, and this time she had chosen a ship. Her grandfather had told her it was the most challenging thing he had ever created for her. No ships existed in Orabel, and it was only rarely that one would come anywhere close enough to be visible from the shore, so he had only vague memories to instruct him.

Emery loved the little ship, but now that she'd seen a real one up close she realized it wasn't perfect. The hull wasn't quite the right shape, the sails slightly larger than they should be.

She turned the figurine over in her hands, frowning. Her grandfather, in his whole eighty-six years, had never seen a ship properly before. Had never set foot off the island. Had never known anything else. All because he'd been born with abilities he'd never asked for.

The unfairness of it burned in her chest, heating her arms, her legs, making her want to get up and do something.

Well, now she *could*.

"Are you angry with me, Grandfather? At us?" Emery whispered, staring at the wooden ship. "For agreeing to go."

Her grandparents had always been protective. They had

sworn to Emery's parents they would keep the twins safe, and they had. But now Emery and her brother were going to leave their protection, and the protection of the entire island, to go somewhere they could so easily get killed, somewhere their parents may have already *been* killed.

Her grandparents had always been protective. They had sworn to Emery's parents they would keep the twins safe, and they had. But now Emery and her brother were going to leave their protection, and the protection of the entire island, to go somewhere they could so easily get killed, somewhere their parents may have already *been* killed.

"My dear, no!" Her grandfather wrapped an arm around her shoulder and pulled her close. "Are we terrified for you? Of course. But we are also so proud of you both. You two have inherited your mother's bravery. I'm sure that is why the gods have chosen you."

"They chose *him*, don't forget."

He squeezed her shoulder and chuckled. "Ah, there was only room in the sacra's fire for one of you. The gods know you are both equally worthy. And more to the point, that wherever one of you goes the other will follow."

Though the burning in her chest remained, her grandfather's reassurance had at least lifted the weight of guilt from her. She leaned into him, taking in his familiar scent, mixed with pine and woodsmoke, trying to store as much of it as she could in her mind.

"I'll find mother," she promised. "Somehow. We'll find a way to bring peace. And we'll save Ayana."

But even as she said the words, the weight of them felt heavy in her mouth. Those were such huge promises. What if she couldn't keep them?

But her grandfather only said, "Of that, I have no doubt."

EMERY COULDN'T SLEEP that night. The fire inside her still burned, and her mind was raging to the point where she couldn't take it anymore. It was time to give up on sleep. She grabbed her lim, stood on her bed, and shimmied out her window. Making as little sound as possible, she climbed down the giant redwood until her feet landed on the dirt path just outside her home.

Darkness still covered most of the island, but the watery violet light of dawn hovered beyond the trees, giving Emery just enough light to see.

She walked without a particular destination in mind, following whatever path appealed to her at random. She just needed to move. A slight breeze rustled the needles and leaves above her and the ferns and flowers growing along the paths. The dirt under her bare feet felt refreshingly cool and soft. Most of the islanders were silent now, asleep or otherwise recovering from the night's excitement.

For the first time since facing the Arch-Elemists and the outsider's scrutiny, Emery's heart stopped racing. She could breathe again.

"Get back here!"

Her eyes snapped over to see a tiny child running out of a home towards her.

"Emy!" The boy launched himself at her, giggling as she caught him.

"Coben, what are you doing up?" she asked.

"Escaping his mother," said Mel, striding from the same tree.

Behind her, Fynn's little face poked out from the doorway. He still looked tired, but not nearly as exhausted as he had the night before. "Coben, best listen to Ma." The other boy added with a playful hiss, "Or the outsiders will eat you!"

Coben shrieked and Mel took him from Emery, hoisting him up onto her hip. "Congratulations, Emery," she said. "And good luck to you both."

"Thank you," Emery replied automatically and then took Mel's free hand. "I promise to do everything I can to bring back a cure."

Mel's eyes filled with tears and she just nodded. "I know you will."

Emery swallowed a lump in her throat. "How's Dray this morning?"

"He and his father aren't home yet. I came back early last night to get the little ones to bed but they must have stayed out celebrating."

Emery thought about the blank look on Dray's face and the apprehensive expression on Aryan's before the meeting had begun the night before. They hadn't exactly looked up for celebrating anything, and she realized she didn't remember seeing them at all afterwards during the festivities. But the whole night had been a blur, she could have just missed them.

After bidding goodbye to Mel and the boys, Emery continued with her wandering. But she was distracted by Fynn's childish warning.

How often had she heard that threat growing up? How many times had such words sent pangs of fear through her?

How many more children would grow up feeling the same way if she and Liam didn't succeed?

She glanced back over her shoulder, watching Mel hold her child close as they went inside, and an entirely different pang rippled through her, a painful emptiness and the longing to know what the touch of a mother felt like.

She turned and continued down the path, eventually finding herself at the Gardens, a huge chunk of land where the elemists grew their food and kept their livestock pens, though the animals mostly roamed free and returned at night to sleep. Fruit and nut trees were arranged in rows and vegetables grew in distinct patches of soil, around which various berry bushes formed lush hedges. The gardens were splendid and plentiful now, thanks to the islander's abilities, but Emery knew if the Withering sapped too many islanders of their strength, they would eventually be unable to tend them adequately, and they'd all starve.

She grabbed a bright red apple to eat while she wandered

through to the fields where goats and sheep grazed and the chickens and geese most liked to wander around. While the islanders only took from their animals what they naturally produced, their milk and eggs, wool and feathers, and they used their hides and bones after they died, she had heard that outsiders *killed* and *ate* their animals. She shuddered at the thought of what she was going to witness out in the world, then tossed her apple core to one of the goats and pushed her way through the foliage at the other end of the Gardens.

The redwoods grew smaller and closer together here, given no one lived in this area. The terrain beneath her feet, now a soft bed of pine needles and moss, grew steeper the further she walked.

To her side a small creek ran between the trees, one of many that began near the cliffs and worked its way down to the central lake. She followed it higher and higher until the land levelled out and the trees gave way to open space. Now she was standing on the edge of a jagged cliff top, nothing but the ocean and sky before her.

She stood on the edge of a jagged cliff top. A cool, salty breeze climbed up the rocks and tousled her hair as she looked down. The cliff was at least a hundred and fifty feet high and completely vertical.

Like everything in Orabel it had a purpose, to keep outsiders out.

And yet, outsiders had entered the island without problem, had even been welcomed by the Arch-Elemists, seemingly without question. What was even harder to comprehend, she would soon be leaving with them, setting out into their world, because they might just be the key to the island's salvation. Her head hurt with the strain of trying to make these opposing realities fit together.

Emery absently watched a fresh water extracted itself from the salt water of the ocean below and climbed up the edge of the cliff next to her, like a reverse waterfall. It was this water that fed the various creeks of the island and continuously granted the islanders fresh drinking water. And it was yet one more aspect of survival that would cease to exist if the islanders lost their abilities to manipulate the water. One more reason why the needed to find a cure as soon as possible.

The sun peeked a golden eye above the horizon, painting the world in streaks of pink, purple and orange. And Emery realized she was about to miss statera for the second morning in the row. Most of the islanders – at least those not sleeping in after the night's festivities – would be rising now to go through their morning prayers in front of the sacra.

She wouldn't make it to the center of the island in time from where she was, and if she were honest with herself, the thought of mingling with her friends and family was daunting right now. She wanted more time to sit with her thoughts. But she was determined not to miss *statera* for a second day in a row.

She stepped away from the cliff edge, giving herself space to move without fear of falling off. Then, breathing deeply and gripping the rough stone with her toes, she fell into the movements, allowing her body to choose the poses. She stretched up into *solid oak*, bent down into *setting sun*, then twisted her waist to shift into *ivy in the wind*, allowing her mind, her soul, to reach out to that of the elements, and of the gods, and she prayed. She prayed to Teralyn for strength, to Tadewin for luck, for Eldoris to keep her curiosity alive and for Pyralis to keep her desire alight no matter what she encountered out there in the world. In the end, wasn't this what she'd always wanted?

A twig snapped close by and Emery's eyes snapped open as she stumbled backwards, catching herself before she came too close to the cliff edge. Tavor was immerging from the trees, shielding his green eyes from the sun's glare. Her heart thundered into a double pace and her hands began sweating once more. For half a moment, her instinct was to reach for her lim, but then she forced her hands down, reminding her body that she was not in danger.

But she couldn't stop from blurting, "What are you doing here?"

"Oh, apologies. I didn't mean to interrupt you." Tavor paused, squinting at the bursts of colours in the sky. "I wanted to catch the sunrise before I headed back to my ship, and then I spotted you." He sighed. "To be honest, it's a bit boring being cooped up on the ship all day, especially after the long journey getting here."

"Have you spent most of your time here on the ship?" Emery asked.

"When not with the Arch-Elemists, yes. Your leaders thought that would be best as to not make your people uncomfortable."

Emery supposed that made sense. It was strange enough seeing the outsider standing on her island's cliffs. Watching him wander through the village probably would have been...unsettling.

Tavor cast her a quizzical look. "Were you praying just now?"

Emery shifted on her feet, suddenly feeling self-conscious. "Yes."

He nodded to himself, as if pleased he'd guessed correctly. "I've seen your people praying together at the sacra. How does it work? Do your gods actually answer? What are those stretches and what are they for?"

Emery couldn't stop a bemused smile from tugging on her lips as Tavor's tone grew more and more excited with every question.

He noticed her smile, and clamped his mouth shut. He looked down, sheepish. "Apologies. I'm just excited to finally be here."

"It's alright," she said, noticing how much younger he looked with that sheepish look on his face. He couldn't have seen more than twenty-two years, if that. "When we pray, we allow our souls to mingle with the elements, and the gods who live within them. This is also how we use our abilities to manipulate the elements, so not only are we connecting with our gods, but we're practicing our abilities at the same time."

Tavor was nodding again as he listened fervently. "Do they speak back?"

"To some people," Emery answered slowly. It felt so odd, almost wrong, to be saying all this to a stranger, and she had to remind herself that Tavor was here to learn about her people so he could help them. "Mostly to the Arch-Elemists. But others have claimed to hear them, too."

"Have you?'

"Well, no." Her cheeks burned with the confession, and she hastened to add, "Most elemists my age don't hear them."

While this was true enough, it still felt like one more thing Emery had fallen behind with and she hoped he didn't ask about her own abilities.

To her relief, he asked, "And the movements?"

"The movements are part of a practice called statera. In order to manipulate the elements, we have to keep our emotions calm because otherwise we can lose control, especially if we're angry, and the movements help with that. It also helps us guide are abilities during the manipulation." She tapped the tip of her lim peaking over her shoulder. "We also practice statera-lim, which is basically the same thing but with the movements sped up for fighting and the addition of our lims."

Tavor eyed her lim with unguarded curiosity. "Fascinating."

Emery shifted again, awkward under his scrutiny. Was it really that fascinating? Did people in the outside world not pray or practice statera?

Tavor faced the rising sun again, clasping his hands behind his back. "What a view." He glanced at her sidelong. "May I ask you something?"

Emery nodded, wondering why he was asking permission now after he just asked her half a dozen questions moments before.

"Why are you not practicing statera with the rest of your people this morning?"

Emery turned to the horizon, too. The pinks and purples of dawn were giving way to blue now. She shrugged, feeling awkward yet again and wondering if she'd ever not feel awkward around this outsider. "I just needed some time alone to think."

She could still feel Tavor's side long gaze on her. "Yes, I suppose you have much to think about after last night."

Emery swallowed, her throat suddenly dry. "It's a lot to take in."

Just standing there, talking with an outsider, was a lot to take in.

"What you and your brother are doing is very brave. Before anything else, I would like to thank you for giving me a chance. And in case it puts you more at ease in my company, I confess I was also nervous to come here. I was worried of your people's reaction. Even after your elders gave us such a warm welcome it took me a while to feel comfortable here." He turned to look at her. "But I do now."

Emery blinked at him. She'd never considered his side of events before, what taking the risk to make first contact must have felt like for him. Most outsiders thought her kind were savages, after all, or so she'd been told.

He looked away first this time, and Emery couldn't help but notice the way the golden morning light gilded his jaw and highlighted his sharp cheekbones.

She took this opportunity to quickly scan his face, all planes and angles in the morning sunlight. Before she could think of anything intelligent to say, a twig snapped behind them and she spun round. The other four outsiders who had accompanied Tavor to the meetings the last two nights stood several paces back in the trees, partially hidden by the foliage. Presumably, the intension was to remain far enough away to give Tavor the illusion of privacy, but close enough to get to him in moments if necessary. Had they been standing there the entire time?

"Why do those men follow you everywhere?" she asked.

Tavor didn't even glance back at them. "The world can be a dangerous place, Miss Aalokin. *Forbiddens* still abound, and they do not agree with what I" – his green eyes met hers – "what *we* are trying to do."

*Forbiddens.* The word covered her tongue with a sour taste. The term had been given to all elemists after their banishment, including, technically, her and everyone else on the island. However, to the people of Orabel, and seemingly also to Tavor – the term only applied to those elemists who remained out in the world wreaking havoc against humans, fighting them and otherwise ensuring that the banishment would never be lifted. Assuming the stories she had heard were true, Emery had never understand why they would choose such a path rather than seek peace.

"There are no...Forbiddens here though," she pointed out. "Everyone here longs for peace and collaboration with your people." She thought back to the more suspicious faces dotted among the crowd at recent events, deciding against mentioning them. Surely even those not yet convinced by Tavor's confidence wouldn't want to harm him or their efforts.

"Nonetheless, peril is everywhere." Tavor glanced back at the four other outsiders. "They are trained to detect danger, even if it seems there is none."

Emery's stomach clenched. *Peril* was indeed *everywhere,* and she was heading straight towards it.

Her panic must have been evident, because Tavor quickly added, "It isn't all bad though, of course. There's a lot of good in the world as well. In fact, I would say there's mostly good. Unfortunately, my line of work has me seeing a disproportionate amount of bad."

She fought the urge to flinch back as he stepped closer, but he spoke softly. "It's not too late to change your mind. You don't have to leave the safety of this island if you don't wish to. I would completely understand."

Emery looked up into his face, so strange and yet so familiar. How ridiculous that a war existed between their two peoples, whose similarities surely outweighed their differences. She had to think of her grandparents, her friends, neighbors, everyone who might never get the chance to leave Orabel if things didn't change. Of Fynn, Ayana, and all the others who might die before she returned, but who could now at least die knowing she was out there, trying to help forge a better world. Of her brother. She couldn't let him go alone. "It was too late the moment you set foot here."

A crash echoed behind them, and Emery whirled again to find at least half a dozen islanders hurtling out of the woods near where Tavor's guards were standing, lims gripped in their hands.

The trees around them were creaking and swaying under the islanders' influence, and a great gust of wind shoved at her and Tavor, causing them both to stagger back perilously close to the cliff's edge, and whipping Emery's hair into her face, momentarily blinding her.

When she shoved her hair out of her eyes, it was to find four of the islanders in a scuffle with Tavor's guards, while two ran straight for Tavor, and for a moment she didn't react, not able to process what was happening.

It was Aryan and Dray, the father and son sharing similar expressions of malice and determination as they rushed ever closer, teeth bared like predators closing in on their prey. She'd never seen such looks of hatred on anyone before, let alone on her own neighbours' faces.

Beside her, Tavor braced his feet, his jaw clenched. His free hand was hovering over his belt, presumably deliberating over whether to pull out a weapon of his own, but he neither moved nor spoke.

"By Pyralis's fire, what are you doing?" she cried.

Ayran and Dray halted just paces away.

"Step away from the outsider, Emery," Aryan demanded. Gusts of wind whipped around them all, ripping at their clothes. "This man cannot be allowed to leave here with our secrets."

Emery's heart raced as realization dawned on her. They were here to *kill* Tavor. Horror twisted her guts, but she did not step away from him. Instead, she moved closer, raising her hands in a placating gesture. "He's here to help us, Aryan. Think of Fynn."

"I am thinking of Fynn," Aryan snapped, and Emery tried not to flinch. Aryan had always been so friendly, always tending to their wounds and caring for them if they fell ill. She'd never seen him like this before. "I refuse to let this outsider reveal our safe haven."

"But Fynn needs a cure – "

"I will find the cure! We don't need him." Aryan raised a hand and squeezed his fingers into a fist. Beneath Emery's feet, the ground began to quake, lose bits of rock falling from the cliff behind her and hurtling into the churning sea far below.

Emery saw Dray's eyes widened as cracks formed in the earth under Emery and Tavor's feet at Aryan's command. Dray had stood by his father silently until then, but now he finally spoke up. "Father, wait, Emery will fall too!"

But whether Aryan cared about Emery's fate, she'd never know. She heard a series of clicks and whistling, and both Aryan and Dray slapped the backs of their necks. When Aryan turned around, she saw a red feather protruding from between his fingers on the nape of his neck. Immediately, the ground ceased its shaking, and the wind faded away.

Behind Aryan and Dray, Tavor's four guards still stood. Two of them pointed strange banana-shaped objects at Aryan and Dray, while the rest of the islanders who'd attacked lay in motionless heaps at their feet. Aryan lurched forward, whether to charge the guards or help his fallen kin, Emery did not know, but he staggered, and dropped his lim. His knees hit the ground, and then he slumped forward onto his face. He did not get up.

Emery's whole body went cold with shocked horror. She locked eyes with Dray in time to watch a look of complete terror cross his face as he too slumped sideways and hit the dirt. Her heart thundered so intensely her vision pulsed. She raced to Dray and dropped to her knees, pulling him into her lap. He was completely limp, but his eyes were open, staring up at her.

She spun on Tavor as he crouched next to her. "What did you do!"

Tavor surveyed the fallen islanders, his expression apologetic. "They're not dead, just temporarily paralyzed."

Emery leaned closer to Dray to make sure Tavor spoke the

truth. Relief shot through her at the sound of Dray's slow breathing.

A bright red feather protruded out of his neck, or at least something that looked like one. She reached to remove it but Tavor caught her wrist.

"Don't. It's laced."

She snatched her hand back. "What does that mean?"

"Our darts are laced with curare. It's a natural paralyzing agent – not poison. I promise you," he said earnestly. "They'll be fine. They just won't be able to move for a few hours."

She didn't know what he meant by *hours*, but that also wasn't her greatest concern right now. "And w*hy* are you carrying a *paralyzing agent* around with you?"

"It's the most effective way to take down F*orbid*d –" Tavor caught himself, cringing. "Sorry, elemists – without causing any real harm to them. And, of course, only if absolutely necessary."

"You're saying that paralyzing someone isn't harming them?"

Tavor looked stricken."No, I – It just renders their abilities useless."

Emery's stomach soured, like she was going to be sick. She'd heard stories of such weapons before, but she'd never imagined seeing them in action. And they hadn't even left the island yet.

"I'm sorry this happened." Tavor stood, his eyes darting amongst the trees as if searching for more danger. His face was pale, and his hands shook.

Emery realized he was just as distressed as herself. Possibly more so. Of course he was. Her people just tried to *kill* him.

A part of her wanted to apologize in return, because she was distraught and disgusted over her peoples' actions. But a part of her was also completely horrified over how easily and efficiently Tavor's guards had taken her people out, and it made it impossible to forget she was kneeling in the middle of a group of varens, people who had been specifically trained to hunt and destroy her.

When the Arch-Elemists approached, materializing from between the trees like ghosts, relief like she'd never felt before crashed over her. Her leaders silently surveyed the scene, gazes travelling from Tavor's guards, to the heap of unmoving elemists on the ground, to Tavor and Emery.

Emery still knelt on the ground with a paralyzed Dray in her lap. Tavor stood just behind her and when she glanced at him, she saw his face had blanched further.

He held up his hands. "I know what this looks like. I can explain –"

"There is no need," Dyzek spoke over Tavor. "The trees have eyes through which we saw everything."

Emery couldn't help but shudder. While it was a relief to know she wouldn't have to explain what happened, to choose a side, it was also a little unsettling to have the rumors confirmed, that the Arch-Elemist saw *everything*. The rumors also whispered they could see off the island too, via the wind and the sea. And that they had ways to silence those who dared to try speaking about Orabel.

Behind Dyzek, Aeolius was using the wind to carefully lift each paralyzed elemist off the ground. "We will take them to the infirmary until the curare wears off, and then they will face consequences for their actions."

Before Emery could contemplate just what those consequences might be, Dray was lifted from her lap, floating on his back on a bed of air like the other paralyzed elemists, leaving her kneeling alone in the dirt, still to stunned to react.

Celosia grasped Emery's hands and gently pulled her to her feet. "You are unharmed, child?"

Emery could only nod.

The Arch-Elemists placed a soft, wrinkled hand on Emery's back and began to lead her into the trees. "I will escort you home and then you must pack your belongings."

"What?"

"For the safety of Tavor and our people, we're afraid we must fast track out timeline. You'll be leaving today."

# Chapter Eight

The next few hours passed in a chaotic blur as preparations were made, but to Emery it felt like mere moments before she found herself standing beside Liam on Orabel's sandy shore, preparing to say goodbye to everyone they had ever known.

Nearly the whole community had come to see them off, spread out along the beach and even spilling into the shallow turquoise water of the bay itself. Further out, the outsider ship floated in the calm water. Over the course of the morning , Tavor's crew had been paddling back and forth between the ship and the shore in small boats, transporting provisions needed for their excursion. Others were scuttling about the vessel's deck, readying the ship for its long, hazardous journey in ways that Emery hoped she would soon understand.

Since the decision they would travel early had been announced, the twins had been bombarded with so many hugs and well-wishes that soon she'd felt completely overwhelmed. However, it had provided some welcome distraction from the moment that now awaited them. The hardest goodbye of all.

Their closest friends and family were standing in front of them, and she tried to hide how much she was shaking at the thought of never seeing them again.

Behind her, the ship that caused so much panic only days before still bobbed in the bay. Emery hadn't realized more outsiders stayed on it, and at the moment these outsiders paddled back and forth between the ship and the shore in smaller boats, transporting provisions between the two. Others scuttled about the vessel's deck, doing whatever sailors did in order to ready ships for long, hazardous journeys.

Emery tried to savor the moment as best she could. She took in their beloved faces, drinking in and storing every detail. Her grandmother's tired eyes, her grandfather's crinkled smile, Fia's freckled cheeks and Grace's golden curls. And Ayana, her brave eyes shining with hope.

But someone was missing.

"Where's Caelin?" Liam asked.

Fia and Grace glanced at each other, then looked down at their feet.

"He's not coming," Grace murmured. "I've tried all morning to convince him."

Emery felt like she'd been punched in the stomach. "Why?"

Grace shook her head. "I...I think he's angry you're leaving... without him."

"But...it wasn't our choice," Liam insisted. "Why didn't he talk to us if he felt that way?"

"I don't know." Tears poured down Grace's cheeks as she threw her arms around Emery. "I'll take care of Ayana until you get back," she whispered in her ear.

"It's going to be so strange without you here," Fia said, embracing Emery next while Grace moved on to Liam. Emery hugged her friend back so tightly it was probably painful, but Fia didn't complain.

Ayana came up to her now, pale lips quirked in a half smile. She pulled both Emery and Liam into a hug, her bony arms stronger than they appeared. "Promise me you'll take care of each other."

Emery's eyes started to burn. "I wish you could come with

us." Emery said. Her eyes started to burn. Gods, what if they didn't get back in time? What if Aya –

Her sister shrugged her frail body away from their embrace. "You know, I can do without mothering you two for a while." Her forced smile started to wobble. "Have fun out there, won't you?"

"You can rely on it," Liam said, his own voice hoarse now.

Ayana grabbed their hands and squeezed. "Promise me something else."

"We won't come back without a cure," he vowed, swallowing hard.

"You'd better not," Ayana chuckled weakly. "But that's not what I meant." She fixed them both with her eyes. "Find our parents. Or at least, find out what happened to them. If things don't go...how we want them to..."

"Oh." Liam's voice cracked. "Of course, Aya. We'll find them, somehow."

Emery squeezed her eyes shut as they all came together in a tearful hug, clinging to each other in the unspoken knowledge that they might never see each other again.

She couldn't help also glancing up briefly, hoping to see Caelin running towards them down one of the paths, having decided not to let them go without saying goodbye after all. But he was nowhere to be seen. A spark of anger flared in her belly but she quelled it quickly. If he didn't want to see them off on this dangerous journey, so be it.

With a heavy heart, she turned finally to her grandparents. Silent tears were streaming down their faces, nearly breaking her resolve. For a moment, she wanted to scream that she'd changed her mind and run back to their tree, vowing never to leave them. Instead, she buried her face in her grandfather's chest, pulling her grandmother and Liam in too, and the four of them stood together for a while in silence, just breathing each other in.

"I apologize for interrupting your goodbyes," a voice that was now becoming familiar said from behind Emery.

Emery untangled herself to find Tavor standing there, one hand resting on his walking stick and the other behind his back. Considering the intense and chaotic morning they had, he appeared remarkable unruffled. Not a speck of dirt marred his coat, nor was a single hair out of place on his head.

Emery fought the urge to smooth down her own flyaway hair as Tavor smiled and said, "

I'm afraid it is time to go."

Liam's expression was strangely blank as he glanced back towards the trees again, no doubt searching for Caelin. Emery swallowed and took his hand. a spark of anger flaring to life in her stomach. If Caelin didn't want to say goodbye, then so be it.

She turned to look at everybody's miserable faces one last time, forcing a brave smile onto her own. "Don't worry about us. We'll be back before you know it."

Liam squeezed her hand.

"We'll miss you," said Grace.

Fia rushed over to give Liam one last hug and Emery embraced Ayana and their grandparents for the final time. She cast everyone a quick, reassuring smile that she hoped didn't betray her terror, then Liam tugged at her tunic and encouraged her onwards. Her legs felt heavy as trees, rooted to the spot, but she willed herself to tear them off the ground, to turn her back to her family and follow Tavor to one of the little boats wedged in the sand. She realized then that, unlike most things in Orabel, it wasn't formed from one solid piece of wood molded into a shape but from many pieces fused together. How...strange.

"Let me take your bags," Tavor offered, and they each handed him the shoulder sacks they'd packed full of clothing that morning. He placed them in the boat, then turned to offer Emery his palm. "May I?"

Emery eyed his hand, not sure what he was asking.

Tavor cast her smile, and elaborated, "May I help you into the boat?"

Her chest tightened. Did she seem somehow incompetent to him?

"Oh, that's alright," she said, determined to prove herself, and leapt into the boat. Sitting down on one of the wooden benches she smiled up at Tavor, but soon stopped when she saw he was still standing in the same position with a frown on his face. Her stomach dropped with realization. Had she just been rude while messing up an outsider custom? "I'm sorry, I'll get out again." She stood up and had half stepped off the boat when Tavor waved his hand and chuckled. "No, please don't. Everything is fine, I was just surprised."

Emery's face flushed as she hovered awkwardly with one foot on the side of the boat.

"Please, just sit. It appears we are both not entirely used to each other's customs yet. But we'll get there."

Emery swung her small sack off her shoulder. Tavor had advised them to wear only outsider clothing while on their journey, of which he would provide for them once they reached their destination. Thus, the twins needn't pack much.

She plopped down again.

Liam clambered in beside her, grinning.

"Well done, you'll make a fine ambassador yet with your *smooth* ways."

She shoved his shoulder, face still burning.

A jolt of panic hit her as the boat lurched forward. Tavor had pushed it off the sand and hopped in himself. A jolt of panic struck Emery right in the chest as the boat lurched forward. She clung to the sides, tapping her foot against the boat's wooden bottom as Tavor paddled them away from the shore, away from her friends and family. Beside her, Liam sat very still. She stole another glance at everyone she was leaving behind. Almost the entire island was still there, waving and cheering. Her hand felt ten times heavier than normal as she lifted it to wave back.

A shadow fell over the boat, and she turned to see the enormous ship looming ahead of them, blocking out the sun as they paddled closer. Soon, their boat was bumping against its massive side, which also seemed to be made from many, *many* separate pieces of wood.

"We must climb up," Tavor said.

He hefted their bags onto one of his shoulders, then offered a hand to Emery.

Though she still didn't need it, this time she accepted the gesture.

Once she had got the hang of climbing the rope ladder, Tavor followed behind her, Liam scrambling up after them.

They were climbing aboard their first ship.

Once at the top, Emery could see it was even larger than it had looked from shore. Everything was wood and rope and canvas. Sailors were hurrying around, climbing and tying and yanking on things, shouting gruffly at one another. They all wore tunics and trousers similar to the twin's clothing. A few eyes wandered over the twins, but no one spoke to them. Dispersed amongst the sailors were varens, distinguishable by their blue-and-black jackets. Emery swallowed down a sudden swell of unease at the sight of so many varens.

Tavor spread his arms wide. "Welcome to *The New Dawn*!"

"The ship has a name?" Emery asked, her curious gaze roving over the three masts which were as tall as trees.

"Of course, all ships have a name." Tavor patted the closest mast affectionately. "And *The New Dawn* is cutting edge. One of the fastest and most comfortable passenger ships out there." He adjusted their bags over his shoulder. "I'll stow your things where you'll be sleeping, I'll be back shortly."

He crossed the ship and disappeared, leaving Emery and Liam alone. They glanced at each other. Liam was still pale, but a smile was slowly lifting the corners of his mouth.

Somewhere below, a man shouted, and drums began to beat. Slowly, the ship began to drift forward. It wasn't moving fast, but Emery still grabbed the railing, her stomach flipping with trepidation and excitement.

It was time.

Liam nudged her, then indicated a set of stairs that led up to a smaller deck at the rear of the ship. Together, they sprinted up the stairs and stood at the railing. From there, they could clearly see the islanders gathered across the bay, some of them still cheering and waving. The twins waved back.

Her throat burned and her eyes stung, but she refused to let the panic take over, the awful thought that this could be the last time she saw her family, the last time she saw home.

She could just make out Fia's red hair in the crowd, and beside her Grace, Aya, and her grandparents, their arms around each other. She stared at their faces, hardly daring to blink for fear of missing that final glimpse, and watched intently as they shrank and began to disappear into the blur of people.

The ship squeezed through the Break, the cliffs suddenly closing in as if to embrace them and then the bay was gone.

For what felt like an age The ship squeezed its way through the Break, the cliffs suddenly closing in around the vessel as if to embrace it. the ship was plunged into semi-darkness as the rough grey stone blocked the world from view. Emery held her breath, and eventually the cliffs spat them back out. She blinked as bright sunlight splashed across the ship once more, and a thrill of shivers rippled up her spine.

She was outside Orabel.

A laugh escaped her, a quick, terrified noise that Liam echoed. Above them, Fia and Grace had sprinted to the treacherous edge of the cliffs, Ayana straddling Grace's back. They were all calling and waving as hard as they could, and the twins waved back just as enthusiastically.

Emery bit her lip, trying to ignore the sharp ache gripping her heart. She waved until her friends grew too small to see once more, and even then she kept waving. It wasn't until Orabel turned into a green-grey mass on the horizon that she stopped.

The twins glanced at each other, eyes wide, and then turned in unison toward the front of the ship. The raced down the stairs leading back to the main deck, ran the length of the ship long the railing until they came across another small set of stairs leading to another smaller deck, this time at the front of the ship.

Ahead of them, the smooth turquoise ocean stretched

endlessly, joining with the sky so far ahead she couldn't tell where one ended and the other began. She'd seen such sights before, of course, but it seemed different this time. This time, she was finally going to find out what lay beyond that mass of blue.

With that thought, her lingering fear began to morph into a more pleasant form of anticipation. Hadn't Tavor himself said there was mostly good in the world? For now, she'd have to trust that statement. She closed her eyes, enjoying the sensation of her long hair fanning out behind her as the wind generated by the ship's gathering speed grabbed at it, running its balmy fingers across her cheeks. She licked her lips, and they tasted of salt and mystery.

"We're doing it," Liam murmured, his voice nearly lost in the wind. "We're actually doing it."

"I know." She turned to look at him. "Thank you. For not leaving me behind."

Liam grinned. "Well, I need someone trustworthy to verify all the amazing feats I'm going to perform, don't I?"

Before she could tease him back, Tavor appeared at her side so suddenly she nearly jumped. "How are the two of you holding up?

Tavor said, appearing at Emery's side so suddenly she nearly jumped.

"Great," Liam replied.

"Excellent." Tavor gave them a magnanimous smile, his cape flapping like a pair of wings behind him.

Emery glanced behind them, torn between wanting to watch the approaching horizon finally change, and her curiosity about how the ship worked. She frowned as she examined the still furled sails. "How are we moving without sails?"

Tavor leaned over the side of the ship and pointed down. "We're rowing. For now."

Emery leaned over as well, and saw dozens of oars sticking out of the ship's hull, dipping in and out of the ocean in perfect unison with the drumbeat.

"Isn't sailing faster?" Liam asked.

"Yes, but we haven't left the Barren Sea yet." At the twins' blank looks, he appeared surprised. "Don't you know? Your island is located within the Barren Sea, many, many leagues away from the continent. And any other land, for that matter."

"What is the Barren Sea?" Emery asked.

"That." Tavor swept his arm out, indicating the calm turquoise waters surrounding them. "It gets its name because it's empty. There's no land, no currents, and no wind. No wind means useless sails. We have to row until we leave the Barren Sea."

"How long will that take?" Emery questioned curiously.

"About eighteen days."

Liam let out a low whistle. "The Barren Sea must be huge."

"Indeed." Tavor nodded. "No one actually knows how large it is. Ships rarely explore the area, let alone attempt to sail through it. It's easy to run out of supplies or become lost. And there are no islands, at least that we know of, besides Orabel, so no hope of respite or salvation if something befalls us."

Emery gazed at the retreating horizon where Orabel had already vanished from sight. It had been genius of the Arch-Elemists to raise their island in the middle of a windless place. There had been wind *on* the island, but Emery had not realized, like most everything pertaining to her home, the wind was under the Arch-Elemists influence.

An ache of longing rippled through her chest as she wondered how far away Orabel was already.

A man approached, glancing at the twins briefly before giving his attention to Tavor. He stood straight-backed with his hands clasped behind his back. This was the closest Emery had ever been to an outsider excluding Tavor, and though she felt the urge to step back, she instead scrutinized the man's attire. He wore a shorter version of Tavor's black and blue coat, just like all the other varens she'd seen thus far, only his had the silver stitching along the hems that adorned Tavor's guards' jackets. She wondered if it indicated a ranking of some sort. His skin was a few shades darker than hers, his black hair was cropped close to his head, and as Emery studied his face, she realized he was indeed one of the varens who had been guarding Tavor back home.

"Commissioner," said the man, his accent different then Tavor's. "We have a situation."

Tavor sighed and turned to face him. "Already? What is it, Anders?"

The varen – Anders – said, "We found a stowaway."

Two more men came forward, dragging a third along with them. Emery's mouth fell open and her heart began to gallop as she recognized the low-hanging head, the shaggy hair falling over the young man's face.

Emery's mouth fell open.

"Caelin?" Liam breathed.

Caelin lifted his head, a smug little smile tugging at his lips. The varens held him firmly, but he seemed otherwise unharmed. Still, the sight of her friend in their grasp like that caused Emery's pulse to race for a whole new reason.

"You know this boy?" Tavor looked at Emery, one eyebrow quirked.

"Yes," she said hurriedly. "He's our friend."

Tavor crossed his arms and peered down at Caelin. "Care to explain yourself?"

"We found him in the hold, sir," one of Tavor's men said. "Inside one of the barrels that was *supposed* to contain water."

Emery glanced at Liam, heart in her throat. His lips were squeezed together, as if he were somewhere between amusement and fear for Caelin.

Tavor frowned at him a while longer, then nodded at the varens holding him. They quickly let go, but Tavor's tone did not soften. "You do realize you've cost us a week's water rations. That could have dire consequences if the weather turns against us."

Caelin's smile slipped away. "My apologies. That was not my intention."

"So much is clear. But what was?"

Caelin cleared his throat and rubbed his arms where he'd been held. After a moment, he looked up at Tavor, his eyes brighter than Emery had ever seen them. "I wish to come with you."

"Why?" Tavor's arms were still crossed but, he seemed more curious than angry now.

"I want to protect them." Caelin nodded at the twins. "Like your guards protect you."

Warmth crept into Emery's belly, but it didn't quite melt away the fearful chill across the rest of her body. If Caelin stayed with them, it would mean one less person to say goodbye to, but it also meant one more person she cared about being in danger.

Tavor took a while to reply. "I can assure you, er..."

"Caelin Airakin."

"I assure you, Caelin, they are well protected."

"I can fight. Really well."

Tavor glanced at Emery again, and she nodded.

"He's the best of our generation," Liam confirmed.

"I can show you." Caelin held out his hand to the varen, Anders, and Emery realized that the man was carrying his lim.

Anders held the lim further away from Caelin, and instead looked up at Tavor. "I'm not sure about this, sir. Isn't it some sort of weapon?"

Tavor glanced at the lims still strapped to the twins' backs. "Give it to him."

The varen blinked, then slowly handed Caelin his lim. Caelin snatched it, bent his knees into a fighting stance and then paused. He eyed the three varens and then Tavor warily. "I'm not attacking, I'm just showing you my skills."

When Tavor nodded the go ahead, Caelin immediately launched into a series of slashes and spins that caused the men around him to reach for their belts. Tavor held up a hand to calm them, and unlike earlier there was no firing. Caelin continued his assault on the air, moving rapidly from *rushing river* to *fleeting storm*, from *rolling hills* into a myriad of other movements they had each practiced day in day out, although none of them could make it look this effortless.

Tavor stroked his chin, eyebrows traveling higher and higher as he watched Caelin move. Finally, he clapped his hands together. "Enough."

Caelin ceased his swinging. He'd barely broken a sweat.

Tavor placed his hands behind his back. "Thank you for that demonstration. However, while I don't deny your obvious talent, I already have one extra elemist aboard to worry about. I don't need another."

Emery felt her face burning.

"The question is what to do with you. I should probably have the ship turned around and drop you back off." Tavor quirked an eyebrow again. "Or have you thrown overboard. That would be usual practice with stowaways."

Liam stepped forward, beginning to argue for Caelin, but the latter spoke over him.

"I'm not an elemist!"

"I'm sorry?" Tavor asked.

Caelin was staring at the ground, face reddening. "I'm not – I don't have the abilities the others have. I was born without them." His gaze flicked to Emery and Liam before returning to the ground. "That's why I made sure to become the best fighter."

Tavor's gaze bore into Caelin. "This is the truth?"

Caelin nodded, and finally lifted his eyes.

Silence fell, as if the very ship was holding its breath. Emery couldn't decide what she wanted to happen. Part of her was so happy at the thought of also having Caelin by her side, but she knew he'd be much safer staying home, at least until their mission was successful. *If* their mission was successful. Back on Orabel, he wouldn't have to worry about varens or storms or pirates or the countless other dangers that could befall them out here.

Tavor took a step towards Caelin, and to Emery's surprise placed a hand on his shoulder. "Perhaps we can find a place for you after all. Although" – he tapped Caelin's lim,– "we'll have to find you a better weapon. I'm afraid a simple stick won't get you very far out here."

# Chapter Nine

To Emery's surprise, it did not take long for a routine to immerge aboard *The New Dawn*. On that first day, after Tavor decided to allow Caelin to stay aboard, he showed them to their cabins. Emery and the boy's had fallowed Tavor through a door opening onto a set of wooden stairs that descended below decks. As Emery followed Tavor down, away from the fresh air and sunlight, she immediately felt choked by the tight space and no matter how many times she descended into the bowels of the ship after that, the feeling never stopped gripping her.

Tavor had paused as the stairs levelled out in a room that seemed to stretch the entire length and width of the ship. But though the level had no interior walls, and Emery could stand upright, the ceiling and floor where much closer to each other than she was used to. "This level is for storage, rowing, and guns." Tavor explained. "You won't be spending much time here."

Indeed, men sat on benches lining each side of the ship, rowing to the rhythm of the drum Emery had heard earlier. One man sat in front of all the others, pounding the drum at a grueling speed, and singing some sort of metrical tune.

Emery only managed a quick glance that first day though,

before Tavor led them further down, until the stairs ended in a tight hallway.

Lanterns hung from the walls, lighting their way with flickering orange light as Emery and the boys followed Tavor along the long corridor. She felt as if they were travelling through a tunnel underground, except everything was made from wood. The floor, the walls, even the doors set into the walls at regular intervals were fashioned from oak planks. Upon further inspection, Emery noticed each door donned an etching of a different plant on its surface, and she assumed it was so one could remember which room belonged to them.

"This level is the berth. The crew sleep back behind us. My men are in these cabins. And yours are just up ahead." Tavor explained. "Ah, here we are."

Their little group paused before two doors set across from each other. One door's etching was that of an orchid, and the other a lilac.

"We are tight on space aboard the ship and had only expected one more guest." Tavor cast them an apologetic look. "We were able to clear out a second room, but I'm afraid you boys will have to share. Emery, you'll get your own cabin."

When Tavor pushed open the door with the orchid on it to show them Liam and Caelin's room, Emery couldn't contain her gasp. It was much, much larger than she'd expected, larger than their rooms back home. And so...fancy. Everything was awash in shades of pale green and cream. A big bed stood in one corner, covered in thick blankets and plump pillows. A squat chest sat at the end of the bed, the lid open and already containing Liam's bag. Two ornate chairs and a small round table sat in the center of the room upon a plush carpet. Lanterns hung from the walls, but they remained unlit at the moment, because shafts of buttery sunlight spilled through the large window at the opposite end of the room as the door.

"Whoa." Liam and Caelin said in unison, and then Liam added, "We will have no problem sharing this room."

When Tavor led Emery across the hallway to her own cabin,

it was to find the exact mirror to the boys' room, except everything was in shades of cream and lavender. Emery stared open mouthed at the extravagance of it all.

Beside her, Tavor chuckled. "It's a little different than what you're used to, I know."

Emery could only nod.

"I will leave you to get settled, and I'll have someone fetch you for dinner in a few hours. Feel free to remain in your cabin or wander the ship at your leisure."

"Thank you," she said.

As soon as Tavor left, shutting the door behind him, Emery had set about exploring her room. The carpet was deliciously soft beneath her bare feet, and she spent a few seconds simply wiggling her toes in the fabric. She ran a hand over the smooth wood of the chair and the table, before moving to stand before the large window. She placed a hand on the glass too, marveling at its smoothness and clarity. Glass was a rarity back home. Sometimes elemists who were skilled with sand or flame or both would create little glass bowls or figurines, but Emery had never seen anything like this window.

Beyond the window, the calm, turquoise water flowed on by. The cabin was low enough on the ship that it created the illusion Emery was standing upon the surface and she was almost surprised when she couldn't feel sea spray on her skin.

She turned back to her room, noticing a door. When she opened it, she found a small room with a washing basin, and wooden bench set into the wall with a hole in it, which, upon further inspection, she realized must be for relieving oneself.

Emery closed the door and made her way over to the huge bed next. It was at least double the size of her bed back home, maybe even triple. With a surge of excited giddiness, Emery belly flopped onto the mattress and sighed at the softness of the blankets and pillows. She rolled onto her back, and all the thrills and tensions of the last few hours slowly seeped from her muscles. She'd never been more comfortable in her entire life.

But even though the bed was pure luxury, and the room itself was beautiful and comfortable, Emery didn't end up spending much time in her cabin besides to wash and sleep. During the early evenings, Tavor always invited them to his own cabin for dinner.

That first evening, a knock at the door jolted Emery awake from a dreamless sleep. She had not meant to fall asleep, and after a moment of panic as she gazed blurry eyed at her surroundings, she remembered where she was, and leapt up to answer the door.

The varen Anders stood in the hallway, clad in his black and blue jacket. Emery's pulse jumped, erasing some of her grogginess. She resisted the urge to run back in her room to snatch up her lim, and instead stood tall. "Yes?"

"Commissioner Thantos wishes to invite you and your brother, and of course your friend, to his cabin to enjoy supper with him." Anders's gaze lingered on Emery's sleep mussed hair. "I'll give you a moment to clean up."

Emery cheeks burned as she ducked back into her room, splashed water from the washing basin onto her face, and quickly finger combed her hair, still not fully awake. When she immerged from her room again, Liam and Caelin stood in the hallway with the varen. The two of them looked groggy too, as if they also had just been woken from a deep slumber.

The varen silently led them along the cramped hallways and up the stairs to the main deck. Emery blinked as they immerged into daylight, and she realized the sun was nearly touching the horizon. She'd slept the whole afternoon away. Crossing the deck, their guide stopped in front of a double wooden door with trimmings carved into the likenesses of sea hawks. Anders knocked quietly and when Tavor beckoned from within, the varen opened the doors, bowed, and then left.

Emery could hardly contain her awe as the doors swung inwards. Tavor's rooms were even more lavish than her own. Everything was black, blue, and silver, just like Tavor's clothing the night he had made his first address on Orabel. Lush curtains, the deep color of the ocean at night, hung on either side of a massive bay window, revealing the setting sun beyond. Silver trimming curled along the curtains' edges like vines, and they sparkled in the light cast by the sconces on the walls. A large bed sat in one corner of the room, neatly made up with blankets of the deepest blues and darkest blacks. In the opposite corner, a desk cast mostly in shadow was covered in neat piles of what looked like white bark, and beside them a set of peculiar shining instruments Emery couldn't quite make out.

At the center of the room was a polished mahogany table, behind which Tavor was standing and smiling at them. His long, indigo coat was draped over the back of his chair, leaving him in a loose white tunic that almost looked too ordinary on him. "Please, sit." He swept a hand to indicate the three empty chairs beside his own set around the table. Liam and Caelin claimed two of them immediately, leaving Emery the one to Tavor's right.

She examined him from the corner of her eye as she made her way around the table. His pine-green eyes seemed to dance in the light of the sconces, and she was once again struck by how young he was.

"Thank you," she murmured as he pulled the chair out for her, another custom she would have to get used to.

Moments later, two men strolled into the cabin carrying platters of food. There were freshly-baked breads and slices of cheese, apples cut up and arranged to look like flowers, green and purple grapes, succulent strawberries, chopped carrots and celery, and potatoes slathered with melted butter.

"Your elders where kind enough to give us many provisions, but I'm afraid they won't last long out here. We had best eat them while we can."

Emery's stomach growled at the sight of all the food, and she realized she hadn't eaten much all day. She didn't reach for anything though, anxious that she might accidentally blunder another custom if she did.

But when Tavor told them to dig in, she wasted no time.

After piling a little bit of everything on her plate, she took a bite of the still steaming bread and sighed.

Tavor placed a few items of food on his plate too, but he didn't eat right away. Instead, he leaned forward in his chair, curiosity alighting his features. "I understand all this food came from your island's gardens. How does that work exactly? You can grow anything? How?"

His questions came out rapid fire like they had when he asked Emery about her statera practice that morning. It was hard to believe that had only been earlier that day. Regardless, his eager curiosity was endearing, and she smiled around her mouthful of bread. She chewed faster so she could reply.

Liam beat her to it. "Well, not everything. We can only grow something if we have the seeds. Everything we can grow back home is because of the seeds the Arch-Elemists and their families brought with them when they created the island."

"But with the seeds, you can grow anything? At any time of year?" Tavor asked. "Because of your gifts?"

"Yup," Liam said through a mouthful of mashed potato.

"Fascinating."

"How does it work out here?" Emery asked.

"Well, we have gardens, too," Tavor said, leaning back in his seat. "But they're large and called farms. We can only grow certain things in certain places, and it takes months to get a crop."

"Months?" Emery quirked a brow. "Then how do you feed everyone?"

Tavor frowned. "It's not easy. Some seasons can be hard and if the weather doesn't cooperate crops can fail, and food becomes scarce." His expression brightened. "But once we bring peace between our people, this is something we can fix!"

Emery swallowed another mouthful of bread and asked the question that had been burning in her chest for days. "How did you find us? How did you find Orabel?"

"Growing up, I heard rumors about a place only meant for elemists," Tavor said.

Emery exchanged a startled glance with her twin. There weren't supposed to be any rumors about Orabel. No one outside of the people who live on the island were supposed to know about it, and on the very rare occasion when someone broke the rules and left, like her mother, the Arch-Elemists supposedly had ways to silence them if they ever tried to speak of Orabel. Namely, by ripping the air from their lungs so they couldn't talk at all.

"I followed these rumors all the way to the Barren Sea. I had no luck at first, given how vast it is, but then one day I heard what sounded like voices on the wind. I couldn't make out where on earth they were coming from, but...they guided me."

"The Arch-Elemists?" Liam asked.

"Yes."

Emery sat back in her seat, mulling over this information, once against struck by the enormity of the Arch-Elemists' powers.

"I also understand that once your abilities awaken, you can, in theory, use all four elements? Is that correct?" Tavor asked.

"Oh yes," said Liam. "But usually, we tend to be very good at using one and less so the others. Even then, we're usually only particularly skilled in manipulating one aspect of that element. It's all quite hard to determine until we start to practice."

"What do you mean?"

"Well, you might be best at manipulating earth over the other elements, but your skill might lean more towards dirt and rock, or towards trees and other plants. For instance, our sister Ayana..." He trailed off, suddenly having to clear his throat.

Emery's own throat constricted too, wondering if they would ever see her again.

Tavor leaned closer to him, as if to offer moral support. "Your sister is particularly skilled with...plants?"

"Flowers, mostly." Liam stared at is plate. "Well, she was. Until the illness sapped her abilities."

Emery thought back to Ayana's bedroom, how it had always been filled with flowers she'd grown with her abilities. Over time, these had given way to plants that had grown naturally, which were never quite as spectacular.

"She has the Withering?" Tavor asked gently.

Liam nodded.

"I'm sorry," Tavor said but then he offered them both an optimistic smile. "Hopefully together we can make the Withering a thing of the past."

As the dinner continued, Tavor peppered them with more questions about their lives in Orabel. Between mouthfuls of food, Emery and Liam answered each one, and then asked questions of their own about his world. But Caelin did not participate in the conversation. He picked at his food, his gaze settling upon Tavor every once and a while with barely contained suspicion, to the point that it began to make Emery feel uncomfortable. What if Caelin offended Tavor and Tavor changed his mind about keeping him aboard?

But if Tavor noticed or cared about Caelin's scrutiny, he said nothing. Not until the dinner was over, and Emery, Liam, and Caelin were moving towards the cabin door. "Mr. Airikin, may I have a private word?"

Emery stomach flipped with nerves for her friend, but Caelin appeared unperturbed.

Tavor also cast a reassuring smile. "Don't worry, I won't keep him for long."

Anders, the same varen who'd fetched them for dinner earlier in the evening, escorted Emery and Liam back to their rooms that night. Instead of going to her own cabin, Emery chose to wait for Caelin's return with Liam in his room. Though the sky outside the window had long since grown dark, the lanterns had been lit, bathing the lavish room in shades of gold.

Liam lounged in one of the ornate chairs, but Emery found she couldn't sit still. Though at this point she was fairly certain Tavor would never harm Caelin, she still couldn't shake her unease. She paced in front of the dark window until finally the cabin door opened, and Caelin stepped inside. He held a long object in his arms. And he was smiling.

"What happened?" Emery asked.

At the same time, Liam pointed at the object Caelin carried. "What's that?"

Caelin strode to the bed and placed the object on the pale green blanket. Emery and Liam looked over his shoulder and Emery realized the object was a sheath. Caelin carefully pulled on the hilt poking out of the sheath and Emery instinctively backed away as the weapon was revealed. It's long, curved blade glinted in the lantern light, so sharp it could one of them bleeding to death in seconds.

Blades existed back in Orabel, made from stone or bone and, on rare occasions, glass. But Emery had never seen anything like this weapon before. Nothing as large or deadly.

"What is it?" Liam asked, his eyes wide with eager delight.

"It's a steel sword," Caelin said, his grin spreading wider. "Tavor gave it to me. He's going to teach me how to use it so I can become your official guard. Apparently, he was the top of his class, too. They called him the Viper. Still do."

Every evening onwards, Caelin continued to be invited to Tavor's dinners along with the twins, and when Tavor asked them questions about Orabel and the elemists living there, Caelin joined in on the conversations, whatever misgivings he'd had about Tavor seemingly melting away after their conversation the first night.

And true to Tavor's word, when Emery wandered into Liam and Caelin's cabin early the next morning, they were both already gone, and she ventured above deck to find Tavor and Caelin already locked in battle.

The clashing of the steel blades assaulted Emery's ears before she saw them, and she followed the sound to the deck at the rear of the ship, which Tavor told her was called the afterdeck. Caelin and Tavor slashed at each other with their swords, the wickedly sharp curved edges gleaming in the morning sun with every block and blow. Every once and a while they'd pause while Tavor advised Caelin on his grip or stance or swing, and then they'd start again. Behind them, Tavor's silver walking stick was leaning seemingly abandoned against the railing. She saw no *statera* movements, not even basics such as *whipping willow* or *flowing water.* This fighting style was nothing like their own.

She gave them a wide berth as she made her way round the edge of the afterdeck, and though the sight of them clashing weapons sent her pulse racing it was difficult to look away. Despite his slight limp when walking normally, in battle Tavor possessed the same grace as Caelin and moved just as fluidly and quickly. Furthermore, though Caelin managed to keep up with him, Tavor's years of training with such heavy weapons eventually began to show, and after a while Caelin was panting. Across from him, Tavor had barely broken a sweat.

Liam was leaning against the afterdeck's railing on the left-hand side of the ship watching them with crossed arms, eyes darting back and forth as the outsider and their friend jumped and spun and lunged at each other.

"How long have they been training?" Emery asked when she reached him.

"A few hours already," Liam said. "They're both animals."

Indeed, they were. Caelin and Tavor sparred every morning, often going for hours. During this time Emery often practiced statera-lim. The afterdeck was large enough that Caelin and Tavor could train on one side, and Emery could practice on the other without either interfering with the other. Tavor had not asked whether Emery wanted to learn how to wield a sword too, and in truth, she was relieved. The deadliness of the weapon unnerved her, and she was plenty happy with her lim.

Emery began each morning sitting cross-legged under the rising sun, just like she did back home. But now instead of sitting in the clearing before the sacra surrounded by her people and the peaceful silence of dawn, she sat on the afterdeck of a ship full of outsiders, trying to tune out the clanking of weapons and the gruff voices of the sailors. She closed her eyes, and allowed her mind and spirit to wander, to seek out those of the elements and to mingle with them.

It was much harder out at sea than on her island. Back in

Orabel, near the sacra, each element's presence was rich and plentiful. But out on the Barren Sea, most of the elements were scarce. There were no flames above decks during the day, and any wood aboard the ship had long since died. The only earth Emery could sense was the sand and rock and aquatic plants growing far below in the ocean's depths. Without wind, the air was stubbornly still and stoic, and unwilling to allow Emery to grasp control for more than a moment. The only element easily found and manipulated was the turquoise water surrounding them. But even then, the body of water was too large for Emery to control, and when she tried to separate even a few drops from the sea, it clung stubbornly to itself and refused to do her bidding.

But even if her abilities were stronger and she were able to call the elements to her will, she wouldn't. Tavor had quickly advised Emery and Liam not to practice any elemental manipulation above decks for all the crew to see.

"I chose this crew with care," he'd explained. "Each person on this ship is sympathetic to our cause. But people can be skittish and it's wise to integrate you and your abilities slowly, as to not cause any unwarranted fear."

Emery probably should have felt uneasy about this warning, but instead she was relieved. She'd been dreading the moment Tavor found out her abilities were so weak. She'd happily put it off as long as possible.

As the days wore on, Emery practiced statera as subtly as she could. But the scarcity of the elements was not the only reason why she found it difficult. There were simply too many distractions. As she sat crossed legged on the afterdeck with her eyes close and the morning sun beating down on her, looking for all the world like she was simply dozing off, the feeling of being watched would break her focus. When she cracked an eye, she'd often spot sailors watching her, curiosity and wariness mixing in their gazes. But any time she made eye contact with any of them, they'd look away and return to their work.

When she practiced her statera-lim afterwards, it was even

harder to ignore the sailors' stares boring into her as she eased into the movements, swinging her lim at invisible foes. And there was one stare that was particularly hard to ignore. She'd often glance up to find Tavor watching her as he sparred with Caelin. When their gazes met, he didn't look away like the sailors did. He'd hold her gaze for an extra moment, before his focus returned to Caelin and their deadly clash of swords. And every time, Emery was left with a peculiar jolt in her stomach.

More than once, Emery had considered taking her practices down to her cabin to avoid the stares, feeling awkward under the constant scrutiny. But the elements were even harder to detect so deep in the bowels of the ship, and though the room was huge, it still felt too cramped to properly train with her lim.

So she continued to practice on the afterdeck, because not training at all was out of the question. She'd surely go mad from boredom without it. Every day, Emery kept an eager eye on the horizon, waiting for something, anything, to appear. But just as Tavor promised, nothing ever did. No ships. No islands. Not even a sea creature. Just leagues and leagues of empty, placid blue.

For a place that was supposed to hold unspeakable dangers and the answers to all her questions, right now the outside world was proving to be frustratingly dull. Nothing to do, and nothing to see. Emery had been excited to learn about sailing, and Tavor took her around the ship and taught her the name and use of various parts, no actual sailing happened due to the lack of wind. The sailors took turns rowing and that was about it. And they always kept to themselves, giving Emery and Liam wide berths, though they didn't seem to mind Caelin's presence.

The afternoons were long and tedious. After days of wandering the ship, Emery soon ran out of new places to explore. On one occasion she tried climbing the riggings to burn off energy and to get a new view of the horizon, but the sailors yelled at her immediately to get down, and she never tried again.

It pained Emery to think that Tala was still months away by Tavor's reckoning, and that was if the weather was favorable.

Finally, after three weeks, *The New Dawn* crossed the threshold out of the Barren Sea and a warm wind finally greeted them. Emery thrilled with excitement as the captain, a portly man with a salt and pepper beard, shouted the order to loosen the sails and she watched the sailors scurry about, tugging this and climbing that until the gigantic canvas fell, snapping in the breeze. The oars disappeared inside the hull as the ship continued to slice through the waves, not even slowing down.

With the wind came the waves, *The New Dawn* rocking and tilting with each one they crested. Even after years of honing her balance with statera, moving about the ship took some getting used to.

Even so, Emery gleefully wandered the deck observing the crew, wishing she better understood what they were doing. But when she asked, the sailors just mumbled under their breath and moved away from her, and she soon gave up. She'd find Tavor and ask him.

Dodging flailing ropes and swinging beams, she meandered about the ship searching for him. When she climbed the stairs to the forecastle at the bow of the ship, she instead found Liam standing with his back to her, leaning against the railing. He shifted from foot to foot, fingers tapping on the polished wood of the handrail. Emery knew her restlessness was nothing compared to her twins. Liam didn't know how to sit still, and this long journey full of nothingness was making him irritable. Sometimes he joined Emery with her statera practice, but he rarely practiced with his lim anymore now that there wasn't a teacher around forcing him. He'd found a new toy. Something called gunpowder. His fingers, which still tapped away on the railing, were stained black with the stuff from that morning.

Emery rested her forearms on the railing next to her brother, watching the sea beneath them rush past. The turquoise water she was used had shifted to a deeper cerulean blue and the sun beat down on them harder and hotter.

"If something interesting doesn't happen soon," Liam grumbled, "I'm going to jump off this ship."

As if summoned by Liam's words, a man suddenly cried out from the rigging high above them, "Sail ho! Three points on the starboard bow!"

The sailors' heads all swiveled to face ahead and right of the ship. Tavor appeared on the forecastle, striding to the starboard side, Caelin close behind.

"I guess you'll have to save your watery demise for another day!" Emery said, nudging Liam's shoulder before hurrying to join Tavor and Caelin. Excitement bubbled in her veins. Finally, something new to see.

Emery followed Tavor's gaze but all she could see was a tiny spot of black on the horizon.

Tavor dug something shiny and elongated from his pocket and held it to his eye.

His mouth formed a thin line. "Hmm." Then, seeing Emery's curiosity, he held it up for her to see more clearly. "It's a telescope, it enables you to see objects that are far away as if they were larger and closer to you. Perhaps when things aren't so –"

"Two ships, Commissioner!" the man above yelled, snatching their attention back immediately. "One heading for the other."

"Indeed," Tavor muttered. Without a further word, he strode to the massive wheel that steered the ship. The captain was already standing behind it, gripping it with both hands. "Bring us closer," Tavor instructed.

The captain barked at the crew, "Hands aloft to loose the topsails!" then swung the wheel, and the ship moaned as its huge bulk turned in the water.

The ship skimmed across the sea, but it still took a while before they were able to see the two vessels somewhat clearly. One was racing after the other like a beast after its prey, closing the distance with alarming speed. Emery also noticed the one giving chase had crimson sails instead of while, the colour ominous against the blue sky. The closer they came, the higher the wind picked up around *The New Dawn*, making the crew fight ever harder to keep course.

"They're attacking!" Liam shouted, the wind nearly stealing his words.

Tavor stepped up beside them, one arm behind his back and the other on his cane. "Yes."

"Pirates?" Caelin asked, gripping the railing with white hands.

"Worse," Tavor said. "Forbiddens."

The word sent a shock of cold down Emery's spine.

"How can you tell?" she asked, eyes wide.

"Their speed. Only elemists can move that quickly on the water. And judging by the way they're hunting the other ship, they are not friendly."

Of course. They could manipulate the air and currents to their advantage. And to their prey's disadvantage. Emery watched, transfixed, as the first ship slowed to a crawl while the hunters raced ever closer.

A sailor ran up behind Tavor, his face pale and sweaty. "Sir, the captain would like to know what he is to do."

Tavor's eyes didn't leave the Forbidden ship. "Tell him to get us there as fast as he can."

Emery stared at Tavor, past the hair whipping into her face.

"Are you going to capture the Forbiddens?"

"No."

"Why not?" Caelin called over the wind.

"We'll never make it in time," Tavor said, his voice turning hard, cold. "They're too fast. By the time we reach where they are now, the Forbiddens will be long gone."

A silence fell, save for the roaring wind and waves slamming against the hull. Despite Tavor's words, she noticed the varens lining up in attention on the main deck, readying themselves for something.

"Then what exactly are we – you – going to do?" Emery asked.

"We'll help the survivors."

No sooner were the words out of Tavor's mouth than a burst of orange flames engulfed the fleeing ship.

# Chapter Ten

---

The *New Dawn* raced across the ocean towards the burning vessel, but it seemed they could never get any closer. Emery, Liam, and Caelin stood at the bow, gripping the railing for dear life and watching with dread as the Forbiddens closed the distance between themselves and their prey.

Beside them, Tavor peered through his telescope again, and his face drained of colour. "No. It's the *Audacity*!" He turned to Emery and the boys, his face as stern and serious as she'd ever seen it. "You three stay here." Then he quickly spun on his heel and sprinted to his awaiting varens, shouting orders that Emery couldn't hear over the roaring wind.

The flames had made it to the fleeing ship's sails now, devouring every inch of canvas. Above them, thick black smoke was billowing into the otherwise blue sky. The blackness swallowed both ships whole as the Forbiddens caught up with their target. Even though *The New Dawn* was still leagues away, the wind carried over the sound of dreadful screams.

Emery didn't want to imagine what was happening. She'd heard too many stories about Forbiddens using their abilities to kill, to torture. The same abilities that flowed through her own veins. Disgust and fury battled in her heart. It was thanks to

Forbiddens that outsiders still hunted elemists, their fault that elemists were so feared they'd normally be killed on sight. Seeing them attack another innocent vessel the way they had just done, she hoped Tavor caught every last one.

*The New Dawn* continued its pursuit, plunging into the smoke but then slowing down as visibility became poor. The smoke scratched Emery's throat and stung her eyes so fiercely she almost didn't see the half scorched vessel until they'd drifted right next to it. It was alone now, floating adrift, no longer on fire but with plenty of smoke still curling from its rigging. As Tavor had predicted, the Forbidden ship was gone.

The crew tied the two vessels together, and Tavor asked Emery, Liam, and Caelin to stay aboard while he investigated. He then led a group of men across, weapons at the ready. Emery's hand hovered over her lim as she watched the crew approach a group of sailors gathered together at the center of the vessel, kneeling, bound and gagged and covered with soot. Blackened sails sagged around them like forlorn shadows and one of the masts lay in a broken heap nearby. Something that looked horribly like blood had soaked the wooden planks of the deck, which was littered with weapons and...bodies.

Emery swallowed bile as Liam grabbed her hand. Enough smoke had drifted away now to make out the Forbidden ship retreating far off on the horizon, already no more than a blotch against the sky.

* * *

A KNOCK SOUNDED on Liam and Caelin's cabin door, interrupting a card game the three of them were playing in an attempt to take their minds off what they had just witnessed. Caelin had been able to persuade some of the sailors to teach him the game a couple of days ago, and had even been lent a pack of cards from one of them.

Liam opened the door and Anders stood in the hallway

beyond. The varen nodded a greeting at Liam but then looked at Emery. "Miss Aalokin, Commissioner Thantos would like to see you."

Emery hesitated. "Just me?"

"Yes, Miss."

Emery's heart thudded with the uncertainty of why Tavor would want to see her only, especially since neither she nor Liam or Caelin had seen much of him at all since the chaos of the afternoon. He'd been too busy helping his men deal with the aftermath of the Forbidden attack. It had taken some time to transfer the few survivors onto *The New Dawn*, where they were then taken to the infirmary below deck. Once the survivors were cared for, the varens had gone back for the limp bodies strewn across the scorched deck. Emery had grown closer and closer to vomiting with each lifeless body that had been carried onto *The New Dawn* and then taken somewhere below. There had been so many.

Eventually Tavor had escorted the twins and Caelin down to their cabin, but he said very little, his face pale, and he'd left again almost immediately. A small dinner had arrived for them not long after, an obvious signal that they would not be joining Tavor that night for their evening meal.

Now, Emery hesitated as Anders waited to escort her to Tavor's cabin. She hadn't been alone with the outsider since the morning of their departure, and for some reason the thought left her with damp palms.

Nonetheless, she placed her cards on the bed where they were sitting and got up to follow the varen.

Caelin frowned silently from the bed, but as she strode past her brother, he cast her a mischievous grin that inexplicably caused her cheeks to redden. "Have fun," he drawled, and shut the door behind her.

As usual, Anders said nothing as he led Emery up to Tavor's door. He knocked twice and then left her alone.

Emery fought the sudden urge to grab him and ask what this was about, but the door had already opened and Tavor was standing there, this time in an emerald-green tunic, smiling. "Good evening."

"Hello."

"Come in." The door shut behind her with a quiet click and Tavor walked to his usual seat behind the mahogany table. A small teapot and single lit candle were sitting in the center, along with two cups and a plate of brown biscuits. "Sit with me a while."

Tavor rolled back the sleeves of his tunic and poured them both some steaming tea. Emery pulled at a loose thread on her own sleeve. Tavor had no clothes that fit her, Liam or Caelin properly, nor had they yet come across a port where they could get something more suitable, so they were stuck wearing the comparably bland off-white tunics and brown trousers with which they had left the island.

When Tavor finished pouring, he pushed one of the cups towards her. "I thought some hot tea might help you relax." He smiled again. "You seem a little shaken by today's events."

She shrugged. "I'm alright." But she wrapped her fingers around the cup eagerly, allowing the heat to seep into her skin and melt a small bit of the ice that had crept into her veins when she first saw the Forbidden ship.

"You look...well, disturbed."

She ran a finger along a grain of wood on the table's surface. She *was* disturbed. And disgusted. And a cold had settled deep into her bones. A cold, hollow anger. Those people – the Forbiddens – it was all their fault. Elemists like them were the ones to start the war that ended with the banishment of their people. And they were the ones who still caused so much havoc in the world that the Ungifted still hated elemists, still wanted to see them all eradicated. Her anger churned her stomach. She blew on the hot drink and took a sip to steady herself, pleasantly surprised by the minty flavor.

"Are you alright?" Tavor's voice was soft.

Emery blinked and looked up at him. He blew on his own tea, holding her gaze.

"I just...don't understand. Why do they do it? Attack innocent people like that?"

Tavor leaned back in his chair and sighed. "I've spent my entire life asking the same question."

"And?"

"Most of them seem to be..." He ran a hand over his short hair. "To put it simply, they seem to be out of their minds."

The coldness inside Emery expanded. "What do you mean?"

He shook his head, his eyes far away. She wondered what those eyes had seen over the years. "They just...want to kill. To create mayhem. It's like...there's nothing human left in them."

Emery's stomach churned and she put her mug down. Nothing human. She knew he didn't mean her. She wasn't raiding ships and hurting innocents. But still, the people he was describing this way, as if no hope of redemption remained for them in his eyes, were her own. They shared the same abilities, the same gods, the same ancestors. The same blood.

"No wonder you all hate us," she muttered, staring out the window.

"We don't all hate you." His voice was soft again. "Some of us acknowledge you aren't all...like that."

"How do you tell us apart?"

"The truth?" Tavor dumped a spoon of sugar into his tea. "It's not easy."

Distracted, Emery forgot to blow before taking the next gulp. The tea scalded her tongue and burned all the way down her throat, but it felt like it was slowly thawing the cold anger inside her. There was nothing she could do about the Forbiddens, but she could help Tavor show the world that not all elemists were like them.

Tavor seemed to be gazing at nothing. His jaw rested on his fist as he absently stirred his drink with glassy eyes. She remembered him referring to the *Audacity* earlier, as if he recognized the name. The name of the Forbidden ship, presumably.

"Those Forbiddens today...have you come across them before?"

"Yes. I've been hunting them for years. One of the most ruthless groups I have ever come across." He rubbed his leg, the one that caused him to limp, and his jaw tightened. "Especially the captain, Denzel. His wickedness is unmatched. He's known as the Scourge of the Sea."

"What...has he done?" Emery asked, unsure if she really wanted to know.

Tavor hesitated, then asked. "Did you notice the color of their ship's sails?"

"They were crimson."

"Yes," he said, again hesitating as if he wasn't sure if he should continue. "The sails are crimson because they've been soaked in their victims' blood."

Emery blanched, suddenly feeling ill. She tapped her now half-empty cup from one hand to another, watching as Tavor poured himself more tea. He looked so...tired. "Why are you trying to help us?"

"For a long time after the war, the world was a very dark place. It has gotten better over the years, but there are still shadows. Stubborn shadows. I guess I want to help disperse them, to help the world come back to what it was. Maybe even make it better than it was."

A warmth that had nothing to do with the tea tingled up Emery's limbs. "That's...a suspiciously noble reason. You're telling me there's no personal gain to be had from this?"

A small smile lifted one side of Tavor's mouth. "Well, there is another side to my motivation." His eyes met hers, direct but also...nervous? "My parents were elemists."

Emery nearly spilled the contents of her cup. "What?"

"You heard correctly." He sipped his tea, carefully placing the cup back down. "But I was born without their abilities." He opened his palms out, and for the first time his smile seemed laced with sadness. "I've got nothing."

"Like Caelin," Emery breathed.

Tavor nodded, his eyes sparkling in the flickering light. "I've never met anyone else like me before."

"That's why you let him stay."

He nodded again. "I supposed I saw a bit of myself in him. A little lost, but determined nonetheless."

And brave.

"You told him, that first night." Caelin had been smiling when he'd come back from Tavor's cabin that evening after their dinner. She thought it was because of the sword he'd been gifted. But now she suspected this information was more the reason. Caelin had never met another Ungifted born to elemists either. "But he never said anything."

The realization that Caelin had discovered something so significant to him, and yet didn't even mention it to her, made Emery's chest constrict uncomfortably.

"I asked him not to share the information," Tavor said apologetically. "It's information I don't share with just anyone."

Emery tried not to think too hard about what it meant that he just shared the information with her. "But why? Are you ashamed to have elemists as parents?"

"Of course not!" Tavor said quickly. "It's just...if people were to find out, they may not believe I really *am* Ungifted."

He stopped there but Emery understood the implication. He could be hunted and destroyed just like the rest of her people.

Emery stared at the dregs of her tea, thinking of her own parents. "May I ask you something?"

"Of course."

"Have you ever met a Kathleen Aalokin?"

Tavor scratched his chin. "Can't say I recognize the name. A relative of yours?"

She stirred the dregs with her spoon. "My mother. I thought...maybe, since you've lived and traveled for so long out here, you might have..."

"I'm sorry." He sounded sincere. "The world is a big place. But what would your mother be doing out here? I thought leaving your island was forbidden."

"It is. But she did anyway." Emery kept her eyes on her cup. It felt strange relaying such information. Everyone back home already knew this. But Tavor had shared something personal, and she felt compelled to do the same. "When she was my age, she just left in the middle of the night. Didn't even say goodbye to my grandparents." The thought of her grandparents gave her a jolt of homesickness, but she tried to ignore it.

Tavor frowned. "Then how did you come to live on Orabel?"

"About ten years after my mother left, she returned with my siblings and I. And our father. He was an outsider. I don't know anything about him." Emery swallowed down the bitterness her next words brought on. "They stayed only long enough to ditch us with our grandparents. Liam and I were maybe a year old... they never came back."

"I'm sorry," Tavor repeated, leaning forward to fill her cup again. "Perhaps, when we've done what we set out to do, we can look for them."

"Really?" Emery looked at him then, hope flaring, burning away the last of the chill in her veins.

Tavor smiled. "Of course."

A lump of gratitude, but also fear, started to fill her throat, and her eyes pricked with the threat of tears. "I've tried so hard to dampen my hope, for years. But then when you came, and started telling us –"

"Commissioner!"

Hurried footsteps sounded outside the cabin and two men in varen uniforms burst into the room. One of them was Anders. Blood leaked from a cut on his lip.

The second man slammed the door shut and stood back from it, a sword drawn. "It was a trap!"

Tavor stood up, blood draining from his face, but his voice remained calm. "The Scourge?"

"Yes," Anders panted, drawing his own weapon to face the door as well. "The Scourge is aboard *The New Dawn*. We think the whole attack was a set up. He likely hid in the damaged vessel."

The damaged vessel in question was currently being towed behind *The New Dawn*. Tavor had mentioned earlier he planned to drop it and its surviving crew off at the first city they came across.

"The Scourge is on this ship, now?" Tavor repeated, as if he couldn't quite believe what he was hearing.

"Yes," Anders said, wiping at the bloody cut on his mouth. "He's coming for you."

Emery jumped to her feet, heart pounding in her ears. She immediately reached for her lim...and grabbed only air.

She'd left it on Liam's bed.

"He's stolen a pistol, sir," the second man said. "He's taken down almost everyone. No one saw him until it was too late."

"Miss Aalokin." She jumped at Tavor's address. "Please hide in that corner." He nodded over to the desk. "He won't see you there."

"What about my brother?" she squeaked. "And Caelin."

"They'll be fine," Tavor said, his jaw clenched. "He's after me. He'll come straight here."

She couldn't make herself move away from the door though. Liam was still out there. He might –

"*Now.*" There was fire in Tavor's voice as he grabbed and pushed her towards the desk.

She knelt behind it, hidden now in the shadows of the corner, and cowered deeper as muffled shouts were followed by thuds right outside the cabin, then nothing. The silence was so absolute she could hear the breathing of the three men inside, and the waves slapping the hull beneath.

The double door swung open, slamming so hard against the wall the window rattled. A gust of wind followed, sweeping inside and sending Tavor's belongings flying. The sconces on the wall sputtered and flickered out, casting them into near-complete darkness, save for the lone candle still burning on the table.

Emery peered as far as she dared around the side of the desk. Tavor's men were raising their weapons while Tavor, clutching his cane in his left hand, was edging to his right, towards the weapons hanging on the wall. He had taken no more than half a complete step before a whistling pierced the silence and the two varens simultaneously slapped their necks, removing what in the pale light of the doorway looked like a couple of feathers, just like the darts Tavor's men had shot back on Orabel. They both took a step forward, and then slumped to the ground. Neither of them moved again.

Emery slapped a hand over her mouth as Tavor took another half step towards his weapons, but a different voice froze him in place. "Don't. Move."

The Forbidden – The Scourge of the Sea – stepped into the cabin so silently she couldn't even hear the movement. The air around him whirled in fury, catching his hair and thrashing his clothes so that they moved about like living things. Her entire body shuddered as she saw the pistols he was holding in each hand, the same Tavor's own men had carried, aiming directly at him. If the Forbidden fired, Tavor wouldn't be able to defend himself, and who knew what would be done to him then.

But the weapons weren't the most concerning aspect of the intruder's appearance. His face was twisted into a furious snarl, his eyes burning with a fiery loathing so intense Emery was almost surprised Tavor didn't burst into flames under such a glare. She'd never seen such wrath before, such hatred. He looked as if he wanted to skin Tavor alive.

Tavor's face, by contrast, was the picture of calm, save a slight narrowing of his eyes. "A bit rude to interrupt a man's teatime, wouldn't you say?"

The Forbidden took another step forward, never taking his wrathful eyes off him. He spoke with the same accent as Tavor, and his voice rasped with rage. "I'd say interrupting my entire life seems a little more inconsiderate." His eyes darted to the cane in Tavor's hand. "I've heard rumors your leg never healed properly. I hope you're not expecting an apology." He tossed one of his guns aside, keeping the other trained on Tavor. Emery saw now, or rather sensed, that it was slightly different from the other one. Instinct told her this one wouldn't just paralyze. It would kill.

Tavor spread his arms. "Go ahead. Shoot."

Emery half rose from her hiding spot, squinting through the gloom for something she could use as a weapon, or at least a distraction.

But the Forbidden tossed his second weapon aside too. The wind raging around him died down, but somehow it only left him looking more menacing. "I'm not going to shoot you. I want to *feel* the life leave your body."

Tavor leapt for his weapons, but the Forbidden launched himself over the table, catching Tavor around the middle and the two men went crashing to the ground. In an instant, the Forbidden's hands were around Tavor's throat.

# Chapter Eleven

Emery bit back a scream as the Scourge of the Sea's fingers dug deeper into Tavor's throat. She began to step from behind the desk, but Tavor writhed and bucked enough to dislodge the Forbidden's grip and send a fist into the man's face. Emery heard bone crunch and the Forbidden reeled back into the room, blood streaming from his nose, and with a kick Tavor sent him crashing into the table, nearly upending it. He then began crawling towards his weapons, but couldn't reach them before the Forbbiden had recovered and brought an elbow down onto his back. Tavor collapsed, and the man kicked him savagely in the ribs. Tavor's air rushed out of him, and Emery took another step into the room. She had to do something, weapons or no.

The Forbidden had flipped Tavor over and the two men were now a tangle of bloody fists. Could she launch herself over the table and reach the weapons on the wall before the Forbidden could react?

The wind rose again around the intruder, lifting his hair and clothes.

That was it. The weapon was right in front of her, all around her.

Emery squeezed her eyes shut, muttering a quick, whispered prayer. "I call upon Tadewin, fair goddess of the wind, to lift me up and give me courage. Do not let us lose."

She forced her mind outwards, her soul, her very being. She felt the wind swirling round the room, its playfulness, its strength, its mercilessness.

*Move with me,* she begged. *Obey me!*

She lifted her hands and pushed the air away from her.

*Move!*

But the wind wouldn't listen. She couldn't do it, and Tavor was going to die.

A sickening crack echoed off the cabin's walls and Emery's eyes snapped open to watch Tavor fall to the floor, utterly limp.

The Forbidden knelt over him, panting. He held the gun by its barrel, presumably having just smashed its other end into Tavor skull. Tavor wasn't moving. The Forbidden turned the gun in his shaking hand and pressed the barrel to Tavor's forehead.

"No!" Emery hurtled straight for the Forbidden, snatching the teapot from the table as she went.

The Forbidden's head whipped in her direction, and she tossed the contents into his face.

He cried out in shock and pitched sideways, the liquid wasn't scalding anymore but it was enough to get him away from Tavor. His gun hit the floor with a clatter, too far away for Emery to reach.

The Forbidden rose to his knees and his eyes locked with hers. They still blazed with rage, but for a moment, surprise flickered across his features. And something else, gone too fast to interpret. Then he the fury returned, and in an instant, he was reaching for his gun. Before Emery could react, it was trained on her, aimed right for her heart.

She stood, frozen, staring at the gun, knowing it was too late to run, hoping she could dodge in time.

The Forbidden spat a glob of blood on the floor beside Tavor, who still laid motionless, blood leaking from a wound on his head. The man's eyes flickered from her to Tavor, then back again. He growled a low animal noise and spun to aim at Tavor's chest. His finger tightened on the trigger.

Emery threw herself at him, sending them both to the ground and winding herself in the process. A deafening bang exploded by her ear before she landed half on him, half on Tavor's walking stick. She rolled sideways, wrapping her fingers around the stick as the Forbidden scrambled once more for his gun. He scooped it up, and she swung hard as he turned towards her. The cane caught his temple with a metallic crack that twisted Emery's stomach and the Forbidden slumped sideways, head connecting with the floor with another awful sound. The gun spun out of his fingers, rotating a few times before coming to a stop on the floor beside him.

Emery's ears rang as she watched him lying there. He was breathing, but didn't move again, and more blood began to soak the space between them. Blood that, this time she had spilled, the blood of another elemist.

She stepped forward to check on Tavor, but her knees gave out and she had to sit down for a moment, fighting the urge to throw up. Before she could pull herself up again, three of Tavor's men burst into the room. They moved stiffly, presumably whatever paralyzing agent had been used against them hadn't completely worn off yet.

One went straight to Tavor while the other examined the Forbidden. The third crouched in front of Emery, although she couldn't help noticing the considerable distance he kept from her. "Are you alright, miss?"

Emery nodded, then rose unsteadily to her feet. Instead of helping her, the man took a half step backwards, but she chose not to care. She glanced over at Tavor, still motionless beside the Forbidden. The first man was checking his wounds while the second roughly rolled over the Forbidden and tied his hands behind his back.

"Will he be alright?" she asked. "Commissioner Thantos?"

"He'll live, miss," the man reassured her. "He'll have a nasty headache for a few days though." He looked up at her. "If you don't need medical attention, you should go back to your cabin to rest. The ship's been secured."

Some of Tavor's men were still lying around limp as Emery headed across the deck and down the stairs. She wasn't sure if they were paralyzed, unconscious or...dead. But a delayed sort of panic had set in and she did not pause to find out. She crashed into the corridor's walls as the ship tilted beneath her feet, but finally she reached the boys' cabin and threw herself through the door.

Liam and Caelin were as she had left them, sitting cross-legged on the bed facing each other, a pile of cards between them. Liam was pulling a card carefully from his hand, trying not to spill the rest. "Teralyn's teeth, Emery, no need to break the door."

Caelin, however, looked up at her and immediately dropped his cards. "Is that blood?"

# Chapter Twelve

The next morning, Emery leaned against the ship's wooden railing and stared out at the glistening ocean. The sun was making the water blaze a blinding white. She leaned into the wind and rubbed her stinging eyes. She'd barely slept after the events of the night.

Liam and Caelin somehow hadn't noticed the commotion going on above them. After she'd told them what happened, Liam had scoured her top to bottom to make sure she was unhurt. Caelin had demanded to know every detail, his face turning pale under his shaggy hair.

"I'm sorry I wasn't there," he murmured when Emery had finished. "I came out here to protect you. Anything could have —"

"It's alright," she'd said. "You couldn't have known. Tavor didn't even know." Furthermore, Tavor had nearly been killed. Who knew what could have happened to Caelin?

She'd slept in their cabin that night, or tried to, with Liam in the giant bed beside her and Caelin in the cot that had brought in for him on their first day aboard. Though her bones had weighed her down with exhaustion, every time she'd closed her eyes the Forbidden's bloody, furious face hovered in front of her.

Even now, as the midmorning sun warmed her skin, she felt a little queasy. Caelin and Liam hadn't left her side all morning, looking concerned and somewhat sleep-deprived themselves.

"How did he even get on board?" Liam wondered. He was standing with his back to the ocean, staring at the door that led to the stairs down from the main deck, past the ropes and canvas and crew.

"Tavor's men said the ship that was attacked yesterday was some sort of decoy."

Liam whistled, scanning the rigging. "Maybe he hid somewhere up top, then swung over when no one was looking."

The Forbidden's face floated once more before her eyes, so full of rage and loathing. She could still see his fingers curling around Tavor's throat. The clear thirst for his blood.

Out of their minds, Tavor had called them. They just *want to kill*.

But why? All night, the same question had run circles in her head. Why were the Forbiddens like this, or at least the one who had attacked last night? Why had he wanted to kill Tavor so badly? None of it made sense.

She turned to rest her back against the railing and crossed her arms. Her brother was standing the same way, still gazing at the door across the deck. Behind them, far below in the depths of the ship, the Forbidden was locked away. A small flicker of pride sparked in her chest at being instrumental in that.

But she needed answers.

She pushed away from the railing and headed towards Tavor's cabin. Caelin and Liam followed her.

"What are you doing?" Caelin asked.

"Going to check on her suitor."

She turned on Liam and sputtered, "My what?"

Caelin demanded the same.

Liam shrugged. "Why else did he want to be alone with you last night?"

"I – for tea," she stammered, her face burning. "It was just tea."

"Mhm."

Caelin didn't look convinced either, although he didn't seem as amused.

Emery paused in front of Tavor's door, feeling Liam still grinning beside her. She jabbed him in the ribs. "Shut your mouth. It was just tea."

"Who are you trying to convince?" Liam muttered.

Emery shook her head. Typical of Liam not to take anything seriously, including a Forbidden attack.

She knocked on the door before she lost her nerve. She wanted answers, and she wanted to check on Tavor. The last time she'd seen him he'd been unconscious and bleeding after all.

It had just been tea.

And personal, revealing conversation.

"Yes?" Tavor's faint voice called from behind the door.

"It's – er – me." She closed her eyes so she couldn't see whatever Liam's face was doing.

Tavor opened the door, a white bandage wrapped around his head. He smiled but didn't let go of the door handle. His eyes looked glassy, his skin too pale. "Oh, good. I was hoping you'd stop by." He sounded slightly breathless. "I wanted to look for you myself, but I'm afraid I can't walk far yet. I'm still quite dizzy."

Emery winced at the memory of the Forbidden's gun cracking against Tavor's skull. The telltale bloodstains were also still on the floor behind him. Whatever scrubbing had taken place that morning obviously hadn't been able to get rid of everything. "Is it bad?"

"It's just a concussion. Could be a lot worse. I'm sorry."

"I – what? Why on Teralyn's earth would you be sorry?"

"I promised you'd be safe. We've not even made landfall yet and already I seem to have –"

"She could have died!" Caelin burst through the polite exchange.

Tavor gazed at Caelin. "Yes, and I take full responsibility for that." His eyes slid back to hers and she felt pinned in place. "I hope you can still trust me."

"Of course," she said, mentally kicking herself for responding so quickly.

Liam shrugged, although this time it struck Emery as forced. "I'm just sorry I missed the excitement."

"We won't make any more detours," said Tavor. "Except for replenishing food and water supplies."

"Makes sense," said Emery, although if she were honest with herself, she was a little disappointed to hear she'd see nothing new until they reached the continent.

Tavor blinked a few times, leaning more heavily on the door now. "You'll have to excuse me, I think I need to lie down again."

"Wait." Emery held the door open. "That man. You know each other, don't you?"

Tavor sighed. "As I said last night, I've been hunting him and his crew for years. The Scourge of the Sea is one of the worst I've ever encountered."

"But what has he *done?*"

Beside Emery, Liam's eyebrows rose expectantly.

Tavor shook his head. "Terrible things, Miss Aalokin. The details of which I would rather spare you."

"But –"

"My apologies, but I really must rest." Seeing how haggard he looked, Emery released the door this time. Tavor thanked her and began to close the door, but then paused. "I know you three are curious. I will try to answer your questions soon, I promise."

Emery swallowed her disappointment and nodded. He cast her a weak smile and shut the door. Liam and Caelin turned and walked away, but she was momentarily locked in place. The Forbidden's face was floating before her again, the same word burning across her mind.

*Why?*

She turned to face the deck, and her gaze landed on the door that would take them back down to their cabins.

Or the Forbidden.

The boys had slowed down, seeing she hadn't followed.

"You want to talk to the Forbidden, don't you?" said Liam.

"What?" Caelin hissed.

Emery checked that none of the crew had heard her brother, then nodded.

"Are you serious?" Caelin said, coming closer. "Why?

"I need to."

From the moment he'd stepped into Tavor's cabin, she'd wanted to talk to him. No, before that. Before she'd even seen his ship on the horizon. Before the outsiders had arrived on Orabel. She'd wanted to talk to Forbiddens for the longest time, to ask them why they did what they did. Even now, something was pulling her towards those stairs, towards his scorching eyes. For the first time in her life, the answers she longed for were reachable.

EMERY RAN her fingers along the wooden paneling as they descended the stairs deeper into the belly of the ship.

Caelin glowered in the darkness. "This is a terrible idea."

"You don't have to come," Liam said. "Go wait up top. We'll find you when we're done."

Caelin mumbled under his breath but didn't turn around.

Her stomach squirmed, agreeing with him. Of course, this was a stupid idea. What did she think she could gain from talking to a crazed murderer?

The place the Forbidden was being kept was tucked away at the rear of the ship, on the lowest deck. The temperature steadily dropped the farther they went, and the musky odor worsened. When the stairs ended, they found themselves standing on the lowest deck facing the cargo hold, which was full of coils of ropes, folds of canvas, crates of food, and other supplies. Past all that, the Forbidden awaited.

They didn't come across anyone on this deck until they found two of Tavor's men, wearing his uniform of black-and-blue jackets with silver trim, standing outside a wooden door.

"What are you doing down here?" one of them asked, reaching for the handle of the blade tucked into his belt.

"We'd like to talk to the Forbidden," Liam said as if it were an everyday request.

"Nobody's allowed to speak to him," the second man responded.

"Says who?"

"Commissioner Thantos."

"Well then." There was a hint of relief in Caelin's voice. He turned to leave, but Liam caught his arm.

"I'm sure he'd allow me, *the chosen one*, to talk to him." He flashed a broad smile.

The first guard's eyes narrowed. "He specifically said not to allow any of you down here."

There was a small pause.

"Oh. Well, in that case, we'll be off." Liam spun on his heel and stalked back down the hallway.

Emery and Caelin followed him, no one speaking until they'd walked back through the cargo hold and stood beneath the stairs. Here, the light of the whale oil lantern hanging on the wall barely reached them.

"Why would Tavor forbid us talking to him?" Emery asked.

"Um, perhaps because he's a dangerous lunatic?" Caelin leaned against the wall and crossed his arms.

"Maybe if we talk to Tavor he'll change his mind."

"Do you want to wait for that?" Liam asked. "In which time, something could *happen* to the Forbidden, and we lose our chance."

Emery and Caelin looked at him.

"I could also get you in right now." His eyes gleamed, just as they always did back home when he was about to make mischief. Liam lived for chaos.

"How?" she asked, heart thumping with anticipation.

"Wait here." Liam strode back into the cargo hold, rummaging around until he returned carrying a small cask of something. "Give me a moment with this and I'll have the guards distracted."

"Is that gunpowder?" Emery asked, suddenly feeling apprehensive again.

Liam just flashed a wicked grin. "You two hide. You'll know when it's time."

Without hesitation, Liam darted up the stairs, heading to the gods only knew where.

"Em..." Caelin began. Judging by his tone and the look on his face, he was still against this idea.

But Emery didn't want to hear it. It was too late anyway. Liam was gone and she wouldn't be able to stop him if she tried. She snatched Caelin's wrist and pulled him into the cargo hold. They sank into the shadows behind a large crate, hidden from anyone who could wander through.

The ship above and around them was silent. She could hear only Caelin breathing beside her, the ocean slapping the hull through layers of creaking wood, and what might have been a rat scuttling somewhere in the distance.

*BOOM.*

Emery fell against Caelin, who swore under his breath. The ship shuddered so violently that dust fell from the ceiling and the hull groaned as if in pain. The sound echoed along the corridor, followed by alarmed yelling and footsteps thundering above them. On their level, Emery could hear the two varen guards bickering.

"We shouldn't leave our post!" one of them urged.

"It sounds like we're being attacked again!" the other argued. "I'm not waiting down here to be cornered."

The first guard made a frustrated noise of acquiescence and then two pairs of footsteps raced towards where Emery and Caelin hid. Emery shrank further into the shadows, pressed against Caelin. She felt him holding his breath just as she was.

The varens didn't even glance towards them as they rushed through the cargo hold and disappeared up the stairs leading to the deck above. Emery waited several heartbeats before she released her breath and stood.

"Come on," she whispered, grabbing Caelin's wrist again and pulling him through the cargo hold.

There, at the end of the room, stood the door in the dying light of two sconces, alone and unguarded.

Emery stepped towards the door, but Caelin grabbed her hand. He spun her around, his dark eyes unusually bright in the flickering orange light. "Are you sure you want to do this?"

"Yes. We'll all benefit from having answers."

He gently released her. "I'll watch for the guards." He turned around to face the cargo hold and the stairs beyond.

Emery reached for the door handle, hesitating for a moment when fear washed over her. No, she could do this. She'd already knocked him unconscious, and this time he'd even be locked up. Besides, today she had her lim. She turned the handle and walked in.

Only one sconce sputtered on the wall, so the room was even darker than the hallway, the back part mostly in shadow. Strange vertical branches led directly from floor to the ceiling, cutting the room into sections. She ran a finger along one of them and realized it was too cold and smooth to be wood. They were metal, like the blades Tavor and the other outsiders carried. The room was silent, the sounds of whatever commotion was happening above somehow not reaching here. The sound of her own swallowing was impossibly loud in her ears. She couldn't see the Forbidden though, in fact she could hardly see anything beyond the sconce and the many, many metal branches lining the room. She wrapped her arms around herself, the air was damp and chilly. And stale.

She squared her shoulders and walked in further, ignoring her tingling skin. Then, at the end of the room, where the shadows lay thickest, she saw him.

He was sitting in the center of one of the cages, two rows of the metal branches cutting him off from the rest of the room, trapping him in the darkest corner. He was cross-legged, wrists and ankles bound by further metal. He didn't look up when she approached, just continued to stare at his hands, lying open in his lap. She couldn't see his face, but she felt the *wrongness* coming off him. Chills skittered across her skin, and she considered bolting after all.

*No.*

Pulling herself together, she gripped one of the metal branches keeping the Forbidden locked away and whispered, "Hello."

Despite speaking quietly, her voice seemed booming as it broke the awful silence.

The Forbidden slowly looked up, and Emery fought the urge to step back. Most of his face was still in shadow, but she could make out the slight bend in his nose where Tavor had broken it, the purplish bruising around his left eye, itself no more than a slit now, and the swollen cut on his lower lip. Dried blood caked the side of his face and crusted his tunic, and even more had splattered onto the floorboards beneath him.

She could account for two of these wounds, but the others must have come afterwards.

Even through the shadows and the wounds, she could see his expression was bizarrely blank. Whatever rage that had fuelled him before was gone. His gaze was empty, lifeless, and it was almost more frightening than the wrath it contained last night.

Emery licked her dry lips, refusing to blink when those blank eyes came to rest on hers. "What is your name?" When he said nothing, Emery prodded. "People call you the Scourge of the Sea, is that right? That's what I'll have to call you too if you don't tell me your name."

His gaze bored into hers, and she stared right back, even as her eyes began to water. His mouth tightened ever so slightly, but he said nothing.

She didn't have time for this. Anger flickered inside her.

"Fine, Scourge. Why did you try to kill Tavor? Why are you killing innocent people?"

He didn't move, didn't make a sound. Just stared back without blinking.

Her anger sparked brighter and she smacked the metal with her hand, the ringing sound too loud in the silence. "Come on, there's got to be a reason! Why are you doing this? Why are you choosing to give us a bad name?"

The Scourge's good eye narrowed at the word *us*, but otherwise he gave no reaction.

Emery ran a hand through her hair. "This was clearly a stupid idea." She chuckled despondently. "I thought coming here and talking to you could do some good. I'm sorry I wasted your time." She turned to leave.

"What are you to him?" His voice sounded ragged, as if it hadn't been used in years, and somehow younger than she'd expected.

She turned around. The Forbidden was staring at the spot in which she had stood moments before, still wearing the same dull expression. Her fists clenched as she stepped back under his gaze. Finding his eyes again, she stared him down. "What do you mean?"

The Forbidden's expression didn't change. "Let me put it another way. What is he to you?"

"He's..." He was their savior. The only person to offer her people aid, even the chance of freedom, in a century and a half. He was someone who seemed to understand both sides of the conflict, in fact he *came* from both sides of the conflict. She glared at the Forbidden and said simply, "He's everything."

A flash of hatred flickered across his blank expression, then it was gone. His voice was deathly calm. "Perhaps I should have killed you too."

Emery blinked away the shock of his harsh words, refusing to give him any other reaction.

She nearly leapt to the ceiling as Caelin ripped open the door and poked his head inside. "Em, they're coming back!"

Emery tossed one last glance at the Forbidden. "But you didn't. And now you're here, locked away where you belong."

The Scourge of the Sea's hands curled in his lap, but he didn't say anything.

"Em!"

She turned and ran.

# Chapter Thirteen

E mery and Caelin hurtled up stair after stair until they burst onto the main deck, eyes watering in the sunlight that seemed impossibly bright after the darkness below. In her temporary blindness, Emery ran straight into a solid chest.

"Miss Aalokin?" Tavor's voice was alarmed as his hand gently grasped her shoulder, steadying her. "Are you alright?"

Emery blinked until her vision cleared. Tavor gazed down at her with concern. His face was still pale, the bandage still wrapped around his head. She allowed fear to trickle into her voice and hoped she sounded innocent when she said, "We heard an explosion. Are we being attacked again?"

"No! Nothing like that. We're safe, I assure you." He looked past her towards the bow where a tendril of black smoke wafted from another door leading below decks. "There was an...accident."

"What happened?" Caelin demanded, hand hovering over his sword sheathed at his side and gaze darting about the deck as if he didn't quite believe they were safe. Emery hoped he wasn't overplaying their innocence act.

"Liam got a bit carried away with some gunpowder." Tavor said, a hint of irritation sharpening his voice.

Emery did not have to fake the worry in her own voice this time. "Is he okay? Where is he?"

"He seems fine, but the medic is looking him over just in case," Tavor assured her, but then added. "Though he nearly blew a hole in the ship." He rubbed gingerly at his temples as if warding off a headache. A stab of guilt lanced through Emery. This was probably the last thing Tavor needed in his state. "If you'll excuse me, I must lay down again."

Emery and Caelin wandered silently back to the boys' cabin, where Liam was already waiting. He sat at the ornate table, drinking tea as if nothing had happened. Emery noticed bandages covered a few of his fingers, and his eyebrows were singed, something she would have laughed at if she wasn't so worried about him.

"What did you do?" Caelin fired at him.

Liam sipped his tea. "Things may have gotten away from me."

"Tavor said you nearly blew up the ship!" Caelin cried.

Liam waved his bandaged hand. "An exaggeration."

Emery crossed the room, took one of his hands, and examined it. "Are you okay?"

He pulled his fingers away. "I'm fine. Just a few singes."

"Was Tavor angry?" Emery asked. He hadn't seemed angry, but she suspected he'd been holding himself in check for her sake.

"Let's just say, I suspect if I wasn't *the chosen one* I'd be tossed overboard by now." Liam grinned. Caelin swore at him, but the words were lost on Liam. He looked at Emery eagerly. "So? What did the Forbidden say?"

"Nothing." The disappointment was bitter in her mouth. "Nothing we can work with anyway."

"Oh well." Liam wandered over to his bed. "At least you tried and I had fun. Want to play cards, take your mind off it?"

Emery played a few rounds with them, but couldn't really concentrate. The enigmatic, frustrating conversation she had just had and lack of sleep were forming a noxious haze in her head. A dinner was eventually brought down for them and after they ate, she excused herself to go collapse on her own bed.

But as exhausted as she was, sleep wouldn't claim her. The conversation with the Forbidden – or lack of it – kept buzzing around her head. She could still see him sitting in the dark with his hollow face, fingers curling in his lap as if he was picturing them around Tavor's throat. Or her own. She shuddered, thankful he was locked up far below.

She rolled on her side and stared out the window. Outside, the stars twinkled, and a crescent moon gleamed off the black ocean. The hull of the ship creaked quietly, and the sea rocked her back and forth, until finally sleep took her away.

When her eyes snapped back open, she wasn't sure what had woken her. She didn't feel like she slept long, but the room was distinctly darker than before. She laid there in the darkness, all her muscles coiled and ready, though for what, she didn't know.

The world tilted, toppling her from her bed. She landed hard on her hands and knees, and she stayed there, heart pounding with confusion. Nausea gripped her as the world tilted the other way, throwing her up against the wall. The ship bucked back to its normal position again, and she could now hear some kind of roaring sound in the distance. Clinging to the side of the bed and thanking the gods the furniture was bolted down, she edged along the floor towards the window. The ship swayed violently back and forth, and looking outside, she saw why.

The moon and the stars were gone. Instead, rain fell in torrents and lightning flashed again and again with unnatural frequency, illuminating the sea in eerie light. Furious-looking clouds hung low in the air, nearly touching the monstrous waves roiling along the ocean's surface. The roaring sound was a mixture of thunder and a wind that howled like an angry beast. Mountainous waves clawed at the side of the ship as if trying to tear it apart.

*Sweet Tadewin.*

A wave slammed up against the window so powerfully it rattled the glass. Emery flinched and stumbled for her door, making sure to scoop up her lim this time. The floor shifted just as she turned the handle and she tumbled into the hallway beyond, landing in several inches of cold, salty water. Liam and Caelin's door swung open as the ship listed the other way and they too spilled out in a tangle of limbs, nearly landing on top of her.

Emery made it to one knee before the ship shifted again and splashed her face with the frigid water. The darkness between lightning flashes was intense here, like hands were clamping down over her eyes. All the lights had been extinguished.

"Em! Are you alright?" Liam's voice sounded far away even though he was right there.

"Yes," she sputtered. "Are y –"

"Come on." Caelin grabbed her wrist and pulled her along.

With her free hand, she strapped her lim to her back. "Have you seen any of the crew?"

"Not yet!" Liam shouted over the crash of thunder. "We need to find Tavor!"

Together, they half-blindly stumbled down the hallway, falling sideways every time the ship listed. At times the darkness seemed to swallow them whole, and Emery was unnerved by the water sloshing around their ankles, like they were now in the belly of a gigantic beast.

A flash of lightning blinded them for a moment, and stars spun in Emery's vision afterwards. Another flash illuminated their destination, the stairs up to the main deck.

"We're almost there!" Liam shouted.

They rushed forward and the ship tilted again. Thunder seemed to split the sky apart, so loud Emery's ears rang, and then there was an awful crack. A bizarre silence followed, and then something crashed down above them. Darkness burst into white and orange light, and then the walls and ceiling began to buckle and splinter. The ship bucked and Caelin's fingers slipped away from her. She hit the ground hard, sliding along the floor, water splashing into her nose and mouth, and smashed against something solid. Pain pierced the back of her head and the world flickered into darkness and silence.

When she came to, her body felt light and heavy at the same time. Her mouth tasted of blood and her hearing was only returning in bursts of sound. Thunder. Water. Crashing. Howling. Screaming. Someone screaming her name.

"Emery!"

It was Liam. The terror in his voice forced life back into her limbs.

Caelin was calling out for her too. "Em!"

She crawled towards their voices, but they were muffled, like they'd been buried in earth. Or perhaps she was the one who'd been buried. She tried to shout back, but her voice came out too small. She had no breath. She couldn't see. Thunder still boomed somewhere above, but for some reason the lightning couldn't reach her anymore.

She could feel it now. The suffocating presence of the debris that had gouged a hole in the upper levels of the ship, taking her with them and trapping her in its bowels.

"Emery!" Liam sounded like he was leagues away.

"I'm here!" she cried. Even kneeling up now, the chill water reached her chest. Panic clogged her throat, trying to choke her before the ocean got its chance.

She stood up so the water only reached her thighs, distancing herself from the deadly surface, and took a deep breath. This was not how she was going to die. She started feeling around in the wreckage above her, for something loose she could shift to free herself. But there was nothing.

The ship tilted and she stumbled into a wall. Keeping one hand on it, she let the feeling of the grainy wood against her skin ground her and waded in what felt like the right direction. The darkness was thick as tar, but she tried to sense where the air was clearer, where it might point to a way out. She shivered worse with every step.

*Eldoris, merciful god of water, please don't let this water rise while I'm still in it.*

She paused as a smaller sound reached her ears, in a gap between the thunderclaps and peaks of wind and wave. The water in the corridor was being disturbed, like something was moving through it. No. Someone. Moving towards her.

She stepped backwards, but the person crashed into her. She overbalanced, and a hand grasped her elbow before she could fall. A man said something to her as his hand moved down to grasp hers, but the thunder smothered the quality of his voice. She knew it wasn't her brother or Caelin, and surely the hand was too calloused, too rough, to be Tavor's.

"This way!" Whoever it was, they tugged her in a different direction from the one in which she'd been heading. She didn't care, so long as they got out.

He moved quickly, confidently, despite the rolling ship and now belly-high water that kept slapping them in the face. Finally, miraculously, he was dragging her up a flight of steps and a blast of cool air hit her face. They were just below the top deck now. She nearly laughed with relief.

They turned a corner and lightning streaked across her vision. She blinked as a seemingly never-ending barrage shone through the grate in the ceiling. At least she could see the sky again, in all its blazing-white awfulness. Just ahead of them now was a ladder leading up to freedom.

She turned to thank whoever had quite possibly saved her life, but the words froze on her lips. She stared up at the Scourge of the Sea, his face as bloody, bruised and blank as it had been earlier.

Emery shook her hand as violently as she could, but he held fast. The ship rocked and she tumbled into the wall, yanking him down with her. His grip loosened slightly and she wrenched herself free, jabbing her elbow into his side for good measure. Lurching upright, she careened in the direction of the ladder.

Footsteps sloshed in the water behind her, already far too close. Darkness and light chased each other in quick succession as lightning strike after lightning strike hit, and each time the ladder was a little bit closer. But the Forbidden's hot breath was also on her neck. She leapt just as the ship gave its next heave and landed on the ladder. The wood shuddered as the Forbidden hit the rungs just below her.

Emery clung to the ladder as the ship shot upright again, then began climbing frantically. Cold fingers wrapped around her ankle, but she pulled her leg up and kicked out with the other. With a final heave, she was flopping onto the sodden floor of the deck.

The world around her was in chaos. Freezing rain pelted her face and stabbed her flesh. Wind tore at her hair, her clothes, but she forced her eyes to stay open.

Lightning forked across the sky, over and over, followed by the raging rumble of thunder. Wind had shredded the sails and whipped the ropes in every direction. Not one mast remained standing and half the deck was caved in. A fire raged near its middle, somehow immune to the gallons of rain and ocean water pelting it. Giant waves rolled across the deck, sweeping away anything that got in their way.

*The New Dawn* was going down.

Varens and sailors alike were running in every direction, trying to salvage what they could and readying the lifeboats. Across the ship, Tavor was hunched over by a pair of boats, clutching his ribs as if he were even more badly injured. She couldn't see Liam or Caelin anywhere and panic ripped through her heart.

Emery tried to stand, to run for Tavor but a hand latched onto her foot and began pulling her back towards the ladder.

The Scourge yelled something as he pulled her towards him, but she couldn't hear him over the howling wind. She only saw his mouth move, his eyes narrow. He was climbing onto the deck now, never relinquishing his grip on her foot. She kicked and rolled but he held on. Another monster of a wave rushed across the deck, hitting her like a wall and forcing the air from her lungs. Salty water forced its way into her mouth, down her throat. She choked and sputtered. The ocean pushed her right up against him, and his arms wrapped around her body, so tightly it hurt. The wave retreated once more, dragging them across the deck with it. Emery opened her eyes just long enough to see the Forbidden's face, right next to hers, before a blinding pain exploded at the base of her skull and the world dissolved into nothing.

# Part Two

## *The Forbiddens*

# Chapter Fourteen

When she woke, Emery's eyelids felt as heavy as if they'd been weighed down by a pair of stones. She forced them open, blinking slowly as the shadowy ceiling came into focus. Her stomach clenched in terror as the memory of her last waking moments gripped her, but more so because she didn't know where she was now.

She bolted upright, nausea rippling through her, but there was no water left to throw up, no wind roaring, no thunder or lightning. She clutched the sheets beneath her, felt the gentle swaying of the ship around her, breathed in the warm, slightly musty but reassuringly dry air of the cabin. The ocean lapped pleasantly against the hull, and beside the creak and groan of wood the night was silent. None of the nightmare had been real?

Her pulse refused to slow though, pounding strongest at the base of her skull. A slow, steady beat of pain. As if she really had been thrown head-first into one of the walls.

She gazed at the silver moonlight spilling through the giant bay window and pooling along the walls, across the floor. Her breath caught in her throat as her muddled thoughts finally caught up to what she was seeing.

This was not her cabin.

She remained completely still as she scanned the unfamiliar space. In front of the window, the moonlight illuminated a desk, piled high with objects she didn't recognize. But the rest of the room was too dark to make out details. Had she somehow ended up in Tavor's cabin?

No. The shape was right, but everything else was wrong. The cabin was too small and everything was in the wrong spot.

Panic had her leaping from the bed, but dizziness seized her so hard she fell to her knees.

"You shouldn't move so quickly."

She turned, again too quickly, and colors burst in front of her eyes. The Scourge of the Sea stepped out of the shadows and into the moonshine, the silver light throwing half his face into sharp relief against the shadows behind him.

Emery scrambled to her feet but lost her balance as soon as she tried to turn, the floor seemingly rippling beneath her. The Scourge stalked towards her. She tried to run, but again the floor tilted and tipped, throwing her to her knees, as if the storm was still raging inside her.

His footsteps were right by her ear now. "You hit your head."

She didn't need telling. The world was spinning at a revolting speed, darkness creeping along the edges of her vision. She retched, unable to suppress the nausea anymore, but nothing came up. The Scourge's hand brushed her back. She rolled away and righted herself as quickly as she could, but the world still tilted around her. She groaned at the sensation but began to crawl towards where the door had to be, just beyond the light's reach at the other end of the cabin.

"If you move too fast, you'll black out again."

She ignored him and pressed on, all her focus on reaching the other side of the door. Her crawling was slow and pathetic though, the pain in her head nearly blinding, and she dry heaved again as the Scourge's boots once more tapped the floor next to her ear.

"You're wasting your energy. You've nowhere to go."

A dull, distant horror began to claw her heart. Where were

Liam and Caelin? And what had happened...or been done...to Tavor and his crew?

Finally, she reached the door and used it to climb to her feet, panting with the effort. Her vision tunneling, she tried the handle. It wouldn't open, no matter how hard she shoved or pulled or rattled.

"You're not going back."

The Scourge's voice was directly behind her and she spun, pressing her back against the door. He was right there, so close he could grab her at any moment.

"Stay away from me," she demanded, chest heaving with exertion and fear. Her eyes darted to the giant window. Maybe, if she could get past him, she could climb through it.

Pulse pounding in her ears, Emery pushed away from the door and swung a fist at his face.

He caught it easily, keeping her hand aloft without so much as straining. "You're going to make yourself pass out."

She tried to wrench her arm away, but his grip was too strong and she hated every part of her weakened body for not being able to fight back and deal the blows it normally would. With a roar of rage, she swung with her other fist, but he caught that one too. Shadows danced across her vision, but she refused to let the darkness pull her down.

"There's no point fighting." His voice held no emotion. "You've got nowhere to go. Nothing to go back to."

His sharp words sliced at her heart, but she refused to give in. She kicked his shin, but the blow was a sad parody of what she'd usually be capable of.

He grunted dully, then stared right into her eyes. "The other ship is gone. The sea claimed her. And everyone aboard."

*No. No, no.*

Pain flared along her skull. She struggled against his grip, but to no avail. Her vision began to blur and the darkness thickened. "I don't believe you," she snarled at him, but it came out more of a sob.

A slow, horrible smile broke across his blank face. The first real expression she'd seen him make. "Whether you believe me or not, it doesn't matter. They're dead."

Her heart splintered into a thousand pieces. And finally, she let the darkness swallow her.

⚓

FOR A MIRACULOUS MOMENT, Emery didn't know where she was, or why she was there. She simply existed, and everything was peaceful.

Then, the agony returned, and with it her memories. Her head throbbed, her stomach roiled, her limbs ached. But that was all eclipsed by the yawning pit opening inside her. Her brother was dead. Drowned, probably. She could picture his white, bloated corpse floating in the ocean, Caelin and Tavor's beside him. Their corpses would have sunk to the ocean's inky depths by now, the darkness swallowing them like a monster's maw.

She'd never spent a day without Liam, had never known herself without him. Now he was gone. How was she supposed to function, to breathe even, when he no longer could? And Caelin, he had only left Orabel because of her and Liam. He shouldn't even have been on the ship. Now he too was dead, and Grace also brotherless. The sea should have swallowed her with them.

She opened her eyes and rolled onto her side, the small motion nearly making her gag with nausea. It was daytime. Bright, piercing sunlight stabbed her eyes. Sheets were tangled between her legs. She was back in the bed that didn't belong to her. Stiffening in recognition, she carefully lifted her eyes to the rest of the cabin.

With the sunlight pouring through the bay window, she could now clearly make out the details of the cabin. Everything was made of a mahogany and walnut, from the floors to the walls to the beams crossing the ceiling. The bed she lay in was built into an alcove in the wall on the right side of the cabin, with shelves on either side. Against the wall across from the bed stood a wooden wardrobe, and a chest. A door next to the wardrobe led, presumably, to a small washing room. The huge bay window took up the entire back wall of the cabin, in front of which sat the desk and a few chairs. A pair of thick, wooden double doors loomed at the front of the room, leading to the rest of the ship.

The room wasn't nearly as large or lavish as the cabins on *The New Dawn*, but it still had a cozy, comfortable quality to it. Or it would have, if not for The Scourge of the Sea sitting on a wooden chair in the center of the room, arms crossed, face expressionless, watching over her silent suffering.

For the first time, she could see him properly. Blood no longer coated the side of his head, and he was wearing a clean, cream tunic. His sleeves were rolled up, and Emery noticed one of his arms was entirely covered with tattoos. His other displayed a number of leather bracelets. His golden hair was tousled, as if he'd just left a windstorm, and it was kept from falling into his eyes by an emerald bandana wrapped around his forehead. Though his face bore the stubble of several days, she could still see the youthful skin underneath it. With a jolt of surprise, she guessed he couldn't have been more than a year or two older than herself.

His eyes locked onto hers, and she couldn't look away. There was no rage in them now, rather an endless depth of...nothing. He stared back at her, sitting completely still with his arms crossed over his chest, a blade strapped to his hip. His left eye and nose still looked swollen, but the purple bruising staining his face had lightened by a few shades. How long had she been out this time?

It seemed entirely wrong that the sun should still be rising and setting, as if the world hadn't just ended. Her heart was thudding methodically in her chest, which seemed wrong too. How could her heart continue beating when her brother's no longer did? When Aya's would also stop soon?

And Tavor had been her people's hope for a better future.

Now they'd be stuck living the way they always had, isolated and scared. If the Withering didn't kill everybody first.

*Oh, Ayana. I'm sorry I couldn't save you.*

Emery's eyes stung and hot tears dripped down her cheeks, but she didn't bother wiping them away. When she refocused, she found herself staring right into the Scourge's hollow eyes, which gazed back, unblinking.

Without obvious reason, the Forbidden stood up, leaving as wordlessly as he'd been sitting. She didn't care. All she could see was her brother, floating dead in the ocean, and she allowed the grief and shadows to drag her down once more.

A METHODICAL THUDDING woke her sometime later. Her gaze flicked to the desk. The Scourge sat behind it, throwing a dagger repeatedly at the desk, burying its tip in the wood. She wondered, almost detached from herself, what he planned to do with it.

This time, he spoke. "You should eat."

She hadn't even noticed the plate of food on the bedside table. Her voice came out as dry as her throat felt. "Why?"

"You're no use to me dead."

Her eyes burned again, her jaw trembled, and she bit the inside of her lip to keep it still. She didn't want to be useful to him. The people she cared about, on the other hand... For a start, she would probably never see her grandparents again. At least they'd never know how Liam died. They'd go on thinking he was alright, off bringing peace to their people, not trapped in the skeleton of a ship at the bottom of the ocean.

But Aya, she would wither away, waiting for a cure that would never come.

The Scourge leaned forward in his chair, resting his elbows on the desk. "Did Tavor really mean that much to you?" He asked as if the concept was unfathomable.

Emery closed her eyes and hot tears squeezed their way to freedom as she choked up the words. "My brother."

For a long moment, the Scourge said nothing. Then, "Tavor was your brother?"

"No." She fought to keep a sob at bay. "My...brother...was also on the ship." Her insides felt wrung out and misshapen.

The Scourge sat perfectly still again, but this time his empty expression cracked. His skin paled, a frown tugged on his lips. But only for a moment. Then the blankness returned as he stared at her for what felt like an eternity. Without another word, he stood up and left again.

As soon as the door closed behind him, the sobs broke free. Feeling like part of her had died with them, Emery finally let loose and cried for her brother, for Caelin, for Orabel's lost hope of freedom.

Eventually, when there were no more tears to shed, just an emptiness inside her that resembled a starless night sky, she rolled on her back and closed her eyes, hoping sleep would pull her into its bittersweet oblivion.

Before it could, the door opened, clicked shut again. She kept her eyes closed, stayed on her back. She knew it was him. It was never anyone else. The still-full plates rattled as he exchanged them. She had no energy to move anymore, didn't even feel fear when he stayed there, hovering over her.

His voice sounded a touch gentler than before. "I don't *know* they're dead."

Her eyes snapped open. It must have still been daytime again, for sunlight bathed every inch of The Scourge. He stood by the bed but stared out the window, a plate and mug in each hand. Bruises still lingered on his face, and his nose was still slightly crooked from Tavor's punch.

"What did you say?" Her throat was so dry she barely heard herself.

"They could have gotten off." He looked down at the floor. "Could have gotten on a longboat. They could have survived."

Her heart shuddered, as if it was trying to restart itself.

"There's a chance your brother is alive."

Emery raised herself onto her elbows, her muscles aching and trembling. "Why are you telling me this?" A flash of anger, an almost welcome change from the despair, sparked in her hollow belly. "And why only now?"

He swallowed, finally looking at her. His eyes weren't the blank things they usually were. Something deep, dark and desolate dwelled in them. But before she could analyze it further, he shook his head, returning to his dead-eyed state, and left.

Too weak to follow him, Emery rolled onto her back and stared at the sun-drenched ceiling. Her brother could be alive. He could be out there somewhere, wondering what had happened to her.

Or was the Scourge lying now? Whether he was, or had lied the last time, what was his reasoning in either case? How would either choice benefit him?

A new picture of Liam, Caelin and Tavor formed in her mind. The three of them clinging to a longboat, defying the ocean's rage, refusing to go under. It was possible.

Doubt prowled at the edges of her mind, but she closed her eyes and clung onto this new hope. Even if their chances of survival had been slim, she needed to find out what had happened to them, one way or another. She needed to know, and to find them if they still were alive.

Nor could she give up on Aya. Even if all else was lost, she could still try to find the cure, somehow, and a way to bring it back to her.

It was time she understood the entirety of her situation, the fulness of the Scourge's plan, whatever it took to achieve that. It was time to regain her strength, even if the thought of accepting his food felt like a betrayal of everyone and everything she was fighting for.

She blew out a long breath, trying to calm the nerves erupting inside her belly. Her muscles ached and bones creaked as she edged herself into sitting. The pain in her head had dissipated, but the dizziness remained. She grabbed the mug and plate from the bedside table. It was only water and a chunk of stale-smelling bread, but it represented the first step back to herself. Leaning cross-legged against the wall, she nibbled on the bread and watched the door.

S HE MUST HAVE FALLEN ASLEEP, so exhausted by the act of digesting something again that she'd passed out. Now, outside the window, the world was hidden in darkness, only a quarter moon illuminating half of the cabin.

The Scourge slipped through the doorway as silent as a shadow. His chair remained in the center of the cabin, just outside the moonlight's reach, but before he sat down, he lit a lantern hanging from the ceiling. Warm light illuminated the space, gilding him in gold as he took a seat. He said nothing as he glared at her.

Emery squeezed her fists to keep them from shaking, instinctively wanting to reach for her lim, but it was nowhere to be seen. Had she lost it in the storm, or had it been taken from her?

Refusing to show her fear, she stared calmly back, waiting for him to break first.

Finally, he gave in. "What is your name?"

"What's yours?"

"Captain Sean Denzel."

She blinked. She hadn't expected him to answer so plainly. "And people call you the Scourge of the Sea."

His expression tightened slightly. "Some people do." When she didn't reply, the Scourge – Sean – leaned forward. "Your turn."

She could think of no reason not to tell him, so she relented, "Emery."

"Emery," he repeated, and hearing the infamous Forbidden say her name sent shivers down her spine. "That's an Everwyn word for brave. It suits you."

She hadn't known that. The first elemists to settle in Orabel travelled from all corners of the realm, so they had all manner of names back home. She'd never thought to ask what her name meant or what language it came from.

Annoyed at her own ignorance and not wanting him to notice, she deflected. "How do you know I'm brave?"

A sardonic sort of smile crossed his lips. "Not many people are brave enough to cross the Scourge of the Sea."

She cocked a brow and couldn't stop her own provoking grin from appearing. "And how many people cross the Scourge of the Sea and *win*?"

"Very few." She expected him to sound annoyed at the reminder that she'd knocked him unconscious but instead his tone sounded almost...impressed. And then he asked, "Your accent...it's intriguing. Where are you from?"

The question caught her by surprise. She wasn't the one with the accent, he was. The lilting of his words was almost hypnotizing, just like Tavor's speech.

"It's a strange mixture," he continued. "I can hear some Aedish, maybe Jokulian, a dash of Bazylish. And yet you speak the Royal Tongue. Will you enlighten me?"

Emery had no idea what any of that meant. Everyone spoke the same language back home – the Royal Tongue, apparently. But of course, she couldn't and wouldn't tell him where she was from. She raised her chin and held his stare. "Where are we?"

"In my cabin. Aboard my ship, the *Audacity*."

She'd guessed as much but hearing the confirmation still made her pulse quicken with unease. "How long have I been here?"

"About two days," he said. "You were unconscious for one."

"How did I get here?"

"I brought you," he said simply.

She wanted to ask how, because the last thing she remembered was them both being swept up in a monstrous wave during the storm. She'd hit her head, lost consciousness. And she recalled nothing after that. So how did they get to his ship? But a more pressing question flew from her mouth instead. "Why? What do you want from me?"

The Scourge — Sean — cocked his head to the side. "That depends on your relationship with our mutual *friend*."

Emery swallowed down her growing dread. "Why do you hate Tavor so much?"

A shadow passed over his face and his voice turned hard. He peered at her as if trying to look into her very soul. "What are you to him? Are you family?"

She leveled her gaze at him, noting the green of his eyes and the gold of his hair. So similar to Tavor's. "Are you?"

"No, and I thank all the gods for that," he said, looking repulsed by the very thought. "Are you business partners?"

She continued to stare him down, not responding.

He leaned forward. "Perhaps" — finally, his voice began to show emotion, even if it was disgust — "you're his *lover*."

Emery's face heated, not because of the suggestion that she and Tavor were lovers, but because the Forbidden seemed to think she was so much more than she really was. He thought she was more than just a tag-a-long, more than a request by her brother and a decision that took little thought. She hated the way her own words tasted as she spat, "Maybe I'm nothing to him."

He scowled. "That's clearly not true. You risked your life to save his."

"I had no choice. You were going to kill him."

His hands tightened in his lap, as if imagining his fingers around Tavor's throat once more. She couldn't get the image out of her head, the crack of Tavor's skull as the Scourge drove the butt of his pistol into his head, the blood leaking onto the floor.

"What *are* you to him?" Sean repeated.

Emery crossed her arms and refused to break eye contact, even though her skin crawled under the intensity of his gaze.

They glared at each other, his characteristically empty expression beginning to crack once more as his jaw tightened.

But though nerves squirmed in her stomach, it felt like she was winning the bizarre game they were playing.

"What do you want with me?" she asked one more time. "What do you want from Tavor?"

The Forbidden got to his feet. Even though he stood halfway across the room, he seemed to tower over her. "I don't *want* anything *from* him."

She tried not to shrink back against the wall.

He stepped closer, the lantern's light carving shadows over the planes of his face. "I want to *give* him something."

Emery curled her fingers into fists, ready to leap off the bed if he moved any closer. She couldn't stop herself from asking, "What do you mean?"

"I'm going to make him hurt. And you're going to help me."

"And you think I'm going to agree to that?"

A crooked smile appeared on his face. "As I said, you're no use to me dead. Yet."

# Chapter Fifteen

T he Scourge of the Sea didn't elaborate on his sinister
intentions. In fact, he stalked from the cabin after his
proclamation, slamming the door behind him, leaving Emery
alone on the bed with her heart thundering.

She had to escape, to get out of this cabin and off this ship
before Sean came back and made good on his promise.

Though panic pounded through her veins, she waited several
long minutes to make sure he didn't return before launching
across the cabin for the door. Luckily, the food and sleep had
done her good. Only a slight wave of dizziness hit her as she
crossed the cabin, and the pain in her head was easy to ignore.
But that's where her luck ran out. The door did not open when
she rattled the handle, though truthfully, she hadn't expected it
to. She hurried to the smaller door beside the wardrobe next,
and found a little washing room, complete with a small basin of
water, an empty tub, and a place for one to relieve themselves.
Nothing useful in there.

Finally, she raced for the window, and after a moment of
searching, found a latch that opened a square panel of the glass.
A gust of air rushed into the cabin, bringing with it the scent of
brine and freedom. She glanced over her shoulder at the door,

making sure the Scourge hadn't crept back in with that silent and sinister way he had, before settling her attention back on the open window. It was not a large opening but, thankfully, she was not a large person.

She poked her head through the window, and the wind blew her hair around her face. Below, the deep, dark ocean frothed as the ship left a wake in its path. Above, the quarter moon hung in the night sky, gifting her with just enough light to see by. She wiggled her shoulders through the window, and then her hips, barely squeezing through the tight opening. Pausing, she took a deep breath, very aware that if she were to slip and fall now, there was nothing but ocean to catch her, and she'd likely drown in its dark depths before she ever found land or another ship to rescue her. What she needed was a longboat.

Everything was slippery with sea spray and any handholds she found were small and few between. But she'd rather risk falling in the ocean then allowing the Scourge to kill her. She thanked the gods for all her years of scaling trees and began to climb. The going was slow and painstaking, but eventually she reached the guardrail of the afterdeck, and paused long enough to peak through the gaps in the railing.

The moon cast the deck in shades of silver, mixing with the golden light thrown by a whale oil lantern hanging nearby. The deck appeared deserted, the helm empty. A rope attached to one of the wheel's spokes tied it in place as the ship sailed slowly onwards through the night.

Emery waited, scrutinizing every shadow in case one suddenly moved and revealed itself to be a person. When the deck remained silent and still, she set her gaze on the longboat hanging against the hull of the ship only several paces away and climbed over the guardrail. When her bare feet touched the wood of the deck, she paused again, her skin prickling with unease, and she looked around.

She had the uncomfortable feeling of being watched but she still saw no one. There had to be other Forbiddens on the ship, not just Sean, but she assumed – and hoped – they were all asleep so late at night. She wondered where the Scourge himself was sleeping, since she'd been passed out in his cabin for the last few days. That thought hadn't fully registered in her head yet and now she shuddered at the realization that she'd been laying in a murderer's bed.

With renewed vigor, Emery tiptoed towards the longboat, her bare feet silent against the wooden planks. The pully system attaching the longboat to the ship was cast in shadows, and she squinted at the mechanism, trying to figure out how to free the boat. It clinked when she brushed it with her fingers, the sound far too loud in the silence of the night. She glanced over her shoulder again, making sure she was still alone, and then went back to work on release.

Precious moments past as she fiddled with the thing, but she couldn't figure it out in the dark. She cursed, wishing she'd brought something sharp with her so she could simply cut the ropes instead.

"Need help with that?"

Emery spun, heart hammering in her throat. A man leaned against the mizzenmast, his arms and ankles crossed. A stretch of red lace was wrapped around his head, keeping his shoulder length black hair out of his slightly uptilted eyes. He appeared only a few years older than herself. She was certain he hadn't been there last time she checked.

Emery curled her fingers into fists, wishing again that she had her lim and cursing herself for being in such a panic to escape that she didn't grab a weapon first.

The man grinned, flashing a set of white teeth against brown skin. "I'm Ranit. And you must be Emery, I presume. Pleased to finally meet you."

Emery said nothing, even more unnerved that this stranger knew her name. Sean must have told him. The thought of him caused her pulse to race even faster and she glanced around, trying not to imagine what he might do to her if he caught her trying to escape.

Ranit stepped forward and she caught the flash of steel at his hip.

She fought the urge to flinch back and instead stood taller, bracing herself if he tried to grab her.

He must have read the alarm on her face because he raised his hands in front of him. "Easy. I'm only – "

She didn't let him finish. Darting forward, she dropped into a roll, executing the *rolling stone* maneuver she'd been taught but never thought she'd ever have to use. As she came out of the roll behind the stunned man, she snagged his blade from his belt and pointed it at him.

"Don't touch me," she growled, hoping her voice sounded menacing enough the man didn't notice how awkwardly she held the blade. It was so much heavier than her lim.

Ranit spun to face her, his back now against the longboat and his hands raised before him. "Easy," he repeated. Instead of looking angry or afraid, he made a humming noise and his grin widened. "I understand now."

"Understand what?" she couldn't help but ask.

"Why you have my captain so flummoxed."

Emery didn't know how to interpret that statement. Adrenaline pumped through her veins, and she was surely running out of time before someone else heard their commotion and came to investigate. "Untie the boat."

"I probably shouldn't," Ranit said, shrugging as if he was sorry for the inconvenience. "The Captain wouldn't be pleased."

"I don't care what pleases your Captain," she said, urging as much threat into her voice as possible. "Untie the boat or I'll spill your blood with your own weapon."

He stared at her for a moment, eyebrows traveling up his forehead, and she hoped he wouldn't push her any further. She didn't know if she had the stomach to actually stab someone, and she'd prefer not to find out any time soon.

But once again, Ranit appeared more amused than anything. "Now I really understand."

Before Emery could respond with another threat, and arm

banded across her chest and something sharp pressed into her throat. She froze as a woman's voice commanded. "Drop the blade or I'll spill *your* blood."

Emery dropped the sword. It clattered to the deck. Icy terror sluiced through her veins as her mind raced for a way out of this situation without *anyone* spilling blood. She wished she'd stayed in the cabin.

"Cam, lower your ax." Ranit said. He leaned casually against the rail, as if his life hadn't been threatened moments before. "I have the situation under control."

"She had you at sword point, Ranit," Emery's current captor – Cam – spat.

Ranit shrugged. "Semantics."

The blade at Emery's throat dug in as Cam shoved her towards the railing. "Move."

Now Ranit stood up straight, a look of alarm finally crossing his face. "What are you doing?"

"We're tossing her overboard! She shouldn't be here."

"We can't do that," Ranit said slowly, as if trying to placate a rabid animal.

"It's for his own good!" Cam nearly shouted, pushing Emery toward the railing and the black sea beyond.

Emery's years of training kicked in once again. She allowed one step, and when Cam lifted her own foot, she used her captor's imbalance against her. She drove her left elbow into Cam's ribs, winding her, and with her right hand, grabbed Cam's arm, wrenching it and the ax down, pinning it to her chest. She ducked, twisting Cam's pinned arm and then slipping under it, yanking the ax from her grip. She hooked her ankle around Cam's as she moved behind the woman and sent her crashing to the ground.

Chest heaving, Emery stood over the fallen Forbidden, stolen ax raised and ready. The weapon looked like the hatchet's they had at home, only the head was metal instead of stone or wood, and it was a lot heavier.

Ranit still stood near the longboat, eyes wide, and Cam lay

on her back, staring up at Emery. They both looked as shocked as Emery felt on the inside. A part of her couldn't quite believe she'd just done that. After so many years of learning to fight, it felt wholly different to use the techniques against an actual enemy and not someone she'd known her whole life. It felt...empowering.

If she ever made it home, she'd head straight to Ezra to thank her.

Cam sprang to her feet so fast Emery didn't have time to do anything but back up. Icy blond hair spilled across the woman's shoulders, and she stood at least a full head taller than Emery. Her pale skin was like snow in the moonlight. She snarled with rage and plucked a second small ax from her belt.

She roared as she hurled herself at Emery. "You – "

"ENOUGH!"

Cam skidded to a halt so fast she nearly tripped over her own feet.

Emery turned just enough so she could keep Cam in her sights but could also see the Scourge of the Sea stalking towards them. His gaze flew over the scene, coming to rest on the ax in Emery's fist, and his eyes were anything but blank right then.

Ranit's tone was incongruously bright. "Hello, Captain..."

"What do you think you're doing?" Sean's voice was so calm it made Emery's spine tingle. At first, he thought he was speaking to her but then she realized he was looking past her. "Explain yourself, Camulus."

Cam did not cower under her captain's intense gaze. "She shouldn't be on this ship, and you know it. We need to –"

"We've already discussed this," Sean interrupted, his voice soft but firm.

"This is madness."

"Camulus..." Sean warned, his jaw clenching.

"This has got to end. You lied to us, nearly got yourself killed, and now you're putting the rest of us in danger too. And for what? You know it won't bring her back."

The Scourge of the Sea flinched at Cam's last words. Ranit

cleared his throat, whether in trepidation or preparing to inter-
cede Emery couldn't tell.

Some of the fury in Camulus's face died and she winced. "I'm
sorry, Captain. I shouldn't –"

"Leave." Despite the clearly painful nature of what had been
said, his quiet voice betrayed no emotion. He stared down at his
subordinate with hard, empty eyes.

Ranit approached the pair. "Captain, I –"

"Both of you. Now."

Camulus glared one last time at Emery before stomping
across the deck and disappearing down the stairs. Ranit gave her
a small salute and then followed. Emery met the Scourge's hard
stare, the ax starting to tremble in her hand, her head whirling
with questions but too afraid to ask and risk riling him further.

"Back to the cabin," he ordered.

She bristled, instinctively wanting to defy the demand.

At her hesitation, no doubt noting the way her eyes darted
about the ship in search of somewhere to flee, he reiterated,
"You can walk back to the cabin, or I can take you."

He used that same deadly calm voice he used on his subordi-
nates. And Emery had to admit, it was affective. Her feet moved
almost on their own accord, but she still glared at him as she
strode for the stairs. The back of her neck tingled as Sean
followed her down the steps and into the cabin. The door
clicked shut behind them. When she reached the middle of the
room, she turned to glare at him some more, only to find him
standing right in front of her. He moved so silently she hadn't
realized he followed her all the way into the cabin, and she
fought the urge to back up.

Sean snatched the ax she still held from her hand. She
resisted for only a moment before letting the handle go. The
fight had gone out of her. Despite holding her own against Ranit
and Cam, she suspected that might have been because she took
them by surprise. Sean was watching her every move now and
she was definitely still too weak to take him in a proper fight.

"Are you hurt?" he asked.

Emery blinked in surprise but of course he wouldn't want the goods damaged before he could kill her himself.

"No."

"I would not advise trying to escape again."

Emery scowled, wishing she were taller so she didn't have to glare up at him. "You think I'm just going to patiently wait for you to kill me?"

The Scourge's answering glare was cold and he stepped even closer, so close she could feel his body heat. "If you ever threaten a member of my crew again – "

"That woman was going to throw me in the sea!" Emery burst, not yielding a single step.

"*After* you pointed a sword at Ranit," he growled. "I saw everything."

She raised onto her toes so they were nearly nose to nose. "Then you saw him coming after me first."

"I saw you threatening my family." He didn't yield either, his usual stoic expression cracking with suppressed rage. "You're alive right now because I want Tavor to witness your death. But make no mistake, if you ever threaten my family again, I will not hesitate to immediately throw you overboard myself."

Finally, the Scourge spun on his heel and stormed from the cabin, slamming the door behind him. Emery didn't bother checking if the door was locked. She wasn't going anywhere tonight.

# Chapter Sixteen

After Sean stormed from the room, Emery didn't move, watching the door and bracing herself in case he changed his mind and came back to throw her overboard after all. After several long moments of silence, her adrenaline began to wane, and exhaustion took over. A glance out the window told her dawn was not far off and she hadn't slept all night.

She sat on the bed, still watching the door, her mind whirling with the events of the evening.

Her attempted escape had been a disaster, but it had left her with a valuable piece of information. Sean said he wanted Tavor to witness her death, which meant the Scourge didn't plan to kill her until they found Tavor again, assuming he even survived the storm. Which meant she likely didn't have to fear him barging into the cabin at any moment to wrap his hands around her throat or shove his blade in her heart or whatever he eventually planned to do. She had time, and she planned to use this time wisely so her next escape attempt resulted in freedom. No more acting out of panic.

She'd also been left with questions. Clearly, Camulus did not agree with her Captain's plans. Cam wanted Emery off the ship, and Emery wondered if her effort to throw Emery overboard was a murder attempt or a strange attempt at rescue. Regardless, she wondered if there were other members of the crew who also didn't agree with their captain's plans, and if she could use that unrest to aid in her escape somehow.

Cam also insinuated that the Scourge wanted to get someone back. But who was she? Where was she? And what did Tavor have to with any of it?

With such thoughts tumbling together in her head, the knowledge that she likely didn't have to fear imminent death, and knowing she was going to need all the strength she could get for the days to come, Emery finally allowed her exhaustion to overtake her.

When she awoke next, daylight spilled through window. She had no idea how long she slept but a quick glance around the cabin told her she was still alone. It was time to start plotting her escape.

But first, she needed to clean up so she could feel human again. Dried blood still caked her hair and her clothes stank, encrusted as they were with salt and grime.

She headed for the little washing room. Desperate for a wash but knowing Sean could walk in at any time, she opted for simply dunking her head in the basin of water. The water turned red from the blood in her hair, and she winced as she ran her hand over the bump still on the back of her head.

With her long hair dripping down her back, she went to Sean's wardrobe next and threw the doors open. Inside, a variety of clothes were dangling from hangers or neatly folded on a shelf. She opted for a pale blue tunic and black trousers, both of which hung loosely on her body but smelled a lot more pleasantly. She sniffed one of the sleeves to get a better sense of it. Crisp sea salt, cedarwood, and something balmy she couldn't name.

Feeling a bit more centered, she strode to examine the items on the desk, hoping she could find something there to aid in her escape. A large sheet of the barklike substance she'd seen in Tavor's cabin lay across half of it, white and smooth. Little squiggling lines and long, straight strokes of black and blue covered its surface, along with jagged symbols and roughly-sketched images of sea monsters and ships. A map, Tavor had explained, used for navigation. Emery frowned, wishing she knew how to interpret it so she could use it to find Liam, Caelin, and Tavor. She knew they headed to a place called Dornwell before the storm hit and, if they indeed survived, they'd likely continue the journey there. But all she knew about Dornwell's location was that it was on the coast of the continent to the east.

Her gaze curiously trailed over the various other objects occupying the desk, all just so, as if painstakingly placed in their specific spots; a lantern, a bottle of black liquid, a strange metal device comprised of two connected legs but nothing else, a feather with a metal point placed over the end of its shaft, and a black, eight-sided box. She opened the box, revealing a neat circle of symbols adorning its inside, and at its center a red arrow that always returned to point the same way, no matter how many times she spun it.

The door opened and her whole body stiffened but she didn't look up, as if the Scourge's presence unconcerned her.

A stretch of silence passed. "Are those my clothes?"

"Mhm." She continued to spin the odd little box and watched the arrow quiver but ultimately stay in place.

"What are you doing?"

She finally deigned to look at him. He stood by the closed door with his arms crossed, eyeing the object in her hand. Sunlight glinted off the long blade at his side, the hilt of a pistol strapped to his waist on the other.

Instead of evoking fear, the sight of the weapons caused hot anger to spike in her chest. "I need to entertain myself somehow, don't I? I'm getting bored waiting for you to kill me."

Her shoulders tensed as he crossed the room, but he stopped on the other side of the desk. Forcing herself to appear calm, she spun the arrow in the box again, eyeing his weapons from under her lashes.

"That's not how it works."

Curiosity got the better of her and she looked up at him

again. The morning sunlight was highlighting the golden streaks of his windswept hair, and though his face remained generally blank, the corners of his mouth seemed to be lifting the tiniest of degrees. Once again, she was struck by his surprising youth and his rather ordinary appearance. He looked nothing how she imagined a bloodthirsty Forbidden to look. If she were to pass him on the paths back home, she wouldn't have given him a second glance. Perhaps the alluring lines of his cheekbones would have turned her head but –

She slammed such treacherous thoughts down. He was a monster, and he planned to kill her, alluring cheekbones or no.

Horrified at herself, she schooled her expression. "What is it then?"

"A compass." The Scourge stalked over to the chair in the center of the room, dragging it over with a noise that grated on Emery's taut nerves. He sat so the desk was between them, and Emery noticed the flash of some sort of trinket hanging around his neck. "The arrow always points north. Which means you can always orient yourself."

Emery examined the red arrow, curiosity sparked anew. If she learned how this compass worked, maybe she could use it to find Dornwell.

Taking a quick breath, she raised her chin and held the box out to him. "How does it work?"

He eyed her, arms still crossed, and then slowly leaned over the desk to pluck the compass from her fingers with surprising gentleness. He began rotating the position of the compass on his palm, which she noticed was wrapped with some sort of leather guard. "You line up the north point with the arrow, and then you know which direction you're facing."

She looked down at the device. The red arrow now lined up perfectly with one of the marks in the outer circle, indicating, if she understood correctly, that north lay behind her and east was to her left.

Her gaze travelled to the map. Emery bit the inside of her lip, wondering if it would be wise to ask any more questions. She didn't want him growing suspicious of her new plans. She also didn't like him knowing how ignorant of the outside world she was, nor could she trust anything he told her was truthful.

Nonetheless, curiosity was building up inside her like a river in danger of overflowing its banks. She tapped the map with her finger. "How does this work?"

Sean raised a brow. "You mean the map?"

She nodded, aware of curiosity in his gaze as his eyes flickered across her face. He swept a hand across the map, indicating various places in turn. "These chunks are land, and the rest, the wavy bits, are water. This is what our world looks like from above, very roughly speaking of course."

Surprised by the generosity with which he was offering what *felt* like accurate information, she couldn't help glancing up at him. His voice remained monotone, but his eyes weren't as empty as usual. Something new was there, something that suggested a soul might be living within him after all. She blinked away the thought and looked down at the map again, poking a large, green mass that took up most of the right-hand side. "Where's this?"

Again, the Scourge answered as if this were any regular conversation. "That's Tala, our largest continent. It's made up of several countries." He pointed to a black smudge at the edge of the mass. "And that's Dornwell, the capital. Where the king lives."

Emery's breath caught as she stared at the mark on the map that represented Dornwell, memorizing its location the best she could. But then she lifted her gaze back to Sean, wondering if he'd just given her the location of the exact place she wished to go on purpose.

He held her gaze, giving nothing away, and sat back in his chair. "Are you going to tell me where you're from now?"

"Where are *you* from?" she shot back.

He sighed, but sat forward again, placing a finger on a small dot about halfway down the edge of the Talian mass. "A town in southern Everwyn, about there." He looked up at her, his eyes slightly narrowed, as if trying to peer into her head. Sitting so close in clear daylight, she could see now that his eyes were a deep green. It reminded her of the pines back home, and her heart clenched with longing.

She tore her eyes away, distracting herself by picking up the feather she'd examined earlier. "Why is there metal on this?"

"It's a quill. We use it for writing. Do you...know what that means?"

She did not. She pointed to the container holding the black liquid. "What's this?"

"Ink..."

He gave the answer slowly, as if suspicious of her sudden onslaught of questions. In truth, she just couldn't contain her curiosity any longer.

"This?" She held up a complicated-looking device covered in what looked like many metal-rimmed eyes.

"A sextant. You use it to measure angles, particularly between the horizon and..." She couldn't change her confused expression before he noticed. He almost sounded amused when he offered a simpler version. "It helps you navigate while out at sea."

Emery shot him question after question, and he answered each one with a patience that began to unnerve her. Perhaps it was only a ruse. Perhaps she'd ask one too many at some point, or one he didn't feel like answering, and he'd snap her neck instead.

But the longer their conversation continued, the harder that was to believe. He seemed genuinely...content like this, feeding her curiosity like an indulgent teacher, and it was difficult not to smile whenever he reached over quietly to straighten things she had accidentally – or not – placed in the wrong spot.

Done with everything on the desk, she wandered to investigate one of the shelves flanking the bed. Her spine prickled as she felt his gaze on her back and stroked along the rectangular objects lined up with an admittedly satisfying neatness. "What are these?"

"Books."

She pulled a particularly large one from the shelf and sat down with it, gasping when it fell open in her lap. "I'm sorry, I didn't –"

"It's alright." Was that a chuckle? "It's meant to do that."

More of the same bark-like material spilled up from the book, hundreds of little black symbols covering each sheet. The aroma wafting from them was heavenly, heavy, like almond oil and dried flowers.

She ran a hand over a line of symbols. "How does it work?"

"You read it." Again, the corners of his mouth tilted up ever so slightly. "Then the pages tell you a story. Or give you information."

Emery stared at the pages, at the hundreds of black marks squished together on each one. "You get meaning from these... wiggly things?"

"Mhm."

What a marvelous thing, to be able to preserve stories, or even histories, like this, to protect them against the ravages of time or simple forgetting, rather than having to pass everything on orally, or through pictures of flame or sand.

Perhaps, if her people had been able to venture from their island, they'd have learned about books by now, and how to read them. And who knew what else.

The Forbiddens had helped ensure that remained impossible.

Another hot wave of anger flared under her skin, and she slammed the book shut. "Why do you do what you do?"

He didn't respond.

She turned to look at him, and his eyes were blank and empty once more.

She knew she probably shouldn't aggravate him, lest he go back on his promise to wait for Tavor's presence to kill her. But she couldn't stop her sudden rage. "Why do you go around slaughtering people? Is it *fun* watching innocent people die by your hand?"

It may have been a trick of the light, but she could have

sworn he flinched. He was certainly fiddling with the trinket hanging from his neck. "You know nothing of what you speak."

"Do you enjoy spilling blood?" she pressed him. "Or knowing that your own people are hiding away in terror, generation after generation, because people like you are making it impossible for us to come out of hiding?"

His fingers stilled, his eyes narrowed. "Us? You mean...you're an elemist?"

Perhaps she had been too open, but it was too late to take anything back.

"Whether I am or not is beside the point. We're talking –"

"What are you to him?" he cut in. "Why would Tavor want an elemist on his ship?"

"Because he's a good man."

The Scourge snorted, but there was no humor in his expression.

"He's trying to help!" She bashed the desk, unable to control her frustration any longer. "Why did you try to kill him? What has he done that you want to hurt him so badly?"

Sean's teeth were grinding and his fingers were back to fiddling with his trinket.

"Who are you trying to get back?" she asked. When Sean stiffened, she pressed further, casting him a wicked smile. "Did she leave you for him? Is that why you want to hurt him? Can't say I blame her – "

He stood up, chair scraping against the floor as he shoved it back.

Flinching, Emery gripped the book as tightly as she could. If he swung his blade at her, would it be solid enough to act as a shield?

"Bite your tongue before I rip it out," he growled, that spark of fury in his gaze flaring to life.

Emery swallowed down her fear. She'd clearly pressed him too far, her temper getting the better of her. But she couldn't show weakness now. "Were you born so violent and bloodthirsty?"

He stalked around the desk towards her, his voice low and menacing. "Has it occurred to you that we're *not* all violent and bloodthirsty?"

Emery stood her ground as he kept approaching. "I've heard the stories."

"Stories can be skewed."

Just like the night before, he stalked so close he had to stare down his nose at her. She glared right back up. Again, she felt his heat, and the book she clutched to her chest was the only think separating them. The bookshelves dug into her back, but she refused to shift.

"I saw all the dead bodies you left on that ship you set on fire," she spat. "I watched you try to kill Tavor."

The memory of watching Tavor and his men gathering the corpses made her feel sick and the memory of watching the Scourge's fingers dig into Tavor's throat fanned her own rage.

She stared right into his wrathful eyes. "I wish I killed you that night in Tavor's cabin."

Something dark flickered behind the wrath but his voice remained eerily calm. "Do you?"

He pulled a dagger from his belt. Emery's grip on the book tightened even more but he flipped the dagger so he gripped its by its blade, offering her the hilt. "Here's your chance to right your mistake."

Emery stared at the dagger but didn't take it. Was this some sort of trick? If she tried to take it, would he just stab her?

In one quick movement, he yanked the book from her grasp, tossed it to the floor, and pressed the dagger's hilt into her palm. Her fingers gripped it automatically. He guided the dagger's blade so it rested above his heart.

"Go ahead, kill me. Sink down to my lowly level."

Emery's eyes darted from the dagger to his face, which was as frighteningly calm as his voice. He dropped his hands to his sides, and Emery was certain there was no way he could stop her from driving the dagger into his chest. This was no trick. She realized Tavor had certainly been right about one thing. The Scourge of the Sea was truly insane.

"You'll be making the world a better place, won't you?" he said.

Emery swallowed, her fingers tightening on the dagger. It would be so easy. All she had to do was shove and he'd be dead. She'd save the world from his cruelty. Save Tavor from his vengeance. Save herself from certain death at his hands.

But she did not want to sink to his level. She was no murderer.

She shoved him back as hard as she could and bolted. Straight and true as an arrow, and nearly as quick. She slammed into the door, the dagger held tightly in her hand and turned the handle.

It was locked.

The key must be on his person. She turned and pressed her back against the door, bracing herself to fight. She didn't care about an escape plan any more. She couldn't stay aboard this ship, in this cabin, with this mad man for another moment. She had a blade. She just needed to get through the door, sprint for the nearest longboat and cut it free.

He already stood in front of her. He had moved so quickly, so quietly, like a ghost.

The dagger gleamed as she held it out in front of her. "Let me out!"

He crossed his arms, such a casual movement. "I doubt you've really thought this through."

"And why's that?"

"You're shoving a dagger in my face, and you think I'm just going to set you free on my ship?"

"If you want to prove that you're not as terrible as the stories say, let me out."

He sighed, as if suddenly exhausted. "Give me the dagger."

"Give me the key and I'll think about it."

He stepped forward. "I'm not –"

She slid to the side in a move that clearly surprised him, then leapt up and swiped her elbow sharply into his temple in *bee sting*. She still couldn't bring herself to stab him, but this blow should stun him for a few precious moments.

Sean reeled backwards and Emery launched herself at him, searching his pockets frantically for the key.

He recovered faster than expected, grabbing her arms and pushing her away. She whipped her armed hand out of his grip, catching him in the face with the dagger as she did so. He swore in pain and they both froze. A cut opened, stretching from his cheekbone to his jawline. She couldn't tell how deep it was, but blood began dripping from it in an instant.

She'd never hurt anybody like this before, and now fought the stupid impulse to apologize. Sean was gritting his teeth but seemed to be glaring more at the dagger than at her, as if he couldn't quite believe what had happened.

Coming to her senses, Emery dove for his pockets again. Warm liquid fell on her as he grabbed for her arms, and she felt sick. Suddenly, both her wrists were in his hands and he was holding her – and her weapon – firmly at arm's length. She pulled and tugged, tried to kick him, but he dodged every blow.

"That's enough!" Blood sprayed from his mouth, and terror began to prick Emery's insides. He was so damn strong, even with her skills she couldn't pull out of his grasp, nor angle the dagger to stab his wrist.

But he just...held her there, glaring at her, blood dripping to the floor from his face. He didn't strike back, didn't even touch her except to hold her in place.

"Why don't you bloody do something?" she cried. "Just kill me! Get it over with."

He didn't say anything. The only sign he had even heard her was that he transferred both her wrists to one of his hands, keeping his eyes firmly on hers. She tugged with all her strength, but still couldn't pull away from him. He reached for the dagger, gripping the blade, and pulled it from her hand, seeming not to care that it was surely slicing his palm. She gulped as the dagger came away in his grasp, muttered a prayer and prepared for him to plunge it into her.

He sheathed the dagger at his belt.

The surprise as he released her nearly sent her falling backwards. He stepped towards her again, but she held her ground, refusing to let the terror and confusion inside her show.

The Scourge held her gaze, blood dripping from the cut on his face, down his neck and onto his now crimson-stained tunic. He came closer still...

...and continued past her to the door.

"Please." She turned to face him. "Just let me out."

He didn't so much as look back. He produced a key from somewhere inside his tunic and unlocked the door, leaving a smear of blood on the handle as he turned it, and stepped outside.

But...he didn't close it behind him. He left it open, about an inch, the key still inside the lock.

# Chapter Seventeen

E mery wrapped her arms tightly her around herself, not letting her eyes leave the doorway. Four finger-widths of space told her she could walk right through and finally leave the room. Crisp sunlight filtered through the gap, a gentle breeze gliding across the cabin to her face, bringing with it the fresh aroma of the sea. This meant that, like on Tavor's ship, the captain's cabin stood on one of the decks.

She held herself back from following Sean immediately. This was such a sudden change of direction from him, it had to be some sort of trick.

But time crawled by, and nothing happened.

That didn't mean someone − or something − wasn't lying in wait for her on the other side.

Feeling something tickle her cheek, she swiped a hand across her face to get rid of it. Her sleeve came away bloody. The Scourge's blood.

He wasn't going to kill her just yet, otherwise he surely would have just done so.

She took a deep breath. Beyond the doorway, the wind sang to her, beckoning her onwards. With her hands in fists at her sides, she marched out, ready to fend off whoever or whatever might attack.

Sunlight stabbed her eyes and glorious heat engulfed her, caressing her skin, sinking through to her bones. Once her eyes got used to the new brightness, she was able to take in the assault of blue around her. She stood on the deck of a large ship, though it wasn't as large as *The New Dawn* had been. The boards beneath her, as well as the railing and masts, were all of dark mahogany. As on the other ship, ropes hung everywhere like thousands of vines. Crimson sails billowed above like wine-soaked clouds. Or blood, if the stories were to be believed.

More importantly, there were people ahead of her. Ranit stood with a mop suspended over a bucket, looking shocked to see her out in the open. Another man with flaming-red hair and beard and a bundle of canvas in his arms came to a stand-still upon seeing her. Yet another man, gangly and with white-blond hair, paused his climb up a rope ladder to her left.

When she made eye contact with the third man, he immediately scurried higher into the rigging. Ahead of her, the flame-haired man dropped the canvas and reached for the blade strapped to his waist.

"That won't be necessary," came a voice behind her.

She spun round to see Sean leaning, arms casually crossed, next to the door she'd just exited. Blood still leaked from the wound on his face, soaking into his tunic.

"I let her out," he reassured the men. "Aleksy said we should let her stretch her legs."

Emery studied Sean's bloodied face, not that it gave anything away. She was certain that Aleksy – whoever that was – had said no such thing.

"But your face, Captain," the redhead said, his own pale and wide-eyed.

"An accident," the Scourge replied coolly.

The man eyed Emery's bloody sleeve, then his gaze travelled to her face, his eyes narrowing as he no doubt took in her suspicious lack of wounds. Beside him, Ranit was still holding his dripping mop as if he'd forgotten about it.

"I said, stand *down*," Sean insisted

The redhead reluctantly slid his weapon back into place.

"Just ignore us, gentlemen," Sean continued. "Our guest and I are going for a little walk."

Ranit silently lowered his mop and returned to wiping the deck. The redhead stomped off, glaring back at Emery over his shoulder. Her skin crawled with fear, but she kept herself standing tall, glaring back with as much conviction as she could muster.

Sean stepped closer, arms still crossed, but he was gazing past her at the ocean. He seemed to be waiting for something.

She crossed her arms as well. "What trick is this now?"

"You wanted to be let out," he replied. "So here you are."

"And you're just...letting me out?" She raised her eyebrows.

He shrugged, still gazing at the sea. "Where would you go?"

She didn't let it show on her face, but her heart sank at his words. It was good question. Forbiddens scurried everywhere, and the ship was surrounded by water. And she couldn't try to talk to any of the crewmen to ask for help with their captain watching

A dark-skinned woman with a mass of long braids appeared at Sean's side, holding a white rag with which she began dabbing at the captain's face.

Sean dodged the attempt, grabbing the rag for himself. "Thank you, Aleksy. It's fine."

Aleksy's dark eyes flicked briefly to Emery. Thick spiraling scars covered half her face, running from her left eye down to her jaw. "You may need stitches, Captain." Her accent differed from Sean and Tavor's.

"No, I don't. Thank you, Aleksy." There was an obvious dismissal in Sean's tone.

Aleksy and her captain glared at each other for a moment, until finally she relented and stalked off. Sean crossed his arms again, albeit now using one hand to press the rag against his cheek.

"Well, off you go then." He waved the rag at Emery. "Lead the way."

"I thought *you* were in charge. Where am I supposed to go?"

"Wherever you wanted to go so badly that you stabbed me." His voice was unnervingly emotionless.

Emery turned, trying to get some idea of the ship's layout and where she was within it. It seemed similar to *The New Dawn*, with the forecastle deck at the bow, the afterdeck at the stern, and a long stretch of lower deck between them both. The captain's cabin was located beneath the afterdeck, so she decided to turn to go up the stairs leading to that deck. The Scourge followed.

She had developed decent sea legs by now, but behind her, Sean walked, as if he'd been born at sea. Her spine prickled from the sensation of feeling him behind her, but she kept going, wandering along one set of railing, then another, keeping an eye on the unchanging horizon and trying to ignore the way the crew stopped to stare wherever she passed.

She wandered the afterdeck's circumference, but there was nothing particularly encouraging to see. She had hoped the horizon would reveal something to her, a speck of green that signaled land onto which she could try to flee, or maybe a second ship with which she could communicate for help, or even swim to. She passed the longboat she'd tried to take the night before and didn't dare eye the release mechanism for too long with Sean watching her every move.

She was well and truly trapped, and Sean knew it. No wonder he didn't stop her from wandering for as long as she wanted, only continued to follow her as if she were a toddler learning how to walk with minimal supervision. She felt him tense every time she got remotely close to one of his crew, as if expecting an altercation to erupt at any moment. Then, when Emery spotted Cam, wearing a triangular hat with her silver hair streaming down beneath it, he went further still, stepping in front of her and steering her away from Camulus.

With Camulus's part of the ship out of bounds for now, there was nowhere else to explore but below decks. She couldn't face going down into those dark, cramped spaces with Sean so close all the time, so she reluctantly wandered back to the cabin.

Sean followed her inside, stopping at the doorway himself and not saying anything. He had managed to clean most of the blood off his face, but the wound was still red and swollen. She winced inwardly at the sight.

"Sorry for stabbing you," she said, almost involuntarily. He had kidnapped and threatened her, after all. "Even though you deserved it."

He didn't reply, and Emery glanced about the cabin, not sure what to do next. Then a question that had been bugging her burst from her mouth. "Is there a brig on the ship?"

"Aye."

"Why aren't I in it?"

She recalled the dark, dank cage that Sean himself had been locked inside aboard *The New Dawn*. Though suspicious of his reasons, she was certainly grateful he hadn't done the same to her.

Again, he said nothing.

"Where are you sleeping?" she asked. "Why aren't you sleeping in your own bed?"

"If you'd like me to join you in my bed," he said slyly, a crooked grin lifting the corner of his lips. "You need only ask. You wouldn't even have to stab me first."

With that, he slipped from the cabin, shutting the door behind him.

She checked the handle. It was still unlocked.

THE SCOURGE DID NOT RETURN that afternoon, and Emery spent the time pouring over the map on the desk. She couldn't decipher the characters indicating location names, but she tried to at least commit to memory the shape and position of as many land masses as she could.

Just as the sun began to dip outside the window and Emery's stomach began growling with hunger, the door opened. Her pulse skipped but she didn't move from the chair behind the desk.

But it was not Sean.

Aleksy, the woman who had brought Sean a rag for his wound earlier, stepped into the cabin carrying a mug and a plate of food. She wore a long brown leather jacket over a white tunic, tight black trousers, and boots that reached her knees. The beads woven into her mass of braids tinkled as she slowly approached the desk. A blade flashed at her hip.

Emery's fingers wrapped around the quill, wondering if its sharp metal tip would work as a weapon.

"There's no need for that," Aleksy said, her accent heavy and unfamiliar. "I'm the ship's medic. The captain wanted me to bring you dinner and to check on your head."

Emery sat a little taller. This was her chance to find out if Aleksy disagreed with her captain's plan just as Cam did. Perhaps Emery could enlist her help for an escape.

"Has your captain tired of overseeing his prisoner himself already?" She watched the other woman's face for any reaction that might tell her how she felt about the situation, but Aleksy's expression remained impassive.

Placing the mug and the plate on the desk, Aleksy asked, "How does your head feel? Any dizziness or nausea?"

"It's still sore," Emery admitted. "But not much dizziness or nausea anymore."

"May I examine the wound, please?"

"No." Emery did not want this stranger – this Forbidden – to be so close, even if she was a medic and, presumedly, the one who had taken care of her wound when she had been unconscious. What if this was a ruse to keep her calm so she wouldn't put up a fight when the death blow came?

"I mean no harm," Aleksy promised, her face still impassive and impossible to read.

Emery studied her. "How do I know that's not a lie?"

"I suppose you don't," Aleksy said. When Emery still didn't relent, she added, "I can't leave until I examine your head. Captain's orders."

"Do you do everything your captain commands?"

Aleksy looked Emery dead in the eye. "Always."

Emery's heart sank but she kept her face expressionless. She supposed she had her answer whether Aleksy would help her escape.

"May I examine your head, please?" Aleksy repeated.

"Fine."

Emery sat still as the other woman strode around the desk, moving slowly as if to not startle a wounded animal. Her neck prickled at the stranger's close presence behind her, and she still gripped the quill just in case, but she was inclined to believe this woman didn't intend to hurt her. Emery hissed as Aleksy gently moved her hair out of the way, her locks tugging on the wound.

"It's healing well. The tenderness should be gone in a few days."

Aleksy stepped back and Emery turned to look at her. The spiraling scars on the side of her face caught the light of the setting sun and Emery wondered how she got them. They did not look accidental.

Aleksy seemed to be hesitating to stay something. "The captain also ordered no one to harm you."

"So he can deal the final blow himself?" Emery asked.

Once again, Aleksy's face revealed nothing. She was harder to read then Sean.

"Keep your wound clean," she said, and left without a backwards glance.

THE NEXT MORNING, dawn danced beautifully across the horizon, rendering the sky fluffy and pink. A soft blanket of mist slithered over the ocean's surface. Standing in the center of the cabin and admiring the view, Emery practiced statera. Though she shifted through each position easily, her body reveling at the familiar movements, her mind was too consumed with thoughts to try calling the elements.

All night, she had lain awake trying to decide her next move. She needed to find a way to have a closer look at the longboats and figure out how to work the mechanism that released them. She could perhaps also peek down below, see if she could find where the crew kept their rations. She wouldn't be able to escape right away, but she could hoard food and water and watch the horizon. As soon as something – anything – appeared, she could make sure she was ready to grab a longboat and get off the ship.

The main problem, of course, was that anything she did alone would almost certainly arouse suspicion. She'd have to be clever how she approached this.

Remembering how patiently, perhaps even enthusiastically, the Scourge had talked her through the items on his desk and shelf, a strategy had begun to present itself.

Done with statera and ready to execute her plan, she threw her hair in a braid, beads clinking as she did so and headed for the door. A cool breeze greeted her as she stepped onto the deck and nearly tripped over Ranit.

He sat cross legged on the deck with his back to the door, lightly strumming a red lute and humming along to the quiet tune. He jumped up, a warm smile on his face. "Good morning, Ocean Eyes."

"Are you guarding the door?"

Ranit's smile only widened. "Of course not! You're allowed to leave at your leisure.

Emery narrowed her eyes at him.

"...But I'm here to follow you when you do," Ranit relented. "Can't have you making any more mischief."

That's what she'd figured. She would have been shocked if Sean allowed her free range on his ship.

"How'd you wind up with this job?" She couldn't imagine any of the crewmen being happy with the task of minding her.

But to her surprise, Ranit said, "I volunteered."

"Why?"

"Let's call it curiosity."

"About why I have your captain so flummoxed?" she guessed, remembering his words from the night of her botched escape.

He winked. "Precisely."

"What do you mean by flummoxed?" she asked.

"I mean baffled, confounded, flabbergasted, perplexed, mystified," Ranit sang each word, punctuating them with strums of his lute. His voice was smooth as honey.

She crossed her arms. "I know *what* it means." When Ranit said no more and simply kept strumming, she asked, "Where is your captain?"

Ranit pointed the head of his lute towards the bow.

When Emery began to walk that direction, he followed, continuing to strum casually on the lute. The morning light filtered through the pink clouds, caressing her cheeks but lacking the punch it would carry later in the day. The deck seemed to be deserted, save for them, and the sight of the empty ship stretching out before her seemed like something out of a dream. The wind whistled through the rigging above, and the wood beneath her bare feet creaked, but only quietly. She breathed in the salty air and deliberately took her time as she worked her way along the vessel. The open sky and fresh air began to cleanse her of the uneasiness and fear that had been wrapped tightly around her throat since she had first woken on this ship. Without anyone else around, she could almost forget why she was there, and that dozens of Forbiddens were sleeping beneath her. And that one currently strode next to her.

In truth, Emery didn't mind his presence. It gave her a

chance to gather more information of her own. "I suppose trying to convince you to help me off this ship would be a waste of my breath."

"Sorry, Ocean Eyes. But it would."

"You sure are a loyal lot," she grumbled.

"Aye."

Emery watched his face closely. "Why follow a man like that?"

Ranit met her gaze, as if scrutinizing her reactions just as carefully. "A man like what?"

Emery opened her mouth but the words got stuck. She wanted to say bloodthirsty or violent, but Sean's own words floated through her head.

*Has it occurred to you that we're* not *all violent and bloodthirsty?*

Certainly nothing about Ranit screamed violence or blood-lust. But perhaps that was by design. And while Emery had laid awake the night before, Sean's words running through her head, she'd thought about how she'd attacked him multiple times now, and he had never once retaliated, never once laid a hand on her save to protective himself from her blows.

But she had watched him try to kill Tavor, witnessed the destruction and death he had left in his wake when he attacked that ship.

Emery didn't understand what it all meant. She felt like she had pieces of a puzzle that didn't fit together.

Finally, she settled on the things she knew for a fact. "A murderer. And a destroyer of peace."

Ranit strummed his lute a few times, as if picking his next words carefully. "That murderer and destroyer of peace is my best friend."

Emery stared at him in surprise. Obviously, she'd realized he was loyal to the Scourge and must at the very least share some of his values, but she had not expected that kind of relationship.

"He gave me a home. He gave all of us a home when we desperately needed one," Ranit continued. "I would follow that man to the underworld and back." He looked down at his feet.

When he met her eyes again, his typically jovial expression was serious. "And I follow him now, even though he is lost and searching for a way back."

Emery frowned, not understanding. "I thought he was searching for someone."

Now Ranit looked confused.

"Cam said his plan won't bring *her* back. Who is she? And where is she?"

"Ah." He bit his lip, again seemingly choosing his words with care. "I'm sorry.

Though I am a storyteller, that's not my story to tell."

They'd reached the stairs leading up to the forecastle.

Ranit bowed, his tone back to cheery. "I'll leave you to it. I bid you a good morning, Ocean Eyes."

"Why do your call me that?"

"Because your eyes," he sang, strumming his lute once again, "are the blue of the ocean at twilight."

Emery raised a brow. "How did you know my eyes were blue? The only time you saw me up close before this was at night."

Ranit gave her a mischievous grin and tilted his head towards the bow. "I was not the one who made the observation."

# Chapter Eighteen

Not sure what to do with the insinuation that the Scourge of the Sea had not only noticed the color of her eyes but had mentioned it to Ranit, Emery slowly made her way up the steps to the forecastle, leaving Ranit behind.

The deck appeared deserted, and Emery thought Ranit must have been mistaken. Then she spotted him.

Sean was lying on his stomach about halfway along the pointy beam that stuck out from the front of the ship – the bowsprit, she thought it was called – staring at the water. One of his arms was dangling down, as if he'd originally thought he could somehow reach down to the surface and then not had the inclination to pull it back up again. He was so still he could have been part of the ship, and didn't seem to notice her.

But something was different about him. The tension that always seemed to be wrapped around him like armor had... vanished. The hollowness usually carved into his expression had melted away, leaving behind...something else. She glided further to the side so she could see his eyes better. He was just peering down at the water, into the sea's dark depths, and despite everything she knew he had done, everything she feared he would yet do, her stomach shrank in on itself at the expression in his eyes.

He looked like he wanted to throw himself in. She fought back the sudden and ridiculous urge to ask what was troubling him, to offer some sort of comfort.

She stepped back a little so it wouldn't be so obvious she's been watching him, then cleared her throat.

The Forbidden lay there for a moment, then turned his head towards her. The blank mask was back, and to her surprise Emery now found that emptiness worse to look at than his earlier pained expression.

He climbed to his feet and, with surprising grace, walked back along the beam and hopped down in front of her. The cut on his cheek was no longer swollen, but it stood out red against the rest of his tanned face. His eyes, the same emerald as the cloth pushing his windswept hair off his face, had gone completely blank again, as if he had pulled a pair of shutters across them.

He didn't say anything, and she fought the urge to scuttle back to the cabin. Instead, she crossed her arms, as if he didn't intimidate her in the slightest. "I'm bored."

"Are you?" His voice was as vacant as his eyes.

"You brought me here, the least you could do is offer me some entertainment."

He scratched the stubble on his jaw, the movement so... normal it distracted her for a moment. "And what exactly do you propose?" She shrugged and stared past him at the pointy beam at the front of the ship. "Teach me about sailing."

Sean cocked an eyebrow, as if genuinely amused.

"You owe me that at least."

He ran a hand through his hair, pushed the cloth band further up his forehead. "Alright then. What do you already know?"

She suppressed the flicker of joy and relief coursing through her. One step closer to releasing a longboat. "I know the big wheel steers the ship."

His other eyebrow rose, another phantom grin threatening to invade his empty expression. "What else?"

"The sails catch the wind and make the ship move."

"Good enough for now."

This time she had to smile. Even faint praise was encouraging at this point.

He shrugged and starting walking back towards the rest of the ship. "Come on then."

Sean put together a vague plan as they walked, deciding it was best to start from the bottom of the vessel and work their way back up. He led Emery down floor by floor, ladder by ladder. These lower decks weren't like Tavor's at all. Instead of tight hallways, the spaces below were wide and open, although the ceilings were still low enough to give the impression of having been swallowed by a gigantic beast. Whale oil lanterns lit their way.

Eventually, they came to a square hole in the floor with a metal grate covering it. "This is the orlop deck," Sean explained. "We're now going to go down into the hold, which is the base of the ship. At its lowest part it's called the bilge, which is where water collects and needs to be scooped out if there's a leak, or" – he hesitated, not meeting her eye – "a bad storm, and so on."

Emery had to fight off the feeling of panic as she made the final descent and the dark, damp air of the hold settled around her. Sean led her to what felt like the other end of the boat, past stacks of boxes and barrels loaded nearly up to the low ceiling. She peered into any open ones standing around, making sure not to be obvious, but most appeared to be quite empty. No food to steal easily then.

At the far end of the hold, he opened a rickety wooden door and beckoned Emery to peer inside. It was a small, shadowy chamber, mostly shrouded in darkness, but she could make out the same vertical branch-like things behind which Sean had been locked aboard Tavor's ship. This room was smaller though, and even danker.

"The brig," Sean said behind her, and her heart climbed into her throat, convinced he was going to shove her inside and lock the door. "You already know what it's for."

She tensed, ready to leap to the side and fist him in the face. But he just reached round her to shut the door again, the sudden click making her jump, then began leading her back the way they'd come. She shook her hands out to get rid of the tension in them, making sure to follow him at more of a distance.

They returned to the orlop deck via the same square hole through which they'd come, and Sean dragged the grate back over it. Even more barrels lined the walls here, along with coils of rope and folds of canvas. There were also rows of large metal devices Sean introduced as *cannons*.

Emery ran a finger along the cold, smooth surface of the one closest to her. "What are they for?"

"Shooting holes in things. Or people."

She withdrew her hand.

Near the front of the ship on the same level was the berth, which was where the crew slept. Emery felt uneasy at the prospect of disturbing anyone given how her interactions with them had gone so far, but once she and Sean arrived pretty much everyone had already departed to begin the day's duties. They hadn't seen anyone belowdecks though, so she assumed they were above. The berths themselves were rather cramped, a dozen or so hammocks hanging sporadically from the ceiling while the rest of the space was taken up by small chests that Emery assumed held the crew's personal belongings. Emery wondered if this is where Sean slept while she occupied his bed, but she didn't ask, her face heating when she remember his comment the last time she brought up their sleeping arrangements.

On the opposite end of the level was the kitchens, a long room full of wooden tables and benches bolted to the floor. The flame-haired man was in the far-left corner, but he didn't seem to pay her any mind this time, or his captain. Above him, a wide hole had been cut into the ceiling, allowing shafts of sunlight to fall onto a narrow wooden box filled with dirt. Numerous plants had sprouted from it but looked like they had all died at various stages of growth. The man was crouching next to a new sapling, concentrating on helping it to grow with such intensity his forehead had begun to sweat. The plant twitched, grew a little taller, then lay still. The redhead cursed, and Emery realized she was looking at a tiny, sad version of the gardens back home. Surely these Forbiddens should be able to grow something better than these few shriveled plants.

The Scourge watched her, as if daring her to ask about it. When she said nothing, he led them back above deck, pointing out objects and explaining their functions as he went. As they reached the capstan – used to lower and raise the anchor – a short, elderly man began wandering towards them, staring at Emery. His skin looked as thin as the petals of a flower, and his face seemed to be made entirely of wrinkles. His snow-white hair stood straight up from his skull, and his eyes were of different colors, one olive and the other a milky, opaque white without a pupil. It may have just been the suddenness of his appearance, but something about him chilled her.

"Smythee," said Sean, his tone not unkind. "Not right now, maybe you could –"

But Smythee had already grasped Emery's hand and was shaking it with surprising vigor, a toothless grin stretching across his droopy face. "You're finally here! I've waited so long!" Unlike his grip, his voice was as frail as his appearance. "It's such an honor, an honor I tell you! Can't believe this day's finally come!"

"Er...thank you?"

He began coughing, although it soon turned into a chuckle. "Happiest of days, happiest of days." Finally, he released her, letting life return to Emery's fingers.

"We'll be off now, Smythee," Sean said. The patience in his voice and the way he patted the old man on the back didn't sit well with her.

*That's because it's all a show,* she reminded herself. *He kidnapped you, remember.*

"Alrighty, alrighty, bye-bye, bye-bye," Smythee muttered, ambling away, still giggling to himself.

Emery watched his retreating back. "Is that man...well?"

"No." Sean was watching him too, a small frown tracing the edges of his lips. "Hasn't been since the day I met him."

"What happened to him?"

"I don't know."

The sun climbed higher as they continued the tour. The crew scurried about doing their chores. Emery made sure to keep her distance where possible, but even when they ended up close to someone, no one looked directly at her. They nodded at their captain, but would then sweep their eyes down and away from her, as if she carried a disease they could catch just by making eye contact. Once again, when Emery spotted Cam, this time busy drawing fresh water out of the sea and into buckets with her abilities, Sean made sure to stir her in the other direction.

One crewman was noticeably younger, fourteen or fifteen at most. His face was round, his eyes doleful, and sandy hair spilled out from his hat in little curls, reminding Emery of the sheep back on Orabel. He was struggling to tie a finicky knot, and she had to hold herself back from offering to help him. To her relief and surprise, Sean took a moment to tie it for the boy himself.

"Thanks, Captain," the boy murmured, and scurried off to do something else.

She watched him go, wondering how a crew of fearsome Forbiddens could be made up of senile old men and scared teenagers.

The only crew member who gave her any kind of attention was Ranit. He was sitting on a crate, red lute in his hands, strumming away and watching Sean lead her across the deck. He let their eyes meet, even smiled at her, and then he began to sing.

*Adrift at sea, about to drown*
*Our captain heard the most beautiful sound*
*From the deep immerged a mermaid so fair*
*With shells and pearls and coral in her hair*
*The waves, they crashed and the winds, they sighed*
*And he was lost in her ocean eyes*
*She pulled him to land, through the storm she braved*

*Back on the sand and our captain was saved*

Emery's cheeks heated and she glanced at Sean, who sent Ranit a withering glare. As the next verse began, Sean tapped Emery on the shoulder and their tour continued. Like back in his cabin, he answered every one of her questions quickly and patiently, but he never properly smiled, never gave any sign he was taking some kind of satisfaction from the exchange. She was grateful, in a way. It helped her remember who was teaching her, why she was on this ship in the first place.

By the time the sun reached its pinnacle in the sky, Emery's mind felt ready to burst. She leaned against the railing on the starboard side, watching the cerulean waves roll by. She wiped sweat from her brow. It was hotter than she was used too. Sean stepped forward to rest his forearms on the top bar beside her. They stood in silence, and...it wasn't uncomfortable.

His sleeves were rolled up, revealing the tattoos adorning his entire left arm. They were all in greyscale and depicted a variety of seemingly random images. Curious, she studied what tattoos she could see out of the corner of her eye, spotting a compass, a sea beast, a constellation she didn't recognize, and a ship that resembled the *Audacity*. In the center of his forearm, seemingly out of place, was a beautiful lily. And printed on his wrist was a series of symbols like the ones in his books. Of course, she had no idea what they meant.

Her face heated as he caught her looking at them. "They're tattoos."

"I know," she said, her voice coming out harder than she meant. At this point, judging by her severe lack of common knowledge, the Scourge probably thought she was an idiot and it bothered her more than it should. "But what do they mean?"

Sean tilted his arm to look at the tattoos himself. He shrugged. "Different things. Different parts of my life."

He didn't elaborate and Emery sensed that if she asked anything more, he wouldn't divulge. Her eyes snagged on the mass of leather bracelets on his other wrist. Some appeared worn out and fraying, others new and bright. "What are those for?"

Sean's gaze shifted to his wrist. "Mementos. I collect one every time I go somewhere new."

Emery's eyes widen. There were so many of them, he must have travelled all over the world. Unbidden, a spark of jealousy lit in her belly. She plucked at one. "Where's that one from?"

"Jokul." At her blank expression, he continued. "It's a frozen land up north. Lots of snow."

The only snow Emery had ever seen was a small pile when her grandmother made it out of water after Emery and Liam had begged to see what it was like. Emery couldn't imagine an entire land of snow. "And that one?"

"Aedan. Slightly less north. Mostly mountains."

She'd never seen a real mountain either and wondered what such a place would look like. "This one?"

"Antilla. Down south. A bit too hot and humid for my liking."

Emery continued to pluck at his bracelets one by one and he gave her the name of each place with amusement building in his voice. When she glanced up at him, he was watching her face carefully, and she realized he was probably waiting for her to react with familiarity to one of the locations, trying to figure out where she was from. But a faint, amused smile tugged on his mouth, too, as if he found her myriad of questions as fascinating as she did.

She realized her hand was still on his wrist and she stepped back, increasing the distance between them. They'd been close to each other all day, and not once had she felt unsafe or uncomfortable. That wasn't good. It meant she was falling into a false sense of security. He must have realized too. Why else would he have agreed to her requests so easily?

She had to break the seemingly amiable atmosphere.

As if on cue, a shout rang from high in the riggings. "Sail ho! Six points to starboard!"

All the air seemed to be sucked from the ship, and for a

moment Emery could only take in the fierce beating of her heart.

Sean began to cross the deck. Emery followed him, new hope burning in her veins. He climbed partway up the starboard rigging, holding onto the ratlines with one hand, telescope already in the other, and began scanning the horizon with the device. Emery squinted in the same direction. A dark smudge was now visible in the distance.

"Colors?" Sean called.

"Antillian!" the voice cried from above. "Cargo ship!"

Emery's heart felt like it was spinning in circles. Her brother could have been saved by a cargo ship. He could be on this very one.

Sean lowered the telescope and gazed at the ship. A deep frown etched its way onto his face, and he played with the trinket hanging from his neck again.

The redheaded man who'd futilely been trying to grow plants below deck stepped up to him. "Captain, there's nothing left. We've only got food for a few days. We need to resupply."

An older man, with a wild mane of silver and a beard to match, also came over. "We could also make a stop somewhere. Find food that way."

"With what coin?" the redhead asked. "We spent the last of it on hardtack."

Sean closed his eyes and ran a hand over his face. Then, he looked right at Emery, seeming to search her face as if she somehow had the answer to his dilemma. "How does she bear?" he called up, still watching her face.

She stared back, unsure what to make of his sudden focus on her.

"Broad on the port beam."

Sean looked at the silver-maned man. "I'm sorry, Billy," he said in a voice so small it almost didn't seem like his.

The man's expression saddened. "Don't be. Give your orders."

Sean leaped down and headed towards the helm. "Hands

aloft to trim topsails! Ready the guns and raise the Antillian flag, we're taking her!"

The crew acted accordingly, climbing the rigging, tugging on various ropes to make the desired adjustments. The angle of the sails changed, and a flag of blue and green matching that of the cargo ship rose into the air, fluttering like a discolored leaf. Beside it, a smaller, white one was also hoisted.

Emery followed him to the gigantic wheel. "That's spineless trickery," she growled. "Luring them in with a false sense of security."

*Like you're trying to do with me.*

He shrugged, his face expressionless. "The less they struggle, the better for everyone."

"You can't do this to innocent people!"

Something briefly flashed behind his eyes. Could it be... shame? It was gone just as quickly. "What if they aren't?"

"What do you mean?" She crossed her arms, genuinely wanting him to make a case for this. To give her some insight, finally, into his motivations, his side of the ongoing conflict that he himself was helping to perpetuate.

His eyes iced over, making her own skin feel cold. "I suggest you barricade yourself in my cabin. This might get dangerous."

# Chapter Nineteen

S ean heaved on the wheel of the *Audacity*, and Emery clung to the railing as the ship changed course, hull and rigging creaking in protest. Around them, the crew scrambled about, preparing themselves to unleash horror on the other vessel.

"You're just going to capture it?" Emery asked.

Sean stopped the wheel abruptly, the bowsprit now pointing directly at the cargo ship. "No, we're going to raid her."

Blood pounded in her ears like a drum. She couldn't let this happen. She'd seen it before, the destruction these Forbiddens left in their wake. But she had to think quickly. They were already speeding towards the other ship like a sea monster towards its prey.

"Trim the sails!" Sean shouted. "Slow her down! We don't want to alarm them!"

Her mind whirled like a storm. She had to find a way to stop this.

"Emery." The ice in his eyes had melted a little, enough to make him appear mildly concerned. Hearing him say her name though, made the storm inside her rage more angrily. "I really think –"

"NO!" She spun on her heel and sprinted the length of the

ship. No one tried to stop her. She didn't stop running until she reached the bow, nearly crashing into the railing. She flung her arms up and waved at the cargo ship. It was so close already. Too close. "Go back!" she screamed, willing someone to see her, hear her. She knew she was blowing her chance at escaping with them, but that would have been a futile hope anyway. Letting them come close enough for her to jump across would have meant coming too close to be savable, she'd have just doomed them alongside herself. "Turn around! They're going to –"

A hand slapped over her mouth as someone started dragging her backwards.

"Apologies, but we don't need you making this any more difficult than it already is." Sean's breath was hot in her ear, sending shivers skittering down her spine.

She plunged her teeth into his palm.

He swore and released her mouth, but just as quickly lifted her off the ground and continued hauling her back the way they'd come.

She shrieked a few more warnings, but soon had to admit defeat.

"I'm sorry." And he actually sounded sincere. "But this is for the best."

She kicked and clawed at his hands, swung her elbows back, on one occasion catching him in the eye, but he never lost his grip. Nor did he strike her, or squeeze too hard around her middle, just continued carrying her back across the deck, not putting her down until they reached his cabin.

As soon as her feet touched the ground she bolted for the door, but he beat her to it, blocking it with his own body. "You really are brave, Emery." Even now, he didn't sound condescending. More like...admiring. A new bruise was already forming around his left eye, and for a moment she felt a twinge of guilt.

Then the thunderstorm roared inside her again, and the feeling disappeared. "Let me out."

"I'm sorry." He darted out, locking the door behind him.

She shouldered the wood repeatedly, until she felt raw and

tender, but it didn't budge. Her breath seared her throat as she stepped back, ears straining, but no sounds pierced the silence that seemed to have swallowed the ship.

She closed her eyes, reaching for the elements, hoping she might be able to blow the door off its hinges, to set fire to it, or persuade the wood to curl in on itself and let her through. But the wood was too far dead to manipulate, there was no fire in the room to call upon, and she only managed to create tiny gust of wind that didn't even shake the door.

Grinding her teeth and cursing her abilities for still not awakening fully, she sprinted for the window. But the latch wouldn't open. How was that possible? She would have noticed Sean somehow locking it from the inside, surely.

But then she noticed the thick ice coating the outside of the window frame. It wasn't locked. Someone had frozen it shut.

Cursing, she glanced around the room, looking for anything she could use.

Her eyes landed on that damn chair from which Sean watched her all those times, sitting there still and sinister.

She picked it up and threw it to the ground, smashing off two of its legs in an immensely satisfying way. She picked one of them up, enjoying its weight in her hands. It wasn't as long as her lim, but it was a lot better than nothing.

She grabbed the compass and the map from the desk, stuffing both in her pockets, before backtracked to the window, tightening her hold on the chair leg. She swung at the glass, but the leg simply bounced off. The second time she swung more violently. The glass shattered, and a gust of wind burst into the room, bringing with it the salty scent of freedom. She swatted the remaining shards away with the chair leg, then poked her head through, wind blowing hair from her braid and around her face. Below her, the deep ocean frothed.

Above and away from her, the sound of shouting rolled over the snapping sails and slapping waves.

Sticking the chair leg into the back of her clothes, she hauled herself out the window and began to climb. Ocean spray chilled her back, and the wood was extra wet and slippery from the ice, but she gritted her teeth and pressed on, pretending she was climbing an oddly shaped tree back home. In the rain.

Once she reached the deck, she paused her climbing long enough to look through the railing before making her next move. The *Audacity* was pulling up alongside the other, grey hooks with ropes attached flashing through the air to pull them closer together.

She was too late.

In front of her, Ranit was at the wheel now, telltale lute strapped to his back, just a few feet away but unable to see her.

Her eyes slid to the lower deck, though she couldn't see much from where she was hiding. Mind racing with potential ideas, her eyes followed the length of the closest mast, then skimmed across the horizontal spar that held the sails in place...

...nearly touching that of the other ship.

She could make that leap.

Ranit didn't notice as she lowered herself down behind him, but there was no way past without him seeing her. Heart thudding loudly in her chest, she edged forward, tightening her grip on the chair leg. Then, the board she stepped on creaked sharply in protest.

Ranit whipped round, pistol already in hand. But his face relaxed upon seeing her, and he lowered the weapon. "Ocean Eyes. How did you get out?"

"Your captain's going to have to replace his window."

"Bugger." He sighed. "Look, I won't say anything. Just make your escape quick." He glanced at the chair leg in her hands. "And don't hit anyone with that thing, please."

"I – what?"

"You can go, I won't try to stop you."

It took a moment for his words to fully register. Was this another kind of trick?

As she stared at him, trying to decipher what his real agenda might be, a smirk twisted his lips. "It's too bad, though. It's been fun having you aboard."

"*Fun?*"

The smirk faltered. "Well, I get why you're mad. Or scared, or whatever. But I swear by Roark himself, Sean would never hurt you."

"And why would I believe that?"

"Well, has he?"

Emery swallowed her answer. No, he hadn't. But that didn't mean he wouldn't.

"One question though, before you leave."

She paused, suspicion immediately rising again. "Make it quick."

"Why were you on the Viper's ship?"

"The Viper?"

His head tilted, as if he was confused that she didn't understand. "Tavor."

"I – " She'd forgotten about the nickname Tavor's fellow varens had given him. Apparently, Forbiddens called him that too. Thrown off, she countered, "Why are you here?"

"Alright, I'll go first then." Ranit adjusted the lacey cloth holding his hair back. "Short version, I lost everything. I found Sean. Or rather, Sean found me. Now, all I have is this ship and the people on it. Oh, and her." He reached back and patted the neck of his lute. "Your turn. Feel free to give me the long version."

"Short version," she said slowly, buying herself a moment to run what he'd just said over in her mind. "Freedom."

"Ah." His grin returned. "A dream we share." He stepped to the side, gesturing to the rest of the ship. "Best of luck to you then."

She inched along, keeping an eye on him until she had to turn around to climb. Sliding the chair leg once more into the back of her clothes, she grasped the nearest hanging ropes and began pulling herself up the mast. Despite everything, her spirit hummed at the feeling of climbing again.

The farther she climbed the more of the two decks she could

see. The men on the cargo ship were already cowering on their knees, releasing their weapons in surrender.

The Forbiddens stood on the *Audacity's* deck below Emery, facing the cargo ship. They all held weapons aloft, except for two of them.

The Scourge of the Sea was standing in the center of his group, his arms spread wide, a rogue wind tearing at his clothes and golden hair, twisting around him like it meant to devour him.

In front of him, Smythee was beginning to stalk across the plank that now connected the ships, his wispy hair lifting in the currents Sean had created and his giggling carrying up to Emery's ears. The other crew recoiled as he approached, and his laughter turned hysterical. She realized there was a lit torch in his hand. The flame flared and fire began to slither along his arm like a blazing snake, then coiled down the length of his torso. The flames curled around his legs, draped themselves across his shoulders and slid along his other arm, coming to rest on his open palm. He was wearing a robe of flames.

Some of the cargo ship's sailors began to pray.

Shaking with apprehension, Emery hauled herself up onto the first spar, then crouched against the mast, trying to think what to do.

Sean was now following the old man along the plank, coming to stop at about halfway. "We will not harm you." He didn't speak particularly loudly, but his voice nonetheless seemed to boom between the two vessels. "As long as nobody tries anything stupid. If any of you so much as twitches in the direction of your weapons, my friend here will have some...fun with you."

Smythee cackled as some of the sailors flinched again as his flaming torso flared brighter. None of them moved after that, except to bow their heads and allow the Forbiddens to cross and tie their hands behind their backs.

Emery didn't move either. There was nothing she could do now to help. She couldn't fight off Sean's entire crew with a chair leg and her own minuscule elemental power. Even if she did climb across, if Smythee decided to burn the other ship down anyway she'd be worse off than now. There was no choice but to sit in the rigging, wait, and hope someone in Sean's crew might make a mistake, something she could use to her and the other sailors' advantage.

Aleksy and Billy moved to stand behind the bound crew, keeping watch. Their faces were blurred from such a height, but Emery was certain they were grimacing, as if they'd rather be doing anything else.

Sean was now in the middle of the deck, not far from the captives, being approached by the red-headed man. "Well Rooney, what is there?"

"Not as much as we'd hoped, Captain." The other man was holding a roll of parchment – the same material as the map back in Sean's cabin – and was scribbling on it with a thin stick of charcoal. "Lots of trading goods, obviously. Rum, spices, whale oil, canvas, sugar. But not many provisions." Sean ran a hand over his face, and Rooney cleared his throat. "There's some salted beef, but it looks old. A few crates of biscuits, but the stuff Farley's inspected is full of weevils. And there's four barrels of water."

"That's it?"

"That's it," Rooney replied gravely.

Sean looked up at the sky, then closed his eyes. "Take three barrels of water, and half the beef. Grab the hardtack, weevils or no. One roll of canvas. One barrel of oil, we're low on that. Take the sugar. Leave the rest."

Rooney glanced up from his scribbling. "But Captain, the spices catch a fine –"

"I said, leave the rest."

The redhead sighed, "Aye, Captain," and disappeared below deck.

Unease prickled the base of Emery's scalp. Why were they taking so little? If they were going through all this trouble to capture a ship and raid it, why not take it all? Why be so...merciful?

It didn't take long for the crew to haul over their measly booty. Soon, only Sean remained on the cargo ship, the wind he'd created long since dissipated. "The nearest port is only a day's sail away," he said to the captive crew. "We've left you with more than enough provisions to get there."

"Sea wolves," one of them spat.

Ignoring him, Sean turned back towards the *Audacity*, and for a moment it looked like shame and anger were warring in his face. Just as quickly, they were gone, and his usual blank mask was back. Head held high, he crossed the plank back to his ship.

Emery's skull ached. None of this made sense, but could it really be a trick? What would be the point?

Nonetheless, this was her chance to escape, to get back to her brother, and she had to take it.

The Forbidden crew pulled back the plank and hauled in the hook-ended ropes. In moments, the two ships were drifting apart and Sean was shouting orders to sail away.

Emery tiptoed along the spar as the topsails unfurled above her head. The ship shuddered, and she resisted the urge to look down as she took a deep breath and leaped across the short gap to the cargo ship.

# Chapter Twenty

E mery spent her first moments of freedom clinging to the mizzenmast of the cargo ship, watching the Forbiddens sail off into the field of blue. Everything she had just witnessed sat heavy in her head, refusing to make sense.

It didn't matter. She was free of that ship. All that mattered now was finding Liam, Caelin and Tavor, and continue the mission together.

The sailors below her had managed to free themselves from their bindings. A large man wearing a hat with a feather stuck in it, presumably the captain, was shouting orders, while the others hurried about, readying the ship to sail again. Beside her, ropes wiggled and tightened, and sails slowly unfurled. One nearly slapped her in the face, and she took it as a sign to find more solid ground.

She took her time climbing down the mast, the wind pushing softly against her back as if hoping to aid her if she slipped. Five feet remained when she decided to drop the rest of the way, landing on a deck displaying more nicks in its wood than the Forbidden ship.

One man immediately spotted her. His eyes bulged, and he let go of the rope he'd been tying down. With a zipping sound, the rope uncurled from its cleat and was sucked up into the rigging, followed by alarmed shouts as a sail fell out of place. The man scrambled away from her, tripping over a fold of canvas and catching himself hastily on the railing.

She held up her hands, showing they were empty. "I'm sorry, I didn't mean to –"

A second man pulled out a blade and stepped between them, bushy eyebrows scrunched together in hatred. "It's one of them! Maybe there's more still aboard!"

"No!" Emery's heart dropped all the way to her feet. "I'm not with them. I'm –"

"Shut your foul mouth!" he snarled, slashing at her.

She dodged his steel and pleaded, "I swear, I wasn't –"

The feather-hatted captain sauntered over. "What's this about?" Then he saw her.

"It dropped from the rigging, sir."

All the crew seemed to have crowded round them now, yelling and pointing weapons at her.

"I'm not one of them!" Emery shouted over the roar.

Even though she was. The same blood ran in her veins.

"Bullshit and lies!" one of the men spat.

"Throw her overboard," the captain ordered.

The crew surged forward. One of them grabbed the chair leg stuffed in the back of her clothes. She managed to fend off several attacks, but there were just too many. Soon, two men had seized her by the shoulders and begun dragging her to the edge of the ship. Emery's stomach twisted as she continued pleading. "I escaped! They kidnapped me! I snuck away during the raid. I came to ask you for *help*!"

The captain ordered the crew to pause, and Emery sagged with relief. The honesty in her voice must have broken through.

He raised an eyebrow. "Is this true?"

"Yes. The captain captured me. I've been their hostage."

"Hostage, eh?" The captain scratched his chin, then smiled. "Gents, heave her overboard."

The crew surged forward again, taking her with them. "Wait – I'm telling the truth!"

"Oh, I believe you, miss," said the captain. "But if they kidnapped you, they'll be wanting you back. And we're not going to stand in their way."

Words withered and died on Emery's tongue as more men crowded in to push her forward, the stink of their unwashed bodies suffocating. She tried to kick, bite, or beat her way free, but she was too far outnumbered, and the crew half pushed, half dragged her all the way to the edge of the deck. The water below had never seemed so far down, or so dark.

"Wait!" She forced her way around to face the captain, who seemed to be watching without pity. "At least let me have a boat. Please!"

The captain played with the feather on his hat for a moment, then sighed. "Alright. Release one of the boats!"

A few of the men grumbled but did as he asked. Then they unceremoniously lifted her up into the longboat still dangling high above the ocean.

She twisted to the captain again. "What about food? Water?"

He shook his head. "Sorry, lass. You're Forbidden friends took most of ours.

Without another word, he turned on his heel and marched away. Emery had just enough time to clutch the sides before the sailors unfastened the pully holding the boat in place. She bit her tongue as it was lowered in halting lurches that felt almost as sharp as freefall down onto the water.

"Good luck, girlie!" one of the men shouted as the little boat began drifting away from the ship.

Above them, the remaining sails unfurled and the vessel began to cruise away from her. This was freedom then. She had made her choice, tasted it, and now the people she had staked all her hopes on were callously leaving her to die.

Fear, anger, and humiliation made her blood steam, and a scream began to rise inside her. She choked it off. No one would hear her, or care. She had to save her strength, and think.

She twisted on her wooden bench and searched the horizon. To her right, the cargo ship was slowly shrinking into the distance. To her left, the Forbidden ship was still visible but barely. There was nothing else, just the endless blue expanse and unforgiving sun.

She had no food. No water. No shelter. If another storm whipped up, she would drown. Despair began to seep into her heart. She tried to ignore it, to concentrate on what she did have; a paddle, her wits, a map she couldn't read, a compass she barely knew how to use, the clothes on her back that weren't even hers.

*Oh gods.*

Giving up wasn't an option though. Not for herself, nor for Liam and Ayana. Determined to fight for as long as she could, Emery lifted the oar and dipped it in the water, letting the anger towards the men who'd done this to her propel the longboat on. Its prow now pointing straight at the cargo ship, she began to paddle after it, alternating between left and right. There was no way she'd be able to catch up, but she reasoned they were most likely now heading towards land. If she could keep following until the ship disappeared, then kept going forward in a reasonably straight line, she might just make it.

Might.

She glanced over her shoulder and her heart lurched. The *Audacity* had turned around, and it was sailing right for her.

Panic seized Emery so fiercely her limbs practically moved of their own accord. She began paddling as fast and as hard as she could, and her sorry little boat skimmed the sea with even greater determination.

*Thank you, Tadewin, for making the day so calm.*

She looked over her shoulder again. The Forbidden ship had already grown twice its size on the horizon. They were coming for her.

Then, the boat tilted so violently she nearly dropped the oar, and had to clutch the sides to keep herself from flying out. When it fell back down, it spun for a while in slow circles.

Emery stayed frozen where she was, eyeing the water in all directions. There were no big waves rolling, no reef in sight, nothing that should have sent her rocking like that.

The boat bucked again, making her teeth clank together. Emery dunked the oar back in the water and began paddling furiously. The wood was torn from her grasp so quickly that splinters pierced her skin, and she could only watch as the oar sunk down into the ocean. On the surface, only a ring of ripples remained.

Something huge and dark moved underneath, and Emery pressed her mouth shut to stop herself from screaming.

The boat rocked again, and she whimpered. The huge thing beneath her was at least four times larger than the tiny scrap of wood on which she was now bobbing, utterly exposed. Whatever it was, it began moving away from the boat, presumably to turn itself around and attack with better aim. The thing was just a dark shape, a blob of shadowy terror, but her imagination easily filled the gaps with scales, tentacles and fangs.

She placed herself in the very center of the boat, folding herself as small as she could. It shuddered and pitched again.

*Blessed Eldoris, Pyralis, Tadewin and Teralyn, please, don't let me die like this.*

A long, red tentacle appeared at the front of the boat, creeping along the wood like a horrible snake. Its suckers stuck to the grain as it searched, and Emery scrambled further back. The tentacle found the bench on which she'd been sitting and slowly wrapped around it. Then it squeezed, sending shards of wood flying everywhere, stinging Emery's cheeks and forehead. Blood began to drip from her brow, but she kept her attention focused on the terrible limb moving towards her.

She waited until the tentacle was nearly touching her with its bright tip. Then she pounced, grabbing one of the shards that used to be the wooden bench and stabbing down. The limb shot out of the boat, blue blood leaking from its wound.

The boat was thrust into the air, landing with a jarring thud on the water. Something crunched behind her, and Emery turned to see half the boat crumbling away into the sea. Water began rushing in, and within moments she was clinging to what little was left, legs already fully submerged.

A cold, slippery tentacle curled around her body, its suckers clinging to her skin. She stabbed it again with the shard, but this time it did nothing.

She began clawing at the beast with her bare hands, scraping it deep with her nails, but all it did was squeeze her tighter. A terror she had never known gripped her as she began to gasp for breath, her mind filling with images of Liam and Ayana. Of Caelin, Grace and Fia, her grandparents. Of Tavor. Even of Sean. He had at least shown her some kindness, even if it had been part of a greater plan. A plan she would now never get to hear.

The tentacle began to pull her under, and she made one last, fierce attempt to squeeze out of its grasp.

It didn't work. Cool water filled her ears, stung her eyes, as she was dragged beneath the ocean's surface.

Something whipped past, narrowly missing her shoulder, and pierced the tentacle. A long metal blade – a harpoon, Sean had called it. The tentacle released her, and whatever nightmare it belonged to bellowed so loudly the water vibrated.

She broke the surface, gulping in the sweet air. The *Audacity* was right there, its crew standing by the railing, some brandishing weapons, others yelling at her to swim.

Beside her, the tentacle rose again, slamming down on what remained of the boat and yanking it down into the abyss. She began swimming frantically towards the ship, picturing a yawning mouth opening up beneath her. Something smooth touched her foot, then her calf, her thigh. She screamed, swallowing brine, and kicked out, but connected with nothing.

Something splashed down beside her. She turned, ready to tear the tentacle apart with her bare hands, but instead it was a head that popped up, flicking wet hair out of its eyes. It was Sean, clinging to a rope with one hand, reaching for her with the other. She swam straight to him, relieved beyond all reason that it was now his arm wrapping around her. They began to be hoisted up, dangling ever further over the water once more. A tentacle shot up after them, but a second harpoon ripped through its flesh, and the beast dove down with another water rippling roar.

Emery clung to Sean as they swung over the railing, heaving in breaths that felt like they weren't fully reaching her lungs, until they had the solidity of the deck back under their feet. But as she tried to pull away, he turned her around and looked straight into her eyes, his own a little wild.

"Emery." The sound of her name sounded so jarring in his voice, in such a...familiar tone. As if she weren't a prisoner who had just been recaptured. As if she...mattered to him. "Everything's alright. You're safe."

Her vision blurred with tears of fear and frustration and a myriad of other emotions she couldn't process right then. She yanked herself free of Sean's grip. But her knees were shaking so violently, she couldn't keep herself upright anymore. She collapsed onto the smooth planks, her whole body trembling now. Before she could scramble to her feet again Sean's arms were under her and he was striding to his cabin, carrying her back to her prison.

She didn't put up a fight.

# Chapter Twenty-One

The wind howled through the still open window in Sean's cabin, the ocean beyond sparkling red in the light of the fading sun. Ever since Sean had deposited her back there, Emery had been sitting behind the desk, hugging her knees with her head pressed against the wall beside the window. Looking out had helped ease the turmoil in her head, but the fear and humiliation still seethed under her skin. The way those men had been prepared just to toss her into the sea, like she was nothing, like something diseased and totally unwanted...and she kept feeling the tentacles wrapping around her wrists, her ankles, pulling her under.

She'd now be digesting in the beast's belly if it hadn't been for the Forbiddens. Sean especially had taken great risk to save her life, literally leaping into the reach of a monster to pull her back to safety.

After he'd brought her back to the cabin and set her on the bed, he'd repeatedly asked if she was injured. She'd insisted she was fine, despite the quaking of her limbs. Wanting to be alone with her torrent of emotions, she then asked him to leave. He only hesitated for a moment before slipping through the door and shutting it quietly behind him.

Since then, all through the afternoon and into evening, no one had so much as come to the door.

She shook her head and buried her face in her hands. Why had he gone to such lengths to save her? Just to have the pleasure of killing her himself when the time came? Was his vendetta against Tavor so extreme? She couldn't believe that, not anymore. He had *chosen* to rescue her, chosen not to harm anyone on the cargo ship, even though the options of letting her die and leaving the other sailors with nothing would arguably have been easier.

She had to talk to him. She needed answers, and she also owed him some sort of thanks.

She opened the cabin door to a soft murmuring of voices. As she began to step out the voices hushed, and someone began to sing.

> *Oh, the sea is a grand and wondrous thing.*
> *With its waves that crash and its winds that sing.*
> *It's a place of adventure and mystery,*
> *where anything is possible, as long as you believe.*
> *With a compass in hand and a heart full of dreams,*
> *we'll explore the world and chase down our schemes.*
> *With a song on our lips, the sails fill with a crack,*
> *we'll dance with the waves and wind at our backs.*

People were sitting in a circle further along the deck. In the center, a whale-oil lantern was burning, illuminating their faces, and fending off the darkness of the incoming night. Ranit faced her, the gold trimming on his lute catching the light beautifully. He was strumming the strings and whistling through his teeth, then resumed his song. The tune sent chills across Emery's skin.

No one seemed to have noticed her yet, so she crept closer along the shadows by the railing, studying the faces rendered pale by the lantern's light. Nobody was singing with Ranit, they were just sitting there, staring into the glow, or at their hands, or at nothing at all. Nor did any of them seem particularly to be enjoying themselves. She could make out Aleksy, Smythee, Rooney, Billy, and the one who was still a child. Then the sailor who had scurried up the rigging the first time she'd stepped out of Sean's cabin, and Camulus. Sean wasn't among them but judging by the way the others kept glancing towards the bow she had a pretty good idea where he was.

Camulus's white-blonde hair gleamed as she turned to glare at Emery. Her cover was blown.

Ranit grinned at Emery, then looked at each of the other's faces as he began the next verse. Several of the other crew turned to her briefly, and though none of them smiled, they didn't seem as overtly suspicious as before. Some of them began to mutter along with Ranit's tune, and eventually to sing themselves. Their voices rose in strength and began to harmonize, and Emery realized; Ranit was trying to cheer everyone up. Her heart twisted in her chest, even though she didn't know what had brought them so low now. She edged closer to the circle, keeping herself mostly in shadow.

It also occurred to her how small this crew seemed to be. There were certainly fewer hands available than on Tavor's vessel, or the one from which she'd just been thrown, possibly fewer even than she would have thought necessary to sail a ship of this size. Or to wreak havoc on the seas.

Billy, the man with the silver mane, picked himself up and headed towards her. His hair was even more impressive up close, bright, and wild, both on his head and face, and deep lines etched the skin around his piercing blue eyes. He began tugging on his beard as he got close. "Hello, miss. Er...my name's Billy."

"Pleased to meet you, Billy." She smiled, feeling a sudden warmth towards him, perhaps towards all of them. "I'm Emery."

"Aye, I know." He tugged on his beard again and looked down at his feet. "Are you going to him?"

"Yes."

"He may not talk to you, be warned. He's...in a mood."

Emery swallowed. "I'll take my chances."

He nodded as if he'd expected such an answer. "Could you

give him this then?" He held out a hard biscuit. "He hasn't eaten anything all day."

Emery studied him. This man was acting more like a concerned father than one criminal talking about his captain – an even more infamous criminal.

She took the biscuit. "Alright."

"Thank you." He looked down at his boots again, his eyes seeming to shimmer strangely, then turned back to join the group.

The crew were singing loudly and clearly now, the words seeming to follow her as she walked towards the bow.

> *So come ye, me hearties, and raise up your voice*
> *In a song of freedom and adventure and choice*
> *For the sea is calling, and the time is right*
> *To set sail and discover all the wonders in sight*

When Emery reached the bow, she struggled to see Sean at first, even by the light of the quarter moon. He had climbed out onto the bowsprit again, but this time he sat on the small plat-form at the very end that held the spritsail topmast secure. In other words, as far from everyone else as it was possible to be without leaving the ship. He was sitting completely still, the only thing about him that moved was his hair being tousled by the breeze.

She took a deep breath and knocked on the bowsprit.

He didn't react.

She cleared her throat.

He didn't move.

"Sean," she called finally, and his head turned slightly. "I think we need to talk, don't you?"

He turned back towards the sea, saying nothing.

"Please?"

No reaction.

She huffed, deliberately loudly. "Fine, I'll come to you then."

She hauled herself up onto the bowsprit and began crawling

along its length. Sea spray had made the wood slippery, and as she neared the platform she almost lost her grip. At her short intake of breath one of his hands shot out, grabbing her wrist and steadying her. She clung to his arm in return, trying her best not to look down, convinced a tentacle would rise up from the froth if she did. Sean pulled her the rest of the way up onto the small platform, where there was no choice but to sit tightly side by side.

Emery allowed her legs to dangle over the edge, and breathed in the salty air. There was nothing to block her view of the stars now, and for a moment she had to gaze at their vastness in awe. When she spotted the constellation the Bow of Eldoris, the familiarity steadied something within her. At least some things didn't change.

She glanced at Sean. He, too, was staring at the twinkling sky, and the blank mask she'd half expected wasn't there. Instead, he looked tense and exhausted.

"Billy asked me to give you this," she said, holding up the biscuit.

A frown brushed his mouth, but he took it anyway. He didn't eat it though, just curled his fingers around it and placed his hand in his lap.

She leaned back against the pole behind them, lacing her fingers together over one knee. "I have several questions."

Sean gave nothing away.

"During the raid, you didn't hurt anyone. You didn't even damage their ship."

"You're surprised." It wasn't a question, or an invitation for her to interrogate him further, but at least he was talking.

"Well...yes. And confused, frankly."

He plucked at the leather guard tied around his palm but didn't respond.

"You just...scared them into submission," she pressed. "Why?"

"Inspiring fear from the outset is the best option if you don't want a fight."

"And you don't want a fight?"

"We never want a fight," he murmured.

"Oh. Why not?"

He played with the trinket hanging from his neck. "That's how people die."

Emery frowned, confused. "Like the people you killed on that ship you set on fire?"

Sean sighed. "None of them were dead, just paralyzed or unconscious."

Emery stared. Searching back through her memory. She couldn't now remember if Tavor had explicitly said those people were dead or if she'd just assumed they were.

"And the fire?" she asked.

"That was just to get the Viper's attention. It was under control."

That nickname again. She studied Sean's face but his empty expression still gave nothing away, and he still hadn't looked at her. "If you don't want to fight or cause damage, why do it at all?"

"We have no choice. It's either that or we starve."

"I don't understand." Back home, everyone took turns working the gardens, and everyone got a share of the food. For other goods, such as pots or blankets, anything that needed to be crafted, people simply made their own or traded with each other according to skill. No one ever went without. "Why don't you just go to land for food?"

"We've no coin."

"Coin?"

For the first time that evening, he looked at her fully. The skin around his eye was stained a violent purple from where she'd elbowed him earlier. "You really are something, you know that?"

She wasn't sure how to respond to that.

He leaned his head against the pole but kept his eyes on her now. "Coin, like silver spades? Or copper diggs? Golden royals? It's what you use to trade for things like food, or medicine, or...

well, pretty much anything. If you don't have coin, simply surviving can become…difficult."

"Then why don't you get it?"

He frowned and looked away again. "We can't."

"Why not?"

His answer dripped with contempt. "Because of our mutual *friend*."

Emery swallowed and looked down at her feet. She still had too many gaps in her knowledge to understand what Sean meant. Most likely it had something to do with the fact that Tavor had been trying to catch him and his crew for years. But surely, Sean had himself to blame for that.

Being reminded of Tavor again immediately made her think of her brother. She missed him so much her heart ached. Not wanting to succumb to that emotion right now, she gritted her teeth and peered instead at the dark ocean beneath her feet. The water was as black as the ink on Sean's desk, it would be impossible even to see something just below its surface. Like the bulbous eyes of a monster.

Shivers shot up her spine and she rubbed her arms where the suckers had left welts on her skin. She also pulled up her feet so that her bare toes would no longer dangle over the water.

"Are you hurt?" Sean was watching her, the concern on his face looking so real she didn't know how to interpret it.

"Just my pride," she said quickly. "You saved my life today. Why?"

Sean's eyes, bled of color by the moonlight, flicked over her entire face before meeting her gaze. He swallowed but didn't answer, and suddenly she felt rather self-conscious, sitting so close together with him. Alone.

She looked up to the sky to diffuse the tension. "Oh, I remember. Because I'm no use to you dead *yet*." She chuckled drily. "For a moment I almost forgot that you kidnapped me in the first place."

A long silence passed, broken only by the crew's distant singing and the slapping of waves against the ship.

Then, after a deep breath, Sean said, "I didn't."

She blinked at him. "What?"

He was staring straight ahead, refusing to look at her now. "I didn't kidnap you. And I never had any intention of killing you. But...I'm sorry. For how things played out between us."

Her mind was truly reeling now. "If you didn't kidnap me, then how am I here? *Why* am I here?"

He ran a hand through his unruly hair, making it stand up even higher. "When the storm began tearing Tavor's ship apart, my cell was smashed in. I escaped and tried to find a way off the ship. Instead, I found you, in the dark, trying to get out too. I wanted to help, but you were too scared of me, understandably at the time. When you ran, I chased after you because I didn't want you to rush out onto the top deck without first assessing the situation. But I couldn't reach you quickly enough."

Emery stared at him as he spoke, unsure if she could believe a single word. But nor did she have any way to disprove his claims.

"And then that wave swept you into me, and you hit your head on the rail." He paused, still not looking at her, still playing with that thing around his neck. "We were both swept overboard into the ocean, and I clung to a piece of debris, keeping both our heads above water until my crew found us."

Emery could not stop starring at Sean, imaging how difficult that must have been. "Why would you do that?" she breathed.

Finally, he looked at her again. "I wasn't going to leave you to die."

She opened her mouth, but nothing she considered seemed worthy of saying.

"It wasn't until it became clear you were going to make it that I started wondering what to do with you," he continued. "And I realized I might have made a mistake."

"A mistake?"

"You were travelling with the Viper. You still haven't told me why, by the way, but it didn't matter at that point. You couldn't be trusted."

"So, you locked me up."

"So, I locked you up. To keep my crew safe until I felt confident you weren't going to be a direct threat to them. To be honest, some of them are still mad at me for bringing you aboard."

"Really? I hadn't noticed." she said dryly, thinking of Cam's effort to toss her into the sea. That hadn't been an ill attempt at a rescue at all. She'd simply wanted Emery gone.

Her legs were beginning to go numb, but she wiggled her toes and tried to ignore it. How could she determine whether to believe him? "If you never intended to kill me, why did you threaten me?"

He looked down at the biscuit in his curled fingers, and shame seemed to cross his features once more. "I did...think about it. Right at the beginning." He shook his head. "But I couldn't. So, I decided to use fear against you. To ensure you'd submit and not fight. I thought if I could get enough information from you, you might become useful in another way." He let out a breath, and a noise startlingly close to a laugh. "But Roark be damned, you have a lot of fight in you."

Emery rubbed her temples, trying to ease the onset of a headache. "Why are you telling me all this?"

"Because...I still don't know what to do with you."

His words hung between them like a blade.

"Then...just let me go."

"I did, earlier." This time he did chuckle. "You think I didn't see you up there?" He nodded at the high rigging.

"You...what?" she breathed.

"I was just going to let you go, at least that way I no longer had to decide what to do with you. But then I didn't have the heart to just" – he gestured vaguely – "leave you to your fate, so I waited around to make sure you were safe."

"And then you saw when they threw me off."

"Aye. And now you're back."

Another silence stretched between them, in which Sean

turned to face the dark horizon but kept glancing at her from the corner of his eye. Her skin tingled under his gaze.

"I'll make you a deal," he said after a while.

"What kind?"

"The next time we make port, you can leave, you can go wherever you want."

"In exchange for what?"

He turned to look at her again, his expression hard. "Give me your word that you won't harm any of my crew."

She stared at him. "You think *I'd* harm *them*?"

"No, not anymore," he confessed. "But I'd still like your word."

Emery narrowed her eyes. "When you gave me that dagger and told me to kill you, it was a test, wasn't it?"

"Aye. And you passed, even though you did end up stabbing me." He didn't look mad about it. In fact, he cast her a devious smirk, as if he thought it was funny.

But her face heated at the recollection of inflicting the red line down his cheek, the bruising round his eye. "That was an accident."

"I know."

Emery rubbed her temples again. This could be some sort of trick, although if it was it was the most bizarre and elaborate one yet. Then again, what if it wasn't?

"I promise I won't hurt anyone." Emery meant it. Not unless she absolutely had to, and even if this was some sort of deception it was probably best to play along for now. "But how can I trust you to keep *your* word?"

He shrugged, his shoulder brushing hers. "The same way I'm trusting you not to slit my family's throats in their sleep."

She jerked upright, the horrible image twisting her stomach. At first, she thought he must be joking. But his smirk was gone. He looked deadly serious. Why would he think she'd even consider doing something like that? He and his crew were the vicious ones. Or at least, they were supposed to be. The more she spoke with him the less things seemed to make sense. She also hadn't missed the way he'd just described his crew as family, again.

Sean was back to fiddling with the trinket hanging from his neck. The more he played with it, the more that blank expression seemed to cloud his face. "If I'm going to let you go free though, I need to know." He turned to look at her, any ounce of emotion absorbed by that void nothingness. "Why were you on his ship?"

Her mouth went dry. "Why did you try to kill him?"

She stared into his empty, uninhabited eyes, willing him to back down first. How did he do that, throw on that mask so expertly it was like he'd gotten up and left even though he was still sitting next to her?

To her surprise, he did relent. "Well, I suppose we both have our secrets."

He got up and began making his way back to the body of the ship. Neither of them would be getting more answers tonight.

# Part Three

## *The Varens*

# Chapter Twenty-Two

A balmy wind blew easterly across the sea, caressing Emery's cheeks and collarbone. Her fingers tightened around the ropes she was holding and her toes gripped the yardarm more tightly. The sails were swollen beneath her, moving the ship ever onwards.

Farley, the man who had at first climbed away from her in panic, was in the crow's nest on the next mast over. She'd since learned that he was Cam's younger brother, and that he shared none of her fierceness. It was also his job to keep watch over the horizon. Right now, he peered through his telescope, sending her an occasional glance. Every time she looked his way though, he snapped his attention elsewhere.

This didn't just happen with Farley. The crew never tried to harm her, but most never talked to her either. They eyed her suspiciously from time to time, but mostly they ignored her.

A week had passed since her deal with Sean. So far, they'd both kept their promises. She never hurt anyone, of course, and he in turn allowed her to roam the ship at her leisure, although she did notice he was never far away. She still wasn't sure if this was part of some larger scheme, but it was becoming increasingly difficult to remember to fear these Forbiddens.

Besides Sean, the only three who talked to her were Ranit, Billy, and Smythee. Not long after the deal with Sean, she had tracked Ranit down and thanked him for letting her go, and since then they had spoken often. Billy wasn't quite as talkative, but also seemed incapable of being unfriendly, smiling at her every time they were in proximity. Smythee approached her on occasion, but he often wasn't lucid enough to hold a proper conversation.

Sean had continued to teach her about the ship and she had continued to learn eagerly, even daring to ask if she could help in some way. She didn't exactly want to make things easier for them, but reasoned that ingratiating herself a little, perhaps earning further trust, couldn't be bad either.

In response, Sean had given her a lot of scut work, starting with swabbing the decks in the mornings using a bucket filled with a mixture of foul red vinegar and seawater. Once that was finished, she moved around below deck, swinging a lamp in front of her that apparently helped dissipate *miasmas* that caused diseases. Then there was the slushing of the masts and spars, greasing them from one end to the other with fat scraped from the meat barrels so that the rigging could move more easily along them.

She made sure never to complain, happy to be doing something that kept her mind off her homesickness, off her friends and family, off her lack of concrete plan beyond getting off the ship. If she went too long without something to occupy her, worry began to creep in like a slow toxin, poisoning her until she couldn't breathe.

She practiced statera every morning, but her mind quickly began to drift each time, even more so than back home. Today, she had simply given up after *leaning elm*, realizing she was lost in her own head, stuck inside the stuffy cabin, wondering, for instance, why she'd never seen anyone aboard the *Audacity* practice statera. She didn't want to ask – or start doing it up on deck – in case this drew more questions her way that she feared to answer, but she also knew she wouldn't be able to bear practicing under a roof for much longer.

She had decided to climb the rigging and gaze out at the water for a while, hoping it would calm her mind. The sea sparkled in the afternoon sun and the horizon was a melted blur of cerulean blue. She was now trying to find the line between the water and the sky, but couldn't see anything to mark the split. No land on which to make port. No ship perhaps carrying her brother. No Orabel to return to.

"Looking for something?"

She turned to find Sean on the yardarm as well, leaning against the mast with his arms crossed. His sleeves were rolled up to his elbows, his tattoos on full display.

She shrugged, almost used to his quiet way of appearing, and turned back to the sea. "Just looking."

His boots tapped on the wood as he stepped closer. "Not much to see, is there?"

"There's always something. You just need to look."

"What do *you* see right now then?"

"I see...the sea, and the sky. All the mysterious creatures that live out there. Faraway lands no one has even heard of yet, people that aren't supposed to exist. The horizon and what's beyond it, what could be beyond it..." She trailed off, wondering how far beyond the horizon Orabel was, how faraway her family and friends were. She cleared her throat and turned around. "I don't know. Lots of things."

Sean peered past her, his brilliant green eyes searching the sea as if trying to find everything she had just described. "And you think all of that's out there?"

"I don't know, don't you?"

His eyes skimmed the horizon once more. "I hope so."

The sincerity in his voice coaxed a smile out of her, and she was surprised to see the corners of his mouth quirk up in response. He gazed at her for so long it began to feel uncomfortable, and she braced herself for questions that she wouldn't be able – or want – to answer.

Instead, he plucked one of the ropes from her hands. "They could use some help down below."

Before she could answer, he had leapt off the yard and slid down the rope, out of sight. She scrambled after him down the shrouds and ratlines to find him waiting for her at the bottom.

"You're getting faster," he said, that almost-smile still there. "But I won."

She narrowed her eyes. "I don't think that was completely fair."

He shrugged and spun on his heel. "Come along."

He led her to the capstan where Ranit, Camulus and the boy with the curly hair were standing. She thought she'd heard Sean call the boy Seadar once, but they'd never been properly introduced. Ranit smiled as they approached, and Emery nodded in return. The other two didn't so much as look at her, the boy choosing to stare at his boots, Camulus keeping her arms firmly crossed, eyes fixed on the ocean beyond. This was the closest they'd been since the night Camulus had tried to toss her overboard, and Emery couldn't remember seeing her interact with Sean at all since then. At least, when she finally did look back, her glare fell on him, not her.

The capstan was drum shaped, with many wooden bars sticking out of its sides like spokes. They each took a spoke, and together, the five of them pushed so the capstan began slowly turning. Emery had learned the capstan's cables were used for hauling things beyond the normal power of men, such as the anchor, heavy cargo, or canvas. Today, they were replacing one of the crimson sails that needed repairing.

As the group worked to turn the capstan, Ranit kept them in time by singing a shanty. Seadar sang along heartily, while Camulus hummed a little. Emery had heard it enough times by now to know the words, and after a while she gathered the courage to sing along as well.

Once the canvas was hoisted and it fell to Rooney and Aleksy, who waited in the rigging, so secure in place, Camulus's eyes flashed at Emery. "You sound like a strangled cat."

Emery blinked back, caught off guard by the fact the other woman was speaking to her, even if it was for a cheap insult.

"Cam!" Sean hissed.

"Well...you sound like...a whale that's beached itself," Emery shot back, then clamped her mouth shut in shock.

The others fell silent as Camulus gaped at her, a dull flush creeping up her neck. Then, a bark of laughter burst from Sean. Only one syllable escaped his lips, but it echoed in Emery's ears, reverberated in her chest. What a lovely, surprising sound, warm and rich and rough from neglect. For reasons she couldn't understand, her pulse skipped knowing she had been its cause.

A slow grin broke across Ranit's face, but Camulus's skin flamed with anger. "Are you going to let her talk to me like that, Captain?"

Sean's half smile still lingered. "You started it, Cam."

The other woman's eyes bulged. She opened her mouth, but whatever she was about to say was lost in as a cry from Farley cut her off. "Sail ho! Twelve points to port!"

"Colors?" Sean shouted, sprinting to the side of the ship with Emery and the others close behind. He got out his telescope, but the fear in Farley's voice conveyed everything they needed to know.

"Varens, Captain! It might be the Viper."

The entire crew froze, and even in Sean's eyes the fear was blatant.

But unlike the Forbiddens, hope flared to life inside Emery. Farley meant Tavor, and if Tavor was on that ship, maybe her brother and Caelin were too.

The vessel was clear on the horizon now, long and sleek like a serpent. It seemed to slither towards them, blue-and-black flag waving from one of the masts, its silver trimming glinting in the sunlight.

If Liam was on board, she just had to wait.

"Ready the sails!" Sean shouted, hurrying to help Seadar haul on a rope. "Get us moving, now!"

The crew scrambled to obey the orders, and soon the

crimson sails fell open, catching the wind and moving the ship forward.

"Bring her about!" Sean yelled to Billy, who was standing at the helm. The older man heaved the mighty wheel, and the ship swung around.

As the ship rocked, Emery twisted to keep the varen ship in sight. It cruised along behind the *Audacity*, not yet close enough to see anyone aboard, but close enough for the panic in the crewmen around her to rise. It even began to crawl under her skin like something contagious, and she couldn't help remembering the awful stories she'd heard about varens growing up, about them hunting down her people and destroying them.

But Tavor wouldn't hurt her. Furthermore, if she was aboard, the others should be safe from him too. All she had to do was speak with him.

She raced to Sean and found him still helping Seadar with the foresails.

"Stop trying to outrun them! This is your chance to get rid of me."

Sean didn't slow as he tied one of the ropes to a cleat. "Sorry, I can't." He sounded surprisingly sincere.

"Yes, you –"

He towered over her with his full height. "I *can't*. If we so much as slow down, we're all dead."

Her heart plummeted. "But what if I talk to him? My –" she fumbled for the right word. "My relationship with Tavor is a lot more positive than yours. I can speak for you."

Sean's expression sharpened. "There's no talking to him. Trust me."

Before she could ask what that meant, he had already sprinted up the stairs to the helm. She followed, taking the steps two at a time, anxious to reunite with her brother, but also shaken by the complete certainty in Sean's voice. He seemed genuinely frightened, for himself and everyone on board.

She tried to force her rising pity down where she couldn't

find it. If Tavor was so bent on capturing them, there had to be a good reason. There had to be.

She reached the helm as Sean was taking over from Billy. For a moment, he closed his eyes and stood perfectly still, only his chest moving as he breathed. Then, a gust of wind picked up behind him, tossing his hair and tugging at his clothes. The wind wrapped around Emery as she moved towards him, so powerful she had to hold her hair down to see him properly. Then the wind swept past them and up into the rigging, bulging the sails to maximum capacity. Emery nearly lost her balance as the ship thrust violently forward.

With his golden hair swirling in the sunlight and the wind ripping at his clothes, Emery found it impossible to look away from him. He looked like the god of wind himself.

What more, given this crew supposedly used their gifts to wreak havoc across the seas, she had almost never seen them use their abilities.

Her musing ended when she realized that this extra speed also meant she was once more being dragged away from her brother.

Camulus stalked past Emery to stand beside her captain. Sean didn't open his eyes but nodded as she approached in wordless understanding. Her icy hair flew around her pale face as she too closed her eyes. Emery couldn't see what she was doing, but felt the ship jolt forward again, now holding an even more breakneck speed. She realized Camulus was manipulating the currents beneath them, the waves behind, sending them ever onwards with a swiftness that was eye-watering.

"They're falling behind," Billy said, clamping a hand on Sean's shoulder.

Sean didn't open his eyes but reached up to pat Billy's hand. The strangely intimate action hit home to Emery that she would now not get to embrace her own brother, again.

She headed to the railing and watched the varen ship disappear into the blue. Her chest felt shredded, the hope torn from her heart.

She jumped when a hand landed on her own shoulder. It was Sean. "I'm sorry," he said again, once more sounding so sincere she didn't know how to react. She searched his face, but it was too difficult to read his expression. The warmth of his palm spread through the fabric of her tunic though, heating her skin and melting the icy disappointment in her blood. When he removed his hand, for a confusing moment all she wanted was for him to put it back, to feel that warmth again.

"Captain!" Farley's voice rang from above. "Something's happening. I don't – they're picking up speed!"

They all whipped round to face the varen ship. It was getting larger again. Closer.

"But how?" Sean's voice was strained. He closed his eyes again, and the ship shuddered as the wind he was generating provided an extra buffet. Camulus's eyes had stayed shut this whole time, but now Emery could see that her hands were shaking.

Ranit came dashing up the steps, his face so pale he looked like he was about to pass out. "Captain, I think they're also using the elements. *Really* using them."

Sean's eyes snapped opened, and the ship slowed ever so slightly. "How would they be doing that?"

"I – they must have elemists aboard."

Emery's chest constricted, cutting off her breath. It was another sign that Liam could be with Tavor. But surely he couldn't manipulate the air so powerfully yet. He'd barely been able to form a small twister back on Orabel. Could her twin's abilities have grown to such a degree already, while her own had barely appeared?

"God," Sean breathed and closed his eyes again, what looked like dread and disgust chasing each other across his face.

The varen ship was now pursuing them at an alarming speed, moving even faster than the *Audacity*. A war began raging inside Emery. Her brother was there, so close she could almost sense him. And yet...a part of her didn't want them to catch up. If what Sean had just said was true, she realized with abrupt clarity that she didn't want these Forbiddens to die.

The varens were so close now she could see men standing on the other ship's deck, all in black-and-blue uniforms with weapons at their belts. She searched for Liam, Caelin and Tavor, but saw none of their faces in the crowd.

A bang ripped the sky apart as something whizzed past the *Audacity*, barely missing the stern and crashing into the ocean beyond. A geyser of saltwater shot into the air and rained down upon the deck.

Cannons.

"Seadar, Smythee!" Sean shouted. "Portside guns, rolling broadside on my signal!"

The two abandoned their positions and sprinted below decks, just as three more deafening booms tore through the air in quick succession. Emery ducked, bracing herself for the impact, and the *Audacity* quaked as at least one of the cannon-balls struck her side.

An arm landed on Emery's shoulders, keeping her down. "Fire!" Sean shouted, right next to her face. His arm stayed around her. "Stay low."

Another series of thunderous bangs sounded, this time beneath them, as if a storm had just erupted in the ship's bowels. The *Audacity* swayed as the missiles left their guns, but Emery couldn't see whether they hit their marks.

"Sean!" Billy's frightened voice was just loud enough over the cannons. "They're coming aboard!"

Sean released her, and they both straightened to see varens throwing grappling hooks across the now only narrow gap between the ships. Already, some were swinging over on ropes, and the metallic *zing* of blades being unsheathed pealed across the deck.

# Chapter Twenty-Three

S ean grabbed Emery's arm. "You have to hide!" he yelled over the clashing weapons. "Doesn't matter where, just stay out of sight." His emerald eyes were burning, just like they had the night he attacked Tavor, burning with hatred and urgency and something else she hadn't been able to recognize back then. Terror.

"Just let me go over. I can reason with him!"

"I will let you go, I promise. But not —"

She yanked her arm free and ran to the nearest ratlines.

"Emery, wait!"

She leapt onto the netting, scrambling up as fast as her shaking limbs allowed, and hauled herself onto one of the spars. She crouched on the beam to steady herself, every breath sharp in her chest. Below her, a swarm of men in black and blue was surging onto the *Audacity*, severely outnumbering the Forbiddens. Nonetheless, the crew raised their weapons and blades clashed. Sean already had two varens swinging at him, but he was dodging and parrying each attack, moving so swiftly and eloquently it was difficult not to become distracted. Instinct urged at her to go back down to him, to help him, but she shook the impulse off. Her instincts were wrong.

They've been hunting him for a reason. He's killed people.

She concentrated on those she needed to find. Liam. Caelin. Tavor.

Tearing her eyes from Sean, she crawled along the spar. Then, righting herself, she leapt across the gap into the other ship's rigging.

More varens were stationed beneath her, long-barreled guns all trained on Sean's crew. Cold prickled along her skin, and again, the fear they might actually be killed struck her so hard it knocked the breath from her. Darting her eyes over the deck, she looked for Tavor amongst the black-and-blue swarm. If she could just find him, perhaps she could put an end to the attack. Her search fruitless, there was nothing for it but to look in the cabin, or even below decks.

She shimmied down the nearest mast as further bangs and screams pierced the air. One man quickly spotted her, reacting much the same as the crew on the cargo ship. He stumbled backwards, aiming his gun at her. "Get back!"

"No, wait!" She threw up her hands, showing her lack of weapon. "I'm not with them. They kidnapped me!"

"Likely story," the man spat, pulling back the hammer on his gun.

"Ask Tavor!" she shouted above the clamor. "I'm part of his former crew!"

The man blinked, then lowered his gun a fraction. "You mean...Commissioner Thantos?"

"Yes! Tell him Em – tell him Miss Aalokin is here. And that she would like –"

"He isn't on this ship," the man hissed, raising his gun to eye level. "And I don't believe a thing that comes out of your filthy Forbidden mouth."

Anger flared in her at his awful words. But then the realization came.

That meant Liam wasn't here either.

Did that mean they really were all dead? That she was trapped out here, alone, with no hope of completing their mission or finding a safe way home? All because of this senseless conflict. The injustice of it all, this new sense of hopelessness, only fanned her fury.

With perfect clarity, she saw the man's finger begin to squeeze the trigger, and her anger exploded. A new wind rose up around her, like a beast begging to be let loose, and she threw it forward. The gust blasted past her, hitting the man full in the face. He fell backwards hard, and the bullet exploding from his gun flew wide. Emery hit the ground as the mast behind her shattered into a thousand wooden shards.

For a moment, she stayed there. She'd done it. She'd manipulated the wind, and not in a small way.

More bangs. More screams. More metallic clashes shredded the air. She scrambled to her feet. Other varens had now seen her and were aiming their guns, swinging their blades, all determined to kill her. She dodged them frantically as she sprinted to the nearest climbable rigging, bullets and darts ricocheting around her. She scrambled up to the highest yard, then pressed her back against the mast, using it as a shield from the ongoing assault. No one followed her up, but they continued firing until a couple of bullets hit the sails, at which point they clearly thought better of tearing holes into something so crucial to their own survival.

Emery's heart pounded so hard she thought her chest might break open. The flames of anger had disappeared, replaced instead by despair at being so thoroughly trapped.

A different kind of shouting began directly below her, and she cautiously looked down. Three varens were shoving a woman and a couple of men with the bladed tips of their rifles, steering them towards the starboard railing. Towards the *Audacity*. The prisoners' tunics were ripped, their trousers looked like they'd never been washed, and their hair was so matted and dirty it was impossible to determine its natural color. Metal chains stretched between their wrists and ankles, and iron collars had been clamped around their necks. Emery's own throat constricted as the varens continued to prod the prisoners, who were already tripping over their chains, and each other, stumbling along like sickly sheep.

One varen yelled, loud enough for Emery to make out, "Use your bloody powers before I blow your brains out!"

They were elemists. This must be why the ship had been able to catch up with the *Audacity*.

But the prisoners just shook their heads in refusal, or perhaps because they had already used up all their energy.

The second captor smashed the butt of his rifle against the woman's head, who immediately crumpled to the floor. The other two prisoners roared in unison and flung themselves at the three varens, punching, kicking and biting. But the fight ended quickly, with another varen turning around to aim his gun at the two men. Emery closed her eyes, but the shots still reverberated through her.

*Holy Gods.*

She sucked in a breath, fighting the urge to vomit. Shaking with horror, she turned to face the *Audacity*. Things weren't much better there. Most of the crew were fighting the varens with blades. A few - Aleksy, Billy, Rooney – were using their pistols, although they seemed never to aim to kill, shooting the varens only in their legs or arms. Nor were many of them using their abilities. No wind whipped through air, no fires flared amidst the fray, no water reared up from the ocean. The only manipulation Emery saw was Cam freezing the sea spray on the deck, causing the varens she was fighting with her ax to slip. Sean was by the helm, blade in one hand and pistol in the other. Varen after varen flooded up the stairs towards him and he was taking them down with his sword. As soon as he had brief respite, he protected the others with his pistol, taking out one varen on the lower deck about to shoot Billy, another who had pinned Smythee in a corner, a third fighting Farley who at that point was relying only on his fists. When his ammunition ran out, he sent down blasts of wind instead.

But he was doing too much at once, and he missed the varen bearing down on Seadar behind him, missed the raising of the man's pistol, aimed straight at the boy. He heard the shot though, because he whirled around just in time to see the boy collapse.

Sean sprinted at the varen. Emery didn't see what he did with him, didn't really care. She couldn't tear her eyes from Seadar's small form, lying motionless on his side. Her vision blurred and the rage blazed in her veins again. Seadar was so young, too young to pose any kind of threat. How could they just shoot him like that?

Sean had reached Seadar's limp body, dropping to his knees and moving his hands over the boy's chest. She couldn't tell if he was searching for a wound or signs of life.

Emery's entire body stiffened as yet another varen began climbing the stairs, aiming his gun straight at Sean's exposed back. She called out a warning, but it was clear Sean couldn't hear her. She had to move, braced herself to make the leap back onto the *Audacity*. But Sean didn't need her warning. He spun, blade in hand, and slashed at the varen's face.

The varen ducked the blow, and Sean threw up his hands. At first Emery though he was surrendering, but then she realized he was trying to use the wind.

Only...nothing happened.

Sean's chest was heaving, his forehead gleaming with sweat. He was spent. Seeing him so helpless in from of that gun made her feel sick.

The varen bore down on him again, raising his gun to fire. But Sean refused to give up. He swung his blade at the other man's ankles. Just as quickly, the varen kicked out, catching Sean's wrist and sending his sword sailing over the ship's railing.

Sean rose, but this time didn't move any further, not even as the varen began to stalk steadily closer, so close the blade at the end of his rifle pushed into his left shoulder. Emery could only see their mouths moving as the two men shouted at each other, and then Sean spat in the varen's face.

The varen snarled, raising his gun to Sean's head.

Instinct took over as Emery sprinted the length of the spar, snatching the first loose rope she could find and hurling herself towards the *Audacity*. Her stomach disappeared as she crossed the narrow gap between the two boats, the ocean's dark depths momentarily beneath her. She grabbed a new rope and released the other, biting her tongue as her muscles flamed and hands burned from maintaining their grip, but she managed to swing the last distance to her target. She careened into the varen, knocking him back down to the lower deck. Then she dropped to her hands and knees, head spinning from what she'd just done.

Sean was already taking her by the shoulders, hauling her to her feet. "Are you alright?"

She nodded, too breathless to speak.

He took a step back, his concerned face settling into its familiar blankness. "Why did you –"

"Tavor isn't there," she gasped.

"I know."

"What?" She straightened so she could look at him better. "How?"

"I realized as soon as they came aboard. These men are too new. They're just trainees, and Tavor never bothers himself with trainees." He bent down to pick up the rifle the varen had dropped. "They're disorganized and hotheaded. That's the only reason we haven't lost yet." He tossed the rifle to her. "You're going to need this."

She ran her shaking fingers over its parts. "No one's trained me how to use one."

"Then stab or swing." He crouched to pick a fallen blade from the ground and then moved to stand over Seadar, who remained on the floor.

"Is he..."

"He's alive. Just paralyzed."

Emery exhaled with relief.

They turned to the deck below, where battle still raged. The metallic smell of blood and the scent of gun smoke singed Emery's nostrils, and so many bodies now littered the ship it wasn't clear who was who. Smythee's maniacal laughter was still discernable as it ripped through the screams and bangs, and then came a burst of flame and he was standing in the center of the ship, torch in one hand and fire coiling around his body like a living thing. Any varens unfortunate enough to be in his vicinity received a burst of flame to their chest, their screams and the stench of burned hair and flesh joining that of the blood and smoke. Many began fleeing back to their ship, but one turned and sprinted up the stairs towards Sean and Emery. He beelined for the Forbidden, tackling him around the middle and sending them both sprawling across the floor. They vied for the upper hand, one moment Sean was on top, the next the varen, fists and feet and blades everywhere. Emery circled them, wanting to intervene, scared she might accidentally hurt Sean.

Perhaps she could use the wind, separate them somehow, then –

Footsteps sounded behind her. She spun, raising the rifle to strike, but a blade crashed against it and it took all her strength to keep her attacker at bay.

The varen's face was streaked with gore, bloodlust gleaming in his eyes. "You disgusting little creature."

In that moment, all the horrible stories she had ever heard about them came to life.

The man lifted his blade to swing again, but this time she blocked him back with an accelerated *arcing moon*, using the rifle as she would once have used her lim. The varen pulled back his blade and jabbed, but she dodged it by spinning into *petals in the wind*.

Emery had trained long and hard for just such an encounter, but fighting a real aggressor was not the same as practicing back home with her friends. This man slashed, parried, twisted in odd ways, following none of the rules she was used to.

She wasn't going to let him get the better of her though. Dodging a fresh blow with *leaning elm*, she caught him on the side of the head with *stinging bee*. He wavered for a moment, granting her a precious moment to think.

Her gaze landed on the railing behind him.

Knowing what she had to do now, she held steady as the varen began once more to rain down on her. She started edging to her right in *spattering of stars*, shifting slowly enough that he wouldn't suspect anything. Sweat was beginning to bead on her forehead as she parried hit after hit, until she thought her arms might snap. It was almost a relief when the railing finally touched her back. Then, as the man lunged to stab her, she stepped out of the way, letting his own momentum topple him over the railing.

At the last moment, he snarled and grasped Emery's tunic, pulling her over the railing with him. She tried to twist and grab on, but the world had already upended itself. She fell for one terrifying heartbeat, and then her ribs cracked as she hit the hard deck below. The metallic taste of blood filled her mouth.

The floor quaked and the blurry outline of another angry varen materialized above her. He raised his blade, ready to strike, but her body refused to move. Her heart practically beat out of her chest as she tried to roll sideways, tried to cry out for help.

A loud crack sliced the air and the varen collapsed beside her. Her vision cleared, and she could make out Ranit standing over them.

"Emery!" He crouched down and tried to help her to her feet. "Are you hurt?"

"I don't know," she slurred, her tongue heavy and bloody in her mouth.

"We need to move," Ranit said, carefully pulling her up. "Smythee's got most of them on the run but –"

Another terrible bang sounded close to them. Ranit cried out and lurched into her, sending them both crashing to the boards. He lay on top of her, not moving.

"Ranit?"

Something warm and wet was seeping through her tunic. She wiggled out from under him and flipped him over, bile instantly crawling up her throat.

From the elbow down, his right arm was a ragged mess. He

229

stared up at the sky, eyelashes fluttering and his chest heaving with shallow breaths.

Another varen was approaching them, gun trained on Ranit. Half his hair was singed, his clothes were smoking, and the look on his face was utterly deranged.

She placed herself over Ranit, shielding him as best she could.

The varen's lip curled into an awful sneer, and his finger squeezed the trigger.

Someone dropped on top of him, knocking the man unconscious. It was Sean, rolling off the varen and climbing gingerly to his feet. In that moment, with his golden hair gleaming in the smoky air, he was the most beautiful thing she had ever seen.

"Ranit needs help!" she cried.

Sean was already kneeling by him, his face drained of color. "Aleksy!"

Aleksy appeared quickly, taking no more than a moment to examine Ranit's arm. She pressed her hands against his ruined flesh and the bleeding ebbed to a crawl. Emery realized she was manipulating the water in his blood to slow it's flow, like she'd seen the healers back in Orabel do.

"Your cabin, now," Aleksy ordered. "We don't have time to get him to the infirmary." The calmness of her voice jarred with the frantic haste of the situation. She then turned to Rooney, who had just thrown a varen overboard. "Fetch my bag!"

Ranit moaned and struggled as they picked him up and carried him to Sean's cabin. Further along the deck, Smythee was using a wall of flames to steer the last varens standing back to their ship, dragging their dead and injured with them. Camulus and Farley were running along the railing, chopping the ropes that still tethered them, and finally the ships were drifting apart again.

Rooney ran into the cabin after them, carrying Aleksy's medical supplies, and Aleksy immediately got to work cutting away Ranit's tattered sleeve.

Ranit screamed as the scissors touched him, and Sean fought to hold him down, speaking softly against his ear.

Emery's head swam as the full extent of the damage became clear. Raw muscle, exposed bone, far too much blood. She reached out and stroked Ranit's hair, her fingers trembling.

"Can you save his arm?" Sean's voice was strained.

Aleksy's expression did not inspire hope. "There's nothing to save. Even if there was, we wouldn't be able to clean the wounds effectively. He'd die of infection in no time."

Ranit tried to sit up, but Sean held him down. "I'm so sorry."

"No!" Ranit wailed. "No! Don't take my arm! Please!"

"It's that or your life, my friend," said Aleksy.

"I'd – rather – die!" Ranit was bucking so hard that even Sean was struggling to hold him. Hating herself for it, Emery placed her hands on his shoulders and pressed down as well, while Rooney came forward to grasp his flailing legs.

"I'm sorry," Aleksy whispered. "But we're not going to lose you."

Sean's face had gone the color of spoiled milk. "Rooney, fetch the saw. And a bottle of ale."

"And something for a tourniquet," snapped Aleksy. "I won't be able to cut and stop blood flow at the same time."

Rooney was gone and back in a heartbeat, taking the lid off a bottle of amber liquid and shoving it into Ranit's still functioning hand. "I'd get drinking if I were you."

Whimpering, Ranit tipped the bottle back and drank like he was trying to drown himself. Rooney handed Aleksy the saw, and Emery instinctively wanted to shrink away from its jagged metal teeth.

"Emery, get out," Sean ordered.

She hesitated. No part of her wanted to witness what was about to happen, but she also didn't want to abandon Ranit to his agony. She stroked his hair again with one hand. "Maybe it's better if –"

"Now!".

Fighting back tears, Emery choked an apology to Ranit and retreated to the doorway.

"I'm going to start now," Aleksy said. "Sean, Rooney, you have to hold him. Tight."

With a quavering voice, Ranit began to sing, "*Oh, the sea is a grand and wondrous thing...*"

Emery dashed the last few steps onto the deck and slammed the door behind her. The others were waiting there, Camulus, Farley, Smythee, even Seadar was sitting groggily against the railing. Only Billy was over at the helm, guiding the ship ever further away from the varens.

"*With its waves that crash and its winds that sing...*"

No one spoke, just stared at the door, rubbing their faces, chewing their lips, all united in terror for Ranit.

"*It's a place of adventure and mystery...*"

Sean, Rooney, and Aleksy were all shouting now, and Ranit's voice was growing louder and more ragged.

"*WHERE ANYTHING IS POSSIBLE, AS LONG AS YOU BELIEVE!*"

Then his words became an incoherent series of screams. Smythee sat down on the deck and began rocking back and forth.

Centuries crept past as they waited, no one going further than a few paces from the door. Part of Emery felt like they were linked now, bonded in some way by this shared horror, at least for the time being.

Suddenly, the screaming stopped.

"He'll have passed out," Camulus whispered, gripping Farley's shoulder so hard her knuckles were turning white.

After another excruciating stretch, the door finally opened, and Rooney and Sean staggered out, their clothes and faces streaked with blood. Sean looked utterly haunted, and he marched straight to the railing and retched over the side.

Once there was nothing left in his stomach, he tore off his tunic and threw it overboard. They all watched the bloody thing sink into the depths.

# Chapter Twenty-Four

Once everything had been done for Ranit that could be, Aleksy took his medical supplies to the infirmary and began looking over everyone else. Fortunately, other than a few deep cuts and colorful bruises, it looked like no one else had suffered any serious injuries.

Emery went down last, hauling herself up painfully onto the table. It hurt to breathe, her ribs protesting every time she tried to expand them. In some ways, it was a welcome distraction from her whirling thoughts. Unoccupied, her mind kept showing her the varen aiming his gun at Sean's head, her entire body recalling the terror that had surged through her at the thought he was about to die, the action she had taken in reaction to that fear. She had tried to remind herself that she didn't care whether Sean lived or died, that he was a criminal wanted for crimes so vile that Tavor hadn't even been able to bring himself to relate them to her. But she knew it was a lie. She did care.

Guilt also plagued her about Ranit. She may not have been the one who took his arm, but he had lost it saving her life, putting himself in the wrong place at the wrong time. Nothing she was going through in this moment compared to his ordeal.

She gritted her teeth while Aleksy carefully examined her

torso, then confirmed she'd bruised some ribs during her fall. "You should limit your movements for a while, let them heal." With that, she turned and began packing away her instruments.

"How is he?" she asked.

"He'll live," Aleksy replied, but added nothing further.

By now, Emery's defenses were utterly exhausted. She also knew she had to take this chance while she had it. "Aleksy, have you ever heard of an illness that makes you...age rapidly, or strips elemists of their gifts?"

The healer turned to look at her, but her face was expressionless. "No."

"My sister – never mind." She squirmed painfully off the table and retreated without waiting for a further response. Aleksy clearly hadn't heard of the Withering, and she didn't have the energy to get into it now. She went up to sit on the stairs to the afterdeck, trying to lose herself in the softness of the encroaching night sky.

For the rest of the evening, the crew rotated in shifts, repairing bits of the ship, visiting Ranit, or sitting around in a bleak stupor. Sean returned to the cabin and never came out. Billy went in and out the most frequently, each time looking more and more stricken, until eventually he stopped altogether. Emery kept to herself, nervously watching the door for a chance to go in alone.

Eventually, the visiting ceased altogether, except for Sean who looked like he wasn't going to leave Ranit's side. She didn't really want to face either of them, didn't know if she'd be able to keep a hold of herself or whether her body or the myriad of emotions running through her would betray her, but she knew she owed it to Ranit.

She took a deep breath, the pain in her ribs quickly clearing her mind. She had to go, before the confusion could return and change her mind.

The deck was deserted now. The others must have finally disappeared to their hammocks, wanting the day to be over just as much as she did.

When she reached the cabin door, she decided to knock and wait. Only when no response came did she slip silently inside.

The metallic stink of blood and the sterile aroma of alcohol hit her immediately. A lone candle was burning on the bedside table, the flame nearing the end of its life. It was casting an orange glow across half the cabin, leaving the other in shadow.

Ranit was lying in the bed and didn't stir as Emery approached. Once her eyes adjusted to the gloom, she could see he was sleeping, the rise and fall of his chest mercifully soft once more. His remaining arm hung limply from the bed, and she swallowed as she saw what was left of the other. It ended just after the elbow, the stump wrapped with a blood-stained cloth. Guilt once more gnawed on her heart.

"I'm so sorry, Ranit," she whispered.

Tearing her gaze from him, she searched the rest of the room for Sean, beginning with a tentative step towards the desk. But the chair behind it was empty.

Then she spotted him. He was sitting on the floor on the other side of the desk, jammed into the corner by the window. He was so still she'd at first mistaken him for a shadow.

He was staring out into the dark abyss beyond the window, still shirtless. A trickle of blood oozed from a wound on his shoulder. He didn't seem to have noticed her, or didn't care.

"Sean?"

He remained silent, unmoving.

"You saved Ranit's life today. And mine. Again." She swallowed, her throat suddenly dry. "Thank you."

Finally, he moved, although he didn't look at her, just gazed down at his hands in his lap. His voice was rough when he spoke. "I'm the reason your life needed to be saved."

She looked into the cabin's darkest corner, for some reason finding it too hard to witness him in this state. "That may be, in the wider sense of things. But you didn't have to do what you did today. You could've just let me die. Again."

She didn't even know what she was trying to say, who she was hoping to convince. Her heart was galloping in her chest as if trying to outrun the stupid, contradicting emotions fighting for control inside her. She was suddenly overwhelmed with the need to retreat and almost turned for the door. But she couldn't leave him like this.

Letting out a shuddering breath, she said, "You should clean that wound."

When he still didn't reply, Emery gathered a clean cloth and the leftover bottle of alcohol and knelt before him.

Finally, he met her gaze. For a moment, his eyes betrayed something beyond that empty expression before he turned his attention back to the darkening sea outside. She couldn't tell what she had seen in them, only that it was deep-rooted and dreadful.

Pouring some alcohol on the cloth, she gritted her teeth. "Sorry about this."

She dabbed the cloth on his wound. He hissed but otherwise made no other reaction. But when her fingers accidentally brushed his skin, she swore she felt him shiver. When she was finished, she set the cloth aside, and sat back on her heels.

"Thank you," he said, his voice so quite she barely heard him.

"Are you...alright?"

"It's not that deep," he said.

"That's not what I meant..."

Sean closed his eyes, and for the space of a breath his blank expression collapsed fully, and a sense of guilt and grief radiated off him so intensely she could feel it herself. Just as quickly it was gone again, replaced by the usual façade of nothing. But she had seen it now, the emotional wound he was carrying, the one from which he was slowly bleeding out.

"I'm fine," he said, his voice once again betraying him.

Emery didn't know what to say, how to push him, so she stood to leave. But he caught her wrist. "Don't go. Please."

He was looking up now, but gazing past her slightly, refusing eye contact. That awful blank expression clouded his face, but his voice had been so ragged. He let go of her wrist quickly.

She swallowed. "Alright." She crossed the room to pull a

blanket from his wardrobe and then tossed it over his still bare shoulders. He could feel his eyes on her as she turned to go sit against the wall on the opposite end of the window. When she lifted her eyes to his, he immediately looked back out at the sea. She followed his gaze and they just sat in silence for a time. The candle on the bedside table burned lower and lower, casting ever more strange shadows over the room. The ship groaned, and Ranit snored softly, but otherwise the night was cloaked in silence.

Eventually, Sean shifted. He still gazed out the window, but he was now toying with the trinket hanging from his neck and his voice had returned to normal, flat as an iced-over pool. "Do you believe in god?"

She wasn't sure to whom he was referring, whether Eldoris or Pyralis or perhaps some other god that existed out here. Carefully, not wanting to give anything away lest he started asking her question she couldn't answer without possibly revealing Orabel, she said, "I believe there must be something out there, somewhere."

"I used to think so too."

"Not anymore?"

"Not for a long time."

"Why?"

Another silence swallowed them. Sean never answered, never moved.

Emery gazed at Ranit's sleeping form, the void where his arm now ended abruptly. Her eyes burned. "I'm sorry. It's my fault Ranit lost his arm."

"No." Sean's head snapped up, and for the first time that night he peered directly into her eyes. "You didn't pull the trigger."

"But he was only there because –"

"*I* brought you all here," he interrupted. "If anyone aboard is at fault, it's me."

The guilt and the grief had fallen back into his voice, and Emery couldn't bear it. "Sean, it wasn't your fault either."

He blinked, staring at her as his blank expression gave way to a quick succession of emotions. Surprise? Disbelief? Pain? They flitted past, too fast to catch, before he shook his head and peered out the window again. "You have no idea what I've done."

It was true. She had no idea what he'd done to become such a hunted man, nor what he so clearly blamed himself for. But she was sure of this. "You're right. But Ranit's arm is a different matter. You weren't there, you couldn't have foreseen it, and you didn't shoot him any more than I did."

Sean continued to gaze at her, his face once more carefully blank. "We'll have to make port soon. Ranit will need medicine."

Emery blinked at the sudden subject change. She should have been thrilled to hear these words, but to her surprise she felt nothing. Her heart lay heavy and cold in her chest. Perhaps the nightmarish day had finally caught up with her, because all she felt was numb.

"Oh," she responded, matching his non-committal gaze, and for the rest of the night they sat in silence, adrift in their own minds until sleep finally took her.

When she awoke to dawn breaking across the horizon outside the window, the blanket was now around her shoulders, and Sean was gone.

# Chapter Twenty-Five

R anit screamed.
   And moaned.
And wept.

For the past two days and nights, his horrible wailing had punctured the air around them, louder than any wind or noise from the sea. Even when Ranit fell into unconsciousness, his cries reverberated around Emery's skull in never-ending witness to his suffering.

Now, at the end of the third day, Emery had come to perch on the end of the bowsprit with her hands clamped over her ears, desperate for reprieve, but even here she could hear him. Guilt still chewed on her insides, and when she slept, nightmares plagued her. Nightmares about missing arms and manic varens, and blood, always so much blood.

The worst part was not being able to do anything for him. They didn't even have medicine on board, nothing to dull the pain except for copious amounts of alcohol, so, when Ranit wasn't wailing from the pain, he was drinking himself into oblivion. Now that was slowly running out too.

Sliding her hands from her ears, Emery braced herself for more screaming. But it seemed to have ceased. She waited for it to start again, but all she could hear were the sails flapping above, the wind whistling in her ears and the crew calling to each other.

Until someone said her name.

Heart thrashing, she twisted to find Sean standing by her, one foot on the platform and the other still on the bowsprit.

"Teralyn's teeth," she breathed, ignoring her aching ribs as she got to her feet. "How are you so silent?"

He shrugged. "Comes with the occupation."

She edged aside so he could step fully onto the platform. Though there wasn't much room for them both to stand, he seemed to be taking care not to touch her. He gazed at the distant horizon, smudges of purple underscoring his glassy eyes, looking exhausted and almost detached from the world around him. He'd rarely left Ranit's side since their last conversation, and Emery suspected he'd slept even less then her these past nights.

"We'll be seeing land soon," he said.

Emery followed his gaze to the smear of blue where the sky and sea collided. A flame of hope sizzled inside her, but she tried to dampen it down. "If we're going to a port..."

"I stand by my promise. You can leave if you wish. Only..."

"Only what?"

He ran a hand through his hair, keeping his gaze straight ahead. "Where we're going...it's dangerous. I wouldn't advise you to be there alone, for any amount of time."

"What exactly are you saying? That you want to keep me here after all?"

"No, I – that's not..." Sean's mouth worked as if he couldn't find the right words. "You can go. You can. I would just...urge you to consider that there are worse places to be than this ship."

"Fine. I'll consider that when I see the place."

But in truth, she had already considered that. After everything that happened, she was certain she was safe aboard the *Audacity*, at least from the crew and their captain. She was sure now that Sean had been telling the truth when he said he never meant her harm.

But if she stayed aboard the *Audacity*, she'd never find her brother. Sean was running *from* Tavor, while she needed to go *to* Tavor. Dangerous or not, on land she would immediately have greater options for finding a way back to her brother, and for searching for a cure. Those were two things she wouldn't give up on no matter the hazards.

The ship creaked as someone – most likely Billy – turned the wheel to adjust the *Audacity's* course. The sudden movement lurched Emery's shoulder into Sean's, and he quickly inched away so that they were no longer touching. She grabbed one of the lines to steady herself and tried to ignore his blatant distancing, annoyed she had noticed it in the first place, even more so that it bothered her.

"So, what's this place we're going?"

He cleared his throat. "Brimlad."

"Is that the island or the village?"

"Both," Sean said. "The island is so small it only has one village."

"And why is it so bad?"

He didn't answer immediately, instead turned to face her properly. "It's a place run by crooks and pirates, with little in the way of laws and alot in the way of debauchery."

"Why go there, then?"

"Varens rarely bother with the place, so it's relatively safe in that sense. And you can find anything there for cheap, including the medicine we need for Ranit,"

Silence settled between them, and together they watched the sun dip below the horizon, casting the world in inky darkness. Not long after, a small orb of golden light appeared, so faint at first that she had to look twice.

"Is that it?"

"That's it."

The golden light began to swell as the *Audacity* skimmed the sea towards Brimlad. Emery clung to the lines, her entire body feeling like it would float away if she let go. Those lights meant land. Those lights *were* land. Not only did that mean finding Liam and Caelin, and maybe even a cure for Ayana and the others, it would also be the very first place she'd set eyes on besides Orabel.

She had dreamt of this moment for as long as she could remember, although never had she imagined she'd be standing next to a Forbidden when it happened. It didn't matter. For the first time since waking up on the *Audacity*, she allowed herself to think about all the reasons she had wanted so badly to come out into the world. To help her sister, to defeat the Withering, the curiosity of what lay beyond Orabel's borders. But also, the painful, driving need to know what had become of her parents. What had happened to them, or why had they chosen not to return.

The golden lights glittered on the horizon, expanding as they approached. Sean, however, barely glanced at them. Instead, she could tell he was watching her face.

"Have you never been anywhere besides your homeland before?" he asked.

Emery bit her lip, realizing she must have been gaping like a fool at the oncoming lights. There seemed little point in lying now. "No. Never."

His gaze lingered on her, intense as any physical touch. She kept her eyes fixed on the lights, feeling her cheeks heat.

"It's a shame this will be the first of the world you see."

She turned to look at him then, but he had already slipped back down the bowsprit to the deck.

He returned a few moments later just as silently. This time, he was holding a long, sleek stick in his hand, with a sheath to go with it.

Her lim.

"If you insist on leaving, you'll probably need this back."

Emery's heart clenched as she took it from him, running her hands over the protruding end. "You've had it all this time?"

She didn't know how to feel. Elation that it wasn't rotting at the bottom of the sea. Despair, thinking how differently things could have gone had she been able to use it this entire time. Anger that he'd taken it. Most of all, relief at having it back in her hands.

Before she could voice any of this, Sean also swung a sack off his shoulder, and held it out to her. "And you'll need supplies. There's a map. Some clothes. A few coins that will at least buy you a meal or two."

Speechless, she took the sack. She'd lost the other map she took in the ocean during the sea monster attack.

Lastly, he held up his compass. She'd placed it back on his desk after he'd saved her, as if she'd never taken it at all. "And you can have this, too."

She looked up at him as her hand slowly closed over the compass, her fingers brushing his, and they momentarily held it at the same time. Whatever initial indignation she'd felt upon learning he'd had her lim this whole time had vanished. Instead, a lump formed in her throat. "Thank you."

He shrugged, as if it was nothing. "I worked hard to keep you alive. It would be a waste to let you die now."

"Right." She didn't know what else to say, and for a moment she held his gaze, trying to figure out this puzzle of a man.

But then he released the compass, his fingers slipping out from under hers. "I'd better relieve Billy at the helm." And he slipped away again.

She watched him go, and then turned back to the horizon, clutching the compass to her chest. It was still warm from his grasp.

The golden lights were now morphing into a vaguely bean-shaped island that looked no bigger than Orabel. Indeed, Sean delicately directed the *Audacity* into a bay that appeared to be larger than the island itself.

The crew scrambled about as they neared the dock, and soon the mooring lines had been cast and the *Audacity* was bobbing snugly between two other ships. With a clank, Farley and

Camulus lowered a plank across the divide between the ship and dock edge.

With her lim slung across her back, the sack around her shoulder, and the compass now safe in her pocket, Emery began her descent from the bowsprit as the crew gathered on deck.

"First things first," said Sean, stepping up to the others. "Let's contact Scal, see if he'll take some of the cargo. Rooney, if you would."

Without a word, Rooney set off into the night at a brisk pace. Not long after, he returned with a portly man who immediately approached Sean. This outsider's slicked back hair gleamed under the whale-oil lights hanging about the ship. His shrewd eyes hungrily scanned the ship as they began to converse, and a smug smile peered through his beard.

Something about this newcomer made Emery uncomfortable, so rather than join the group she wandered over to the railing to get a better look at the island sprawling before them. The night was too dark and the village too far away for her to really see anything, and, though she itched with desire to have land under her feet again, she had to admit she didn't want to go alone, not yet at least.

The crew led Scal down to the ship's hold. When they emerged again, none of them looked happy.

"You're ripping us off and you know it," said Sean, glaring. "That lot is worth at least three royals."

"I don't have to take this junk, you know." Scal's shot. "I've seen better loads today and paid next to nothing for them. Take what I offer or don't. Makes no difference to me."

Sean's anger was melting into dismay. "Three spades will barely get us what we need."

"Not my problem." Scal held out a grubby hand and looked up at him expectantly.

Billy stepped behind Sean and patted him lightly on the back.

Sean frowned, closed his eyes for a moment, then held out his hand.

Scal dropped a few shiny things that clinked like pebbles into the captain's palm. "My men will come by in an hour."

The crew glared at him as he ambled off the ship.

Sean sighed. "You all deserve some fun and rest. Go enjoy a warm meal and an actual bed."

"And the medicine?" asked Camulus.

"I'll see what I can find." Sean looked down at his palm. "I might have enough."

Camulus stepped closer. "I'll come with you."

Sean shook his head. "No. You should all take the night off." Camulus opened her mouth to argue, but he cut her off. "That's an order."

Camulus fumed, but Aleksy put an arm round her shoulders and led her and the others towards the village. Only Billy and Rooney remained behind.

Emery followed them as far as the plank but felt compelled to wait a little longer. Perhaps Camulus was right, and Sean shouldn't go anywhere on his own. With her lim returned to her, they could watch each other's backs while he completed this short mission. It would be for Ranit's sake, and then they could go their separate ways as agreed.

"Billy." Sean sounded more exasperated than anything else. "Go."

"No, I'll stay," said Billy. "I'll watch Ranit and help Rooney supervise Scal's men, you go find the medicine. He needs it sooner rather than later, and your legs are younger than mine."

Sean looked like he was going to argue, but Billy gave him a disarming smile and he nodded instead, seemingly deciding against playing the captain card again. "Alright."

"Be careful."

Sean headed for the plank, slowing when he saw her standing there. "You haven't run off yet."

"I'm still considering."

"I see." And she swore she saw a hint of a smile in the dim light.

"I'm also considering continuing to consider while going with you wherever it is you're going now."

He seemed surprised to hear these words from her, but for Emery such a decision was no longer a hard one. If her choices were uncertain danger or a Forbidden who had never actually harmed her, she'd rather stick with the latter until she got her bearings.

Besides, Ayana also needed medicine.

He led them down the plank and across a wooden structure he referred to as a *pier*. At the other edge, they reached a sandy shore that separated the sea from the mass of foliage obstructing the view of the town. Orange lights filtered through the fern fronds and palm leaves but otherwise Emery could see nothing of Brimlad proper.

She took a moment to wiggle her toes in the soft sand before following Sean. He swayed slightly with every step, as if his body missed the feeling of rolling waves beneath him. Indeed, Emery felt slightly wobbly on her own feet and hoped the sensation didn't last long. She also noticed the scabbard at Sean's hip, the butt of a pistol poking from his belt. Touching the tip of her lim to reassure herself, she wondered what other weapons he'd felt it necessary to carry.

As they crossed the beach and headed for Brimlad, Sean suddenly stopped and turned to face her. "Promise me one thing, at least until you're done considering."

"What?"

"Don't leave my side, for anything. And don't trust anyone."

# Chapter Twenty-Six

E mery and Sean crossed the beach and stepped onto a dirt path that cut through a thin jungle of palm trees and ferns, and led to the outskirts of Brimlad. Despite Sean's warning, Emery's first impression still made her recoil. The ground here was muddy. Dozens of square-sided, ramshackle buildings were littered about, some made from multiple planks of wood like the outsiders' ships and drooping in on themselves as if they were rotten. Their foundations were sinking into the muddy ground and their straw roofs sported various holes, as if the straw had decayed in places and no one had bothered replacing it. Further into the village the buildings were built from piles of stones stacked vertically to make walls.

Grimy men and women clogged the narrow streets, most of them stumbling about clutched half-empty bottles. The men were yelling bawdy songs at the women, who were wearing dresses that were gigantic at the bottom and airy on top, and who had what looked like colorful paint on their lips, eyelids, and cheeks.

Sean frowned at Emery, almost apologetically. "Not what you were hoping for, is it?"

"Not really." She covered her nose with a sleeve to ward off the horrific smell burning her nostrils, one that only grew stronger as they wandered further in.

Even Sean was scrunching his nose. "That would be the sweat of a few hundred sailors and, if I'm not mistaken, human feces."

As he led them further in, Sean's eyes darted over every person and down every street, his hand constantly hovering over the pommel of his blade. He steered them around anyone who appeared in their path, keeping as wide a berth as the narrow streets allowed. The people around them seemed to be turning ever wilder, and Emery had to concede she was glad that Sean was with her.

A group of men had converged at the end of the street ahead of them, and it soon became clear they had congregated over something lying in a heap at their feet. It was another man, sprawled on his back in the mud, his face covered with muck and blood. The others were kicking him repeatedly. He groaned every time, but never moved.

"Hey!" Emery shouted. "What are you –"

Sean pulled her behind him as the circle of men turned to glare at her. "That was not a good idea," he whispered.

"But they're hurting him," she hissed back.

"That's what people do here. They hurt each other."

Sean tried to steer them around the group, but one of the men stepped in their way, bloodshot eyes scouring Emery's body.

"Oy, lookie here!" His rancid breath choked her even from two arms' lengths away. "See this fine lass here."

"She looks a treat," a second one said, licking his chapped lips.

"How much are you worth, lass?" the first man asked. "I bet you're mighty expensive."

Emery glared in response, bile threatening to fill her mouth.

Sean moved so close that their sides pressed together and draped an arm around her waist. "She's already spoken for, gents." The pleasantry in his voice had a frosty edge. "Now, be good lads and back off."

Most of the men eyed Sean's face, then his weapons, and

shrank into the shadows of a neighboring alleyway. The first man, however, slowed his steps so that he fell behind the others, continuing to gaze at Emery like he wanted nothing else in the world.

Emery stared straight ahead as they left the group behind, distracted partly by her crawling skin, partly by the sensation of Sean's arm still around her middle.

As soon as they rounded the next corner and had reliably vanished from the men's view, he removed his arm and took half a step away.

"Thank you," she choked, wrapping her own arms around herself and trying to ignore how unpleasantly exposed she suddenly felt with so much space between them.

As if sensing her thoughts, Sean narrowed the distance again, enough that their shoulders brushed as they walked. The instinct to lean into him was so strong it left her dizzy. Instead, she focused on the way the mud sucked at her feet and squished between her toes. Seeing her glance down, Sean followed her gaze. "I should have given you some boots, too."

"It's fine."

"There might be broken glass though. Just watch your step."

She smiled up at him, bewildered once again by his thoughtfulness. "You're really making it difficult to dislike you."

He sent her an unreadable look. "I could say the same about you." While she had tried to sound light, his tone was heavier, like not disliking each other was a bad thing.

They stopped in front of a wooden building shoved into the darkest corner of an alley. A rickety sign hung over the door, splattered with what Emery hoped was peeling red paint.

Sean let out a breath, then stuck his hand in his pocket. Something jingled.

"What did that man give you earlier? For your goods."

"Coin." He pulled out his hand, which was still wrapped in the leather palm guard, three small circles of silver metal now sitting in his palm. "But not very much."

"This is what you buy food with?"

"And medicine, hopefully."

"Why are these things so valuable?" She prodded them, unable to think of a single use for them, save perhaps making a trinket.

The corner of Sean's mouth quirked up. "They're not. It's just the system."

"Seems like a stupid system."

Sean snorted and turned to knock on the door. "New to the world and you already have it figured out."

"Wait!" Emery swung the sack from her shoulder and rummaged around until she had a handful of coins herself. She offered them to Sean. "Use these too."

"You'll need those."

"Ranit needs medicine more." When Sean still didn't take them, she shoved them into his hand.

With a sharp creak, the door swung outwards, and they both stepped back to avoid having their noses crushed. A relatively short man, about level with Emery's chest, was standing in the doorway wearing a tattered cloak. The hood was thrown over his face, but Emery could make out teeth glinting through the murk, and the giant blade strapped to his back rendered the overall image somewhat terrifying.

Sean was also tense beside her, his voice strained. "I have business with Petter. Is he in?"

The man leaned against the doorframe. "Depends on the business."

Sean glanced up and down the street. Both sides were deserted for the time being, save for a drunken man serenading an upturned barrel. "I need some golden iris."

"And you've brought payment?"

Sean jingled the coins with his hand closed around them.

The hooded man stepped aside, waving Sean into the dark building beyond. The Forbidden swept in, but when Emery made to follow the man held out a hand to stop her. "Not you."

"She's with me," said Sean. His voice was calm now, but Emery didn't miss his fingers closing over the hilt of his blade.

"She's not coming in." The man stepped further into the doorway, as if to stop her bolting past. "She's untrustworthy."

"How so?" Emery demanded. "I haven't even said anything yet."

"Doesn't matter," he sneered. "I don't recognize her face and I don't like the look of you."

"She's fine," Sean insisted. "And we'll be in and out in a minute."

"She can wait out here with me."

Sean stared up at the dark ceiling for a moment, then pushed his way out again. "Let's go back to the ship. I'll come back later."

"No." Emery crossed her arms. "Ranit needs it now. Just...do what you have to do. I'll be fine."

She could come back at a later point herself and see if this place had medicine suitable for Ayana and the others, when hopefully a more accommodating person would be at the door. At least she now knew where to start looking.

"She'll be fine," the cloaked man echoed.

Sean shot him a glare, then ran a hand through his hair.

"I won't go anywhere," she said, and meant it. After what she'd already seen of the town, she was beginning to wonder if it really was worth staying. Her brother, Caelin and Tavor wouldn't have lingered in a place like this, not if they could at all help it, and nothing had so far inspired confidence that anyone would be willing or able to help her find them. Nor did she imagine her parents having ended up here.

Sean sighed and slipped a dagger from his boot, pressing it into her hand and folding her fingers around the pommel. "I won't be long."

Emery stared down at the weapon, so much heavier in her hand than it looked. The metal gleamed in the light cast from the stars above and the distant glow of streetlamps, and she prayed she wouldn't have to use it.

She nodded, and when Sean continued to hesitate, she

turned him around and shoved him towards the door. He cast her a quick look, then stepped into the darkness beyond.

The cloaked man slammed the door behind him, then stood in front of it with his arms crossed.

Emery crossed her own arms in return, careful not to cut herself with the dagger.

The man sniggered, and she glared at him. "So, lass." He leaned against the doorframe again. "That's an interesting accent you've got there. Where are you from?"

She didn't answer, though it amused her that she was the one being questioned about how she spoke. He was the one with the accent after all, and on top of that it was further different from the one Tavor and Sean shared, although not far off Billy and Rooney's.

She squished her toes into the mud. "Where are *you* from?"

"That's not for little lassies like you to know."

She raised an eyebrow but thought better of pointing out that she was taller than him.

The man huffed when she didn't respond but said nothing more. She stared up at the blinking stars and waited for Sean to return.

Soon, it was clear he was taking longer than planned, and her stomach began to churn with nerves. "What's going on in there?"

The man shrugged, making his cloak rustle. "Perhaps he didn't bring enough coin."

She thought of the tiny handful of pieces Sean had with him. "And if he didn't?"

The man shrugged again. "Petter won't like that."

Her fingers tightened around the blade, and she considered stepping closer, demanding to be let in, but a chorus of laughter brought her up short. The men from before were stumbling down the alley towards them, singing and punching each other on the arms. Emery shrank back against the building, folding herself into the shadows, but it was too late. The man with bloodshot eyes had already spotted her.

He threw out his arms, stopping his friends in their tracks.

"Well! If it isn't that lovely treat!" His voice sent shivers up her spine. "Still spoken for, are we?"

Emery stepped away from the wall, holding herself straight and passing the blade slowly in front of her in the hope it would catch the light. "I am indeed. In fact" – she indicated the house next to her – "he's just in there."

The ringleader leered. "Then he won't mind us having a bit of fun with you, will he, while he's...occupied."

She cast a pleading look at the cloaked man still standing in the doorway. He opened the door and Emery leapt towards it but the cloaked man was already hopping inside, giving her an ironic salute.

"Wait! You –"

The door slammed in her face, the fierceness of the locking vibrating through the walls

Her stomach dropped to her knees as the group stepped closer still, but she turned to face them, making sure her voice didn't betray her nerves. "If I'm gone when he comes out, he'll make you eat your fingers."

"I'd like to see him try," the ringleader rasped, bloodshot eyes narrowing, inches from hers now.

Her heart stilled as if trying to hide inside her chest, and she attempted not to inhale the man's sour breath. "He's done it before."

"How much are you worth, lassie?"

Emery didn't quite understand the question. She thought it had something to do with coins and the man offering to exchange them for something she absolutely was not willing to give.

When she didn't answer, he said, "Every woman has her price. Ain't that right, lads?"

The others grunted in agreement, and Emery's bravery began to slip from her like sand through fingers.

The man's voice was edged with frustration now, and something else she didn't want to name. "Well then, if you don't have a price, I guess we shall take you for free."

Terror shot through her, but she calculated quickly. He was getting riled up, she could use that against him.

"I have no price for a man who apparently eats pig dung."

Cursing at her, he sprang forward, and she kicked him straight in his groin. He collapsed, writhing and groaning, and before the others could react, she took off past them, out into the street beyond.

Mud sprayed everywhere as she ran, sticking to her feet, trying to slow her down, but she kept going, clutching her aching ribs, ignoring the sharp pain every time she sucked in a breath. The men were behind her again, shouting incoherent obscenities. She dashed in and out of muddy alleyways and filthy streets, sliding through muck and crashing into walls. She ran until the shouts finally grew distant, until her ribs screamed in agony and her legs burned. Turning the corner into a quiet street, she threw herself behind a large crate and folded herself as small as she could.

The street remained empty but she stayed put for a while, closing her eyes and focusing on breathing, even though the air smelled like vomit and worse. The mud she was sitting in began to suck the heat from her body, and the shivers that came over her made her ribs ache even more.

After she was sure enough time had passed, she peered out from behind the crate, checking the street in both directions. It remained unused and silent, save for the sound of lewd singing somewhere in the distance. If anything, the stillness was more unsettling than having a rowdy crowd to hide behind.

Taking a deep breath, she began to creep along the street, pressing herself against the buildings and keeping to the shadows where she could. She had to be honest with herself, the thing she most wanted to do now was find Sean. She might have weapons and training, she might have a mission to complete – or several – but nothing was going to make her feel safer and more capable right now than being back in his presence.

The realization hit her hard. She *had* felt safe with him. Completely and utterly, and she craved that feeling again.

But where was he? Where was *she?*

Her fingers tightened around the dagger as she turned around, certain she was going in the wrong direction. Facing the right way again, she nearly jumped out of her skin at the sight of a lone figure standing in the middle of the street, clearly watching her.

The person was too short and thin to be any of the men who had been pursuing her, and was just standing there, still, and silent, wearing a black cloak that puddled on the ground behind them. A hood hid their face, reminding her of the man back at the building Sean had disappeared inside, but it wasn't him either.

The figure glided towards her as if drifting on air. "Emery, my dear child," came a raspy, crackling voice. "You have finally found me."

Every muscle in Emery's body tensed at the sound of her name. She couldn't move, couldn't speak. A mixture of horror and wonder gripped her in place.

"I am not going to hurt you, dear child." Two gnarled hands slid back the figure's hood to reveal the weathered face of an elderly woman. "Come with me." She turned and began drifting away again down the dark street, turning only briefly to glance back at Emery. "I have something to show you."

# Chapter Twenty-Seven

Emery clutched her throbbing ribs as she followed the woman down various streets and alleyways. Heaps of rotting trash littered the ground and the mud squishing between her toes was warm and watery. She tried not to think about what she might be walking through, and kept her eyes trained on the woman's back.

The woman drifted along like a ghost, and when she disappeared into a pocket of shadows Emery wondered for a moment whether she had literally glided through the wall of one of the stone buildings lining the alley. Then her eyes adjusted, and a door materialized in the gloom. She shook off some of her unease, but still hesitated before stepping through herself. One thought convinced her though; this woman, for whatever reason, knew who she was. Perhaps she'd been in contact with Tavor, Liam, or Caelin. Or perhaps this meant she knew her parents.

Shadows swallowed her as she stepped into a dim hallway covered in dust and cobwebs. Ahead of her, the woman was climbing a rickety set of stairs, leaving a shining trail on the otherwise dusty handrail. The steps made no noise as she ascended, but then creaked and groaned under Emery's feet, as if they might collapse at any moment.

The stairs led to a tiny chamber with a lonely sconce flickering on the far wall. The dim orange light illuminated the grime on the walls and various cobwebs draped over the furniture, but not much else. Two wooden chairs stood upon a moth-eaten rug in the center of the room and a damp fireplace sat empty in one corner, a bowed bookshelf in the other. The stale air felt like it lingered in Emery's lungs even when she breathed out.

The woman bent over the fireplace. A moment later, flames roared to life, casting eerie shadows across the walls and heating the room to such a degree that whatever clean air had survived until then was sucked away.

"Sit," she said, gliding into a separate room that was so dark Emery hadn't noticed it until now.

Emery edged towards the chairs, the rug spitting up puffs of dust with every step, and lowered herself onto one of them with a loud creak. When the woman didn't return immediately, her grip began to tighten on her dagger. Perhaps this was a trap of some kind, and this was her last chance to bolt. But then her mysterious host drifted back in carrying two chipped mugs. She handed one to Emery, her bony arm seeming to shake with the effort, and wandered over to the second chair. Sitting down, she peered at Emery with her drooping eyes, and a smile stretched her pale lips. "Drink, my dear."

Emery eyed the mug, trying to hide her disgust. It was chipped in several places and looked like it hadn't ever been washed. Inside was a serving of chunky brown water with algae floating on top.

But the woman was watching her with an eager smile.

Keeping her lips firmly closed, Emery raised the drink to her mouth and pretended to sip. The mug had a slightly acrid smell. "Thank you," she said, lowering it to her lap.

"You look just like your mother did at your age."

Emery nearly spilled her water. "You know her?"

"Where is your brother?"

"He's —" The hope faded, painfully, that this woman would know, that perhaps Liam had been the one who had described

Emery to her in the first place. Now, she had to accept she didn't know anything about this stranger, her motivations. As with Sean, she'd have to try not to give all her cards away first. "How do you know my mother? And do you know my father as well?"

The woman said nothing but stood up from her chair with shaky limbs. She left the room again, and this time Emery rose as well, ready to follow her – or flee, depending on what happened next. The woman returned a moment later, alone again, and this time cupping a small wooden box. "For you, my dear."

Emery had no interest in a box right now. "How do you know my family?"

The woman kept moving forward, forcing her to sit back down, then dropped the box in her lap. Emery nearly lost her grip on the dagger as she reached up to stabilized it. The woman chuckled wheezily as she returned to her chair.

The box fit inside the palm of Emery's hand and weighed very little. "What is this?"

"I don't know." The woman cackled.

Emery turned the box over, firelight washing over each of its smooth sides in turn. Symbols curled along its edges, skillfully etched into the dark wood, but she couldn't find any seams. "How does it open?"

"Don't know."

"Can you at least tell me what's inside?"

"Don't know!"

Frustration boiled under Emery's skin. "Who gave it to you?"

"Your parents."

Emery took a deep breath. She had to stay calm. "How do you know my parents?"

The woman stared back as if she hadn't the slightest idea what Emery was saying.

Emery chewed her lip. She had to try a different approach. "Alright. Can you at least tell me who are you? Please?"

"My child." The woman sounded insulted that Emery didn't already know. "I am Great Aunt Liliath."

Emery stared at this utterly unfamiliar woman claiming to be her relation, hope and suspicion warring within her. What were the chances of stumbling upon a great aunt she didn't even know but who somehow recognized her, and somewhere like this of all places?

"Your mother and father made such a darling couple," said Liliath, oblivious to the turmoil in Emery's head. "They were both wonderful people."

A lump began to form in Emery's throat. "Were?"

"Or are," Liliath drawled, as if the difference between those words meant nothing. "One can never be sure these days."

Emery gripped the box so hard she was surprised it didn't implode. "So...you don't know where they are, or might be?"

Liliath stared at her blankly.

Emery centered herself. "Aunt Liliath, are my parents still alive?"

"One can never be sure, my dear," she repeated with a wistful smile.

Emery bit her lip so hard she tasted blood. She'd never felt so close to her parents, and yet she was getting no real information. She studied the woman claiming to be her great aunt, searching for some sort of familial resemblance. But Liliath's face was so wrinkled, her skin so papery, it arguably distorted her appearance. The woman could have been older than anyone she'd laid eyes on before, except for the Arch-Elemists.

The realization struck her. There was at least one test she could give her.

"Aunt Liliath, are you an elemist?"

The woman's smile stretched into a grin and her dull eyes brightened. She raised a bony hand and snapped her fingers. The flames in the fireplace rose and morphed into a ball, hovering like a tiny sun within the hearth. Emery shrieked and jumped to her feet as the flames threw themselves at Liliath, engulfing the woman from head to toe. But like with Smythee, the fire only burned *around* her, then blinked out.

Liliath was gone.

The room was also dark again, save for the lone sconce burning on the wall.

Emery stared at the empty chair across from her. She'd never seen anyone use their gifts like that, to disappear. She wondered whether anyone back home knew it was even possible.

Her entire body shaking, she tucked the box into one of the pockets of her trousers and hurried down the creaky staircase, suddenly wanting to be far away from this building. She walked as fast as she could without running, hurrying down one street and up another without any idea where she was going. All she could see was the giant ball of flame swallowing Liliath in front of her eyes, all she could hear was, *they were both wonderful people.*

If that was true, why hadn't they gone back to Orabel for their children?

"Do what you want to me, you're not getting it back."

The voice blew Emery's thoughts away like a cloud of smoke. Sean.

She stopped in her tracks and peered around the corner of one of the shabby stone buildings. Across the street from her, a group of men were standing in the shadows of a dead-end alley. One of them shoved another in the chest. "Petter will have your thumbs for this, scum."

The shoved man took a step backwards but didn't lose his balance. "He'll have to wake up first."

Emery's heart plummeted. Sean stood tall amongst the other men, but he was surrounded, and the night's soft light illuminated the blood already running from a cut on his lip. She flinched as one of the men punched him in the stomach and he doubled over in pain.

The man grabbed a chunk of Sean's hair, pulling him up hard. "You think you can get away with stealing from Petter? He owns this island. And we know where your friend is." The man nodded at two others, who broke away from the group and slid into the shadows of an adjacent alley. The man finally released Sean, whose carefully blank expression had begun to crack, and gave him a smile that looked especially wicked in the moonlight.

"Unless we get back what's rightfully ours, we'll kill everyone on your ship."

Sean shot sideways, plowing one of his assailants into the alley wall with a resounding crack. The man slumped to the ground, joining a second body Emery hadn't noticed previously. Sean spun and kicked a third man in the chest, sending him sprawling over a wooden crate. The first man tried to grab him by the throat but missed as Sean twisted, bringing an elbow up into his nose. Steel flashed as a fourth man bashed the hilt of his blade into the back of Sean's head, driving him to his knees. Sean tried to get up, only to receive a kick to the chest that sent him flying onto his back.

The first man pinned a filthy boot onto Sean's chest with a stream of curses, stemming the flow of blood from his nose with a beefy hand and flicking the tip of a broadsword against Sean's throat. "I've had about enough of you."

Until this moment, the fight had been too quick for Emery to gauge how to intervene. Now, the sight of a sword at Sean's throat forced her from the shadows. She stepped across the street and into the alley with a veneer of calm Sean would have been proud of, and kept her voice clean and sharp. "I think that's enough, don't you?"

The first man twisted, glaring at her with bloodshot eyes, and she realized this was the same ringleader and group who had chased her earlier. "Well, I'll be damned. The lass has changed her mind."

Emery shuddered inwardly but kept her expression hard.

"Smart girl, eh Del?" the second man purred, placing his own sword to Sean's throat, leaving Del free to stare her down and start creeping towards her.

Emery forced her back to stay straight, her hands to remain still at her sides, though her grip tightened on the dagger. She allowed Del's bloodshot eyes to wander where they wanted, flicking her own gaze briefly to Sean. Real fear flashed across his face.

"Why don't we talk this through?" she said to Del, who was

barely a few feet from her now. It occurred to her that imitating the language she had been hearing around her might add weight to the suggestion. "Like men."

Del barked a laugh. "You're no man."

"She's got more balls than you," snapped Sean, earning himself a swift kick in the face from Del's assistant.

Emery flinched, but kept her eyes on Del. "I'm sure we can come up with something...pleasing for both sides. Perhaps a trade? We must have something of equal value to whatever you're missing."

Del's smile turned slimy and his eyes began to scour her body, pausing where the collar of her tunic fell slightly open. "I can already think of something."

Emery just about managed to keep her face blank. "That is not on the table."

"Oh, you'll be on a table alright," the second man guffawed.

She could feel Sean's tension rising to match her own.

Del's smile widened and Emery's pulse picked up speed. This was not going how she had hoped. Back home, they talked through everything. If that didn't work, well...

"How about a duel then?" Her voice was calmer than she felt, knowing now how unfairly people fought out here.

Both Del and his second burst into grating laughter.

Good. Let them underestimate her.

She pressed on. "If I win, he goes free. If you win, you get your medicine back."

Del made a show of catching his breath and wiping tears from his dirt-streaked face. "How about if I win, my little darling, we go find that table?"

Emery's stomach curdled. "Fine."

"No!" Sean rolled sideways, kicking the second man's knees out from under him. A scuffle ensued, ending with the sword now pointing at Sean's eye.

Del chuckled at the sight, then turned his vile sneer back to Emery. "Fists or firearms?"

"Non-firing weapons."

He eyed the small dagger in her hand and chuckled again, fingering the sharp edge of his broadsword.

Emery slung her sack from her shoulders and dropped it to the side. She lifted her blade slightly, felt its weight, and made a quick calculation. She wasn't used to its feel, hadn't trained with it for years. It would only hold her back.

Keeping her eyes on Del's, she tossed the dagger to the wall with a clank, then drew her lim and set its end on the ground in front of her, keeping her stance loose.

Del frowned. "Is this a joke?"

Anger flared, giving her a boost of bravery. "Less of a joke than all of you struggling to take down one man." She nodded at Sean, whose concern seemed to be mixing with confusion at her tactics.

Del stepped closer, bringing his beefy fingers up to her cheek. "It's a shame we'll have to muddle up that pretty face of –"

With a quick whipping willow, Emery slammed her lim against his inside forearm while driving the palm of her other hand into his elbow. Del screamed as his arm snapped, then doubled over, clutching his now useless appendage. Seizing her advantage, Emery swung up into his face, sending him flying backwards into the mud.

Sean had also managed to topple the other man again, and the two were now writhing around further down the alley. She quickly started circling them, but the corner they'd landed in was so dark she couldn't tell which was Sean and which the man she wanted to strike.

Exploiting her brief distraction, Del rushed up from behind and grabbed her by the throat with his good arm. He slammed her onto her back, driving the air from her lungs and bolts of agony through her ribs. The shock of the fall hurled the lim from her hands, but before she could reach for it Del dropped on top of her, pinning her arms with his knees. His eyes were gleaming in an altogether different way now and blood was gushing from his nose. She kicked up savagely at his back, but all the movement achieved was ripping a chunk of her hair out that had also been trapped beneath him.

Del's functioning hand grabbed her throat as he launched a string of the vilest expletives at her.

Then he began to squeeze, tighter and tighter.

Emery's lungs burned as she struggled furiously against him. Shadows soon began to paint the edges of her vision, and all she could see was Del's blood-drenched smile.

A flash of metal collided with Del's head and he slumped sideways, freeing her at last. She clawed her way out from under him, coughing and sucking in the pungent air.

Sean was standing over him, clutching his sword with shaking hands. Emery couldn't help recoiling from him for a moment. He'd never looked more dangerous, not even back when he'd tried to murder Tavor. His expression was dark and twisted, and he snarled like an animal when Del attempted to rise from the ground. This time though, rather than strike him with the blade, Sean shifted the air between them, shoving Del backwards and pinning him against the wall.

Her attacker gaped up at him in terror. "You're one of them demons!"

"Aye. They call me The Scourge of The Sea."

Del's face paled further. "You – "

Fury burned in Sean's eyes and his voice just as fierce as the wind ripped at his hair and clothes. "And you can tell Petter that if he ever so much as looks at any of my crew again, I'll come for him."

Del nodded in quick jerks. The wind began to soften and he backed away, sliding along the wall until he nearly fell out into the street. Then he ran.

As soon as the sound of his footsteps had vanished, Sean dropped his sword and whirled to face Emery. The rage had died away, and all that remained was distress. He dropped to his knees beside her, reaching out as if to touch her but then stopping short. "Are you alright? Did he hurt you?"

Emery's blood was roaring in her ears, and she simultaneously wanted to cry and launch herself after Del and finish him off. Instead, she threw her arms around Sean and buried her face in his neck.

His body tensed against hers, but slowly his arms settled around her shoulders. Her fingers dug into his tunic as she fought to settle her breath. The warmth of his skin was a comfort against her cheek, and for a moment she just focused on that sensation. The rest of her body had gone numb.

But then new panic gripped her, and she pulled away. "Those other men went after Ranit, didn't they?"

As soon as the words had left her mouth, boots came squelching through the mud towards them. Sean grabbed the sword once more and launched to his feet.

But it was Rooney who materialized out of the darkness, dragging two men, face down, by their ankles behind him. "I stopped them before they could get to the *Audacity*."

Sean breathed a long sigh. "Thank you." But then something seemed to occur to him, and his eyes narrowed. "Wait a minute. How did you know what was going on?"

Rooney didn't answer right. "I was looking for you, to tell you Scal's men finished unloading their cargo."

"Rooney..." Sean's voice took on a quiet, dangerous tone. Clearly, he didn't believe him crewman. "You weren't...following me again, were you?"

Rooney shifted uncomfortably. Then crossed his arms and snapped, "Well, it was a good thing I was, wasn't it?"

Anger darkened Sean's face. "I asked you to stop doing that. I don't need a goddamned minder."

Rooney's eyes flicked around the scene in front of him, from the blood on Sean's face to Emery still kneeling on the ground, to the unconscious bodies surrounding them. "Sean, with all –"

Sean stomped up to him, putting his face right in front of his friend's. "Do. Not. Follow. Me. Again. That is an *order*. Here." He pulled a small bottle from one of his deeper pockets and thrust it at Rooney. "Here's what you need for Ranit, now leave me in peace."

He threw a glance over his shoulder at Emery, opened his mouth as if to say something else, but then closed it again and marched out onto the street, disappearing around the corner.

Emery stared after him for a moment, feeling a little dazed.

"Are you alright?" Rooney asked, pocketing the bottle carefully.

She nodded, slowly scrambling up into standing again. "Thank you."

"I'd better get back to the ship." He started heading out of the alley. "And you should probably go after him." He gestured in the direction Sean had stormed, then melted away into the dark street himself.

Emery reached down to gather her fallen lim. Just beyond it, a incongruously white feather lay in the mud. She felt her hair, her own feather was now missing. It must have come out in the struggle.

Shuddering at the memory, she snatched up the feather, gathered the dagger and the sack she'd cast aside before the fight, and sprinted after Sean, hoping never to encounter that pile of unconscious men again.

# Chapter Twenty-Eight

E mery raced after Sean's disappearing back. Her fighting
drive was gone, and all that remained was a wild sense of
panic. She did not want to be alone in this place, nor did she like
the idea of Sean, injured and distracted, storming around on
his own.

As she got close, he whirled around with a flash of steel, his
blade suddenly between them.

She jumped out of his reach. "Sean, it's me."

He lowered his blade quickly but didn't put it away. "By
Roark, what are you doing coming up on me like that?"

"I –"

"You're free to go," he interrupted. "That's what you've
wanted so badly. Why don't you?"

"I wanted to check you were alright."

"Why did you come back in the first place?" The rage in his
eyes had died down, but his voice was still raised in irritation and
what sounded like bewilderment.

Emery was confused herself now, but then the misunderstanding clicked. He thought she'd run away from him back at
Petter's. He didn't know what had really happened. No doubt
the doorman had also relished not putting him straight.

"You've got it all backwards." She took a step towards him. "Those men just now, they...tried to attack me, while I was waiting for you. Petter's assistant locked me out, and there were too many to fight on my own, so I had to run. And then –" She considered telling him what had transpired in the meantime, hiding in the filthy mud and finding herself completely lost, the mysterious encounter with her even more mysterious "aunt", but the remaining anger in Sean's body already seemed to be evaporating, and she thought better of it. "I'm sorry you got the wrong impression, but that's what..."

She'd been babbling, her whole body starting to shake, but she trailed off as he stepped closer, his eyes searching hers. "No, *I'm* sorry. I should have insisted you come in with me. That sounds –" He cleared his throat. "I think you're in shock."

"I'm done considering." Her eyes burned, and her throat constricted a little. "I don't want to stay here."

"Of course." His voice was soft and his touch gentle as he put an arm around her shoulders. She couldn't help leaning against him for a moment. "You can decide again when we reach the next place."

She nodded.

Sean sheathed his sword and they headed back to the ship through the filthy streets of Brimlad, peering even more cautiously now around every blind corner, down every dark alley. Emery's entire body was trembling, but emotionally she was starting to feel numb, as if the fear had blazed through her veins so intensely it had burned itself – and everything else – away.

They found themselves in a crowded street, at which point they could both relax slightly, and began moving with less obvious hurry. As they passed through the orange light of a lantern, Emery used the opportunity to glance up at Sean's face. Blood was still leaking from the cut on his lip, and a bruise was forming on his cheek.

She wondered if she'd ever see him without a wound on face.

"You didn't have enough for the medicine, did you?"

"I did not."

"But you got it...anyway?" she added carefully.

"I did what I had to do."

Nausea grew in her belly. Is this the world she had dreamed of for so long, where violence was everywhere and simply surviving cost so much? She needed to find a way to erase the faces of those men from her mind. Every time she closed her eyes the group briefly loomed in her vision, eyes glinting with ill intent.

Thankfully, the people here were just stumbling past, singing or laughing or otherwise oblivious to their presence.

"How is everyone here so...happy?"

"That would be the alcohol," Sean answered grimly.

"Right." Yes, a drink sounded great to her right now.

They passed a man and woman sitting on a barrel, so entwined with each other she couldn't tell whose limbs belonged to whom. A tall glass bottle, still nearly fell, sat in the mud beside them.

Emery grabbed the bottle, wiping the top on her filthy tunic, and gulped down as much as she could before she started gagging. The foul taste coated her mouth and burned all the way down into her gut. She nearly spat it out but forced herself to keep it down.

When she turned back to Sean he was grimacing, one hand hovering between them as if he'd made a futile attempt to stop her. "You have no idea where that's been."

"I don't care." She took another swig. The heat of the foul drink was already dulling her anxiety, diminishing the feeling of shaking all over.

Something like understanding joined the disgust on his face. "You might if you wake up diseased."

Emery downed some more. "I just want to forget what happened earlier."

"It won't work." There was a bitter edge to his voice now. "Trust me."

He led them along another series of muddy streets. Emery

found herself beginning to stumble, and at one point Sean grasped her elbow to keep her upright.

She examined the bottle more closely. It didn't seem to be labelled. "What am I even drinking?"

She'd had wine back home before and sampled a few sips aboard *The New Dawn* during dinners with Tavor in his cabin. But this was decidedly not wine.

Sean leaned over to gingerly sniff the bottle's rim. "It's probably just rum."

"Want some?" Emery offered the bottle, sloshing the liquid that was still inside.

"No, thank you."

Emery grinned at his discomfort. The alcohol was eroding the fear that had dogged her constantly, to one degree or another, for the past weeks. Her body felt lighter, like a physical load had been lifted off her. "Go on, have some." She pressed the bottle into him.

"No," he repeated through gritted teeth, and Emery realized his hand was still firmly on the hilt of his sword, his eyes flitting about as if expecting danger at every turn.

She stumbled again, but he caught her before she hit the muddy ground. "Perhaps you should stop, you're going to make yourself sick."

"Perhaps having some yourself would make you more fun," she muttered back, not caring how stupid that sounded in the circumstance.

"It doesn't," he said flatly.

She looked up at him again, but his face was too blurred now for her to make out his exact expression. Her fingers were beginning to tingle.

Finally, the mud beneath them turned to dirt as they reached the path cutting through the trees to the beach. As the foliage swallowed the town behind them and the beach opened up before them, Emery felt like she could breathe easier again. The pier and the *Audacity* were directly ahead of them now, and on either side of the pier the open ocean stretched under a full moon, beckoning them once more. Relief and – she could hardly believe it – joy at seeing the ship again flooded through her. And yet, she wasn't quite ready to go back yet.

She pointed down the beach to where the island curved away and hid whatever lay further along the shore. "What's over there?"

"Nothing," Sean replied. "Just more sand and jungle."

"No people?"

"Not usually."

"Perfect." In this moment, being outside with no people sounded exactly like what she wanted. She took another sip of rum and looked at Sean. "Let's go!"

Without waiting for a response, she succumbed to the urge to run along the beach.

"What are you doing?" Sean called after her, but she didn't stop, reveling in the feeling of flying over the sand, of running away – at least momentarily – from all her fears and responsibilities.

"You're going to break an ankle," Sean called again and she could tell he was running after her.

She glanced over her shoulder to look at him, intent on telling him that, for a notorious Forbidden, he sure worried a lot. But the world spun when she turned and she lost her balance, tumbling into the sand. Delighting in its clean, crumbly texture and ocean scent, she shrugged off her shoulder sack and her lim, and rolled onto her back, watching the stars twinkle above her in slow, lazy circles.

Sean's face appeared above her. "Are you alright?"

"Look how beautiful the stars are tonight." When he didn't respond, she patted the sand beside her. "Come on, just for a moment. There's no one around."

Indeed, a swath of dark jungle loomed behind them, the ocean shimmered with moonlight before them, and the shore stretched empty on either side of them. Sean hesitated, but then moved to lie next to her, leaving nearly an arm's length between them. He sighed, and this time it sounded almost contented. After a while, he said, "Thank you. For what you did back there."

She grunted. "You also saved my life again." The memory flashed again briefly, and she took another sip of her foul drink.

"Only after you saved mine." He rolled over to face her. "What possessed you to do that? Had you been a man he would have run you through on the spot."

She sipped her bottle, suddenly feeling achingly homesick. "Where I'm from, we talk things through, or we duel. Friendly and fair dueling, mind. I wasn't going to stand by and let them" – the memory of a sword pressed to Sean's neck flashed through her mind – "bully you like that."

"Well, it's good to know you've got the skill to break a grown man's arm." He grinned, a real grin like the brightness of the moon coming out from behind a long band of cloud. "Consider me warned."

"You're talking like it's something remarkable."

"I can't say I've seen many women fight like that."

"Oh." The ache in her heart sharpened. She knew it was supposed to be a compliment, but it only reminded her how out of place she was in this world. She didn't belong. She poured more of the awful drink into her mouth. Her stomach was starting to churn but she didn't care. "Why were you so angry with Rooney? He was just looking out for you."

Sean looked up at the stars again. "That was wrong of me. He's a good friend. I just..." He shook his head, then cast the bottle a sidelong glance. "I've changed my mind. May I have some?"

She handed him the rum as he sat up. He stared at it for a moment, then launched the bottle into the ocean with a distant splash.

"Hey!" Emery sat up and her head began to spin.

"You'll thank me in the morning." Sean fished around in his breast pocket, then offered her a small glass vial full of liquid. He cleared his throat. "This is for you."

Emery took the vial, turning it over in her hand. It was difficult to make out its color in the pale moonlight, but she thought it looked pink. "What is it?"

"Medicine, against pain. It's not a lot, but hopefully it will help. I may have taken more than we strictly need for Ranit." He looked away and began playing with some sand.

"Aleksy mentioned you'd hurt your ribs."

Emery squinted at his blurry face, her heart swelling. "Was it taking this extra bit that made Petter send those men after you?"

Sean shrugged.

"Thank you, you really shouldn't have."

He looked at her then. "While you're on my ship, your well-being is my responsibility."

Her earlier thought popped in her head, and this time she said it out loud. "For Mister Notorious Forbidden, you sure worry a lot."

"You forget I'm *Captain* Notorious Forbidden. It's my job to worry." He looked tired even as he said it, and for the first time, she realized what a burden that position must be.

She also didn't understand how someone so young-looking could find himself in that position. "Sean, how old are you?"

"Nineteen."

It didn't seem possible.

"How are you already the captain of a ship? And one of the most feared" – she wondered whether she should say *Forbidden* to his face, especially after what he'd just done for her – "pitates out there?"

"Pure talent." He rubbed his face and stared up at the sky.

"Tell me. Please."

"You know, you're very nosy when you drink." He looked at her again, but he sounded weary rather than annoyed. "And even more persistent."

She held his gaze and raised her brows expectantly.

He sighed. "I'd have thought you already knew."

"Why?"

His face darkened and he looked away. "The company you keep."

273

Even her addled brain could figure out he meant Tavor. "He didn't tell me anything specific."

Sean's brows knitted together, but then the old blankness returned, slowly wiping his expression clean. "What if I tell you and you don't like what you hear?"

"Well, if you don't tell me, I'll have to rely on what I heard growing up about... elemists like you, and I'll continue to assume the worst." She resisted telling him she didn't anymore, not after everything she'd seen. "Or you could educate me."

Sean rested his elbows on his knees, not looking at her. "Fine. But I don't really know where to start."

"How about the beginning?"

He took a deep breath. "Well, when I was younger, around sixteen, I took over my father's small merchant shipping company. But I didn't like the office work. I liked being on the sea. Since the company and the ship were mine, I appointed myself as the helmsman. I was good at it, so no one cared that I was relatively young. It was a good gig. I got to see the world, and with the money I made I was able to help my family." He paused, staring down at the sand.

"But then, we were offered a lot of money to make a delivery for this" – hatred began to lace his voice – "man. I boarded my ship one day, ready to set sail, and there he was, standing there with that smug..." Sean's voice began to tremble with rage, and Emery gently placed a hand on his arm. His muscles tensed at her touch. "Usually by then I would have seen the cargo papers to know what and where I was delivery, but I hadn't. When I asked him what the goods were, he wouldn't tell me, just handed me a map with the route and told me to get on with it. I obviously didn't want to set sail without knowing what I was carrying, so I went down to look for myself. But there was nothing there, just my crew's rations. I didn't understand what was going on until I heard voices coming from the brig. I went over to investigate and found a load of people locked up there. They looked absolutely terrified and refused to answer any of my questions. You know, who they were, why they were there. I then checked the map and realized I was supposed to travel to Abyssus."

"Sounds ominous."

He looked at her then. "It's a place elemists are taken and locked away. They go in, and never come out." He took another deep breath. "And I...was clearly supposed to deliver them there."

Emery felt her blood run cold. "I'm guessing...you didn't?"

He went back to playing with the sand. "I went to back to the man and said I wouldn't do it. We argued, and very quickly he said that if I didn't do my job it would no longer *be* my job. I told him where to go." Sean chuckled drily, then licked his lips. "He then replied...that if I didn't deliver the prisoners, he'd tell everybody I was an elemist in hiding, and that I'd be hunted by varens for the rest of my life."

Emery could understand the fear that would have triggered; it was, after all, the main reason almost no one had ever left Orabel. "Did he know you actually were one?"

Sean shook his head. "I don't know. But it didn't matter, his word against mine would have been enough."

She turned further towards him and hugged her knees. "So, what did you do?"

Sean's hands had turned to fists pressing into the sand. "What I had to. I set sail later that day, and we kept going for a week straight."

"You went to the prison?"

"No." He turned to look at her again. "I came here."

"To Brimlad?"

He nodded.

Emery's mind was whirling with questions. "But your crew – how come they –"

Sean seemed grimly amused by her confusion. "Oh, they weren't happy. But by the time they realized the course I was taking them on they knew they had to see it through if they didn't want to run out of rations. They abandoned ship as soon as we were on dry land, and no doubt ratted me out. I've been on the run ever since."

"So, you just...let the other elemists go?"

"Yes. But not before telling them to get better at hiding who they were."

"I don't understand." She rubbed her forehead, the beach spinning now. "*That's* why you're on the run?"

"In a nutshell."

"But that's...so different from what I've heard." Rationally, she knew he could be lying, but her heart told her otherwise. "So, you really do just raid ships because you can't stop anywhere longer enough to make coin? Because that's the only way you get to eat?"

He nodded again.

"And..." She fiddled with the vial, almost feeling bad for asking the next question. "You've never actually...killed anyone?"

He was staring down at his own hands now, tucked in his lap like when she'd first found him locked in Tavor's brig. The careful neutral mask settled across his features again. When he spoke, it almost sounded like he was trying to convince himself as much as her. "Not intentionally."

Emery rubbed her eyes with the heels of her hands, trying to clear her head from the drunkenness she already regretted. "But where did the stories come from? How did you become known as the Scourge of the Sea?"

At this, a roguish grin crossed Sean's lips. "Ranit is very good at making up tales. Whenever we do make port, he spreads the stories with his songs." He shook his head with obvious affection. "Then we just play the parts when we have to."

Emery opened her mouth to tell him he was damn good at playing that part but thought better of it. Instead, she said, "So I'm guessing your crimson sails aren't really dipped in blood."

Sean chuckled, and her heart twitched at the rare sound. "It's just dye. Ranit was sure proud of that rumor though."

Another thought struck her. "None of you really know how to use your abilities well, do you?"

Sean laughed again, only this time it was full of sarcasm. "What gave us away?"

"The fact that, other than you and Cam, none of you seem to ever use them."

"Aye. I'm alright at compelling the wind and Cam has some skill with water. Rooney can grow the odd plant on a good day and Aleksy has been trained to heal using the water in a person's blood. And Smythee, when's he'll willing and lucid, can somewhat control fire. Otherwise," Sean confessed, "none of us really know what we're doing."

It made sense, once Emery thought about it, considering it took years for elemists to master an element, and that was with proper training and without the fear of getting caught doing it.

She rubbed her brow. "We need to get me to Tavor. If I can talk to him, tell him how much of a misunderstanding —"

Sean let out a blunt, humorless laugh. "Talking to Tavor won't do anything."

"You don't know that. I've —"

"I do know." He looked up again, the now familiar fury flashing in his eyes. "It was him, Emery. Tavor was the man who did all this. He was the one who threatened me in the first place."

For a moment, Emery was unable to comprehend what he was saying. Why would Tavor do something like that? "There... must have been a misunderstanding between you. I'll talk —"

"There was no misunderstanding, Emery."

Emery wanted to bury her face in the sand. It was almost impossible to marry the measured Tavor she knew with the malice Sean was describing. She took a deep breath, centering herself within this spinning universe. "No wonder you want to kill him."

"That's not —" Sean stopped himself, and his anger seemed to bleed away, leaving behind that awful, empty mask.

"It isn't?"

"No." But his voice lacked all emotion, and he didn't elaborate.

"Then what's going on? You're clearly...hurting."

He looked away and stared at the ocean.

Once again, she thought back to Cam's comment about the mysterious woman Sean sought to get back. Emery wanted to ask about her, but the last time she brought her up, he'd become instantly furious, and she didn't want that to happen again. But maybe she could help find her. "I don't know whether I can fix this, but if you let me try, there's −"

"You can't fix what he's done."

His face was too painful to look at anymore, so she gazed down at her hands, burying them in the sand. Nausea nipped at her insides as she recalled one of their early confrontations, one pointed question he'd asked. It was a stupid, unimportant piece of information, at least to her, but maybe it would help him trust her more. "Just to be clear, Tavor and I aren't...lovers. We never were."

"What?" She looked up, and Sean was blinking in confusion.

Had that been the wrong thing to say after all?

"I just...wanted you to know." Her tongue was suddenly thick in her mouth. When he didn't say anything else, she flopped back on the sand, her head too heavy to hold up any longer. "Do you know what happened to the elemists you set free?"

Sean lay down as well, propping his head on his hand. "Some wandered off, and I have no idea what happened to them. Others chose to stay with me...and became my new crew." A hint of happiness returned to his demeanor. "We've sailed together ever since."

"Wait." Emery turned her rum-addled head to face him. "Your crew are all prisoners you saved?"

"Aye. All except for Billy."

Emery looked up at the sky, her heart heavy at the thought of what they all must have been through. A new kind of disbelief and horror began to grip her. Tavor had said that varens were different now, that they were able to distinguish the good elemists from the bad and acted accordingly. How could they have made so many mistakes? She rolled onto her side and tried to get up, but the ground was spinning so quickly she felt like she was about to fly away.

Sean reached out to steady her. "Are you alright?"

She leaned into his side and grabbed his hand, letting him be the anchor that kept her from falling over. "We can fix this," she murmured, feeling sleep start to pull her down. "There has to be a way."

A sad smile crossed Sean's face, and he edged closer so she could lean properly against him and ride out her last rum-soaked moments of consciousness. "I'm afraid some things can't be fixed."

# Chapter Twenty-Nine

W hen Emery woke, they were both still on the beach. Sean was asleep on his back next to her, one arm stretched under her head like a pillow, the other tucked against his chest. He was still holding her hand, their fingers intertwined.

Not wanting to wake him, but needing to shift, she tried to pull away gently, but his grip on her hand only tightened, and her heart somersaulted.

She took a moment to absorb their surroundings. The beach remained empty save for the two of them. The wind rustled the palm trees behind them, and gulls cried out as they flew above the calm waves rolling against the shore. Considering Sean's cautious nature, Emery was a little surprised he allowed them to stay on the beach all night. Perhaps he thought the spot was secluded enough to be safe. Or that he'd scared Petter's men so badly that they wouldn't be a problem. Despite these points, Emery had the sneaking suspicion he'd stayed up most the night to keep watch anyway.

In the distance, the sky was glowing a fiery red as the sun climbed above the horizon, pink clouds swirling round its orange orb like great wisps of smoke. The world looked as if it had burst into flames. Emery had never seen such a perfect sunrise, and it was almost enough to distract her. A terrible pain had begun to pound behind her eyes and her stomach writhed with nausea. A bitter taste coated her mouth and she'd never felt thirstier in her life. But that would all have been nothing if it weren't also for the confusion that had returned with her consciousness.

Even now in her sober state, she had no idea what to make of Sean, even less the conversation they'd had the previous night. If what he'd said was true, his great crime, the one that had condemned him to this life of persecution, had been...setting a group of innocent people free. He'd never killed anyone, never even meant to harm anyone, and yet he and the people he'd saved now spent their days fleeing or fighting for their lives.

On the other hand, he could have lied. Made the entire thing up. Her instincts told her he wasn't lying, nor did she want to believe it, but at this point she had no way of knowing either way.

She allowed her eyes to roam across his face, a face so at ease in sleep it was difficult to believe it was his. His eyelashes touched his cheeks and the thin scar she had given him, one that matched a small one above his eyebrow and another near his temple. The rising sun lit his tousled hair on fire, the stubble along his jaw, and his lips were slightly parted as he breathed slowly and, for once, peacefully. A sudden urge to kiss him came over her, and she almost jerked away. What an absurd, outrageous thought, there must still be liquor in her blood.

She tried again to extricate her hand without waking him. As their palms brushed, she could feel every callus on his skin. But there was also something else, something that felt different, like it didn't belong.

Carefully, she turned their hands, and this time she was able to pull slightly out of his grip, enough to see his palm properly. Her stomach dropped as she took in the horrible burn that scarred the center of his palm, its edges raised and white. The shape matched one of the symbols she had seen in his books and maps, one vertical line, and two horizontal lines, one coming from the vertical line's top and the other from its center. She realized with sadness that this was the hand upon which he usually wore a leather palm guard, as if he wanted to hide the scar from the world.

Sean's fingers shifted, curling around her hand, but it wasn't the light grip from before. This time he began to squeeze so hard it hurt. He was still asleep, but the peace had left him. His jaw was clenched, his eyes moving back and forth under their lids. He began muttering something, his expression pained, and clutched her hand even harder.

She forced herself not to pull away. She'd had enough night-mares to recognize he was having one. "Sean," she whispered, nudging him with her other hand. "Wake up."

His head began thrashing from side to side. "Please," she could make out this time. "Don't." The terror in his voice seemed so raw her own pulse sped up in response.

She blew gently on his face. "Sean, you're dreaming."

His eyes flashed open, and he sat up so fast he nearly smashed into her. He gasped for air and looked around wildly. When he finished surveying the beach and his gaze landed on her, he collapsed back on the sand and threw his free arm over his face. His wounded hand was still clutching hers, pressing it against his thrashing heart.

"It was just a bad dream," she murmured.

His breathing slowed and his pulsed eased, but his entire body trembled. It was unnerving seeing him like this.

With gentle coaxing, she was able to lower the arm from his face. He looked like he wanted the earth to swallow him whole. An onslaught of questions flooded her mind, but she knew this was not the time. Instead, she gazed over at the burning dawn. "I get nightmares too, sometimes."

She felt his head turn towards her, but he didn't say anything. After a long silence he sat up again, gave her hand a final squeeze, then let go so he could push himself upright. She tucked her hand into her lap, not liking how cold and empty it suddenly felt.

Sean walked down to the shoreline and splashed water on his face. When he returned, one of his hands was in his pocket, the other fiddling with the shiny round trinket hanging from his neck.

"What is that?" She pointed at the object, partly out of long-standing curiosity, partly to distract him from the nightmare that was clearly still troubling him.

He looked down as if surprised to find the thing between his fingers. "Oh. It's a timepiece."

"A what?"

The tiniest of smiles lifted his lips. "It's for telling the time."

Emery didn't understand. One could already judge the time of day by the sun's height. This device had to be more specific somehow. "How does it work?"

"To be honest, this one doesn't. Not anymore."

"Why do you wear it then?"

The smile instantly vanished. "It...belonged to someone I cared about." He stuffed the trinket under his tunic and cleared his throat. "How are you feeling?"

Emery took the hint. "My stomach feels like I poisoned myself."

Sean smiled again and offered her a hand. "You'll feel better after some food and water."

Dizziness overcame her as she took his hand and let him pull her upright. She stood still for a moment, fighting the urge to vomit. "Well, I'm never drinking that again."

"I did warn you."

After she grabbed her lim and he grabbed the sack, they began walking along the shore, heading towards for the pier and the *Audacity*.

"Thank you," she said. "For not dumping me in a corner somewhere."

Sean chuckled. "I've handled worse. You should see Ranit after he's had a few."

The fact he had taken care of her the way he had, neither abandoning nor trying to touch her in ways she didn't want, also spoke beyond itself. It was further proof he wasn't the awful Forbidden she had thought him to be. That Tavor had been mistaken.

They were walking so closely now that the back of their hands began to brush. Part of her longed to take his hand again, but the rum-fueled boldness that had coursed through her veins during the night had vanished, and common sense was taking over once more.

Their hands brushed again, but this time it was Sean's fingers that reached out and hooked themselves into her own. A dizziness that had nothing to do with rum came over her.

This was an altogether different kind of trouble.

Keeping her eyes fixed ahead of them, she shoved her other hand into her pocket. Her fingers brushed something soft, and she remembered the white feather she had lost yesterday. She pulled it out to examine it better, it was hardly white anymore. Her heart clenched and she stopped walking, suddenly overcome with nostalgia.

For seven years she'd carried this feather in her hair to honor one of the geese who'd provided her people with eggs and down. How many parts of her would this world try to strip away? How many times would it succeed?

She realized Sean had also had to stop, and was now watching her silently, and her cheeks heated. What a fool she must look getting teary-eyed over a dirty feather. She made to shove it back in her pocket, but Sean stepped closer.

"Wait." He held out his hand. "May I?"

Slowly, she laid the dirty, crumpled feather in his outstretched palm. He walked with it to the edge of the ocean, and she worried briefly that he was going to toss it away. But then he bent to the water and simply rinsed it, returning with a conspicuously whiter feather. He took a moment to straighten out its crumpled edges as best he could, then stepped closer again. He held the feather up, near her head.

"Would you like it back in?"

She nodded.

He pulled a lose thread from his sleeve. He carefully separated out a lock of her hair, and she felt him gently but firmly tying the feather back where it belonged. When he was done, she reached up to touch it. To her surprise, his configuration felt both comfortable and secure.

"Perfect, thank you."

"I know my knots." A tiny smile graced his lips, and he reached out to touch the feather again. "You look more like you again." His fingers brushed her cheek and she felt almost dazed by the touch, by his kindness. They were standing so close now she could count the shades of green in his eyes, could see the way his gaze flickered down to her lips.

Twigs cracked and metal sang as a dozen men in black-and-blue uniforms poured from the jungle onto the beach. The varens surrounded them so quickly that Emery's dazed mind couldn't process it quickly enough for her to reach for her lim before their gleaming blades and pistols were pointing straight at them.

"Captain Denzel," said a strangely familiar voice.

Sean went rigid for a moment, then he reached for the blade at his hip despite the mass of weapons trained on them.

Blood rushed to Emery's head as she realized who had spoken, who it was now strolling towards them across the sand.

"Not like you to pay so little attention to your surroundings, but I see you've been distracted by a –"

She stepped between Sean and the speaker, and Tavor broke off midsentence. For a moment, he stared at her as if she were a ghost. He himself looked much the same, his hair gold in the sun, his deep-green eyes sharp as ever, his cape billowing and making him look twice as impressive. But she'd never seen him lose his composure like this before. "Miss Aalokin," he stammered. "You're alive."

Before she could reply, a varen who seemed slightly shorter than the others burst from the circle and launched himself at her. Emery screamed and beat at the man as he threw his arms around her so forcefully they both dropped to the ground, but after a breathless moment she realized he was *hugging* her.

"By the gods, you're alive!" It was Caelin, almost crying into her neck. "I can't believe it!"

Tears of joy and relief welled up in her own eyes. "You made it too."

Tavor was alive. Her friend was alive, warm, and breathing in her arms. Did that mean Liam...

The air shifted suddenly and the varens around them began shouting. She pulled away from Caelin to see Tavor's eyes flicking between Sean and herself, as if trying to make some kind of urgent decision. Sean's blade was raised, the wind he had summoned tugging at his hair and clothes, and every inch of him was trained on Tavor.

The commissioner seemed to snap out of whatever conflict he had just been in and turned to glaring purely at Sean. "I wouldn't do that if I were you." His voice was cold now. "We know where your crew are, four on your ship and three others at the Rusty Anchor. We know one of your old men is still on the loose somewhere, but we'll locate him soon enough."

Sean's blade lowered a fraction but the buffeting wind he had created remained, whipping Emery's hair into her face as she tried to get up and stand between him and Tavor.

For whatever reason, Caelin was holding her down.

She tried to squirm out of his grip. "Let go of me. I need to –"

"And we will let them all be," Tavor continued. "If you come quietly. Stop resisting, and they can all go free."

For a moment, Sean stood where he was, shaking with rage. Then, his sword fell from his hands and the wind died away.

Tavor nodded, and half a dozen varens fell forward. An instant later, irons were around Sean's wrists and ankles.

Tavor looked over to Emery, still struggling against Caelin. "It's alright," he said with much greater warmth.

Caelin loosened his grip, enough for them both to stand up, but didn't let go. She resisted the urge to fight more viciously, he was clearly suffering from the same misunderstanding that had made Tavor come after Sean so hard.

Tavor stepped towards her, shaking his head. "We need to get you to my ship's medic." He turned to one of the varens. "Alert the medic that he will be needed immediately." The varen nodded and took off down the beach.

"I'm fine," Emery insisted. "But we need –"

"There's blood all over you," he interrupted. "I couldn't possibly –"

"It's not mine. Please, just –"

But he was already turning back to the other varens. "Take him to the brig. And sedate him."

The six guarding Sean began marching him away, and it almost pained her to see him not fight back. He just looked back at her, his eyes blank.

She had to fix this. "Tavor, he's not –"

But Tavor nodded again at one of the varens – Anders, she realized – who smashed the butt of his pistol against Sean's skull. Emery cried out as Sean crumpled. He'd have hit the ground had it not been for the chains dragging him along.

She whirled at Tavor, any relief at seeing him again turning to anger. "He wasn't fighting! He did exactly as you asked!"

"Precautions, Miss Aalokin. He's a dangerous man."

Before she could argue further, Tavor grabbed her other arm and, with Caelin, began steering her along the beach. "We must get you to the medic," he repeated. "And then, I imagine you'd like to see your brother again."

# Part Four

## *The Elemists*

# Chapter Thirty

"I'm so happy to see you alive and well, Miss Aalokin," Tavor said to Emery as she was marched across the beach with the rest of their party towards Tavor's new ship, which had been moored on the side of the island opposite from the town. Caelin still clutched her arm, as if he was scared she'd disappear again if he let go. "Rest assured, the monster who stole you from us will be locked away and will do you no further harm."

Indeed, Emery could just see Sean's limp form as the varens half carried, half dragged him along up ahead, the chains around his wrists and ankles clanking horribly. Her chest caved in to see him like that. She needed to stop this, now. "Tavor, he – "

"I can only apologize for all of this," Tavor continued. "None of it should have happened. I vowed to keep you safe, and I failed, quite drastically. I would understand if you never forgave me."

"There's nothing to forgive. He – "

Tavor cut her off, his expression apologetic. But he also seemed anxious. "Thank you for being so gracious. Ah, good, the medic is waiting for you."

They approached Tavor's new ship, which bobbed languidly just off the shore in a deep cove. A lone figure stood by a row of longboats pulled up onto the sand. Caelin, and Tavor guided Emery towards the figure – presumedly the medic – while the varens loaded Sean and themselves into a few of the longboats and began rowing the short distance to the ship.

Emery was whisked into a longboat herself, Caelin sitting beside her and the medic across from her. The man immediately took her wrist to check her pulse. Tavor climbed into a separate boat.

Despite her protests, as soon as they reached the ship Emery was taken straight to the medic's cabin, where Tavor and Caelin waited outside while the man poked and prodded her. She trembled with anxiety over Sean's wellbeing and anticipation over her coming reunion with her brother, barely registering the examination or what the medic was saying loudly enough for the other two to hear through the cracked door. Dehydration, bruised ribs, hand-shaped marks across her throat. These were unimportant right now.

Her brother was alive.

Sean was chained and unconscious.

Joy and despair warred inside her, making everything feel surreal as the medic ushered her from the room and reassured Tavor that she would be just fine with some water, food and sleep.

Tavor and Caelin both exhaled with obvious relief, and before Emery could speak, Tavor said, "Mrs. Aalokin, you should get some rest. I apologize, but I must go deal with our prisoner. I'll have a meal sent down right away and I will come see how you're faring as soon as I can."

With that, he turned and walked briskly down the corridor towards the stairs leading to the bowels of the ship.

Caelin, tried to lead Emery down an opposite corridor but she resisted. "I'll be right back"

She tugged out of Caelin's bewildered grip and hurried after Tavor

"Tavor, wait!"

His indigo cape swished as he turned. "Is everything alright?"

"Um...well, *I'm* fine. But we need to talk. About Sean."

Tavor glanced at the other varens in the hallway. "Come with me." He gently took her wrist and tugged her into an empty cabin, shutting the door behind them. With the light streaming through the porthole, she could see his expression shift from that of a stoic commander to a genuinely concerned friend. It struck her then how difficult it must be for him to constantly maintain his air of leadership, to never show any doubt or weakness, while his men were around. His voice was soft when he said, "I promise, he won't ever harm you again."

"That's the thing." She wiped her palms on her trousers. Apparently even after everything, being alone in Tavor's presence still made her hands sweat. "He never did. Not once."

Tavor's eyes narrowed. "Then...where did the bruises on your neck come from? And why are you so dehydrated?"

"I – Um..." The warmth of discomfort bled into her cheeks, and she looked pointedly away from his face. "I was...attacked last night. I don't want to go into the details, but Sean...saved me." She met Tavor's eyes again briefly, to ensure he'd registered what she'd said. "He put a stop to the attack." She looked away again. "Afterwards, I just wanted to forget what happened, so...I drank. But again, Sean tried to stop me, and in the end, he threw away the bottle before I could finish it."

Tavor's expression softened, but his voice had an underlay of pity she didn't care for. "Miss Aalokin, he may not have physically hurt you, but he will have been playing with your head. That's what he does."

"But –"

"He has kept you on his ship this whole time, surely against your will."

"He set me free at Brimlad," she urged. "When you found us, I had *chosen* to go back with him. His crew are also –"

"He didn't set you free," Tavor broke in, seemingly without any doubt that this was true. "He just made you feel like you were deciding to stay with him."

Emery's pulse began to pick up speed, she didn't like how

Tavor's words were getting under her skin. "He's saved my life on multiple occasions, most of the time putting himself at risk in the process."

"Your life was in danger because of him in the first place," Tavor insisted. He closed his eyes for a moment and took a deep breath. "If I'd only known –"

"Whatever the background," Emery interrupted, "he didn't have to save me. He didn't have to risk his life for me. He chose to, more than once. That must tell you something."

Tavor was unwavering. "It will all have been part of lulling you into a false sense of security."

Tavor's voice was soft, like he was explaining something to a small child, but what hit her most was that he was echoing her own early concern about Sean. Emery's pulse began to race faster still. Her own worry had slowly disappeared, she'd even forgotten about it until now. Did that mean Tavor was right, that Sean really was –

"He wanted you placid," Tavor pressed on. "So that when the time came, you wouldn't fight him." He grunted in dry amusement. "He was probably planning to use you as a way to get back at me."

Emery's breath turned to short, shallows bursts. Sean had insinuated exactly that, right at the beginning of their discussions. But then he had changed his mind...or had he just fooled her into believing that? An abyss of mistrust yawned open beneath her, but there were still things to cling to. "Sean told me how he became an outlaw. How all he'd done to *deserve* that status was to set some elemists free."

Tavor barely raised an eyebrow. "Is that what he told you?"

Emery's blood pumped in her ears as she pressed on. "He also told me...that you were the reason behind this. That you threatened to expose him if he didn't obey you, even though you didn't even know he was an elemist at the time." Tavor remained unreactive, and she took a shaky breath. "Is this true?"

"Yes." His honesty was so blunt she was compelled to step away from him. "I did know he was an elemists and I did threaten him. I was trying to give him a chance to redeem himself for other crimes he had committed previously." Tavor was practically pinning her in place with his eyes. "He'd burnt people's houses down using his abilities, Miss Aalokin. With people inside."

Emery could only stare at Tavor, her mind a mess of whirling thoughts. She couldn't imagine Sean doing something like that, hurting anyone in such a way. She'd also only seen him manipulate the air until now, never fire. But...perhaps this was all part of a story he had woven for her during her time on the *Audacity*.

Anger laced Tavor's words as he bashed the end of his silver stick against the floor. "He's also the reason I need this damned cane."

Emery could only stare at the object clutched by his pale hand. Both men made such good arguments, but which version could she trust? Could she trust either of them?

"Can I speak with him?"

"I don't think that would be a good idea. In fact, I insist that you don't." Tavor's voice softened again. "I know you've been through a lot, Miss Aalokin." He stepped forward and placed a gentle hand on her shoulder. "But you're safe now. He can't hurt you, I promise." He nudged his chin in the direction of Liam's cabin. "You should go to your brother. He's missed you terribly." His hand lingered for a moment. "As did I."

Emery was so taken aback by his confession, she couldn't react before Tavor dropped his hand and slipped back out the door. By the time she recovered enough to follow him, he was already descending the stairs at the end of the corridor. The gloom had all but swallowed him when Emery asked, "What will happen to him? To Sean?"

Tavor turned, and his teeth seemed to flash especially bright as he answered. "He'll be taken to Abyssus, where he'll never again see the light of day."

His words seem to ring in the silence of the corridor, and Emery whirled as a hand gently touched her shoulder. But it was only Caelin.

"I'm sorry," he said, pulling his hand away. His face was a picture of concern. "Are you alright?"

She answered honestly. "I don't know."

Certainly, she'd never been more confused in her entire life. She needed time to analyze all this new contradicting information and to sort through the hurricane of emotions whirling inside her.

Caelin gave no indication he overheard the conversation and much to her appreciation, he asked no questions as he led her back down the corridor to stop in front of a plain wooden door. And suddenly the knowledge that her twin waited on the other side momentarily eclipsed everything else.

Caelin turned to face her, giving her arm an affectionate squeeze. He opened his mouth, shut it, and then said, "I missed you so much."

She hugged him, her throat too tight to say anything back.

When he released her, he began playing with his sleeves. He glanced at the door, then back at her, his jaw working nervously. "He's in there," he said softly. "But I need to warn you, he didn't take your...death very well."

Her death. Of course, the whole time she'd been terrified she had lost them both, they had been thinking the same.

"He's continually blamed himself," Caelin continued. "He's seen himself as the reason you were out here in the first place. I've tried to –"

"I know." Emery placed a hand on his shoulder. "I'm sure you've done everything you could. Thank you, for...looking after him."

"Don't thank me yet," he said grimly.

She turned towards the room in which her brother was waiting, and took a deep breath, forcing the air through her constricted throat. Caelin opened the door for her, and she stepped inside.

This cabin was much smaller and much less lavish than the ones on *The New Dawn*. Even though daylight was falling through a small porthole in the wall, a bent and misshapen candle was burning low on a small table next to a narrow bed wedged in the corner. In the mixture of white and orange light, a slender figure was laying, unmoving, on the bed, facing away from her.

Her brother.

She stepped further into the room, heart spinning out of her chest. "Liam?"

Liam slowly unfolded himself towards her, and light hit the side of his face. Caelin's warning hadn't quite prepared her for his appearance. His hair was longer, shaggier, and, for the first time since they had begun the transition from childhood to adulthood, the shadow of facial hair streaked his jaw and neck. His cheekbones stood out painfully from his gaunt face.

He stood up with a jerk, and for a moment the twins just stared at each other.

Then, he stepped closer his eyes running over her face. Shaking, he reached out for her, and she met his hand with her own.

"I'm here," she choked, smiling shakily. "I'm alive."

Liam's knees gave out. He crumpled to the floor, burying his face in his palms, silently sobbing. Emery dropped beside her brother and threw her arms around him, her own shoulders shaking as he hugged her back. All the hope she'd had to cling to these past weeks collapsed into relief, and she could no longer stop the tears from falling freely. His chest was beating against hers, their hearts pressed together. They were both still breathing, both hearts still beating.

He spoke at last, his voice thick with sorrow. "I thought you were dead."

"So did I. Both of you."

She looked up at Caelin, who had followed her into the room. She tugged him down as well, and the three of them sat there for a long time, arms wrapped around each other as if letting go would mean losing each other once more.

They only untangled themselves when food and drink were delivered to the door, though they remained sitting in a circle on the floor with the trays of food in the center.

As Emery gulped nearly an entire mug of water in one go, Liam stared at her as if he still couldn't believe she was real. "How are you here?"

She wiped water from her chin. "It's a long story."

"We've got time," Liam said

"Actually, I need to do something first."

Liam and Caelin both looked at her quizzically.

Now that she'd finally been reunited with her brother and her racing thoughts had had time to settle, she knew what she had to do. But she chewed her lip, not knowing how to explain her dilemma in a way they would understand. In the end, she opted for simplicity. "I need to see Sean."

Caelin choked on his own water.

Liam just tilted his head. "You mean the Scourge?"

"What on Teralyn's earth for?" Caelin demanded.

Her pulse began to pick up again. "I don't think he deserves to be locked up."

"What?" Caelin hissed. "He kept you prisoner, Em."

"Only at the start. By the time we reached Brimlad he'd agreed to let me go."

"But he didn't." Caelin sounded furious already. "You were with him when we found you, and you were covered in blood and bruises."

"The blood wasn't mine. And the bruises...he didn't cause them."

"What are you trying to say?" asked Liam.

"I'm saying..." She sighed and leaned back against the wall, fiddling with her feather. The feather Sean had so expertly, and gently, resecured in her hair. "I'm no longer convinced he's the monster Tavor thinks he is. In all the time we were together, all the opportunities he had, he never once hurt me. And after everything I've seen out there, I –"

"Are you sure you weren't just seeing what you wanted to see?" Liam asked. "Or what he wanted you to?"

No. She wasn't. She was so far from sure about anything that her stomach roiled with uncertainty. "I'll be more certain once I've spoken with him again."

"Absolutely not." Caelin's sounded horrified. "He's messed with you already. Don't risk falling for more of his tricks."

"He saved my life," she hissed, irritated that everybody seemed to think she'd been played for a fool. Did they really think that little of her judgement? "Multiple times."

"So? That was probably part of his strategy."

"When do you want to talk to him?" Liam asked, his voice surprisingly placid.

"Liam!" Caelin snapped. "You can't be serious."

Emery turned to her brother. His faith in her instincts warmed her heart, making it easier to feel a little more certain herself. "As soon as possible."

# Chapter Thirty-One

The cramped hallways felt ready to close in on them as the trio silently padded over the floorboards. Caelin's lantern cast an orange glow around them but the darkness beyond it was thick, reminding Emery uncomfortably of when she'd been trapped back on Tavor's ship, fearing she was about to die. Until Sean had taken her hand and guided her to safety, even though she hadn't understood that at the time.

The damp, musky scent of the ship's innards did nothing to help the feeling that the walls were about to swallow her, and the knowledge that neither she nor Liam were supposed to be anywhere near the brig had her constantly checking over her shoulder even though they hadn't yet seen anyone. They'd waited until midnight before venturing down here, hoping most everyone excluding a few guards would be asleep.

Waiting had been torture.

Emery had wanted nothing more than to sprint down to the brig to see Sean, to fight through the varens with her lim if she had to. But a plan was slowly brewing in her mind, and she knew she had to be patient, to not completely give herself away.

Emery, Liam, and Caelin had spent the entire day in Liam's cabin, and Emery had been able to distract herself a little by recounting nearly everything that happened to her since being separated from them. She left out a few small details though, namely the more... *personal* moments between her and Sean that she didn't wish to discuss.

When she'd finished, Liam spoke first. "I can't believe you got to see a sea monster before me."

Caelin stared at him in shock for a moment, but Emery had laughed. There was her Liam, with his own sense of humor.

After they puzzled over Liliath and her fiery disappearance, and then took turns trying and failing to open the box she'd given Emery, she had finally demanded, "Now you two need to tell me how you survived. I thought..." She paused for a breath. "I was scared you'd drowned."

Both Liam and Caelin had dropped their gazes.

"We tried to find you," said Liam, hands folded in his lap. "After we got separated on Tavor's ship."

"But his men dragged us up to the top deck and into the longboats," Caelin continued.

"We didn't want to leave you." Liam's voice was quavering now. "We knew there was a chance −"

Emery grabbed his hand. "You didn't have a choice. The ship was going under."

"Then we should have been willing to go under with you!" Liam snapped. "It's my fault you're out here in the first place. My fault any of this happened."

"It's not." She squeezed his hand. "You think I'd have let you leave home without me? And anyway, I'm here to tell the tale, aren't I?" She smiled, hoping it would inspire him to relax, but his blue eyes remained trained on his lap, refusing to meet hers. "What happened once you were in the boats? Where did you go?"

"We paddled to the closest bit of land," Caelin replied. "Tavor managed to get word to someone, and this ship showed up with more varens to collect us."

"We decided to keep heading to Dornwell," said Liam. "I

knew you would never have forgiven me if I'd given up and gone home now."

"You're right, I wouldn't have." Emery glanced at Caelin, who had begun playing with one of the shiny buttons on his black-and-blue jacket. "Why are you dressed like one of them?"

Caelin had shrugged. "Tavor's been training me. I want to be as helpful as I can, too. You know, help sort the good from the bad, bring about peace. He's made me part of his guard."

Emery swallowed her discomfort. It was bizarre to see her friend in a varen uniform, and, truthfully, a little unsettling.

Now, Caelin still wore his uniform as he walked several steps ahead of her and Liam, no doubt wearing the stony face with which he'd left the cabin. He hadn't wanted this but had come along anyway. In the end, he knew he wasn't going to stop her, and that, among them, it was he who had gained the most trust from the crew should anyone cross their path.

He stopped them above a set of stairs leading to the lowest deck. Holding the lantern high, he turned to Emery. His face was still hard. "You're sure about this?"

She couldn't afford to hesitate. "Yes."

He sighed through his nose. "Hide over there then." He pointed to a large chamber where barrels and crates were stacked against the hull. "I'll let you know when the guards leave."

As Caelin descended into the belly of the ship, Liam and Emery crept into the room and crouched together behind a crate. Caelin's footsteps echoed down the stairs until he reached the bottom, at which point it sounded like he was in a chamber of some kind.

"What are you doing here?" an unfamiliar-sounding man asked.

"I'm here to relieve you," Caelin answered flatly.

"Already?" said a second man.

"What do you mean, already?" Caelin snipped. "It's my shift now." A pregnant pause. "Did the two of you fall asleep?"

The first man now sounded less suspicious and more perplexed. "Where's Anders then?"

"Must be running late," Caelin responded smoothly. "I'm sure I can manage a few minutes without him though."

One of the others sniggered. "Yeah. This thing won't be harming anyone in his state."

Bile clawed up Emery's throat, but she stayed put as booted feet climbed the staircase and two black-and-blue clad varens wandered by, yawning and stretching. Once they had melted into the darkness and she could no longer hear their footsteps, she whispered, "How much sway does Caelin have around here now?"

In the low light, she thought she saw Liam shrug. "Tavor's been training him personally, and the others respect how good he is with weapons." A slight bitterness crept into his tone. "It's almost like he's one of them now."

"Do you not trust them?"

He shrugged again. "They've given me no reason not to."

Emery wanted to press him further, but knew they needed to use this opportunity while the varens were gone.

They crept down the stairs to find a small landing, in which Caelin was standing by a single wooden door. The orange light of his lantern blended with the yellow light of the wall sconce, flooding the cramped area and illuminating his unimpressed expression.

"Best be quick," he said. "When they get back to their quarters they may realize it's earlier than I suggested."

"And if they do?" Emery asked.

"I'll have made an honest mistake." His dark eyes looked unconcerned. "Tavor won't punish me for getting the time wrong." He seemed suddenly so much older, more self-assured than she remembered him. Had the few weeks they'd been separated really aged him that much, or had this change already been underway without her realizing?

"Thank you," she whispered.

He nodded, then broke his austere demeanor with a wink. "Anything for you."

She had to chuckle, and for some reason tears pricked the

back of her eyes. His appearance may have changed, but he was still her Caelin, still the loyal person who would never fail his friends.

"Let's not waste time," said Liam, taking the lantern from Caelin and opening the door to the brig.

Emery followed him into the chamber with her heart lodged in her throat. The air here was noticeably cooler, and terribly stale. Panic bubbled in her chest as they stepped into a half inch of water, and she had to assure herself that they weren't sinking.

The lantern swung in Liam's hand, its light cutting through the darkness, illuminating dozens of rusty vertical bars. There seemed to be nothing else to the room, just lines and lines of bars making up at least half a dozen cells. The twins moved cautiously through, every step sloshing the small layer of seawater. Emery's pulse climbed higher with each empty cell they passed, until they finally reached Sean's. Seeing him, she dropped to her knees in the cold water, not caring how quickly it soaked her trousers.

Sean was lying on his side in the darkest corner of the cell. He didn't move as they approached, didn't even open his eyes as Liam raised the lantern and its light fell across his face.

"Gods," he breathed.

Purple bruises sullied Sean's cheeks and jaw, and one of his eyes looked swollen. A trickle of blood was leaking from a wound on his head, staining his ear and neck. The rest of him looked less bloody, but presumably only because he was literally lying in a pool of water. The first time she'd seen him in a cell he'd been sitting up, and she'd been both angry and terrified of him. Now, her heart splintered at the sight of him. She would have given anything just to see him open his eyes again.

"He must have put up a serious fight," Liam mumbled, crouching beside her and placing the lantern on the floor.

"No. He didn't." She took a deep breath, her insides writhing. "They must have done this to him after we came aboard, when he was already chained up."

And unable to defend himself.

"Sean?" She flinched as his name echoed off the barren walls.

Sean's eyes slowly opened, locking onto her own. The blankness was back, but this time it didn't frighten her. Instead, her fingers curled around the cruel bars, wishing she could tear them open and get to him.

"What did they do to you?" she whispered.

He blinked, the movement sluggish, and otherwise stayed still.

"They've paralyzed him," said Liam, his face twisting in disgust.

Sean's eyes were still on her, and he blinked again, slowly, as if it cost him great effort.

Liam moved forward, leaning against the bars much like Emery had. His eyes swept across Sean's limp body. "I don't know exactly what you have, or haven't, done," he said, and his voice wavered slightly. "But you've kept my sister in one piece. And for that, I can only thank you." He cleared his throat and turned to Emery. "I'll give you two some space." He then stood and sloshed back through the room, leaving Emery alone with Sean.

She stared into his fathomless eyes, feeling powerless to do anything else in that moment.

She didn't know if he'd really been tricking her all this time, lying to her with every breath, or if he'd even secretly intended to kill her in some dastardly moment, thinking it would somehow hurt Tavor enough to constitute revenge in his eyes. She couldn't tell whether she now only saw in him what she – or he – wanted. But she did know one thing with certainty. He had saved her life, multiple times, when it would arguably have been easier, and more self-preserving, to have left her to her fate. If she focused on that, and if she listened to what felt like her own soul speaking to her, then, despite anything Tavor, Liam or Caelin had said, she knew he didn't belong down here. She knew he wasn't a monster.

She leaned her forehead against the cold iron bars, gazing straight into his blank eyes. "I'm going to get you out of here."

# Chapter Thirty-Two

E mery had been given her own cabin and decided to head back there after the encounter with Sean. She needed some time alone to process and calm down from what she'd just seen. Sleep eluded her the rest of the night though. She could think of nothing except Sean, alone and injured in that dank cell, unable to pick himself out of the cold water. If he was kept like that for any length of time, there was a risk he would catch a chill, become sick, or even...

Many times, she almost threw back her blanket and got up, the urge was so strong to head back down to the brig, to see if there was something she could do right then. But she knew that other guards would be there, and too many questions would arise if she appeared on her own at this time. The last thing she could afford now, for Sean's sake, was to make herself look suspicious.

So she spent the rest of the night alternating between tossing and turning, and fiddling with the compass Sean had given her, letting the red arrow spin and spin as if it could point her to an answer.

When morning came, she hauled herself up into sitting, leaned back against the wall and rubbed her scratchy eyes, accepting she'd just have to start the day.

A quiet rap on the door seemed to echo her decision, and a varen stepped into the room. She fought the urge to reach for her lim, reminding herself that Tavor's men wouldn't hurt her.

"Commissioner Thantos would like to invite you to breakfast."

After the two of them had roused Liam, the varen led the twins up two decks and across the ship to Tavor's new cabin. Caelin they left behind to sleep a little longer, given he had been up during the night on watch.

This time, the doors to Tavor's cabin were of a light, plain wood, and inside it lacked the lavishness of his last one. A medium-sized bed sat in one corner, plain, off-white blankets pulled taught along the mattress, and a square chest crouched in the corner opposite. Cups of tea were steaming on a round wooden table in the center of the room, and that was it. Emery realized with empathy that Tavor's former belongings were probably all rotting at the bottom of the sea.

Tavor was standing with his back to them in front of a giant window at the back of the cabin, the only thing that really resembled his last quarters, although this too lacked his old deep-colored curtains, or indeed any curtains at all.

Emery was vaguely aware of him turning to greet her and Liam as they stepped into the room, but she found herself too distracted by the window to respond. She stared at the corner where the shimmering glass met the wooden wall, and for a moment she was transported back to Sean's cabin, seeing him sitting on the floor by the large window, curled in on himself in the shadows, radiating with a grief he hadn't yet shared with her.

"Miss Aalokin, are you alright?" Tavor's voice broke through her thoughts, and she blinked the vision away. His worried face was in front of hers, Liam's close behind.

She moved her hand to rest on the side of her chest. "Yes, sorry. My ribs are still a little sore."

Tavor frowned. "Should I fetch the medic?"

"No, it's alright. But thank you." Her ribs did still hurt, but she had better things to worry about.

She and Liam took their seats at the table, and he subtly raised an eyebrow at her. He knew she had lied.

She looked away, not wanting their host to pick up that anything was on her mind.

Tavor was standing behind his own chair across the table from her now, his hands resting on its back. "Are you sure?" Dark smudges had appeared under his eyes since yesterday, and his skin almost matched the white of the sugar cubes displayed in a little bowl on the table. He hadn't slept well either. "He might have something to ease the pain."

She gave him her most convincing smile. "Honestly, I'd much rather he kept it for when someone really needs it."

That seemed to satisfy him finally, and he sat down as well. Beside her, Liam had started making a tower out of sugar cubes. He was unusually quiet.

Emery glanced out the window and her breath caught as she spotted familiar crimson sails on the distant horizon. "The *Audacity*," she blurted.

Tavor sighed and followed her gaze. "Yes, I'm afraid they've been following us at a distance since we left Brimlad. They'll be wanting their captain back."

Emery felt ill with anxiety. "Do you think they'll attack?"

"No, I don't believe they'll risk the fight."

Emery tried to hide her rising panic. If they did attack, how many people would get hurt on both sides?

Luckily, Tavor misunderstood her fear. "I promise you, we can handle them if they do attack." He assured gently. "You are safe."

This did not make her feel better. She tore her gaze away from the horizon and stared at the table. As men began strolling in carrying plates laden with fresh fruit, rich-looking biscuits and honey, Emery could still feel Tavor's gaze on her. She busied herself plucking strawberries from some of the platters, stuffing biscuits into her mouth, but eventually she had to look up at him.

He was leaning forward across the table, and when she

looked up, he reached forward and placed his hand inches from her own. "I can't apologize enough for what happened to you. I – We never thought he would have taken you. We thought you – Well, we thought both of you...were lost. Otherwise, we would have stopped at nothing to get you back."

She met his pine-green eyes, but all she saw were Sean's blank ones staring back at her. She blinked and looked away. "You have nothing to apologize for."

"But he hurt you, Miss Aalokin." Tavor kept his voice soft. "Physically and mentally, and for that I can never stop apologizing. I failed in my duty to keep you safe from him." He took a labored breath. "To keep the world safe from him."

*But he never hurt me.*

She almost said it, but knew it would be pointless, perhaps even counterproductive. Tavor's hatred for Sean clearly ran as deep as Sean's for him. She knew now there was no fixing it, with either of them.

"That's an awfully large responsibility for one man."

He slid back in his chair, looking smaller in his exhaustion. "It is my duty but also an honor."

Not knowing what else to say, Emery fiddled with the stalks of the strawberries she'd eaten as Liam's gaze shot back and forth between them. Again, she was struck by how little her brother was adding to the conversation. Usually, he ran the conversations.

Tavor cleared his throat and continued more brightly. "Miss Aalokin, I assume your brother has filled you in that we have been on route to Dornwell as previously planned?"

She nodded. "I know."

"Although of course, given what all you've been through, I would completely understand if either of you would prefer to be returned home immediately."

She nodded again. "Thank you for being so considerate."

"I was wondering, however..." Tavor shifted in his seat, looking down into his cup. "I was *hoping* that, with your return, you might both, perhaps, choose to stay." He looked up again, specifically at her. "Do you think you still have it in your hearts to help me? To continue the mission on which we set out together?"

Emery looked to Liam to be the first to respond. This was her brother's decision. He had been chosen for the task, after all, not her.

But Liam just looked back at her, as if waiting for her to answer for them both.

She didn't understand. Liam had always been the one with the answers, the louder, bolder of them both. Her "death" must have really shaken him.

Next to him, Tavor looked simultaneously hopeful and resigned.

Then she realized what was happening. They weren't looking to her because they saw her as a leader, but because they believed that, out of all of them, she had been through the most challenging time. It was her choice because Liam wouldn't continue if she wasn't comfortable with it, and Tavor knew he couldn't achieve his own goals without them.

But she wasn't damaged by her experience, certainly not in the way they both seemed to think. The world was damaged though, and everything she'd seen during her time on the *Audacity* had only proved how much the world needed them to act. Someone had to do something about the violence and confusion continuing to tear this horrendous, damaging rift between Ungifted humans and elemists. If they said no to his plans now, who was there to step in?

She gazed back at Tavor, confident in her decision. "I still want to help you." She glanced over at her brother. "I'm sure Liam feels the same."

He gave a curt nod, then smiled. "Amazing how someone coming back from the dead can boost morale."

Tavor sat up a little straighter. "You'll help me? You'll stay in Dornwell, be my ambassadors?"

"Yes," said Liam.

"For a while at least," Emery added more cautiously. "Until it's clear we're making progress."

Tavor let out a long breath, then got up and strode round the table, clasping hands with Liam, then doing the same with Emery. His palm and fingers were warm against hers, his skin softer than –

Sean. Lying in cold seawater, unable to pick himself up. Sean, who –

"Thank you," Tavor gushed. "This means everything to me. We *will* make the world a safer, more peaceful place by doing this. I promise."

The cabin suddenly felt stifling, and Emery stood up. "You'll have to excuse me, I think I need to retire for a while."

Tavor seemed unsuspicious. "Of course, you must still be exhausted. Rest as much as you need, and don't hesitate to ask if there's anything –"

"I'll be fine, thank you. I just need to lie down for a bit."

When Emery was halfway across the deck, she realized Liam was strolling up beside her in the warm morning sun. "You're thinking about the Scourge," he said quietly.

She didn't answer. She didn't need to, and the fewer words spoken out loud on the subject the better, out here in the open.

"When are we breaking him out?" he continued as matter-of-factly as if they were discussing what they'd just eaten.

She gazed at the horizon, at the ship with crimson sails far in the distance. "Tonight."

A warm, briny wind tugged at her hair and the sun beat down on her head, and for a moment she could breathe easier over the enormity of what she was planning to do that night. She wondered if this was how Sean felt before he released the prisoners who became his crew. Certainty that she was doing the right thing, trepidation at what the potential consequences might be.

# Chapter Thirty-Three

As soon as Caelin finished his morning training with the varens, the twins asked him back to Liam's cabin and told him their intention to free Sean.

"That's the worst idea I've ever heard," Caelin scoffed, crossing his arms and stepping further into the room away from them. "You've both lost your minds."

"He shouldn't be down there," Emery pressed. "Let's be honest, Tavor hasn't told us much about him. And what he has, very little fits the person I've spent the last few weeks with. Or his crew for that matter."

"How can you be certain though?" Caelin countered. "That he hasn't fooled you? That he isn't just talented at tricking people?"

Emery straightened. "Whatever he is or isn't, he saved my life, and I owe him."

"We're going to do it," said Liam, cross-legged on the bed. "The question is, are we doing it with or without you?"

Caelin scowled and glared at the floor. "If I did help you..." He closed his eyes and sighed. "How do you possibly want to pull this off?"

"Gunpowder." Caelin's head snapped up, and Liam grinned at

him. "And you."

"We can't use gunpowder again," said Caelin. "That would be far too suspicious."

"I didn't say we had to make anything explode."

Emery glanced at her brother, who was practically shining with new enthusiasm. Apparently, in the weeks since their separation, he had taken it upon himself to learn everything he could about the volatile powder the outsiders used, both out of interest and as a distraction from his grief, in much the same way that Caelin had thrown himself into his new training.

Their friend chewed his cheek for a moment, then uncrossed his arms. "Go on."

"From what I heard the medic say to one of the varens," Liam continued, "if you *ingest* gunpowder, even a little, it can do...interesting things to your digestive system."

"Like food poisoning?"

"Very much so."

"And what, dare I ask, are you planning to do with this information?"

"Sneak it into the crew's food," said Emery. Caelin looked surprised that she would suggest this, but she shrugged. "It's not hugely supervised, and apart from Tavor and us everyone eats the same stuff."

"And if everyone gets sick at the same time," Liam added, "they'll probably just think their food's gone bad."

"Probably," Caelin echoed, with less confident emphasis.

"We'll pour a small amount of gunpowder into the pots before dinner, so this evening the entire crew will end up eating some. Apart from Tavor and us."

Caelin's disgruntlement was slowly softening into intrigue. "Which would mean...even the guards becoming sick, and not being able to make their shift."

"Which is where you come in," Liam confirmed. "Out of the three of us, it would make most sense for Tavor to ask you to watch the cells, since you're his little *prodigy*."

Caelin squinted at Liam. "What, and you think I'm just going let him out?"

"Of course, not." Liam's glee began to waver a little, and Emery looked down to avoid meeting Caelin's eye. "We'll have to make it look like you put up a fight."

⚓

During that evening's dinner, Emery made every effort to keep a steady conversation going with Tavor. As soon as they sat down she began peppering him with questions about Dornwell, what they'd be doing once they got there, and he seemed delighted to answer everything she threw at him. Caelin and Liam also made their efforts, and when the food finally came a small wave of relief flowed through the three of them.

They also took their time leaving Tavor's cabin afterwards, then quietly went to sit in Liam's cabin until a knock sounded at the door. An Anders's head poked into the room, and Emery felt a pang of guilt at the sight of his sweaty forehead and tight face. But then she remembered the way he bashed his pistol into Sean's head and she didn't feel as bad anymore.

"Mr. Airakin," he addressed Caelin, then paused for a moment, looking like he was suppressing the urge to be sick. "Commissioner Thantos has asked for you."

"Of course." Caelin stood up and followed him out.

The twins waited for as long as they could bear before sticking their heads into the hallway. The ship creaked and groaned around them but was otherwise silent. Emery's stomach flip-flopped as they crept out and through the shadows, making their way to the bowels of the ship where, hopefully, only Caelin and Sean would be waiting for them.

They managed to reach the top of the stairs leading down to the brig undisturbed, at which point Liam caught Emery's wrist. "Are you certain about this? Because you won't be able to undo it."

Despite the slight tremor the question sent through her, she was certain. She had to be. "Yes."

They took the steps down and pushed open the damp, creaking door to the brig. As before, a lone sconce was flickering on the wall, washing the cells with orange light and deep shadows. Once more, cold water welcomed Emery's bare feet as she pushed into the room, and the musky air trailed chilly fingers over her skin.

Caelin was standing outside Sean's cell, glaring down at him with his arms crossed. He turned as the twins entered. "Everyone's puking their guts up. I hope you're proud of yourselves."

Liam's expression caught somewhere between a grin and a grimace. "I am a little."

Emery rushed past him to check on Sean. He was still on his side, eyes closed, but there were new bruises on his jaw and cheek, a new cut slashing through one of his eyebrows.

"Sweet Eldoris," she breathed. "What have they been doing to him?"

Sean's eyes flicked open, and this time he lifted his chin slightly and his hand twitched towards her.

"His last dose is wearing off," said Caelin. "And I've given him some antidote to help it go faster."

Caelin pulled a small mechanism out of his pocket, constructed out of a mixture of glass and metal. The paralyzing agent inside was an unassuming, dull yellow, but the long, sleek needle protruding from one end made Emery's skin crawl.

Emery turned back to Sean, who was still watching her. His mouth opened a fraction, as if trying to speak, but he didn't quite seem able to. He rolled onto his stomach and tried to pick himself up, without success.

"The rest should start to wear off pretty quickly now," said Caelin, then handed Liam the curare, as well as a little silver key from another of his pockets.

"Perfect," said Liam. He pocketed the curare, but his confidence was clearly beginning to wane as they reached the point none of them were looking forward to. "Are you ready?"

Emery's heart was hammering. "You don't have to, Caelin.

We'll understand if —"

"I know." Caelin planted his feet wider, lifted his chin towards Liam. "Better make this count, because you're never doing it again."

Liam's grin returned, but he swallowed as his hand formed a fist. "Sorry."

"Just get it over with." Caelin closed his eyes.

Liam hesitated for a moment, then swung into Caelin's face with a horrendous crunch. Caelin stumbled backwards, clutching his nose, while Liam spun in circles, shaking his hand and spewing obscenities. "Are you made of stone?"

Caelin removed his hands from his face. "How does it look?" Blood streamed from his nose, and already a darker hew was spreading under his eye.

Emery winced. "Convincing. Now let's get a move on."

Liam jammed the key into the cell door's lock and turned. As soon as the mechanism clicked, Emery flung open the door and rushed inside, dropping to her knees beside Sean in the icy water. He had managed to raise himself onto one knee and arm, and she grasped his other arm to help him up. His entire body was shaking, she hoped from the effort and not from being cold through.

"What —" His voice was weak, his speech slow. "What... are...you..."

She stroked the wet hair from his eyes. "We're getting you out of here."

Sean started shaking his head, but she ignored him. His lips were blue, and fresh blood was leaking from the wound splitting his eyebrow.

"Can you walk?"

In answer, he tried to get his legs underneath him, but then lurched sideways. She managed to catch him before he hit the ground, but he hissed in pain as her hands landed against his chest. She couldn't tell what this new injury was but investigating would have to wait.

Liam and Caelin entered the cell beside them, any trace of

enjoyment gone from Liam's face. The curare was back in his hands, and he was fingering it nervously.

Emery turned to Caelin, knowing it was probably too late. "You really don't have to do this."

Caelin held his arm out towards Liam. "You know we can't stop now."

"I'm sorry," Liam said.

Caelin sighed and closed his eyes. "It's alright."

"No," Sean breathed, struggling weakly against Emery. "Don't –"

But Liam was already pushing the needle into Caelin's skin, carefully squeezing the mechanism at the other end of the device to inject him with the paralyzing liquid. The dose administered, Liam pulled the needle back out and a bead of blood blossomed on Caelin's skin. Almost immediately, he sagged into Liam, who lowered him gently into the chill water and set him down beside Sean.

"I'll admit, this...is...not..." Caelin's words began to slur. "Not...how I ex...pected...this...jour...nnn..."

Emery grabbed his hand as he struggled to make any further sound. When his mouth stilled and gaze began to soften, she fought against the panic and guilt rising in her and squeezed his hand, hoping he could feel it. "I'm sure it won't be long before some of the others recover and come down here to check on things." She didn't want to leave him like this, didn't want to leave him at the mercy of the varens or other crew, but they had to make it look like he'd lost a fight with Sean, with no involvement from them.

He nodded weakly, then his head slumped back against the wall and his entire body went slack. As gently as he could, Liam arranged his limbs so that as little of him as possible was in the water, while Emery prayed she'd made the right decision.

"Liam," she said when Caelin was as comfortable as he could make him. "I need your help. Sean can't stand without both of us."

His lips pressed tightly together, Liam came over and threw

317

one of Sean's arms over his shoulders, and together they heaved him onto his feet. Sean struggled to keep his own legs underneath him, but between them they managed to half drag, half carry him out of the brig. Emery fought the urge to go back for Caelin as well, tried to reassure herself that he'd be fine. She'd seen numerous times now how this paralyzing agent worked and then wore off. He wasn't in danger from it.

The next challenge was getting Sean up the short flight of steps to the floor above, but, with a lot of grunting and shifting of weight, they managed. Thankfully, they also didn't encounter anyone as they began inching along the ship's dark hallways.

"Wait," Sean mumbled at one point, head lolling on his shoulders. "Stop."

"No," Emery hissed, even though her shoulders were aching under his weight. "We need to make sure you're safe."

By the time they reached the next flight of stairs, Sean's legs had regained some of their function. As his weight began to ease on their shoulders, he also began to struggle against them, trying to drag his arms down their backs and dig his feet into the floorboards.

"What are you doing?" Liam kicked his feet, making him lose his balance and have to lean on them again.

"You can't," Sean urged, fear piercing his voice. "He'll be furious."

"He won't find out it's us," Emery insisted as they dragged him on. Only one more deck until they made it outside.

"He...always...finds out."

His words sent shivers down her spine. But even if they were caught, what would Tavor do? She, Liam, and Caelin were instrumental to his great plan. How would punishing them, driving a wedge between himself and his new allies, serve his purpose?

"We're almost there," she whispered.

Footsteps thundered behind them as they approached the final stairs. They melted into the shadows behind a stack of crates, just as a man in varen garb hurtled past them on wobbly legs. He nearly tripped twice going up the steps, and a moment later they heard retching. Soon after, a second varen stumbled past, also heading up to the top deck.

"We didn't think that aspect through," mumbled Liam.

"How many do you think are up there?" Emery asked.

"Who knows. Hopefully they'll be too busy to notice us."

Emery's body began to shake as they hauled Sean to his feet, and a cold, fearful sweat dripped down her spine.

"Take...me...back," Sean panted, then wrenched his arms so hard both twins lost their grip. He fell onto his hands and knees. "You don't...understand."

"Sean, listen to me." Emery took his face in her hands. His eyes were glassy and wide. "I am not going to let you rot down there. You're not a monster, so I'm not going to let you be treated like one."

He swallowed and grabbed her wrist, his grip so weak he could barely hold on. "You...don't –"

"Em," Liam hissed. "Another one's coming."

They dragged Sean behind a set of water barrels next to the crates as a third varen stumbled up to the stairs, only this one didn't make it further. He leaned against the other side of the stairs to them and vomited, the wet sound and smell turning Emery's own stomach.

"Quick," Liam whispered, hauling Sean to his feet. "And both of you keep your mouths shut unless you *want* us to get us caught."

Sean didn't say anything as they all but dragged him up the last set of stairs, but he continued to struggle against them. He wasn't strong enough to fight them off fully, but the fact he was trying at all was making Emery increasingly nervous.

Just before they reached the top of the stairs, Liam went to scout out the situation above deck.

Sean grabbed her hand. "Emery." His voice was still soft, but there was greater strength behind it now. "You can't do this."

"Yes, I can. Your crew's waiting for you. We can't let them down, can we?"

"What?"

"They've been following us." She knew she had to take this chance to ask him, before he left. "Tavor told me...you set fire to people's homes." Sean seemed to shrink into himself slightly. "Is that true?"

He took a while to meet her eyes. "It was an accident."

"And did you...damage Tavor's leg in some way?"

His expression hardened. "That wasn't."

Emery's mouth opened to ask why, but Liam appeared at the top of the steps. "Let's go!" He helped her heave Sean up the rest of the way, who had at least stopped fighting them now. "They're only a few up here," Liam whispered. "But the long-boats at the stern seem deserted. We just need to be quick."

Up on deck, they avoided the pools of light cast by the whale-oil lanterns and kept clear of anything that looked or sounded like a person. As Liam had said, the stern appeared to be empty, and they went straight for the closest longboat strung up against the ship's side.

"Get in," Emery urged Sean. "Just get in the boat and go."

Liam let go of Sean, but Emery kept hold of his arm to steady him as he leaned against the railing. His legs were just about able to hold him upright. He turned to look at her, his eyes still huge, blood leaking from his eyebrow into his eye.

Her throat suddenly felt sore at the realization she'd most likely never see him again. "*Now*."

"I can't." He sounded almost emotional himself. "And you can't stay."

"Sean," Emery pleaded, her skin prickling with the knowl-edge that someone could spot them at any moment. "Don't worry about me. We'll be fine. But *you* need to leave."

He grabbed her hand, more firmly this time. "You don't know...what he is. He –"

"Tavor? He's...trying to help us. There's clearly been some terrible misunderstanding between you, but –"

"No. That's not –"

They all fell silent at the sound of footsteps echoing nearby.

"Get him in the boat," Liam hissed to Emery, then began

tiptoeing in the direction of the noise. She reasoned he could buy them time by bumping into whoever the footsteps belonged to, pretending he had fallen ill himself and stopping to commiserate with them.

She turned back to Sean, whose mouth was slightly open as if preparing to say something else. Something she couldn't risk.

She surged onto her toes, grabbed his face, and silenced him with her lips against his. He went entirely still, didn't even breathe. And then he sighed, his body relaxing into hers. One hand cupped her jaw, while the other found the small of her back, and he pressed her closer, deepening the kiss. Heat rushed through her body, until she forgot where she was, what she was supposed to be doing.

"That wasn't what I had in mind!" Liam whispered sharply, stepping back towards them.

Emery pulled away and Sean, for a moment, seemed newly drugged. Steeling herself to the task of saving him, she shoved him in the chest and toppled him into the longboat.

Liam was already working the lines, trying to tug them free. But Emery came prepared. She would not be defeated by a longboat again. She yanked Sean's dagger from where she'd sheathed it at her waist.

She felt the longboat move as Sean shifted his weight, trying to pick himself up again. "Quick!" she hissed at Liam.

Liam produced a knife of his own and, in unison, they slashed at the ropes. The boat dropped into the darkness below, the slap of wood on water so loud that Emery winced, bracing herself for someone to rush their direction to investigate the sounds. But the gods decided to be kind, and everyone on deck was seemingly still too distracted by their own woes to notice.

Liam grabbed her elbow and tried to pull her back the way they'd come. "Let's go."

"Hold on." She quickly stepped to the railing and peered over, but there was nothing to see but darkness.

Sean was gone. And though it's what she wanted, something in her chest seemed to crack just the same.

# Chapter Thirty-Four

They heard the shouting when Caelin was found all the way from Liam's cabin. It hadn't taken all night, but long enough for the waiting to become unbearable and drive them to start pacing the room, worrying about him being alone in the cold water, unable to move. In Emery's case, the worry had also been about Sean, out on the open ocean in a tiny boat, with no guarantee his crew would find him by sunrise.

The shouting seemed to reach its peak, with footsteps banging so dramatically through the ship that puffs of dust were knocked from the wooden beams above them. The twins waited a few more moments before leaving the cabin, then made their way up to the main deck, feigning confusion at the varens sprinting about, most of them clutching a weapon in one hand, their stomachs with the other, faces shiny with sickness and panic.

Tavor was standing beside the remains of the pulley system they had destroyed, one hand gripping his stick, the other gestured wildly. He was yelling at two varens, his anger burning bright even though Emery couldn't make out what he was saying.

"What's going on?" Liam asked as they stepped over to him.

Tavor whirled round, blue cape swirling behind him, and he

stared down at them with lightning in his eyes. "You shouldn't be up here," he said, clearly attempting to keep his voice steady. "It may be dangerous."

"Dangerous?" Liam asked, all innocence. "Why?"

"The Forbidden has escaped. Again." He glared at the two men, who scurried away like mice.

"Escaped?" Emery forced her voice into a high squeak. "What about Caelin? Is he alright?"

A muscle pulsed in Tavor's jaw as he tried to keep his fury in check. "Your friend is fine. The Forbidden overpowered him, but he's not grievously injured."

Real worry began to leak into Emery's act. "Where is he?"

"With the medic." Tavor closed his eyes and took a deep breath. When he opened them again, his tone was softer. "Please, go to him and don't leave his side. You'll be safer down there."

"Why are you this worried?" She indicated the cut ropes, the missing longboat, then made her tone as sympathetic as possible. "Don't you think he's long gone?"

"Perhaps. But he's done this before, tricked us. He may still be at large. Please, I'd rather you were safely below decks."

The twins nodded, Emery hoping she looked convincingly terrified.

A varen, still wobbly on his feet, led them down to the medic's room on the level below. Caelin was lying in one of the small cots, still and silent. Emery went over to him and took his hand. He didn't move, and his skin felt cold and clammy, but otherwise the medic assured them he was fine, just sleeping off his ordeal. She clung to the fact that Sean was now free again, at least from his cell and the terrible fate Tavor had planned for him.

THE VARENS SEARCHED the ship well into dawn, from the lowest deck to the highest point of the rigging. Tavor's shouts rang out from various places as he unleashed his fury on his men, shouting orders until he grew hoarse. Meanwhile the twins stayed with Caelin, who at some point woke up and underwent a second check from the medic. Thankfully, he remained unharmed save for his very bruised face.

Tavor interrupted his supervision of the search briefly to check in on him. To Emery's surprise, he offered no criticism, only an apology for asking him to perform such a sensitive task with so little training. It was clear his words hurt Caelin's pride, but he said nothing.

It seemed no one suspected him, or the twins, of helping Sean escape. The Scourge of the Sea had simply vanished from the ship like a phantom. Emery knew she should be happy, relieved, but instead dread gnawed at her insides. It had all been too easy for comfort.

When morning came and the search for Sean had finally been called off, she went to lie down in her cabin. Sleep still eluded her though. She couldn't stop thinking about how hard Sean had fought against his own escape. He'd been afraid, but it seemed more so for her than himself. Why?

It didn't matter. He was gone now, and hopefully safely back with his crew. She had freed him, in much the same way as he had once released the elemists that would become his friends, and now she would never see him again. Never again see his tentative smile, nor hear his even rarer laugh.

Never again kiss him.

Her heart suddenly felt very heavy.

She'd kissed other boys before, even Caelin once. They'd been eleven and had just attended their first binding ceremony. Watching the two lovers pledge themselves to each had enthralled them so much they had reenacted it together with their own childlike imitation, then kissed once before giggling, wiping their mouths and swearing never to tell anyone else about it.

But Sean's kiss, just remembering it made her feel like the world was spinning. She tried to fall asleep again and again, but each time her senses came alive with the memory of his lips on hers, his hand on her back as he pulled her closer.

None of it mattered. He was gone, and she was going to Dornwell to help bring about peace.

Even in her exhaustion, she eventually had to give up trying to sleep. She rolled out of bed, strapped her lim to her back and blearily crossed the hall to poke her head into Liam's cabin. He was passed out, snoring softly. She found Caelin in his own cabin, much the same way.

Sighing with envy, she wandered up above deck. Late-afternoon sunlight was squeezing through a layer of white cloud, casting the ship in a hazy golden glow. Sailors were scurrying around, calling to one another as they pulled ropes and tied off knots, and varens were marching up and down, a few still looking a little green. Every one of them avoided eye contact with her, sidestepping with pressed-together lips if she seemingly got too close. She was happy to avoid them as well. She hadn't forgotten the way the other varens had attacked and injured her and Sean's crew, the way even Ungifted humans had already tried to kill her.

She snaked her way through to the prow and gazed at the bowsprit, deciding it was stubbier than the *Audacity's*. Had Sean made it back there? Was he sitting on his own bowsprit now, staring once more into the distance with his hollow gaze?

She jumped as a hand grasped her shoulder and spun round, reaching for her lim.

"Apologies." Tavor took a half step back. "I didn't mean to startle you. I called out a few times, but you must not have heard."

Her pulse should have calmed at the sight of him, but instead she found it speeding further. "No, I'm sorry," she sputtered. "I'm...tired, I'm not sleeping well."

His eyebrows raised sympathetically. "I'm sorry to hear that. Are you otherwise...alright?"

She nodded and turned to lean against the railing, not

wanting to look him in the eye for too long. On the horizon, the sun was starting to descend in earnest. "A little shaken perhaps."

Tavor came to stand next to her, planting his forearms on the railing. "We will catch him again. I promise."

She gazed at him from the corner of her eye. None of his earlier fury remained. There was even a tiny smile lifting the corner of his mouth as he stared at the weakening sun. The soft light blurred the sharp edges of his jaw and cheekbones, making him look almost...happy.

"Don't take this the wrong way, but you seem strangely pleased for someone who's prisoner has just escaped."

"Oh, he'll show up again. In the end, I am the cat." He turned to her fully, and she felt compelled to face him, not liking the sound of where this was going. "And he is the mouse." His smile came into full force, and he continued brightly, "Now, we have more important things to concern ourselves with."

It was difficult to turn away from him, his smile so radiant and convincing, almost enough to dull the gnawing anxiety in her stomach. She smiled back at him, as confidently as she could. "Dornwell."

"The future."

# Chapter Thirty-Five

After three weeks of sailing in changeable weather, they awoke one morning to cries of "Land ho!" Emery, Liam, and Caelin rushed up to the top deck, and there it was. Dornwell's hulking mass lay in front of them, slowly expanding on the horizon.

The three found themselves a place on the bow where they weren't in anyone's way. From there, they drank in every feature as the morning wore on and Dornwell grew larger on the horizon, until it took up their entire field of vision. At the glorious sight, anxiety and excitement warred inside Emery. Finally, she was getting to see this city, to step out into it for the first time. But it was a city full of people that hated her and she couldn't help worrying about what was to come.

The most obvious impression of Dornwell so far was that it was huge, far larger than Brimlad, perhaps even larger than the entirety of Orabel. It was also very...grey. Every building she could see, and there were so many she couldn't even count them. Even the sky, nearly blocked out by the city now, was smothered by steely clouds that mixed with great plumes of slate-colored smoke rising up from various buildings. Dornwell also sported very few trees. Next to no greenery interrupted the endless field of dullness.

The docks, made up of dozens of long wooden piers built right up to the city, morphed into view as they neared. Ships of various shapes and sizes bobbed in the pewter water, the shades of their sails and flapping flags the only spots of real color Emery could make out so far.

Except for the people. Sailors and merchants were moving up and down the various piers stretching out into the port, loading or unloading goods, their clothes possibly the greatest collection of colors she had seen in one place outside the gardens back home. Yellows as bright as bananas, pure tomato reds, periwinkle blues, leafy greens...The faint echo of the gardens' splendor made her momentarily intensely homesick.

"Aya would have loved this," she breathed.

"She would," Liam agreed quietly.

The ship reached the port, and Tavor and his men set about mooring against one of the piers. The three went to meet him at the ship's waist just as his men were finishing tying the mooring lines and placing a plank across to the pier.

"Well." Tavor's smile was bright again. "How do you find your first sight of Dornwell?"

Emery struggled to find the words to capture how she felt about the immense construction in front of them. "It's...impressive."

"Bigger than anything we've ever seen," Liam added.

Tavor's smile widened. "You've barely seen anything yet."

He led them off the ship and out into the docks, a group of varens coming up behind them and enclosing them on all sides, hands ready over their weapons.

"Precautions," Tavor said, catching Emery's concerned reaction before she could wipe it off her face. "It can get rowdy here on occasion."

Between the varens, various details caught Emery's eye as they walked. Besides the wonderful colors of the clothing sported around them, there were also fabrics she'd never seen before, styles of tailoring she could never have imagined. One group that passed them wore shiny emerald tunics that were so long they reached their ankles, with sleeves that dragged impractically on the ground. Another group wore only tight, maroon-colored vests and breeches with silver straps across their chests. There was also a significant number of varens marching up and down, always in groups of four, always with hands hovering just over their weapons.

Merchants had set up stands along the docks, some displaying swathes of satins and silks, jars of cinnamon and jasmine, bundles of raw sugar cane, others carrying an array of sleek weapons, shiny trinkets and piles of rolled-up scrolls. All around them, sailors shouted to one another and sellers called out their wares. At one point, a dirty-looking child wheeled a wagon full of sea creatures passed them, crying, "Oysters, crabs, clams, cuttlefish and cockles, all fresh from Ruhette!" Gulls cried overhead and men haggled in front of stalls and by the sides of ships. The sea slapped the hulls and the wind whistled through the rigging. The sea's briny aroma intertwined with that of the sizzling meats hanging from some of the stands, as well as a strange metallic smell that Emery couldn't quite place.

Tavor glanced back at them, his eyes bright. "It's a lot to take in, isn't it?"

The three of them agreed.

"Dornwell is a massive port," he continued. "Merchants and travelers come here from all over the realm to sell and trade for things you can't find anywhere else."

He stopped them in front of a contraption that sparkled in the weak sunlight. "This is a carriage. We'll be using it for the next leg of our journey."

The carriage looked golden and pearlescent, a small cabin with a low door on either side sitting on top of a set of large wheels wider than Emery was tall. Two huge creatures were tethered to its front, pawing at the ground with gigantic hooves. These must be the *horses* about which she had heard numerous stories. They towered over her, and she flinched as one of them reared back its broad head with a thundering cry, tossing its tawny mane.

Tavor chuckled at her reaction. "Don't worry, they're quite tame."

Between the horses and the cabin, a man was sitting on a wooden seat. He had leather straps in his hands connected to various bands tied around the horses' heads and in turn connecting the beasts to each other. Before she could interrogate how kind this was to the animals, Tavor herded her and the others inside, then stepped up himself and pulled the doors closed. As soon as he sat down, the carriage jerked into motion, rattling out of the docks and onto a stone-covered road. Behind them, four varens clambered into a second carriage and followed them closely.

Even inside, the carriage was inlayed with gold, and the cushions they were sitting on were of a crimson fabric so soft that Emery had to resist the urge to rub it against her cheek. Across from her and Caelin, Tavor smiled at the three of them in the same fatherly way as earlier. "I'm so pleased finally to be able to show you all my home. We'll go straight to the castle where you'll be staying."

They passed grey building after grey building. At first they were small and at times seemed to lean against each other, but the further they went into the city the taller and wider they became, the straighter and higher they stood. Some of the people wandering the streets here were also dressed even more flamboyantly than those back at the docks. It was difficult not to feel overwhelmed.

A monster of a building began to loom ahead of them, larger than any she'd seen so far. It had to be taller than two of the greatest redwoods in Orabel combined, and ten times wider. No, much more than that. Unlike the other buildings, it also seemed to be constructed entirely of white marble, so white her eyes watered looking at it.

As they neared the enormous building, they approached a giant wooden door, reinforced with what looked like some sort of shining orange metal. Extending from either side of the door and encircling the building itself for as far as she could see was a massive wall made of the same white stone. Guards were standing by the door, and even more were marching along the top of the protective wall. Instead of wearing the varens' black and blue though, these guards wore plain white.

The giant doors opened, and the carriages rolled through, entering the castle grounds. Great swaths of manicured grass dotted with palm trees flanked the long driveway. At last, they reached the castle itself and the carriage slowed to a stop.

The four varens jumped out of their carriage, jogging over to surround them again on all sides. Their driver also stepped down and swung open the door on her right. Tavor climbed out, then turned and offered her his hand. She didn't need it, but knew now that politeness meant she should take it anyway. She let him support her as she stepped down from the carriage, and then all she could do while the other two descended was gape at the building stretching to the sky above them. It seemed to be made entirely of towers, each ending in a spire. Hundreds of arched windows stared down at them like too many eyes, and giant falcons of white marble perched on the walls, looking ready to swoop down at any moment.

"Gods," Liam and Caelin breathed together.

"Welcome to Daehaven Castle," said Tavor, sweeping his arms wide and walking backwards towards the castle's large double doors. "The home of the Rexleys, our royal family, and now, of course, yourselves."

More guards in white flanked the castle's doors. When the guards saw Tavor leading his group towards them, they bowed their heads and swung the door open, making the wood groan.

Tavor marched straight in. Emery, Liam, and Caelin followed, the varens still surrounding them, and the castle swallowed them like a giant, stone beast. The inside was as unbelievably large as it looked on the outside. Everywhere was white stone, with colorful tapestries on the walls depicting events from an unfamiliar history and crystal chandeliers hanging from the ceilings casting rainbows of light over everything.

There were also people other than guards here, adorned with extravagant clothing and ridiculously high hairstyles. As Tavor led them along, the castle people watched the newcomers pass from the corners of their eyes, scattering like flocks of birds if any of them returned their gaze.

The corridors stretched on for leagues as Tavor marched them up and down, until Emery had lost all sense of where they were in relation to the main door.

"How many Orabels do you think you could fit in here?" Liam whispered.

"At least one and a half," Caelin answered.

"This must all seem a little daunting," Tavor said, turning to Emery.

"You don't happen to have a map for this place as well, do you?" she quipped.

He smiled. "Trust me, soon you won't have any worries finding your way around."

Finally, they stopped in front of a nondescript oak door. "Caelin, you can follow Anders here," Tavor said, nodding at one of the varens accompanying them. "Since you'll be continuing your training with them, I thought it might be nice for you to stay in their quarters as well. They can show you the ropes from here."

Caelin looked to Anders, who seemed surprisingly happy about the suggestion.

"Sounds good to me," he said to Tavor. "Will you send for me later then?"

"Yes. I'll fetch you after we've all had a chance to freshen up."

Caelin wandered off with Anders, and Tavor turned his attention to the twins. "I'll take you both to your rooms in a moment, but first I'd really like to show you where we'll be meeting with the king and other significant dignitaries once our plan is under-way." His green eyes were sparkling with excitement. "I've waited for so long."

Hope rose giddily in Emery's chest as she took in the oak door. After all this time, all the travelling, dangers and mishaps, they were finally here, united in their determination to make a positive difference, able to begin the work itself.

"Ready?" he asked.

"Yes," she said, echoed closely by Liam.

Cold air swept through Emery's hair as Tavor swung the door open and led them inside. The chamber was murky with darkness. She couldn't see anything directly in front of her, but off in the distance, or even below it seemed, a dull orange glow drew her attention.

"Watch your step." Tavor's voice echoed off the walls. "We're going down a set of stairs."

"Why is it so dark?" Liam asked.

"You'll see in a moment."

The twins followed him down, the three remaining varens trailing behind. The chill in the air gripped them tighter the further down they went, and the dread in Emery's heart resurfaced. She tried to ignore it, keeping her eyes on the glowing orange rectangle at the bottom of the stairs.

They reached the lower floor and entered a room that looked exactly like the ones in which Sean had been locked aboard Tavor's ships, only this one was huge and made of stone. A single low-burning torch on the wall illuminated a vast number of iron-barred cells, so many they disappeared into the shadows on either side of the chamber.

"What is this?" Liam demanded.

Emery's anxiety crested like a wave, and she started to back out of the chamber.

Only to feel Tavor's solid chest behind her, his arms wrapping around her.

"Liam, run!"

She gasped as something sharp pricked her neck, and with a cry Liam swung his lim at the nearest varen, but the other two took hold of him in an instant. Emery tried to kick and twist her way free of Tavor, but a sinister warmth was already seeping down from her neck, spreading itself across her whole body like a heavy blanket. Her feet barely managed to move, and slowly, though her heart galloped wildly, her body stopped responding completely. Her head lolled back against Tavor's chest, and she felt it vibrate as he spoke.

"I may have forgotten to mention a few things." Holding her tight with one arm, he ripped her lim from her back with the other and began dragging her towards the closest cell. "Welcome to Daehaven's dungeon." Terror pricked her skin like hot needles as Liam screamed after her and tried to free himself. "This is your home now." Tavor tossed her into the cell. She landed flat on her back, the hard stone smacking the air from her lungs and making her skull ring from the impact.

She couldn't respond, couldn't even turn her head to watch as the varens dragged Liam away. She could only lie there as Tavor slammed the cell door closed, locking her inside, and listen to Liam's shouts fading away as the varens dragged him further into the dungeon, before his shouts fell silent altogether.

# Chapter Thirty-Six

As a final insult before he and the varens left, Tavor snuffed out the dungeon's only light, leaving behind a thick, smothering darkness. Emery felt it press down on her like a living thing, and the silence was so absolute she couldn't hear anything beyond her own frantic heartbeat and breathing. The fear that gripped her now was like nothing she'd ever felt before. Not only was she trapped in physical darkness, but also within her own body. Her mind roared like a high wind trying to command her limbs to move, but her muscles refused to work and her bones were just dead weights pinning her to the cold stone floor.

Tears welled in her eyes at Tavor's betrayal and cruelty, her fear for Liam − and Caelin, who right now was probably being dragged down to join them − and frustration at how powerless she was to do anything but wait for the curare to wear off. Beyond these raw emotions though, there was also deep confusion. How could the Arch-Elemists have let this happen? The gods had spoken to them, told them to trust Tavor. Was this another terrible misunderstanding then, like whatever had set Tavor so savagely against Sean, or had he somehow managed to... trick the gods?

The darkness around her kept its secrets, including where exactly Liam was being held. He could be no more than a few cells away for all she could tell, equally unable to move or speak.

Or was he...

No, she wouldn't allow herself to think that. Tavor clearly wanted them alive, he wouldn't have gone to all this trouble just to kill them upon arrival. But what his true intentions were, she could only speculate as the chill of the stone below began to seep into her bones, and none of it was good.

FOOTSTEP SOUNDED as someone descended the stairs. A light flared to life, impossibly bright after such complete darkness. Emery's eyes watered as she tried to determine how long she'd been lying there, whether she had fallen asleep. She still couldn't move, not even to wipe the tears from her face. The new light illuminated the cracked stone walls around her, and she could at least move her eyes to make out a dribble of water leaking through a crack where the nearest wall met the ceiling.

Her insides tensed as the clink of a key in a lock broke the silence and, with a creak, her cell door swung open.

"I hope you're well rested, Miss Aalokin." Tavor's voice was full of pleasure and pride. "Our work awaits."

Footsteps approached her and two varens crouched down to slide their hands under her armpits, heaving her upright. She dangled between, one of them grabbing the back of her head to keep it straight on her shoulders. Tavor was standing in the entrance to her cell, the lantern he was carrying rendering him as a collection of black and orange angles.

"The curare should begin to wear off in a moment." He spoke as if they were discussing the evening's dinner plans. "I hope. We don't have all the time in the world."

She had no choice but to stare back at him, for a brief moment glad the terror couldn't register on her face. Sure enough though, as he adjusted the cuff of his jacket like a bored child, she could feel her fingers twitch back into life.

The varen holding her head let go. It fell forward, but slowly, painstakingly, she managed to lift it enough to glare up at Tavor.

"Good enough for now." The earlier excitement returned to Tavor's eyes. "Shall we?" He whirled and marched off into the darkness, his lantern scattering and shifting the shadows as he went. The varens dragged her after him, toes scraping against the uneven floor, until they came to the fifth cell down. "There's our little Chosen One."

Emery's breath caught in her throat when she saw Liam on his belly behind the bars, half hidden in shadow. He was alive and had managed to raise himself up on one elbow, face screwed up with the effort. His mouth fell open as their eyes met, but he couldn't get any words out.

"Time to begin our first experiment." Tavor unlocked Liam's door, then stepped inside and casually leaned against the rusted bars running along the side of the cell.

Liam glared up at him, just about managing to slide his foot along the ground and get one of his knees underneath him. If he was frightened, he gave no indication.

"When you're ready," Tavor drawled. "We need you in a semi-fit state after all."

Liam pulled himself up into kneeling. "Burn...in... Pyralis's... fire," he slurred.

"Ah!" Tavor grinned. "Perhaps now we're ready."

Feeling the first glimmer of strength return to her, Emery tried to pull out of the varens' grasp, but her attempts were so pitiful they barely noticed.

Tavor crouched in front of Liam, like an eager father before his toddler. "Now, show me what you can *really* do."

Liam spat at Tavor's boots, although the glob sadly landed inches short.

"I thought you might say that." Tavor stood up again, beckoning the varens to bring Emery inside. She dug her feet into the ground, again too weakly to make a difference. "Which is why it was so considerate of your leaders to give me two of you. It will make things so much easier." He produced a pistol from one of his pockets, pressing its cool barrel against Emery's forehead.

She tried to choke a warning to Liam, to tell him not to give in to the threat, but she couldn't force her tongue to make anything more than a few gurgled noises.

Tavor pressed his gun deeper into her skin. "Show me what you can do, or I'll blow your sister's head off."

For the first time, Liam's glare betrayed fear beneath its surface. "What do you want me to do?"

"Show me what makes you so special. The gifts that meant you were chosen."

"I've already shown you! Many times," Liam nearly growled.

Tavor canted his head to the side. "We both know you were holding out on me. A little gale here and frozen puddle there can't be all the special chosen one can do."

"I'm not special!" Liam snapped. "That *is* all I can do!"

"Show me," Tavor repeated calmly. "Or she dies."

Perhaps he really was serious. Emery could feel her pulse quicken against the end of the gun. She didn't want to die, not like this. "Liam," she managed to say, trying to keep the terror out of her voice. "It's alright. You can do this."

Liam looked from her to Tavor, his eyes wide. "Why are you doing this?"

"Show me what you can do," their captor growled. "Or I shoot *right now*." He pushed the barrel even harder against Emery's forehead, making her gasp in pain and fear.

Liam flinched and raised his shaking hands in the air, squeezing his eyes shut. The varens tightened their grip on Emery's arms as Liam concentrated, but an agonizing amount of time passed in which nothing seemed to happen other than sweat breaking out across his brow. Then, the dust on the stone floor began to rise in front of him. At first it was only by an inch, but then it began to spin, picking up speed and height, until a tiny twister of grime was swirling in the air between them. It grew larger and larger until Tavor and the varens holding Emery had to step back.

Liam opened his eyes to see what he had created, whereupon it quickly collapsed back to the floor.

Tavor looked down at the dust, and from the corner of her eye Emery saw his lips curl into a sneer. "I think you can do better than that."

"You said you wanted peace!" Liam spat at Tavor. "Why didn't you just march into Orabel with soldiers if this is all you want to do with us?"

Tavor pushed the barrel even harder into Emery's forehead and she bit her lip to keep from crying out. "Try again, or you'll be cleaning her blood off the floor."

"Is this your way of making the world a better place?" Emery asked, hoping to steer Tavor's attention away from Liam, to make him say something that would offer some sense. "Of creating a *lasting peace?*"

Tavor's anger flashed to her now. "That's exactly what I'm doing."

Rage began to hum in her veins. "I thought you *sorted* us," she hissed. "The innocent from the guilty."

His breath and disgust were hot against her face. "There are no innocents among you." He turned back to Liam. "You're not going to make me ask again, are you?"

Liam closed his eyes again, holding his shaking hands out in front of him. This time, the dust picked up into a slightly bigger twister. He had to concentrate so hard the tip of his tongue poked through his lips, but after a few moments the effort proved too great, and the debris collapsed once more to the ground.

But instead of looking disappointed, Tavor appeared... intrigued. "How interesting."

Emery had no idea what he could possibly find interesting in this situation.

He cocked his pistol, the click vibrating into Emery's skull.

Sean had tried to warn her about him. If only she had listened.

"Wait!" Liam cried. "I'll try again! Just let me get my strength back."

"Too late I'm afraid." Tavor turned to Emery, his face half hidden by the barrel of the gun. "It's a shame really. Your sister's such a beauty."

He pulled the trigger.

# Chapter Thirty-Seven

E mery squeezed her eyes shut as Liam screamed her name, bracing for the bullet's impact, for death, for her spirit to leave her body and join the elements around them.

But none of that came.

Slowly, she opened her eyes. Tavor was examining his pistol with a furrowed brow. "Not loaded." He looked back at her. "How fortunate for you."

Emery's still-weak knees began to buckle but the two varens held her in place. She was trembling so hard she had to clamp her teeth together to keep them from chattering.

"You bastard." Liam's eyes were glassy with unshed tears as he tried to pick himself off the floor, instead lurching forward onto his hands and knees. "You're sick."

"Why are you doing this?" she asked, hoping her pleading tone would make Tavor see sense.

Instead, he let out a dramatic sigh and kicked Liam in the ribs, sending him further into the cell. "Because your kind are a plague on this earth and need to be eliminated."

"How can you say that?" She watched her brother squirm in pain on the floor, then twisted to face Tavor. "After all the conversations we've had. When your own parents were elemists! What about them?"

He turned and stepped right up to her, his eyes burning with so much hatred she could practically feel heat coming off them. "They were the worst of all."

She was thrown by the level of hurt behind his rage, wondered what painful memories could possibly be brewing there, but he was clearly not going to be receptive to any questions at this time. She had to try a different angle.

"But we're not. We were going to help each other." She searched his face, looking for any semblance of sympathy, of understanding. "Weren't we?" He offered no response. "There are sick people on Orabel." Her voice threatened to break as her thoughts raced back to Ayana, growing weaker by the day. Perhaps even – "If you don't help us find a cure –"

His teeth flashed in the lantern light as his face almost touched hers. "They'll just have to die then, won't they?" Before she could argue further, he whipped a needle from his pocket and pressed it into her neck. The curare's warmth raced through her veins, rendering her muscles useless once more. "Take her to her cell. We're done for now."

"Where's Caelin?" she breathed as the varens dragged her away. Not having seen or heard him down here with them was almost worse than knowing he was also a captive now, also being treated this way, and not...

"Oh, don't worry." Tavor smiled coldly at her. "You'll see him soon enough."

ONCE MORE, Emery had to lie helplessly in the dark for an undetermined amount of time. At least this time she knew Liam wasn't far, but she couldn't work her mouth to call out to him, to check he was alright. All she could do was wait on the cold stone floor, fear and anger chewing up her insides.

Torchlight once more banished the complete darkness, but she could no longer draw comfort from this. Shadows meant nothing. Light meant Tavor, and further mindless cruelty. A key turned in the lock of her cell and the door slammed open, but when she'd been thrown in her head had lolled to face the back wall and now she couldn't see who was stepping inside.

Tavor, if it was him, didn't speak. There was just a soft clatter, and the door clinked shut again.

She found the strength to start making her head turn the other way, felt the awful weight holding her down slowly begin to ebb. A tin plate with a small lump of bread on it was sitting on the floor just inside the cell, along with a tankard of what she hoped was water. Beyond it on the wall outside, a lit torch had been left behind in a small act of mercy. Her mouth watered and stomach cramped with hunger at the sight. She didn't want to eat any of Tavor's food, but she refused to die in his dungeon either, which meant not starving.

She flexed her fingers, worked her toes, and slowly, her muscles began to return to her. With effort, she rolled onto her belly and crawled over to the plate, digging her fingers into the gaps between the stones. The bread was hard and she had to chew it for a long time, her jaw not yet back to strength, but with gulps of the water it went down.

As she ate, she pulled Sean's compass from her pocket. They took her lim from her back and Sean's dagger from her hip, but Tavor hadn't bothered searching her pockets or taking anything else from her. He knew her well, knew she wouldn't have anything useful to get her out of this cage. She was left with the compass, the vial of medicine Sean had also given her, and the little box from Liliath.

She held the compass to her chest, taking comfort in the fact that Sean wasn't in these dungeons with her. At least he'd gotten away. She thought about the person Sean was searching for, the mysterious woman Tavor had taken from him. And Emery wondered if she was in these dungeons too, hidden by the darkness.

As soon as she had emptied the plate and tankard, a dart whistled into her shoulder. She looked up to see a varen stepping into the torchlight, gun still raised in her direction.

Not such a merciful gesture then, he just needed something to see by.

She swore at him as her body went numb and slumped back to the ground.

Satisfied she no longer posed a threat, the varen briefly opened the door and took the dishes away.

ECHOING footsteps woke her from a fitful sleep. But they passed her own cell, accompanied by a hand-held light, stopping instead somewhere in the distance. Tavor murmured something and her brother's voice answered. She clung to the sound, the reassurance it offered that he continued to live, and was well enough to talk.

They spoke for some time, too softly for Emery to make out anything. Then their voices grew angrier, their words bouncing off the stone walls in a cacophony of echoes that made it difficult to understand them.

Then Liam started screaming.

He continued for an unbearable length of time. Then, just as suddenly, there was silence.

"Liam?" she called, cheeks already slick with frightened tears.

Footsteps approached. It was Tavor, strolling up to her cell with a torch in one hand, cane in the other. "Don't worry, he'll survive." His eyes swept across her, and his voice shifted to a mocking imitation of concern. "Oh, do you feel left out? It'll be your turn soon."

EMERY HAD EATEN at least three more meals of hard bread and the latest dose of curare was just seeping from her system when she felt the vibration of footsteps return. Light pierced the darkness once again and Tavor opened her cell door. Her pulse began pounding as he stepped inside, followed by giant boulder of a man. The newcomer towered over Tavor, but it was the metal rod and flaming torch in his massive hands that caused her the most concern.

Tavor's silver cane gleamed in the light of his lantern. "Good afternoon, Miss Aalokin. It's time for our own experiment."

The glee in his voice made her spine tingle, and she dragged herself as quickly as possible into sitting.

"Ah, good. You're in a decent state already."

She glared up at him, wanting to ask about Liam but her tongue was still heavy in her mouth. Behind him the door was open, taunting her with the impossibility of escape. And someone else standing there.

"Caelin?" Emery managed to say, her heart leaping in her chest. But when she took in her friend's stony expression, his varen uniform, and the fact that he wasn't in chains or otherwise restrained in any way, her heart began sinking again. "What..."

Tavor looked at Caelin, too. And smiled. "Come in and shut the door behind you."

To Emery's bewilderment and horror, Caelin did what he was told, and the door clanked loudly shut. Her friend moved to stand next to Tavor and stared at the ground, avoiding her probing stare.

A cold dread settled over her skin. "You're...helping him?"

Tavor placed a hand on Caelin's shoulder. "Caelin has come to understand and agree with what I'm doing."

Caelin cleared his throat, still not looking at her. "I want to help bring peace."

"How...is this...bringing peace?" Emery asked, incredulous.

"Tavor has a plan. He just needs information," Caelin said slowly. "Do your part and do what he asks." A warning underscored his tone, one she couldn't interpret.

Shock, horror, and hurt churned her nearly empty belly. But the slowly building rage also present burned the last of the curare away. "How can you do this to us? To your people?"

Finally, Caelin looked up and the iciness in his gaze made her flinch. "They've never been my people. I've always been an outsider. But out here, I'm not."

Tears pricked Emery's eyes, but she refused to let them fall. "Caelin, we're your friends."

His gaze somehow turned colder. "You've always used me."

"What?"

"Friends don't paralyze you and leave you in a dark, wet cell." Caelin's eyes shimmered as if he was fighting back tears himself. "You couldn't stand seeing the Forbidden in a cage. But you didn't care about leaving me in one."

Emery's breaths came in short bursts. "I – you – that's not –"

"Enough of this," Tavor cut in. If he was surprised to hear of their involvement in Sean's escape, he didn't show it. "We have an experiment to perform." He crouched in front of her. "Now, you know what I want. Show me what you can do."

Emery had to tear her gaze from Caelin to glare at Tavor. "Liam –"

"He's fine. But if you want him to continue to be, I suggest you do as I ask. Immediately."

Emery took a deep breath and straightened, but panic flickered in her chest. "I...can't. Not just...like that, on demand. My abilities have barely fully awakened."

"I wouldn't lie if I were you. Don't forget, I have your brother at my disposal."

Images of Liam, sprawled out bloodied and broken, swam before Emery's eyes. Like Sean had been. She looked back to Caelin, her heart splintering. "Caelin, please."

He looked away.

"Quickly now," Tavor demanded. "I've got other things to do today."

Anger clawed up inside her, and she closed her eyes, letting it rip through her, letting it sharpen her focus. She raised her hands, becoming keenly aware of the air around her. It was stagnant, but there was a hidden fury within it at being locked away for so long. She screamed inwardly, filled with her own rage, and a wind reared up around her, making her hair rise from her shoulders and whip around her face. When she opened her eyes again, Tavor had stepped away from her, cape billowing behind him, and the large man's torch shuddered in the gale. Like Liam, she had created a twister, only this one was so large it had encompassed the three of them.

The surprise diminished the force of her anger, and the wind began to die away. Her hair and Tavor's cape fell to their former positions and the torch's flames returned to normal.

Tavor grinned. "Well, that was certainly better than your brother's display." He turned to Caelin. "This is why it's always good to have multiples. Far more accurate results."

Caelin nodded, eyes wide, and Emery's stomach twisted at being spoken about in such a way. Like breeding cattle or a crop plant.

Tavor turned back to her. "Do it again."

Anger started to warm her blood once more. "Why are you doing this, Tavor? We already showed you are abilities while we were travelling." Tavor's smile faded, but she pressed on. "What was the point of all our discussions, all your grand speeches about peace and friendship, if all you really wanted is to tort –"

His cane whipped out so quickly she couldn't react before the wide end collided with her face, sending her flying backwards. When she managed to recover, blood was streaming from her nose and lights were exploding in front of her eyes.

"First of all, never speak to me like that again." Tavor wiped the end of his cane with his cape as if it were contaminated. "Second, why would I possibly prejudice the experiment by alerting my test subjects before the time is right?"

Emery spat blood from her mouth. "Why experiment on us in the first place?"

Tavor rolled his eyes, then looked at the Caelin, who

remained stony faced and staring at the floor. "She doesn't learn, does she?"

He swung his cane again, but this time she was prepared, dodging the swing neatly. This did, however, leave her exposed for a moment, and he kicked her in the ribs, hard enough to fell her to the side, gasping for breath.

Tavor set his lantern and cane down by the door to the cell, then crouched in front of her again. "I have to find your weaknesses somehow, don't I?" His voice was sharp, as if he were reprimanding an unruly child. "How else would I do that but through experimentation?"

"Then why not...just...throw us in the brig," she wheezed, "as soon as...we left Orabel?"

He fixed her with his beautiful eyes. "Because you were generously feeding me all the information about Orabel I could need and why would I stop you?" He sighed, and Emery flinched as he reached up to stroke her hair. "And I couldn't risk you escaping the brig.", He grabbed a fistful of her hair and yanked her to the ground. "Darrel, the rod."

Emery writhed and fought against Tavor's grip, feeling her hair tearing out in places, as the giant man knelt beside them, placing the torch and metal rod on the floor. He then wrapped one of his hands around her throat, pinning her down so hard it almost choked her. Tavor picked up the items and stood up, the metal rod flashing as he rearranged it in his hands. One end was bent into a symbol, and after a moment Emery realized where she'd seen it before. The scar on Sean's palm.

Tavor placed the symbol over the flame of the torch and left it there, then noticed her looking at it. "You don't know what this is, do you?"

"It's a...symbol," she choked, deciding not to reveal where she'd seen it.

"Vaguely impressive, I suppose. It's the letter *F*." He spat the next words at her like something poisonous. "It stands for *Forbidden*."

Her heart pounded into the stone floor as she stared at the

348

metal *F* glowing red in the flames. Blood leaked from her nose into her mouth. "But I haven't – Why are you doing this?"

"You have shown yourself to be a monster. It is therefore my duty to brand you as such."

"So you just think all of us who have abilities are monsters, regardless of what we say or do? You've been lying to us this entire time?"

"To be honest, you weren't very difficult to fool."

Emery recoiled as he took the rod out of the fire, floating the *F* ever closer to her face. The big man's fingers tightened around her airways so she could barely draw breath, let alone fight back. She tried to summon the stone beneath her, grasp the air around her, or compel the flame on the torch, but her she couldn't concentrate enough through her panic.

Tavor grabbed Emery's right wrist and pinned her hand to the floor, palm facing up. The look he gave her was sadistic and terrifying. Then he held the rod out to Caelin. "You will do the honors."

Caelin stared at the glowing end of the rod, a muscle straining in his jaw. Slowly, he reached to take it from Tavor.

"Caelin, please! Don't do this!" Emery begged. "I'm your friend!"

Caelin stepped closer and when their eyes met, his dark eyes held none of their familiar warmth. He was a cold stranger.

"Caelin – "

He brought the glowing end of the rod down.

She screamed as the pain seared through her hand and blackness flickered at the edge of her vision. She tried desperately to pull away, but she was trapped. The smell and sizzling of her own cooking flesh was almost too much to bear on top of the pain.

Then came the rage.

The air reacted to her fury and it surged up around her, shoving Tavor, Caelin, and Darrel off their feet. The burning sensation remained though, and she cradled her injured hand as the wind tore a defensive barrier around her. A giant, blistering *F* had been burned into her palm, just like Sean's. She tried to scramble to her feet, but her legs shook so badly she couldn't gain her balance.

"I knew it!"

Blinking away tears, she looked up at Tavor, on his knees near the cell door, grinning at her with glittering eyes.

He struggled to his feet, wiping the dust from his trousers. "I knew you weren't showing me the extent of your powers. You were lying."

Emery's whole body was shaking with pain and anger. But a numbing shock was taking over. As her surge of rage waned, the wind dying down with it, she stared at her friend, at who she *thought* had been her friend. Caelin slowly sat up but didn't climb to his feet. He remained by the door, staring at the brand he'd put on Emery's hand, his face empty of emotion.

Tavor turned to Darrel. "That's all for today."

Tavor and Darrel grabbed their things, the rod's end once more an unassuming grey, and hurried from the cell. Caelin followed, and Tavor slammed the door shut after him, locking it before she could pull herself up and run after them. Darrel set the torch in its bracket on the wall and disappeared from the dungeon. Without glancing back, Caelin followed him.

Tavor lingered in front of her bars. "Your brother was a real disappointment, Miss Aalokin. But you..." He gave her a blood chilling smile. "You are anything but."

Before she could try to summon another wind or press him further, he turned and walked off into the darkness, his boots echoing up the long staircase back to the world above.

Feeling her skin tighten around the burn, she studied her palm in the torchlight. An *F* of scar tissue was already forming there, shiny in the flickering orange. She felt her flesh screaming beneath the brand, felt the permanence of what it would leave behind. The shape would last forever, marking her as a –

Her eyes burned with angry tears as she cradled her trembling hand against her chest. Worse than the pain, worse than the brand itself, was the knowledge that Caelin did this to her.

# Chapter Thirty-Eight

Emery did not let herself cry. She would not let herself break now.

As she stared down at the brand on her hand, she allowed her anger to anchor her.

Beyond the boiling anger and fear, her main concern was understanding why Tavor was doing any of this. Or what *it* even was. Why go through all the trouble of locating Orabel, of gaining her people's trust and transporting her and Liam to the other side of the world just to force them to do things they would have happily done back home had he asked nicely enough? He now seemed to think she was special in some way, and had initially considered Liam to be as well, but he had clearly experienced more impressive feats from Sean already, presumably others as well. So why this sudden conviction that she was the missing piece in whatever horrific scheme he had in mind? And why was he so convinced they'd been hiding the true power of their abilities all this time?

The fog surrounding Tavor's motivations refused to clear, but in the end it didn't matter. What mattered was finding a way out of this mess, then a way back home as quickly as possible to warn everyone that the Arch-Elemists had been wrong.

But they were never wrong.

If that really was true, even this time, then that could only mean...they had known, all along, where they were sending her and Liam. That no cure would come from going with Tavor. The thought twisted her stomach into knots and she pushed it away, the possibility too painful to entertain. They must have simply been wrong. There was a first time for everything, even for those who speak with the gods.

"Liam?" she called into the darkness.

He didn't call back and she could only hope it was because he was paralyzed and not dead.

Emery wiped her nose, still dripping blood, on her sleeve and sat down again, grateful she had at least been allowed to retain control over her limbs this time. Digging her good hand into her pocket, she meant to pull out the wooden box containing the compass Sean had given her but instead grabbed the other wooden box she'd received from Liliath.

She had wanted the comfort of holding Sean's compass, of knowing that somewhere out there, there was still kindness in the world. But the mystery of this box gave her mind something to think about other than Caelin's betrayal.

She shifted again so the box was better exposed to the light and turned it over in her left hand, keeping her burned one as still as possible. The box's surfaces gleamed, the fine symbols etched along its edges squirming and coiling like living snakes. She still couldn't find a seam or keyhole or other way to open it though. Cursing her aunt for not giving her more helpful information, she wiped her nose to get rid of the blood drip building there. As she pulled away, a second drop fell before she could catch it, and fell onto the box.

She nearly dropped it when it started emitting a series of clicks, then sprang open in her hand.

Her blood had been the key.

A yellowed, folded piece of parchment slowly uncurled from within the box, like a bird from its egg. Holding her breath, she carefully plucked it out, feeling she was on a precipice of sorts, then unfolded it. Curling black symbols, very much like the ones in Sean's books, covered the paper. These symbols could very well tell her everything about her parents, perhaps reveal the answers to questions she hadn't even thought to ask yet. And she couldn't read any of them. Why couldn't the scroll contain images or even a map?

Footsteps began descending the stairs. She turned her back to the dungeon's entrance and carefully stuffed the parchment back in the box, then that into the pocket of her filthy trousers.

Someone stopped near her cell door. "Em."

Caelin's soft whisper froze her in place. Slowly, she turned. Caelin crouched at the door, gripping the bars tightly and peering through the gap. The torch was behind him, so she couldn't see his face well, and she was grateful. She didn't think her heart could handle seeing the icy contempt in his gaze again.

"Em, I'm sorry. I'm so sorry. I didn't want to – I had to make him believe – " He choked on a sob and Emery nearly wept when she processed what he was saying. "I need him to trust me. It was the only way."

She knelt in front of him, and he reached for her hand. She allowed him to take her good one. He squeezed it, his touch warm and familiar. Relief rushed through Emery so intensely she grew dizzy.

"Please, forgive me," Caelin pleaded and she responded by hugging him as best she could through the bars. She could feel his hot tears against her cheek. "I'm sorry." He murmured into her hair.

Beyond words, she just held him tighter. He had been so convincing, she had truly thought she'd lost her best friend and now she could barely breathe through the knowledge that he was still her Caelin.

He pulled away, took her hand again and wrapped her fingers around a small vile. "Put this on the burn. It will prevent infection."

"Caelin – "

"I don't have much time. I could only sneak away for a few

moments," Caelin said, glancing behind the towards the stairs. "Hold on a bit longer. We have a plan to get you and Liam out of here."

"We?"

But footsteps on the stairs echoed a warning and Caelin scurried into the shadows. Emery backed away from the door as a varen stepped into the torch's light.

"If you want your dinner, move to the wall." At least it wasn't Tavor.

Emery did as she was told and the guard edged her plate and tankard inside the cell, then withdrew into the shadows. She grabbed the bread and water and swallowed, because she had to. Because she was going to need all the energy she could muster to get out of this place. As she ate, she turned her back on the varen and discreetly smeared some of the salve Caelin had given her onto the burn. Some of the pain immediately diminished, but it still ached terribly.

No sooner had she finished her bread than a dart embedded itself in her skin once again. The varen snuffed out the torch as her muscles turned to water, her bones to stone, and the guard left her lying there in the miserable dark.

FOOTSTEPS BROKE into her hazy sleep, and she blinked against the fresh torchlight slicing through the shadows. Tavor's voice was drifting towards her, sounding gleeful in a way that made her skin crawl. "Here's the girl, Your Majesty."

Emery blinked as her eyes adjusted to the light. Tavor and a much older man were gazing down at her, lying prone on the floor. Tavor's companion was twirling a gnarled finger through a scraggly white beard beneath a crooked nose. He was clad in deep purple-and-white outfit, above which a crown, encrusted with amethysts and opals, sparkled on his head. This, then, was the king.

"She doesn't look like much," he said with the same accent but much less enthusiasm.

"No, Your Majesty." Tavor turned to him briefly. "To be truthful, neither of them are quite what we've been led to believe. But we'll have more answers soon."

"When do you leave?"

"First light. I already have a ship waiting."

The King huffed what sounded vaguely like approval. "And the boy?"

"This way, Your Majesty."

On the inside, Emery screamed questions and curses as Tavor led the king out of her field of vision, towards Liam.

"He doesn't look like much either," said the King.

And despite everything, relief coursed through her. At least that confirmed Liam was still there, still alive.

"His powers aren't as impressive," Tavor replied. "Our plan might be easier to achieve then we hoped."

Before Tavor divulged what exactly that plan might be, he and the King ascended back up the stairs, and Emery was left alone in the dark once again.

⚓

WHEN TAVOR RETURNED, it was with Caelin and Darrel again. Emery avoided Celin's gaze, worried she'd give him away, and looked anxiously for a metal rod in the giant man's hands, but what he was carrying now was arguably more ominous. A brown sack, the right size for a body.

She willed her muscles to fight the curare, the air around her and the flame of the walltorch to come to her aid, but again, the panic muddled her concentration, and all she could do was lie on the stone floor, unble to move so much as a finger.

The cell door opened and Tavor leaned over her. "Time for bigger and better places, Miss Aalokin. Then our experiments can really begin."

She tried to ask where he was taking her, for the mercy not to put her in that sack, not to be killed, but no noise escaped her, only terrified tears.

Tavor's eyes followed hers to the sack, then returned. "Don't worry, Miss Aalokin, I've still got great things planned for you." He grinned. "Abyssus awaits us."

# Chapter Thirty-Nine

"We must get them to the docks, without incident."

"Aye, Commissioner." Darrel's voice rumbled through Emery as she hung, bundled into the sack, over his shoulder. It was difficult to tell where they were exactly, she could only see vague shapes through the sack, but she knew they had returned up the stairs leading into the castle, then, after turning several corners, the air had become much fresher. Perhaps they were in the large courtyard between the castle and the outer wall.

"We'll need to be extremely vigilant." Tavor continued, his voice muffled slightly through the sacking.

Darrel swung around and began walking again, knocking Emery back and forth as they went. In the semi-darkness of her fabric prison, she could barely see the shapes of Tavor and Caelin striding behind Darrel. She imagined there were many more varens surrounding them. She still couldn't move, couldn't scream, couldn't do anything but worry about what doom possibly awaited her, whether Liam had also been stuffed into a sack and were now swinging their way to...

Abyssus. The place from which elemists never returned.

*Please, Tadewin, grant me luck. Teralyn, lend me your courage.*

*And if Caelin has a plan, help it come to fruition.*

Her stomach disappeared as she was flung into the air, then a hard surface greeted her, knocking the wind from her lungs. After a brief pause, the hard surface began rattling beneath her. It was a wagon, now clattering along the cobblestone streets of Dornwell.

As they travelled on, Emery focused on getting her digits moving again. None responded initially, but with a lot of concentration she managed to twitch the last finger on her left hand. Her right palm still throbbed from the branding.

The wagon slammed to a sudden halt, making Emery slide face-first into one of the wagon's sides. Her nose began to bleed again. Alarmed yelling erupted from somewhere off to the side.

Something exploded nearby, making the wagon vibrate and her ears ring. She tried to start moving more substantially as smaller bangs and more shouts filled the air, but the curare hadn't worn off enough. She recited prayers feverishly in her head as metal clashed with metal around her, and then a second explosion upended the world. Emery hurtled through the air for a terrifying moment, then landed even more brutally on the ground.

"Careful!" Caelin shouted. "They're in there!"

"Where is she?"

Emery's heart began to hammer at the sound of the last voice.

"They're in the sacks!"

She tried to call out, but hands were already on her, flipping her around to get at where the sack had been sealed shut. Blood from her nose ran over her mouth as the fabric ripped open and dim light finally spilled into the world again. A hand pushed the bloody hair from her face.

"I've got her!" Relief flooded Emery as Sean shoved back the hood of his rough woolen cloak, revealing a mess of golden hair, and his eyes met hers. "I've got you."

He was real. He was here, and visibly pushing down his anger at what she must look and smell like. Her nose felt swollen, but all she wanted to do in that moment was reach out and touch him, to reassure herself she wasn't hallucinating.

"That bastard," he muttered. "Can you move at all?"

She started to wiggle what fingers she could, but when gunshots ripped through the air he scooped her into his arms. In that brief moment, she was able to see the chaos unfolding around them. The wagon was flipped on its side, and smoke hid most of the street. Through the smoke, she could make out the shapes of other cloaked figures fighting the varens. Just a few paces away, Caelin was locked in battle was Tavor, their blades a blur as they slashed savagely at each other. But then, cradling her head against his chest, Sean ran and all she could see was grey stone buildings blurring past, punctuated here and there by the dark indigo of the night sky.

They were being pursued, she presumed by varens, sprinting and shouting after Sean to yield. He kept running, ducking around corners, sliding into darker and darker alleys, and behind them bangs echoed through the narrow streets and bullets ricocheted off walls, gouging holes in the stone alarmingly close to their heads. She heard Sean's breath catch once and he stumbled briefly, but, before she could try to tell him to put her down, he had already picked up speed again.

Eventually, the shouts began to grow quieter. Sean continued though, circling back on himself, sometimes running in the complete opposite direction, successfully ensuring the last of their pursuers lost track of them. By the time he had slowed down enough to shoulder open a door and slide inside, he was panting with exertion. Nudging it almost closed again, he stumbled further into the building and sat down abruptly, cradling Emery in his lap. It was too dark to see him, but she could feel how perfectly still he was, like a cat, his head angled towards the doorway. His chest was moving against her, up and down like turbulent waves, and his quick breaths were ruffling her hair.

"Sss...ean," she croaked.

His hand found her cheek. "Are you hurt?"

She tried to answer, but her tongue couldn't form more words yet.

Carefully, he ran his fingers along her limbs, checking for obvious wounds. Emery sucked in a breath as he passed over the raw burn on her palm, unable to stop the shiver of pain. His entire body tensed, then began to shake, and she knew it wasn't from fear or the slight chill in the air. He knew exactly what the burn was.

"He's not going to hurt you anymore," he whispered.

"Where's...Liam?" she managed to choke out.

"With Rooney. We had to split up to make it more difficult for the varens to track us." His voice sounded strained, as if speaking through gritted teeth, and his breathing sounded... sharper than it should.

"Are...you...al –"

"I reckon we've got a few more minutes before Farley sets off the next diversion," he continued, cutting through her enquiry. "Hopefully the curare will have run its course by then." He shifted her slightly and dug something out of his pocket. "Speaking of which." His fingers found her wrist and pushed up her sleeve. Something cold touched the crook of her elbow. "This might sting, but it'll help purge it from your system more quickly."

There was a pinching feeling. Almost immediately, the pressure in her chest began to ease, and she could freely wiggle her fingers and toes. "How...did you...find me?"

"We followed you here, but we were days behind and weren't fast enough to get to you before he took you to the castle. Rooney has some contacts in the castle that confirmed you were in there. We spent a few days watching, trying to figure out how to get you out. I recognized your friend walking around with Tavor. I thought he'd betrayed you." His voice still sounded strange, like the words were a struggle. They all came out in a rush. "We got Rooney's contacts to kidnap him and bring him to us. I was surprised when he was relieved to see us and together, we came up with a plan. Tavor had multiple caravans of Varens heading to the docks, but Caelin was able to tell us which one you were in." His voice cracked. "I'm sorry, I should have come sooner. I should have realized –"

Emery managed to lift her uninjured hand to his face and he stopped, turning to lean into her palm with a heavy sigh.

"Why...did you? This was so...dangerous."

"When you freed me –" He paused. "I realized you didn't have a clue what he really was. I couldn't just –"

"You risked...your freedom though. How was that –"

He made a noise somewhere between a faint laugh and a hum. "I'm never free." But then his voice hardened. "And I wasn't going to let him take someone else I..." He cut himself off.

Emery swallowed. "Who did he take from you?"

Sean was silent for long enough she wasn't sure he'd answer. When he did, his voice was thick. "My sister. He killed her. After torturing us both."

Horror washed over her like ice. "Gods, Sean. I'm so sorry."

Suddenly his hatred, his anger, it all made sense. Hot shame hit her next. She'd *taunted* him about her. She opened her mouth to apologize, to beg for his forgiveness –

The building shook violently, throwing clouds of dust from the ceiling, and Sean's arms tightened around her in an instant. Then, a distant roaring filled the silence.

"That's the diversion," Sean breathed. "Can you stand?"

With some trepidation, Emery held onto his shoulder and pushed up onto her feet. She swayed slightly, her legs feeling about as sturdy as blades of grass, but she could stand. "Close enough."

To her surprise, Sean remained seated. "There's a set of stairs behind you. Take them to the next floor, then climb out the first window on your right. You should be able to get to the roof from there, then stay on the rooftops until you reach the southern edge of the city. You'll know you're heading in the right direction because a mass of trees should appear ahead of you. Behind those trees, we have rowboats hidden in a small inlet, ready to take us – and you – down the coast to the ship." He took a shaky breath. "If that's what you want."

Emery's pulse picked up speed. It sounded like he wanted to split up. "What about you?"

"We need to change our plan slightly." The tension was back in his voice. "You go the way I just described, I'll take the same route through the streets."

"Absolutely not, that's much too dangerous."

"Please, Emery –" He inhaled sharply, shifting his position as if he were in pain.

Or injured.

That's why his voice sounded so wrong, why he continued to be so breathless.

That moment he had stumbled while carrying her, she realized with icy fear what had happened.

"Sean." Her voice started to quiver as she searched the shadowy floor for the sheen of blood. "Were you...shot?" When he didn't respond, she dropped to her knees and started feeling around, gasping as she found the wetness starting to puddle beneath him. "Tell me where. Now!"

"My leg," he breathed, and his hand found hers in the darkness. "Emery, I don't want to slow you down. Please, *just go*."

She laughed drily. "If you think" – she started ripping along the edge of his cloak – "I'm going to leave you like this" – she now had a decent chunk of fabric – "you are very mistaken." She pressed the material into his hands. "Here. Tie this around your leg. I can't see where the wound is."

"I will, I promise. But only if you go now, *please*. We're running out of time."

"Then stop arguing and –"

"Emery, I'm –"

"No." She reached up and grabbed his face, fear, rage and every other emotion that had been coursing through her body these past few days boiling to a peak under her skin. Instinct took over, and she kissed him, hard, on the lips, then pulled away. "I appreciate the rescue, but I'm taking over now. Tie your leg and stand up."

Instead of doing any of this, Sean pulled her closer, and brought her mouth back to his. His fingers raked through her hair as his lips moved against hers and every nerve ending in her body seemed to come alive.

Maybe it was possible to burst into flames and survive.

"You know," Sean mumbled, pulling away and resting his forehead against hers. "You can't just kiss me every time you want me to do something."

"Why not?"

"Because it bloody works."

She grinned as he grabbed the strip of fabric and started tying it in place. "I could always use violence instead."

"I think I prefer your current method."

When he was done, she helped him to his feet. He couldn't put much weight on the injured leg, but with his arm draped over her shoulder they could both hobble with relative speed towards the door.

"This isn't going to work," Sean said, panting already. "We should split –"

"Shut up or I *will* use violence."

They pressed their ears to the door and listened. A wind was howling outside, and in the distance the dull roaring continued. Otherwise, the city seemed quiet, empty almost. She guessed it was late into evening.

Emery cracked the door open, revealing a sliver of street dimly lit by the stars above and a streetlamp somewhere further down. "I don't see anyone," she whispered.

"Wait a little longer."

When they both felt it was safe to venture out, their progress was painfully slow. Now that they were in the light, Emery could also catch glimpses of Sean's injury. Blood had soaked through his trouser leg from the thigh down, the strip of cloth tied around it already glistening a deep crimson. When she looked up at him for a moment, sweat was gleaming on his pale face, and he seemed to be clenching his jaw with every step. She wondered how much blood he had already lost, how much longer he could stand this before passing out.

As they turned the corner from one muddy alleyway to the next, shouts erupted behind them and a group of varens jumped out from the crumbling buildings ahead of them. Emery and Sean flipped direction as quickly as they could, only to find more varens had appeared behind them, cutting off any obvious means of escape.

Sean heaved himself off Emery, drawing both his sword and pistol. "Save yourself. I don't care how."

"I told you, I'm not leaving you." She lunged for the dagger at his belt.

His reflexes still admirably quick, Sean twisted out of her reach. "Then" – he dropped his weapons – "we should surrender."

"What?"

"He wants us alive, doesn't he? For his sick...whatever he wants to call them. If we go willingly, we might get a better chance to escape than if they're forced to overpower us."

So, he was only going to fight to buy her time. He hadn't expected to win.

She tried to summon enough energy from the air around them to use against the encroaching varens, to send them all flying with a burst of tornado. But she was still too weak, or perhaps secretly too scared of bringing further harm to Sean if she tried anything.

There was no choice then but to sink to their knees on the cobblestones, place their hands on their heads, and watch as the varens advanced from both sides. The first to reach them cracked his pistol against Sean's head and Emery sucked in a breath as he slumped sideways. She forced herself not to move as another stepped up behind her. Pain exploded at the base of her skull, and the image of Sean lying on the hard ground winked out.

# Chapter Forty

"I knew you'd show up sooner or later." The voice was murky through the haze in her head. "Like a rat, you always come crawling back."

Tavor.

Emery opened her eyes a crack. Everything was blurred, like the world had melted. She could make out browns, greys and oranges, then, as she blinked, the colors began to twist into solid forms. Brown wooden walls, grey iron bars, an orange flickering sconce, and by her head, a pair of black, shiny-buckled boots.

She examined their owner as best she could without moving her head. Tall. Dark hair. Weapons strapped to his belt. It was Anders.

"Tell me where the boy is," Tavor continued.

"Roark damn you."

Sean.

She peered in the direction of his voice. There were two blurred figures, one standing over a second on the other side of the room. She blinked again and the standing figure morphed into Tavor. Sean was slumped in front of him, his back pressed against the wall. A small corridor with a row of bars on either side separated her from them, and beneath them all the floor rolled and creaked, with something pounding on the wall behind her.

They were in the brig of a ship.

Out of the corner of her eye she spotted a red dart sticking out of her thigh. She tried to wiggle her fingers on the hand trapped under her body.

They moved. As did her toes.

It was unclear how long she had been unconscious, or at what point she had been administered with curare, but she wondered whether whatever Sean had given her was still working, actively combatting its effects. She eyed Anders again. He was standing quite casually, arms folded comfortably against his chest. He clearly wasn't worried she might spring up at any moment and attack him. She had to keep it that way.

"Is he with your crew?" Tavor pressed Sean again, and Emery wondered whether he was talking about Liam, Caelin, or indeed someone else entirely. "You people are pack animals, I know they're around somewhere. And trust me, it will go better by them if the information comes from you."

Sean glared up at Tavor, fury burning so hot in his eyes that Emery could feel it across the room. Tavor hadn't bothered paralyzing him then, she guessed because his wound incapacitated him enough, or because he wanted him to talk immediately. Worryingly, the tourniquet had disappeared from his leg, and blood was trickling once more from the bullet hole.

Emery had to force herself to stay limp as Tavor swung a fist into Sean's jaw with a loud crack. "Tell me where they are!"

Sean responded with a single, elegant spit of blood onto the floor.

"I'm not in the mood for *games*." Tavor slammed the end of his cane into Sean's wounded leg, making him groan through clenched teeth.

It took all of Emery's will power not to leap up and try to get across to them. She squeezed her eyes shut and focused on keeping her breathing calm.

"Fine." Tavor turned to Anders. "Give him some motivation."

Without hesitation, the varen kicked her in the ribs. She managed to remain still, but couldn't stop the noise of pain escaping her throat. "She's awake, Commissioner."

"Good. Bring her over."

A breeze began to whisk the air inside the brig, stroking Emery's face and catching the end of Tavor's cape.

"Ah ah ah!" Tavor held up a scolding finger at Sean. "I wouldn't do that, or she'll be getting a knife instead. I don't think any of us want that, do we?"

The breeze died away but the rage in Sean's eyes remained. He was trembling from head to foot now, fists curled so tightly his knuckles had turned white.

Though her veins also hummed with anger, Emery stayed limp as Anders heaved her over his shoulder and negotiated his way through the two cell doors.

"Looks like you've taken quite a fancy to my friend here," Tavor said with suspicious lightness. "I suppose I see the appeal. She's spirited, and her face is more pleasing than most." Anders dropped Emery painfully onto the wooden floor between them. Tavor gazed down at her, eyes sparkling, then smiled at Sean again. "So, you're going to tell me where the boy is, or it soon won't be as nice anymore."

He gestured to Anders, who fetched something from the corner of the cell she couldn't see. Sean's horrified expression told her enough though, and as she felt the presence of heat wash over her cheek she knew what this new torture would entail.

Fire.

Tavor's smile faded, his handsome face transforming into something fiendish. "Tell me where he is, Denzel."

A muscle in Sean's jaw flexed, but his lips remained together.

Tavor sighed. "I don't want to do this, you know. Tavor said, sighing. But you leave me little choice."

Out of the corner of her eye, Emery saw the flash of a grey rod, its end glowing red hot. She glanced back at Sean, who's eyes were now on her.

"And just like with Lily," Tavor continued, "you'll have no one to blame but yourself."

Out of the corner of her eye, Emery saw the flash of a grey rod, it's end glowing white. She glanced back at Sean and finally he was looking at her. The rage in Sean's eyes died, that awful, blank nothingness swallowing his expression once more. The empty Sean had returned, the husk of the fighter she knew him to be.

She shook her head, just a fraction, hoping only he would see it, that he'd understand.

*Don't tell them.*

"It's funny, don't you think?" Tavor mused. "How we've come full circle. First Lily. Now her." He nodded down at Emery. "How many more will suffer and die because of your stubbornness?"

Sean blinked, his empty eyes shimmering with tears, and tore his gaze up to Tavor. "Please, don't. She's not a part of this."

Tavor grinned. "What? Not sure you can go through it again?"

And with abrupt realization, horror and fury sluiced through her in dizzying torrents. Tavor was making Sean relive his sister's death.

Sean glanced down at her, and Emery jerked her head again, a little harder this time.

Tavor set his cane against the wall near Emery's head. "I've heard stories about how you handled Lily's death. Not very well by the sound of it."

*Don't talk. Don't give in.*

"Last chance, before you regret this forever." Tavor took the metal rod from Anders, the *F* glowing white hot above her, like a streak of lightning in the dark room. "Where's the boy?"

Sean's eyes went wide as the *F* descended towards her face, and she pressed her own lips together to avoid crying out. The heat of the rod was coming ever closer to her cheek. She would have to roll out of the way, grab Tavor's cane and –

"Stop!" Sean burst.

Before he could say anything else, Emery flung her hand out

and grabbed the cane, smashing the hard metal up between Tavor's legs. He tumbled backwards with a shriek of pain and outrage. She got to her feet and kicked the rod from his hand, sending it careening across the cell.

Anders tackled her around the middle, pushing her back against the bars, but Emery dug her feet in under him and threw him off. Meanwhile, Sean had hauled himself up and collided with Tavor in a flurry of limbs and weapons.

Anders found his way to his feet again, and unsheathed his sword. "Put down your weapon."

Emery clutched Tavor's cane all the tighter and shook the hair from her eyes. "Make me."

They began to circle each other, weapons raised, until Anders lunged forward with his blade. She blocked the attack, stepping into *arcing moon* and thrusting up the cane, rendering his blow little more than a sharp vibration in her arms and shoulders. He swung again at her head, her feet, her heart, and each time she blocked him. In turn, she tried to kick his knee out but he side-stepped her, thrusting an elbow at her face. She managed to duck in time, catching him in the stomach with *whipping willow*. It didn't seem to faze him though, and she had to spin quickly to avoid another attack.

In the other half of the cell, Sean and Tavor were locked in their own battle. Neither appeared to have a weapon in hand and were instead plowing into each other with fists, knees and elbows. Sean didn't appear to notice Tavor's blows, his entire face now aglow with the inferno of rage behind his eyes, as if he had finally let it lose. The fury radiating off him rippled the air, making tiny waves that swept across everything. He and Tavor fell to the floor, and he began punching their captor in the face repeatedly, until Emery realized Tavor had fished his pistol from its holster.

"Sean, look out!"

Sean smacked the gun from Tavor's hands, sending it skidding out of reach.

Tavor responded by kicking him hard in the chest, shoving

him backwards and buying himself time to scramble towards the gun. Thankfully, Sean managed to recover quickly, despite the state he was in, leaping on Tavor and pulling him away from the weapon again.

Forced to spin into a new position to dodge Anders's next attack, Emery lost sight of their fight. Anders's sword clanked against Tavor's cane with every blow, and Emery started to feel her body growing tired after such a stretch of forced inactivity and lack of nourishment. Sweat began to slide into her eyes, and her arms trembled more and more with each swing and parry. She had to end this fight.

She waited until Anders lunged again, then swung into the inside of his sword, stepping close enough to bring the cane vertical and hook its broader end where his blade and handle met. Jerking her wrist, she twisted the cane down and out, then, with the full force of her desperation, flicked the sword from his grip. It sailed through the bars and landed with a clatter outside the cell.

Before Anders could recover from the surprise, she rammed the top of Tavor's cane under his jaw, snapping his head back as hard as she could and flinging him against the bars. He slid to the floor and didn't get back up.

She returned her attention to the fight on the other side of the cell. Sean had managed to roll on top of Tavor, pinning the commissioner's arms in place with his knees. He was also holding the pistol in his shaking hands, digging the barrel into Tavor's forehead. "I should have killed you long ago."

Tavor wasn't struggling though, just gazed up at Sean without any indication of fear. "You couldn't do it the last few times. What makes you think you'll be able to now?"

Sean roared and jammed the pistol into Tavor's skin, so hard his forehead began to bleed. He cocked the pistol and his finger began hovering over the trigger.

Tavor laughed, the unsettling sound bouncing off the innards of the ship. "You're weak, Denzel. You can't do it."

"Shut your damned mouth!" Sean roared but didn't shoot.

"Go ahead," Tavor said calmly. "Do it for Lily. I'm sure she'd love to see what you've become."

Sean smacked Tavor's head against the hard floor. "You don't get to say her name."

"Then hurry up, I'm getting bored."

Emery's heart thundered as Sean's finger tightened over the trigger. His entire body was trembling now, so violently it looked like he was about to grind himself into dust. His eyes flicked from Tavor to something Emery couldn't see, then his focus returned to their captor. Emery braced herself for the bang, for the mingle of horror and relief at seeing Tavor's brains burst onto the floorboards.

But instead, Sean lunged off him, scrambling for whatever was on the other side of them. It was the metal rod, the symbolled end still glowing faintly with heat. Before Tavor could react, Sean swung it round to face him, and pressed the *F* down onto his cheek.

Tavor screamed, drowning out the sound of his flesh sizzling. Emery gagged as he jerked and flailed, but Sean didn't relent. "This is for Lily!" he snarled, pressing down even harder. Tavor's screaming escalated.

Something plunged into Emery's shoulder, making her jerk around in pain and shock. Ander's angry brown eyes met hers, before he ripped the small dagger from her flesh again, its serrated edges biting through her, causing even more damage.

She screamed, stumbling away from him, knowing she had to raise Tavor's cane and fight him off, instead feeling her legs turn to water and seeing the floor rise to meet her. Sean was yelling her name. On the floor now, she twisted towards the sound of his voice, he had dropped the rod and was scrambling over to her. A warning cry bubbled up in her as Tavor reared up behind him, but before she could make a sound the pistol had cracked him over the head. Sean fell down beside her as she clutched her shoulder, pressing against the wound with already blood-soaked fingers.

Tavor kicked him in the stomach, howling a string of curses, then flipped him over and began striking him in the ribs. Sean feebly tried to block the blows, but blood was now also welling from his head, and he was clearly dazed. Tavor gave him a final, savage kick and turned on Emery, the giant, blistering *F* on his cheek shimmering in the torchlight.

"Suits you," she croaked.

Tavor booted her right where Anders had stabbed her. Fresh, blinding pain rushed in, making her retch whatever sad remnants remained in her stomach onto the floor. Tavor marched back around Sean and grabbed him by his hair. "I am done with you, once and for all." Sean was squinting at their surroundings as if he had no idea where he was.

Dragging Sean with him, Tavor grabbed the pistol from the floor and held it to Sean's temple, cocked the pistol, and then paused. "On second thought." He gestured with his head to Anders, who wrenched on Emery's injured arm, forcing her to sit up. Blood poured from her wound and her vision began to blur in and out of focus. But beyond the pain and fear, anger was also curdling her veins.

"Tell me where your brother and his idiot friend are," Tavor said, his jaw clenched with pain, "and I won't shoot him in the head."

"I...don't...know," she said, and it was true. Sean had explained the plan for getting them back to the *Audacity*, but that didn't mean that's where they were.

"Don't lie to me, not now." Tavor shook Sean violently, eliciting a groan that made her knees feel weak all over again. "You can both still bleed to death, even if we don't shoot you. *Nobody* has time for lying."

Sean blinked heavily, his blurry gaze resting on Emery's face as he slowly came back to consciousness. He looked like a ghost of himself, all fire burned from his eyes, leaving behind only emptiness.

"Where are they?" Tavor poked at a patch of his blistered skin and hissed with pain and fury.

"I thought Liam was such a *disappointment*," Emery choked. "What do you want him for so badly?"

"Like I'm going to tell you anything." Tavor pressed the pistol harder to Sean's head. "Now, where is your brother?"

The anger bubbled away under Emery's skin, and she started channeling it to form a tiny breeze within the brig. The sconce on the wall flared briefly, but neither Tavor nor Anders seemed to pick up on it.

Tavor sighed. "To be honest" – he tipped his head towards Sean – "you'd probably be doing him a favor letting me kill him. I mean, look at him." He shook Sean again, with no response. Sean's eyes had glazed over once more, not focused on anything. "He's probably lost too much blood already." Tavor bent to Sean's ear, speaking just loud enough for Emery to hear. "You know, my men brought stories back to me about you, out at sea, all kinds of interesting things." He chuckled. "Is it true, you once tried to destroy yourself, and couldn't even do that properly?" Sean closed his eyes and Tavor laughed again.

Emery was trembling with rage now, letting it escape in a trickle that began to commune with the wood of the ship. The boards of the hull creaked and moaned as she willed them to start separating, so slowly the water seeping through was hardly noticeable.

Tavor let go of Sean's hair and instead took hold of the time-piece hanging from his neck. "This looks familiar. Ah yes. It didn't belong to you originally, did it? I suppose you wear it to remind yourself how you failed her. How droll."

He yanked the chain back hard, cutting into Sean's throat, twisting tighter and tighter until Sean started feebly clawing at it as he struggled to breathe. Tavor hissed into his ear, "And that attack on my ship. So sloppy, so unlike you." He smiled, despite the pain it must cause his burnt face. "I know now what that was about. You didn't really want to kill me, did you?" He rolled his eyes to the ceiling, pretending to muse. "Or maybe you did. We can want two things at once, can't we?" He sneered down at Sean again. "But your primary reason was much sadder, wasn't it? Go on." He nudged his shoulder, as if he were encouraging a shy friend, and Emery felt like she was burning alive with protective rage. "Tell her. It wasn't me you most hoped would die that night, was it?" His hand switched from the chain back to Sean's hair, yanking his head so he had to look at Emery. "Tell her how you hoped to provoke me into killing you, since you were too much of a coward to –"

"Enough!" Emery unleashed her remaining fury, and the elements heeded her call. A gale picked up and began whipping through the brig, tossing Anders into the nearest wall. He flopped to the floor, and she prayed that this time he really wouldn't get up again. The sconce on the wall flared, the flame growing to a staggering height, the wooden planks around them began to bend and splinter further, and water burst with increased force through the holes she had created, rushing straight towards Tavor.

But he didn't look scared. If anything, he seemed...intrigued? "The rumors are true –"

The wall beside them exploded and a plank hit him in the chest, sending him flying backwards. Sean, finally free from his grasp, slumped onto his side, unmoving.

As Emery crawled towards him, Tavor recovered and took aim with his pistol.

A fresh wave of saltwater rushed onto him, joined by a wall of flames stretching from the wall torch to encase him on all sides. He screamed as the flames engulfed him, and Emery just managed to grasp Sean's hand before the ocean fully invaded the brig, sucking them all out through the broken hull into the deep, dark waters of Dornwell's bay. Her lungs burned with the effort of holding her breath as she clung to him, too weak now to swim for himself.

Finally, their heads broke the surface and glorious, salty air rushed into her lungs. Sean gasped in her arms and she nearly cried with relief. But she had to hang on to the last of her anger, the force that was enabling her to will the ocean to sweep them towards the shore. The ship they had been on was engulfed in flames and there was no sign of Tavor or Anders above the surface. She couldn't worry about them now. She closed her eyes, focusing on the land ahead of them, on what looked like the trees just beyond the city that Sean had told her to run for before they'd been captured, but she could already feel her anger slipping away, and with it her control.

It wasn't only her anger fading, but also her vision and the feeling in her limbs. She could barely keep her arms from slipping off Sean before the last wave spat them onto the sandy shore of the inlet. They lay on their sides, facing each other, panting sand from their mouths as the seawater caressed their feet. Over his shoulder, through the trees, she could see the end of the pier alight with flames, flames that were also jumping from ship to ship. Then, from the trees, a mass of black figures came running in their direction, buttons and weapons glinting silver.

Varens, and there were only moments before they reached them.

Sean caught her gaze and turned, eyes half closed, hair plastered to his forehead, to see what had caught her attention. He rolled back to face her, his breaths coming quick and short. "Run," he murmured.

But they both knew neither of them would be getting up again.

She coughed out a quick laugh, the pain in her shoulder searing hot and blinding. "After you."

Even as his voice became so small that she could barely hear him, Sean managed to sound impressed. "You absolutely destroyed that ship."

"You...destroyed...his face," she panted back, darkness dancing at the edges of her vision. "That was...a nice touch."

"At least we took him down with us." A smile flickered on Sean's lips. "Remind me never to make you angry." He lifted his hand as if to touch her cheek, but his fingers fell in the sand, just short. His eyes closed. "I'm glad I got to meet you, before..."

"Sean?"

He didn't respond.

Emery reached out and stroked his battered, beautiful face. "Sean?" He already felt cold.

She swallowed hard, accepting it was better this way. The varens had already descended on them, dropping to their knees, taking aim, the barrels of their muskets rising like a dozen black eyes.

*Please, let Liam and Caelin live. If nothing else, let them be safe.*

Emery closed her eyes as the varens around them pressed down on their triggers.

# Chapter Forty-One

Emery's eyes snapped open to darkness, and her heart began pounding immediately. It had been a dream, the threat of Abyssus, the rescue, their triumph and execution. She was still locked in Tavor's cell in the castle dungeon, unable to move, unable to breathe properly. She would never escape from this darkness.

A flicker of orange light appeared, making her eyes sting. She squeezed them shut and her heart started pumping so hard her chest hurt. What was he going to do now?

Someone grabbed her hand and she moaned in fear, yanking it away.

"Emery, it's alright."

The voice wasn't Tavor's, and...she'd been able to move.

She whimpered in a confusion of relief and fear, and a warm, calloused hand touched hers again. "You're safe. Everything's alright."

No, it wasn't. Pain was everywhere. Her head, her ribs, her hand. Her shoulder was the worst, a searing, throbbing pain eating away just below the joint. She'd been stabbed, she remembered now. Her breath caught as everything else came rushing back. The wall of sand erupting from the beach just as the varens were about to shoot, flinging them into the air and then swallowing them and their weapons completely. The shouts behind her, then Aleksy and Rooney kneeling beside her and Sean, saying things she couldn't register before falling into oblivion.

Warm fingers gripped her own, gentle but anxious. "Emery, look at me."

Her eyes snapped open, and there he was. There were stitches on his forehead beneath his tousled golden hair, and he was terribly pale, but he was *alive*. She squeezed his hand, making sure he was real.

Sean reached out with his other hand and caressed her cheek. "Welcome back."

He was sitting next to the bed in which she was lying. An actual bed. They were back in his cabin, gilded by the orange light of a candle.

"How long was I...gone?"

"Three days, save the times someone could persuade you to eat or drink something."

Emery couldn't remember a thing. There was just the bittersweet lingering of what she thought were their last moments together, then nothing until now. "I thought you—" She sucked in a short, shallow breath to stop herself from welling up.

"So did I for a bit." His fingers tightened around hers. "But we didn't. We survived." He sounded like he couldn't quite believe it either.

"Your leg? Your head? Are you – "

"I'm fine, I promise," he hurried to assure her. "I just woke up a few hours ago myself, but I'm healing." He searched her face, as if trying to convince himself she was really alright. "I think you were out longer because you exhausted yourself."

"What about Liam?" she breathed. "And Caelin?"

"They're safe too, everyone's here," Sean said. "Caelin even found a way to snatch your weapons from back home and hide them. He insisted on going back for them during our raid. You're all quite attached to them, aren't –"

Overwhelmed with relief, Emery couldn't hold her emotions

in anymore. Heaving sobs ripped from her lungs, and Sean climbed onto the bed next to her, wrapping his arms around her. She clutched her shoulder, every sob sending a ripping pain through the wound.

"He lied to us," she gasped. "And for such a long time, even after he got to know us. Said he wanted peace, but then – all he wanted – I don't even understand –"

"That's what he does," Sean murmured. "He tricks people. You're far from the first. He's as slippery and deadly as a snake. That's why they call him the Viper."

"Gods." She wiped her face. "No wonder you hated me at first."

"I never hated you." Sean leaned his head against hers. "I really tried though."

She gazed up at him, acutely aware of the warmth of his body against hers, the weight of his arms. "Why did you save me then, from the storm? I would have let me die."

"No, you wouldn't." He took a deep breath, struggling to meet her gaze. "I saved you...because you had so much life in you. I couldn't bear to watch it end." She squeezed his hand, and finally he looked at her. "Plus, in a way, you had already saved my life that night."

"What do you mean?"

He looked down, clearing his throat before speaking with a thickness in his voice. "What Tavor said...he was right. I never intended to leave that ship alive." Heart already heavy for him, Emery reached up and touched Sean's cheek. He closed his eyes and leaned into her touch, then laughed hoarsely. "And then there you were, throwing tea in my face, stopping me from making the greatest mistake of my life." He opened his eyes. "Later, I realized you had saved me, in that moment. Woken me up. I couldn't then just let you die, could I?"

His green eyes were unusually clear and readable. There was no rage in them, but she remembered the way they had burned when looking at Tavor. But also, how quickly grief had been triggered in him, devouring that wrath. Tears welled in her own eyes again as she recalled Tavor taunting Sean, forcing him to relive the final moments of his sister's life.

She glanced down to where the lily was tattooed on his forearm and traced it gently with a finger.

"Sean," she said softly, carefully. "I'm so sorry about Lily."

The familiar blankness immediately began to creep over his face, behind his eyes, but now she saw it for what it was. A defense mechanism for when he was feeling too much. He was shutting down.

She brought his face closer to hers. "No. Don't go away, please. Stay with me."

He blinked, as if in surprise, and the blankness didn't quite take hold. He swallowed hard as he gazed into her eyes, and she felt him trying to cling to this moment, to her, not to be swept away once more by the abyss of sorrow and guilt. "Lily," he choked, swallowing hard again. "Lily was my younger sister. He captured us both. And – and he..." Sean broke off, unable to continue.

She didn't say anything. Didn't want to risk pushing too hard and causing him to fold back in on himself.

"He shot her." His voice was strangled, like every word cost him. "After he'd tortured her half to death in front me. And I – I couldn't –"

He buried his face against Emery's neck, and she felt helpless to do more than stroke his hair, kiss his temple. "I'm sorry," she whispered, new tears of fury and horror pricking her eyes. "I can only half imagine what that must feel like...but I'd have wanted to kill him too."

There was a quick knock on the cabin door, then it opened. Sean and Emery disentangled themselves as quickly as they could, but Liam and Caelin were already standing in the doorway, staring at them.

Sean stood up and cleared his throat, not looking at anyone. "I'll leave you to your reunion." He limped past Liam and Caelin, shutting the door behind him.

For a moment, the two of them continued standing there, looking befuddled, but then they both dashed to the bed.

Caelin reached her first, carefully wrapping his arms around her. "Gods," he breathed. "We thought you were dead. Again."

"I'm alright." She patted his back. "Just...sore." Even as she said it, exhaustion weighed down her limbs and fresh pain rippled in her shoulder. But Caelin didn't let go. "I'm sorry, Em. For what I did. I'll never forgive – "

Emery pushed him away just far enough that she could look into his glassy eyes. "You *saved* me, Caelin. You saved both of us." She pulled him back into an even tighter hug, marveling at the strength it must have taken for Caelin to do what he had to do in that moment. "Thank you."

When Caelin eventually pulled away again, he sat at the foot of the bed, wiping at his eyes. Drained already from the exchange, Emery had to lie back down again.

Liam stepped up to her, taking her hand in his. Like hers, a white bandage was now wrapped around it, no doubt masking a still healing burn of his own. He sat down on the chair next to the bed, his eyes wide and glassy. There was a host of bruises on his face, a cut on his lip, but otherwise he seemed to have suffered no further harm, physically at least. When he finally spoke, his voice was hoarse. "I really thought...this time..."

She blinked hard, pushing back the tears that were threatening again. "I know, I had the same fear about you." She squeezed his hand and glanced over to Caelin. "Both of you."

"You can't do that to us again," said Liam.

"I didn't have much choice in the matter," she joked, her voice starting to tremble. "And I survived, didn't?"

"Barely," Caelin said softly. "Neither of you were conscious when we found you. You'd both lost so much blood..."

Liam broke then, giving into his tears.

She pulled him onto the bed beside her and put an arm around him. "I'm here, Liam," she soothed. "I'm alright"

"Only because Aleksy was able to immediately stop your

bleeding when we found you," Caelin explained. "If she wasn't able to do that with her abilities, she said she didn't think either of you would have made it back to the ship. Even then, she had to stay with both of you for hours, making sure her hearts kept beating."

"You were so pale. You looked dead." Liam sniffed. "It was... terrible." After a while, he regained his composure. "I'll kill him," he said flatly. "I'll make sure he never again has the ability to hurt you, or anyone, ever again."

"I think...I might have already taken care of that," said Emery. "I can't swear to it, but I did...set fire to him. And then... the ocean took him. If Sean and I only survived with Aleksy's amazing help, then I don't know..." She trailed off, unsure whether she actually wanted having killed someone on her conscience, even someone like Tavor. She wondered what happened to Anders and if anyone else had been on the ship when it burned.

"Good." Liam took a deep breath, pulling himself up to lean against the wall by her pillow.

"I still don't understand what Tavor was trying to accomplish," Emery said.

Liam and Caelin exchanged an uncomfortable glance. "I do." Caelin said. "He told me a fair amount when he was trying to convince me to join him...kept saying we were *the same*." Caelin shook his head as if trying to rid himself of the idea, and Emery was reminded uncomfortably of the words he'd said to her before Tavor made him brand her. How he'd always felt like an outsider on their island. She wondered how much truth he'd actually drawn on during that painful speech but now was not the time to ask. Caelin continued, "He wants to round up everyone in Orabel and turn it into a new prison for elemists."

Emery's stomach clenched with horror. "Doesn't he already have his precious Abyssus for that?"

Caelin sighed. "He says it's getting full, so he needs somewhere else to store Forbiddens."

"I'm starting to think there's no such thing," she grunted.

Liam rubbed his bruised face. "I still don't understand his

logic." He scoffed. "If you can call it that. Why not just attack us from the start? Why go through all that trouble to gain our trust if in the end that's all he wants to do? Or why take us all the way to Dornwell and not try to overpower and experiment on us where he found us?"

"Tavor said something in one of our early conversations," said Emery. "Something about growing up hearing rumors about a place where only elemists lived, or only meant for elemists? I can't remember exactly how he phrased it, but maybe they suggested those of us on Orabel are stronger than others. Maybe his understanding meant he felt he had to be more careful, isolate a few of us first."

"Exactly," said Caelin. "He needed to find out what he was *up against*, as he put it."

"What do we do now then?" Liam asked.

"I think we have to go home and warn everyone," said Emery.

"But how do we get there?"

Caelin smiled and it was almost jarring in such a conversation. "I found a map."

"In the castle?" Emery asked

"Yes, in his office, while I was pretending to be his loyal little protégée." Anger had swept into his voice, and Emery wondered if Tavor's betrayal hurt Caelin worst of all, even if was trying to hide it.

"That's brilliant. But...can you read it?" Emery closed her eyes and pictured the map that she had tried to memorize what felt like a lifetime ago. She wished she'd been able to learn how to read it properly.

He grunted affirmatively. "I've learned a thing or two since we left Orabel. We just...need a boat."

"We could probably ask the crew here to take us," said Liam.

"No," Caelin snapped. "No more strangers in Orabel."

"You can't blame them for what happened," said Emery. "They all just saved our –"

"Yes, and Tavor also did and said a lot of nice things at first, didn't he?" Caelin's voice had started to rise and with obvious effort, his next words came out softer. "I am not saying they aren't trustworthy. But I don't think our people will react well to more strangers showing up given how...things turned out. And regardless of all that, need I remind you that it's forbidden to even tell outsiders about Orabel, let alone to take them there?"

"But Tavor and his men already know. Do you think it would matter anymore?" Liam questioned.

"Perhaps not, but do you want to risk having the breath sucked from your lungs if you try?" When Liam just swallowed, Caelin looked at Emery. "I'm thinking of the crew's safety, too. If we just show up with a group of outsiders and our people don't react well, people could get hurt on both sides."

Emery felt a painful emptiness open inside her at the thought of leaving the *Audacity* behind now, its crew.

Sean.

But Caelin was clearly not for persuading, and she understood the logic in keeping their risks to everyone as low as possible going forward. "What's your plan then?"

"I learned a lot about sailing while I was training with the varens. I can take us home. We just need a boat of our own."

Emery took a deep breath and lay back down again. "Well, at least we're surrounded by people who'll know where to get one."

# Chapter Forty-Two

The next time Sean came to check on her, Emery sent Liam and Caelin from the room. She had to be the one to tell him, but she at least wanted to do so alone, on her own terms.

"How are you feeling?" Sean asked, gingerly sitting down beside her.

She had to tell him now, rip the bandage off quickly.

"We need to go home, Sean." She swallowed, nodding at the closed door. "The three of us."

"Of course, I can imagine you're all home –"

"I mean immediately."

He went quiet then, giving away nothing. After a moment his face brightened slightly. "You can stay, you know. All three of you."

Her mouth went dry. "We don't have a choice, Sean. I'm sorry."

"Then...we'll take you."

She shook her head, taking a deep, painful breath. "We have to make our own way."

"Oh."

"It's...complicated," she tried by way of explanation, not

knowing what she could say that wouldn't sound like an insult or give Orabel away.

"Alright then," he said, hands folded carefully in his lap. "What's your plan?"

AS EMERY HAD PREDICTED, Sean was able to offer a solution to their lack of boat. They would return to Brimlad, where vessels would occasionally be left behind for one reason or another. He didn't ask any further questions, and when the conversation was done, he left. After that, his visits became less and less frequent, until they stopped altogether.

It took two weeks to reach Brimlad, a little less time than on the journey from there to Dornwell, thanks to more favorable weather. For the most part, Emery remained bedridden, unable to move around much. Aleksy warned her early on not to risk ripping her stitches, but she also had no energy. Dizziness, pain from the wound on her shoulder, and sheer exhaustion kept a strong hold on her, nor could she bring herself to risk crossing Sean's path, seeing how much her decision was hurting him. It would also just make her own sadness worse.

The crew had grown considerably warmer towards her at least, now they knew they had nothing to fear, and a few times a day most of them took turns visiting her in the cabin. Aleksy came often to check her wounds, Seadar and Farley brought cards and taught her some of their games, and Ranit amazed her with his own recovery. He was the same bright soul she had encountered before the horrific varen attack, proudly showing off how he had taught himself a configuration for playing the lute one-handed, singing for her and, ironically, lightening the mood in the cabin more than anyone else. Billy wandered in and out to chat pleasantly, and Rooney made sure she didn't go hungry. Only Camulus and Smythee kept their distance, and Sean.

With a couple of days' sailing left, Emery was finally able to start walking around the cabin again. The next day, as they began to near land, she carefully climbed up to the top deck to watch Brimlad growing bigger on the horizon. Silently, Sean came up to stand beside her, and for a while they remained there, side by side, neither saying a word, watching the mass of brown and green form into detail in front of them.

She cleared her throat. "Are you sure it's safe for you all to return to Brimlad?"

"Petter's men won't be bothering us again."

Another silence settled between them. Eventually, she forced herself to look up at him. He didn't look back, instead kept his gaze blank and off to the side. "Sean, I –"

"I should probably take over the helm," he said, leaving her to greet Brimlad alone.

THE BOAT BOBBING up and down in Brimlad's steel-blue waters was tiny, with only one mast and a short deck. It was small enough for three people to sail, which was exactly what they needed. The white paint across its hull had been rubbed off along one side, thanks to the waves constantly scraping it against the pier. Its sails were intact though, and no leaks could be found. It was seaworthy.

But it was going to be a long voyage home.

Staring down at the little boat from the pier, the boat she, Liam and Caelin would now have to sail by themselves, Emery tried to enjoy the warm sunshine on her face, the fresh salt breeze in the air, even if it was tinged with Brimlad's fetid stench. Even if the remaining pain in her shoulder and her hand, and the whirl of emotions in her chest made it difficult to enjoy anything. Only the familiar weight of her lim's smooth wood against her back made her feel calm. At least she could move again without fear of ripping her stitches.

The boat had been abandoned months ago, the harbormaster had told them, though no one knew why, or by whom. He was, crucially, willing to give it to them for a barrel of rum, something Sean's crew had thankfully been able to steal on their last raid before the rescue in Dornwell.

They had their way home. It was time to go.

Liam and Caelin shook hands with the crew first, thanking them one last time for all their help, and bade them farewell. They then hopped aboard the boat and began packing away the supplies Sean's crew had helped them procure. Emery alone remained on the platform, putting off her own goodbyes a moment longer. Then she turned round, no excuses left.

She began shaking hands with the crew one by one, except for Ranit and Billy who both insisted on giving her a hug. Though she had barely gotten to know most of them, her heart was heavy at the thought she would probably never see them again. Any of them.

Camulus was the last to approach, her ice blond hair hiding her pale face until the last moment. She hadn't visited Emery once during her recuperation, so it was a surprise to see her reaching out to shake her hand. She then cleared her throat, retracting her hand gently. "I think...I owe you an apology."

"You...do?"

Camulus shrugged. "I should have maybe...given you more of a chance."

Emery smiled at her sadly. "Let's speak more on our next trip then?"

"Sounds good." Camulus nodded her farewell and turned to join the rest of the crew walking back into Brimlad.

Emery's breath caught as she watched them shrink, knowing who was left.

When she turned back, Sean was standing in front of her, hands firmly in his pockets, face carefully expressionless.

She could barely look at him. "I, um...guess...this is goodbye."

He nodded curtly, keeping his eyes from hers. "If you think

that's best. I still don't think you three sailing off on your own is a good idea..."

It probably wasn't, but they didn't have a better one.

"Thank you," she whispered through a tightening throat. "For everything." All words were inadequate for what he'd done, for all the things they'd been through together, but these would have to do.

"I could...say the same to you." He slowly held out his hand, the leather palm guard wrapped around his hand once more, hiding his burn from view. He held a small, braided length of rope. "Um...this is for you."

Emery stared at it, momentarily confused.

"It's a bracelet. Like mine you like so much." She looked back to his face, which had turned slightly, adorably, red "It's made from rope from the *Audacity*. So you won't forget about us."

As if she could ever forget about him. She couldn't force words passed the lump in her throat, so she mutely held out her wrist. He tied the bracelet carefully, his fingers skimming her skin and sending goosebumps up her arm.

When he was finished, he went to pull his hand away but she grabbed it, squeezing his fingers.

"Stay safe," she said, feeling stupid that this was the best parting she could think of. Feeling the heat rise in her own face, she tried to let go, but he held on. And before she knew what was happening, he pulled her close, crushing her in his arms, though he was careful with her shoulder. The tears she'd been fighting to keep back welled up as she buried her face in his chest, wrapping her arms around his middle.

"Stay safe too, please," he murmured into her hair.

She didn't know how long they stayed like that, but all too soon, he let go. Without saying another word, he shoved his hands in his pockets and limped away, keeping his eyes on his feet as he left the docks and headed up the dirt path into town. He glanced over his shoulder briefly, then disappeared from sight.

Feeling empty, she turned back to the boat, fingering her new bracelet. Caelin was busy unraveling a length of rope, but Liam was watching her, offering a sad smile once their eyes met. She ignored him, instead gazing back at Brimlad, digging her hand into her own pocket. It met the little brown box from Liliath. She pulled it out, tracing the symbols with her thumb. Inside it lay the piece of parchment, along with the promise, perhaps, of finding out what had happened to her parents.

When they first arrived in Brimlad, Emery and Liam had tried to track Liliath down, wondering if she might have more answers about their parents or even if she knew of a better way to for them to get back to Orabel. But they found no traces of her.

A whole new emotion coursed through her.

Now she'd probably never get another chance to look for them. Once they brought their news back to Orabel, the Arch-Elemists would probably never let anyone in or out again. It would mean none of them, including Ayana, if she still lived, would ever have an answer to the question that had plagued them their entire lives.

And Ayana...they were returning without a cure. What would happen to Ayana, and everyone else who'd been struck by the Withering? What would happen to the island?

The ship rocked slightly as Liam clambered up beside her. "Are you okay?"

"I think we're ready," Caelin said before she could answer, climbing onto the pier as well, the boat rocking gently behind him.

She swallowed the lump that had formed in her throat and burst, "I don't think I can go with you."

Caelin's eyes opened wide. "What?"

But Liam just grinned, as if he had seen this coming.

"I'm...going after our parents. And I'm going to keep searching for a cure."

Caelin's mouth opened and closed a few times before he spoke. "That's absurd. We can't split up again."

"Well, technically, we can," said Liam.

Caelin stared at him. "You agree with this?"

"Well, I'm not thrilled about Emery not being with us," Liam admitted. "But –"

"We might never get another chance," Emery finished. "I need to do this, now."

"No," said Caelin. "We can't leave you behind again."

"It's different this time, Caelin."

"How? Because we know now just how bad the world really is? I don't –"

"She won't be *alone* this time," said Liam. "She'll have people to help her. People who...care about her, genuinely this time." Emery's face heated up as Liam turned to her. "Won't you? You'll have people who've *proved* we can trust them."

"It's not them I'm worried about! It's everyone else out here." Then a look of realization dawned on his face. "Wait." He jerked his head towards Brimlad, to where the captain of the *Audacity* had disappeared. "Is...he the reason you don't want to come home?"

"No," she snapped, angered and embarrassed by the insinuation. She couldn't deny her feelings for Sean had, perhaps, a small part to play in her decision, but he was far from the only reason. "We've waited so long for our parents to come back, or reach out to us in some way. And they never have." She swallowed. "They probably never will. Which means someone needs to look for them. Or at least find out what happened." She glanced at Liam. "And if there is a cure out here, I need to try to find it for Aya."

Liam nodded.

Caelin took a deep breath through his nose, then seemed to deflate. "I understand. But then how are you going to find your way home? The two of us will have the only map, as far as we know."

Emery smiled. "I had a lot of time to study it while I was stuck in bed. I think I should be able to make a copy."

Caelin chewed on his lip for a while, like he was trying to find another argument. But then he sighed and threw his arms around her. "I swear to Eldoris, if anything else happens to you out here..."

"I'll miss you too," she said into his shoulder, soaking up his warmth one last time. "I'll be alright. I promise."

He pulled away, quickly rubbing a hand over his eyes, and nodded.

When it came to her twin, Emery found that saying goodbye wasn't as difficult as she had thought it would be. They'd proved they could live without each other now, and this time they knew they weren't losing each other, just going separate ways for a while. They'd find each other again. Sooner or later. When she'd found their answers.

They stood in an embrace for a long time. When they finally parted, Liam's mouth quirked up, although his voice trembled a little as he spoke. "Don't come home until you find what you're looking for."

"I promise." She pulled the little vial of medicine Sean had stolen for her the last time they were in Brimlad out of her pocket. "Give this to Aya. It's not a cure but it might still help." He took the vial and then gave her one last hug.

Blood humming in her veins, Emery watched them climb back down into the boat. Caelin took the wheel as Liam prepared to release the main sail. Emery untied their mooring lines and tossed them onto the deck, then stood back and watched them drift into the open water. She had to keep telling herself they'd be okay without her. Caelin had learned a lot about sailing while he trained with the varens, and Sean had given them both a quick course during the time it took them to get to Brimlad while Emery was stuck in bed. They didn't need her.

But her heart floundered as she watched the boat grow smaller and smaller, and, for a half a moment, she had to fight the urge to jump down and swim after them. Then, once they were nothing but a white dot on the horizon, she pushed down her jitters and strode back towards Brimlad, clutching her sore shoulder.

She wasn't sure where to find Sean. But the crew had talked

about a tavern called the Rusty Anchor when they first arrived, and she thought that was as good as place as any to start. The muddy streets looked completely different in daylight, fewer people about and less ominous-looking shadows. Even the buildings appeared a little less dingy.

After several nearly empty streets, she spotted a sign with a crude painting of an anchor outside a more rickety-looking building. Emery took a deep breath and pushed open the grimy door, squinting into the dimly-lit interior. The place was nearly empty, but broken tables and chairs littered the dirty floor and the smell of the place – lingering body odor, stale ale, meat cooking – was enough to steal her breath for a moment.

She stepped inside, picking her way through the jungle of furniture and mess, and there they were, sitting around a circular table in the back of the tavern. Aleksy, Rooney, Billy, and Camulus were playing a game of dice, Ranit was strumming on his lute experimentally, Smythee was asleep, and Seadar was laughing at Farley's attempt to charm the arrestingly-corseted woman placing plates of food around the table. Sean, by contrast, was sitting beside Ranit with his arms crossed, staring pointedly away from everyone.

Emery's chest began to flutter. What if they wouldn't help her? What if even Sean said no? Now that he'd had some time to think, he might have decided it would have been too *complicated* for them to stay on the ship together, that they both had enough to navigate without –

It didn't matter. Then she'd find someone else who could read, another ship to board, another way to find her parents and a cure.

Ranit spotted her first, breaking into a grin and elbowing Sean in the ribs. Sean glared at him, but then followed his gaze, lips parting slightly as his eyes met hers. He stood up instantly, sidestepping the others, who started murmuring when they realized what had pulled him from his stupor.

"What's wrong?" he asked as soon as he reached her.

She motioned to the door, and he followed her out into the

daylight. Emery's heart was beating so quickly she felt sick, but at least it was easier to breathe out here.

"What's happened?" he asked again. "Are you alright?"

She nodded, forcing herself to breathe properly, then look up into his green eyes. "I've decided...not to go home yet. Liam and Caelin are going without me."

He blinked a few times, his face difficult to read. "What changed your mind?"

"There's something else I need to do first." She clasped her aching shoulder and he almost reached out to touch her, then pulled back. Deep breath. "And I was wondering..."

He cocked his head as she trailed off, waiting patiently.

"I thought that, maybe, I could...work for you, as part of your crew, in exchange for passage?"

Sean was examining her with curiosity. "Passage to where?"

"I don't know yet. Where are you going?"

Sean lifted his eyes towards the shimmering sea, just visible between the leaning buildings. "I don't know. Maybe south, to Ruhette or possibly further, somewhere like Bazyli. We don't have specific plans."

It must have shown on Emery's face that she had no idea where those places were. Sean smiled, and her face began to burn in embarrassment. "I'm still...new...to these parts."

"Are you finally going to tell me where you do come from?"

"In time, maybe."

A tiny chuckle escaped Sean's lips and her heart twitched. But then he slowly shook his head, as if bemused, and her heart sank. "Does that mean...we don't have a deal?"

"No, Emery." The panic fluttering in her chest dispersed as he stepped closer and brushed the feather in her hair. "It just means you remain a mystery to me. But now that you're going to be part of my crew" – he pulled back slightly so they could look at each other again – "I'll have some more time to puzzle you out, won't I?"

She gazed at him for a moment, his hand still lingering in her hair, needing a moment for what he had just said to sink in.

Then, all she could do was grin, and resist the urge to kiss him then and there in the sun-drenched street. "What is your first order then, Captain?"

He glanced back at the tavern, strips of warm light splashing across his face, then he gently traced a strand of hair back behind her ear. "Care to join me on a walk?"

"Sounds better than cleaning the decks."

He laughed, and the Scourge of the Sea offered her the crook of his arm. She took it, and together they wandered out into the muck-strewn streets of Brimlad, into Emery's new life. Not as a naïve newcomer to this world, but as an outlaw.

# Acknowledgments

I started writing this book 16 years ago, when I was just 14 and had no idea what I was doing. I wanted a book about pirates and magic and badass heroines and morally grey antiheroes. At the time, I couldn't find one, so I decided to write it myself. The book transformed immensely over the years (thank goodness) as did I (also thank goodness.) After countless edits and rewrites and rejections, it's become the story I've always hoped it could be. So, the first person I want to thank is me, or more accurately, all the past versions of me who refused to give up on these characters and this story. We did it, we're finally here.

Thank you to my parents, who provided me with a childhood in the woods and on the water, who filled my life with adventures and animals, and who have always supported me in big ways and small.

Thank you to my mom especially, who doesn't like fantasy but likes this book anyway, and who's always insisted on having a copy of every version, including the bits I wrote on scraps of paper and napkins for when they're 'worth something some day.'

Thank you to my brother, who always has my back. We're not twins but we look enough alike that we could be, and while Emery and Liam are not based off us, Liam certainly inherited some of your wit, humor, and nonchalance.

Thank you to my husband, who, without having read a single word of my writing, believed in me so much he was willing to plan our future around it. And still is.

Thank you to my mother, father, sister, and brother in-law for becoming my second family and for everything you do for us.

Thank you to my son, for all the snuggles and giggles that do wonders for morale. I'll be honest, you weren't overly helpful. In fact, trying to publish a book while navigating the first year of parenthood was difficult. A lot of writing and editing happened on my phone while I was nap trapped under a sleeping baby. And I wouldn't change any of it for the world.

Thank you to the friends who have become family, you know who you are. You are the reason I love the found family trope so much.

Thank you to Fritz, who was there when this all started, who was there through it all, but who didn't quite make it to the end. You were supposed to be in this book, but I ultimately had to cut you out and I'm still sad about it.

Thank you to Loki, Ares, and Finn, who have been with us through it all, for better or worse.

Thank you to Antonia Reed, who knows my story and characters almost as well, or maybe even better then, myself, who helped make this story even better than I ever could have imagined. Thank you for going above and beyond for this book.

Thank you to Natalia Junquiera, who somehow plucked the cover of my dreams right out of my head and then made it real.

Thank you to Alana Meyers-Echegaray, who brought my characters to life with uncanny accuracy. Watching the characters who have lived in my head for years come to life with your skill was truly amazing.

Thank you to my many beta readers over the years, bolstering my morale with your love for this story. Thank you for reading some not so great versions of this story but loving it anyway.

And lastly, thank you to you, lovely readers. You could have picked up any book but you chose to read this one and that means everything. I hope you loved Emery and the crew as much as I do.

# About the Author

Legends say K.J. Cloutier was born with a pen in her hand. She wrote her first book at five years old. And now, as an adult, she still loves to write about fantastical worlds and torture her beloved characters (literally and figurately.) When not writing, she's usually daydreaming about writing, while also cooking, travelling, and wandering near the woods or water. She's in real danger of one day being crushed under her forever growing collection of books. She lives with her husband, son, three dogs and a bearded dragon in a tiny house by the lake in B.C., Canada.

Beyond The Horizon is her debut novel.

For bookish updates:
https://www.kjcloutierauthor.com